Planet of the Orange-red Sun
Series Volume 1

When Kingdoms Fall

Planet of the Orange-red Sun Series Volume 1 When Kingdoms Fall

Vic Broquard

Planet of the Orange-red Sun Series
Volume 1 When Kingdoms Fall
Copyright 2010, 2011, 2012, 2014 by Vic Broquard

Second Edition; ISBN: 978-1-941415-18-4

This is a work of fiction. All characters, organizations, and events portrayed in this novel are products of the author's imagination and are used fictiously.

http://www.Broquard-ebooks.com
Broquard eBooks
103 Timberlane
East Peoria, IL 61611
author@Broquard-eBooks.com

Artwork by Crooked Willow Studios.

For Morgan and L. Ron Hubbard

Table of Contents

Chapter 1 Prelude

The dull throbbing of the Trail Blazer 5000 vibrated slightly the water pitcher and glasses on the chrome-plated table, while Governor Andrzej Bohater carefully adjusted his green collar and uniform, a last minute inspection before the impending, all-important first meeting of his High Council. The huge spaceship was making its final approach to their destination, Ashford-5, a remote, marginally inhabitable world located in the outer rim of the galaxy. The thirty-one year old man with coal black hair, eyes, and moustache would be taking charge of this group, the Imperium Settlement Force Thirty-three, the very moment the huge ship landed. Andrzej was fresh out of the Academy on Rigel-3, as were all his immediate subordinate ministers and wife, Irena, twenty-nine. She also had the distinctive black hair and eyes, as did all those from Rigel-3, along with their characteristic light grey or olive-colored skin tones.

"Relax; this will go just as you have planned, dear. Shall I fill the glasses? They should be here any minute. We're about to land. I can tell from the vibrations," she asked, flashing him a flirting smile. Distracted for a moment by her bright red lips, matching inch long nails, and dark eye shadow, Andrzej wished they could have spent more time in their bed this morning. However, the ship's captain had informed him they would be landing at 15:00, and he had to officiate this first official meeting of his cabinet.

Irena was also his Construction Minister. Her job was to get their new landing facilities rapidly built. After all, they needed housing. Their three months in a spaceship had been fatiguing, so little to do. He'd spent most of the time with his wife in their cabin's bed. He took his seat at the head of the chrome-plated table and watched his curvaceous wife as she finished pouring the water. Such a woman, he thought to himself. Just as she took her seat to his immediate left, the others began filing in, taking their places around the table.

General Janek Jerzy, the eldest of the party at thirty-four, took his seat at the governor's right. He was in charge of their two hundred Drugi or security soldiers, but Governor Andrzej hoped they would not be needed. His Psychman, Doctor Cezar Gerwazy, twenty-eight, strolled in, accompanied by his wife, Jolanta, twenty-seven, who acted as his assistant. If there were any trouble, the Psychman would see it was terminally handled. The governor's critically important Minister of Mining, Jurek Kacper, twenty-six, entered behind them with his wife and their Refining Minister, Kassia, hanging on his arm. They made a pair, Andrzej thought, as he mentally undressed the shapely woman.

Doctor Zosia Wiola, their resident physician, came in next. For a moment, Andrzej felt a pang of sympathy for her. She was just about the ugliest woman he'd ever seen, but a most competent medical doctor. Twenty-five and like the rest of his ministers, fresh out of Rigel-3's Academy, Medical Section in her case, Doctor Zosia was armed with all the very latest methods and treatments. Although she was most competent, the governor hoped her services would only be minimally needed here on Ashford-5. She was unmarried, naturally, the governor thought.

Two other single women brought up the rear, Dita Eva, twenty-three, and Luzia Lina, twenty-four. Dita was his Social-Anthropology Minister, while Luzia was his Native Relations Minister. Everyone had coal black hair and eyes, indicative of those from Rigel-3. Dita was attractive, but tended to overdo her makeup, while Luzia was rather plain looking. After the two women took their seats, Governor Andrzej rose.

Sounding rather pompous as befitting a governor, he began, "Welcome to our first official meeting of the Imperium Settlement Force Thirty-three. As you already probably know, we are on our final approach to Ashford-5. Our objective is to establish a proper mining facility on Ashford-5. Here in the outer rim, travel consumes a lot of fuel. The Imperial Planet Scouts have reported Ashford-5 is loaded with psi-crystals from which our desperately needed fuel is obtained. We will be setting up a vital refueling station and spaceport here on Ashford-5." Of course, everyone already knew all of this, but it was his duty to spell out these details for the official record, which began with this meeting.

"You have all been handpicked for this exciting challenge," he continued. Well, he was exaggerating slightly. Everyone was fresh out of their various academies on Rigel-3. Times were hard throughout the Imperium, and this assignment offered all them a significant career boost — that is, if they made good on this project. Psi-crystals were the key ingredient in the fuel used by all the ships in the Imperial space fleet. If they turned this backward planet into a major refinery and supply depot, certainly the Imperium would take note of their achievements. "When we succeed here on Ashford-5, I don't have to tell you that all our careers will rocket. I expect nothing but your very best work in the coming days, weeks, and months." He didn't say years because every one of them hoped and prayed they'd be promoted to more civilized planets long before a year had passed. Many nodded agreeably.

"Now then, the Imperial Directive #5, with which you are all familiar I am sure, says we must not interfere in the local culture, politics, and social affairs of the natives. Ordinarily, we would be bound by this directive. However, in the case of Ashford-5, the obtaining of the psi-crystals supersedes this directive. Fuel is absolutely vital out here in the rim. Thus, we have Imperial Orders to do *whatever* it takes to get the mining and refining of psi-crystals up and running as rapidly as possible."

Murmurs came from both Dita and Luzia. Dita broke in, "As your Social-Anthropologist Minister, I want to go on record as being against wholesale violation of the Imperial Directive #5. We could do irreparable harm to the indigenous life forms on Ashford-5, Governor Andrzej."

"I agree with Dita. We should tread carefully on these primitives," added a frowning Luzia.

Andrzej scowled. "Yes, of course, duly noted. Make no mistake. We're dealing with primitives here, quite primitive if the scouting reports are accurate, and I've no doubt they are correct. The obtaining of psi-crystals is absolutely vital to the Imperium, and we must do what we need to do to get this colony producing the much needed fuel. However, that said,

I'm not saying we wantonly eliminate these primitives, Dita. Rather, we'll do what is needed and no more, but I shall stand for no disruptions from our mining targets as set forth in the official documents of our charge. Therefore, Dita, I'm leaving the cultural aspects in your capable hands. Which reminds me, Luzia, are you prepared to handle the necessary primitive native relations?"

"Aye, Governor, I'm fully prepared to handle any and all such negotiations. I have the ULAT's programmed and ready to go. Of course, our linguistic data is based solely upon the initial scouting reports. Expect me to be updating them as I get more familiar with their language idiosyncrasies," she reported. The ULAT was their Universal Language Translator device, a small portable box that fed a translation of the alien's words into their ears, while speaking their own words translated into the alien language from a small speaker within the box — a highly useful invention now in widespread use throughout the entire portion of the galaxy occupied by the Imperium.

"Excellent, excellent, Luzia. Now then, General Janek, are you and your men set to secure our landing site?"

"Absolutely. The primitives will pose no serious threat whatsoever, you may rest assured of that fact!" he replied antagonistically. "We'll have a perimeter established minutes upon landing. From there, we'll fan out and setup a defensive wall entirely around the initial site. How soon after that are we to expand out for the miners?"

He was looking for a fight, Dita sensed. She thought, against Drugi, what chance have these primitives got? This bothered her considerably. They were about to entirely up-heave the existing culture on this planet, something she personally detested. Dita had spent years studying to be an observer not a disrupter of other cultures, especially primitive ones.

"My teams will be ready to head out to the survey-indicated potential sites the moment you give us the okay," Minister Jurek hastily answered. Then, he launched into an explanation. "Ashford-5 is a most peculiar planet." Dita wondered why. She silently cursed, knowing she'd paid little attention to the geological discussions Jurek had held during their long trip here. "It's a planet almost wholly without any elements beyond gold in the classic Periodic Chart of Universal Elements found on most all inhabitable worlds. The survey has shown that iron and gold here are extremely rare and precious, as well as impossibly hard to find."

Dita thought, now it makes sense. I wondered why the survey reports indicated copper and silver were the main currency among the primitives. I always presumed gold would be. So gold is rare here. Strange. I wonder why? She decided not to pursue it here in the meeting.

"The primitives have evolved enough to make forged weapons from a low grade steel. However, most metallic ores are relatively rare on this world. While there's some tin, there is virtually no element heavier than tin here, save for the rare gold deposits. There's an abundance of silicates in many forms, one of which is our precious psi-crystals. That's what makes this world so extremely valuable to the Imperium. The survey crews have mapped out locations of heavier deposits of these vital crystals. We'll begin by checking out the largest of these. Of course, we'll need Drugi for our protection, and Luzia ought to tag along to interface with the primitives. At least one site is close to one of their settlements."

"Excellent, let's plan to head out first thing in the morning. I want to give Irena time to get her construction crews going first. It might be wise to see if the primitives come to greet us when we land. Probably they won't, but before I send out Luzia, I want to make sure," the governor advised.

"Do my Drugi have complete freedom of action?" General Janek probed. By this, everyone knew he meant did he have permission to exterminate any resisters, protestors, or troublemakers.

"As a last resort, use stun settings, general. That's why we have our own Psychman with us. Apprehend them and bring them to Cezar for Behavioral Modification or a full Mind Wipe, if needed," Governor Andrzej explicitly said, hoping to appease Dita somewhat. He knew she was totally against the abolition of the Imperial Directive #5, but he had to do what was needed to get the precious psi-crystals flowing into the refinery.

Not wanting to be left out entirely, the Refining Minister, Kassia, spoke up. "As soon as Irena has finished her basic construction, my crew will begin setting up the first of our planned three refineries."

"How come the delay?" Governor Andrzej asked slightly confused. He wished he had paid more attention to the initial plans and wondered why the refinery constructions needed to be delayed.

"We need stable power sources and water supplies, governor," she answered, guessing correctly he'd totally ignored her papers she'd sent in with the initial plans. Well, she thought, that's nothing new. He seldom gets involved with the details, but always takes the credit for them. Bosses, I hate them.

"Oh, yes, yes, I forgot," he hastily justified. "Everyone, I know you'll all do your jobs admirably. Yes, I know conditions here in this backwater, primitive planet are going to be quite trying and certainly not what any of us are used to, but chin up! Let's do a really good job of it. I am sure if we do, we'll only be here a short while, before we are all promoted and can return to civilization. Now then, I believe we'll be landing in a few minutes. I suggest we get to our quarters and strap in, though the landing should be a smooth one. Meeting dismissed."

As if on cue, the intercom activated. The captain drawled, "We'll be landing within ten minutes. Secure yourselves for landing. That is all."

Chapter 2 King Aaran Wycombe

The inhabitants called their continent and world Tierra, though at this time, the year 1000, they did not know there was a difference between the two names. Tierra was bat-shaped, some six thousand miles east-west and four thousand north-south at its middle, shrinking to three thousand along its wings. The tall and forbidding Goza Mountains divided the Westerlings from the Midlands, while the rugged Buku Hills separated the Midlands from the Easterlings. While there was a distinctive physical separation between these thirds of the continent, their customs were rather similar throughout, though their languages varied somewhat. Trading routes between the three areas often paralleled the southern coastline.

Each section of Tierra was ruled by local kings. Four kings divided up the Westerlings, while four controlled the Easterlings. Somewhat larger in size, the Midlands had seven kings. All fifteen kings constantly jostled with each other for control of more and more territory. Wars were commonplace, though at this time, only two were ongoing. The Westerlings' Kingdom of Alavera was battling its southern neighbor, the Kingdom of Trujillo, while in the Midlands, the Kingdom of Bettingham was on the down side of its war with its northern neighbor, the Kingdom of Rockton. Many referred to this time period as its Great Realignment.

Down in the extreme southern portion of the Midlands lay the Kingdom of Bashir. Here in the hot lands, the Church of God was firmly entrenched, commonly called the COG. They had established their own Mother City, called Valcia, where the Archbishop sought to bring religion to all Tierra. Each kingdom had its own bishop, who controlled the churches there. From these larger churches, priests fanned out into the many smaller towns and villages, preaching the gospel of COG. At this time, the COG was slowly gaining influence among the many kings and nobles, though not with the villagers. The church's main attack was against the many local "witches."

Even tiny hamlets had their own local witch. While the

COG assigned all manner of wild satanic magical spells to these women, in fact, the women were merely closely attuned to the healing nature of the lands around them. They could trace their lineage back a thousand years and were wise when it came to the healing properties of plants. When a villager was injured or sick, they went to their local witch for assistance. Often they received a potion, which speeded their healing. True, some were known to also distribute poisons and other nefarious potions.

To counter these heretic witches, the COG founded and supported the Medical Academy in Valcia. At this time, every king had their own official COG doctor, whose skills were rapidly becoming accepted in these courts. However, the kings knew better than to outlaw their own local witches. Of course, if you were to ask Archbishop Mata Hatta, who ruled over the entire COG, what his ultimate objective was, he'd tell you total control of Tierra. He was wise enough to realize he would not likely live to see his objective met, but he continued to lay the foundations he fully expected would ultimately achieve his objective.

Just north of the Kingdom of Bashir lay the Kingdom of Bettingham. Farther north, the Wyndl River divided the Kingdom of Bettingham from the Kingdom of Rockton. It was the largest river on Tierra, running from its mountain streams in the northern portion of the Goza Mountains, southeast to nearly the southern tip of Bashir, close to four thousand miles long. Rockton's army was predominately mounted soldiers, striking hard across the Wyndl and then retreating. Bettingham's army was mostly foot soldiers, who were hard pressed to stop the cavalry.

King Aaran Wycombe, now forty-two, ruled from his capital city of Wycombe, home to some twenty thousand and located in the south-central portion of Bettingham. Wycombe lay two hundred miles due southeast of the landing site of the spaceship and their new base on the mountain called Beja and its Plateau Grado. The second largest city of nearly ten thousand, Wyth, lay in the foothills of the mountains, barely a hundred miles north of this towering plateau. King Aaran was a ruthless and greatly feared ruler, who struck fear in his enemies as well as his own subjects.

King Aaran's wife was Misty, forty years old. She, like all her family, had yellow curly hair and blue eyes. In her youth, she had been quite pretty, but as she approached middle age, time and the hands of her husband had taken their toll. Their eldest son, Prince Norwood, a handsome twenty-two year old, was far to the north leading their northern defenses. Palmer, a year younger, was still being trained by his father's sword master, but he desperately wanted to see some action. Their eldest daughter, Ally, twenty, had her mother's beauty. Her long curly hair fell to her waist, but she was also strong willed, often defying her father's wishes. Her younger sister, April was just eighteen and she took after their mother, being quiet and retired by nature.

King Aaran resided in Castle Wycombe, a grey stone fortress sitting on a hill beside the sprawling town. A wooden palisade wound its way around the outer edges of the city, adjoining the castle on its eastern side. Also at the king's court was Bishop Gil Granville, forty-five, whose temper rivaled that of the king. Besides overseeing the COG here in Bettingham, he worked to further the church's influence at court. He'd achieved much of that goal by having brought Doctor Corey Forrest to Wycombe. The young doctor, barely twenty-five, had a sadistic streak that dovetailed nicely with the king and bishop. Doctor Corey was also something of an innovator and inventor of all things dealing with bodies. He'd perfected the Forrest Surgical Blades that greatly aided surgery everywhere. However, he also perfected the Amputator de la Mano specifically to assist King Aaran in doling out his unique brand of justice.

Thieves were a common problem among all the fifteen kingdoms. King Aaran had finally solved it in Wycombe, thanks in part to Doctor Corey. Anyone caught thieving had one or both hands inserted into the mechanical device. When the good doctor activated the pull lever, the sterile, extremely sharp blades efficiently separated the wrist from the arm bone's joint. A blast of exceedingly hot air from the modified blacksmith bellows seared the stub with minimal loss of blood. Within a year, most thieves took their trade elsewhere.

Besides, anyone seeing a one handed person knew instantly he or she was a convicted thief. Embolden by his success, King Aaran used his new tool against others who crossed him in anyway.

Today, King Aaran was fuming. "Who the hell stole the church's tithes bag of silver this time?" Bishop Gil Granville had just reported the theft. "If I haven't got enough to worry about with this war against the vile Rockton raiders, now we've thieves robbing the Church of God. Well, who did it? Captain?" He gave his City Guards Captain a stare that could kill.

Not facing the king, Bishop Gil could not resist a fleeting smile. *This is child's play! Manipulating King Aaran is so utterly easily done!* Seldom does an angry man ever see the truth. Aaran was no exception. Bishop Gil was steadily implementing his COG agenda. One of his primary goals was the elimination of the influence of the witches here in Bettingham. In fact, the bag of silver had not been stolen. He only claimed it had been and quietly reported to the captain it'd been taken by the local witch Babs Wynne.

"Sire, the priest believes it was the witch Babs Wynne," the captain reported what he'd been told. That he had not done any investigation of his own seldom figured into the justice doled out by King Aaran, so why should he bother to either, the captain thought.

"Damnable witches again. Send for Doctor Corey immediately!" King Aaran yelled. He paced his throne room and took a lengthy swill of ale, calming his nerves. Shortly, the small-framed doctor came running into the throne room.

"Ah, good doctor. It seems another witch has been stealing from the COG. Babs Wynne this time. What do we know about her?"

Queen Misty spoke up, "Dear, she helped deliver our children, don't you remember?"

He slapped her hard across her face, bringing tears to her eyes. "Don't ever put me down in front of men! But you do have a point, Misty. She did bring our four children into this world. Okay, I'll be kind to her, but she needs to pay. I know, doesn't she have a daughter?"

Bishop Gil could not believe his good luck. He quickly

10

said, "Why yes, Sire, in fact she does have a twenty-one year old daughter, another witch like her mother." Could he possibly kill two birds with one strike?

"Captain, execute Babs! We'll be merciful only because she was of valuable service to us in the past. However, she must pay — set an example, if we're ever going to put an end to thievery in Bettingham. Doctor, take both of her daughter's hands. That'll set a powerful example. We'll not stand for thievery! Period! Now get going!" *I wish I could put an end to this war with Rockton as easily as this!*

"Yes Sire," Doctor Corey replied with a wry smile, echoed by Bishop Gil as well. He and the captain jogged out of the throne room, but slowed to a walk once beyond sight of the king.

Meanwhile, a red bruise began appearing on Misty's face. "Excuse me, My Lord," she whimpered, covering her face with her hand. She bowed politely and left, heading to her room, hoping she still had some of the healing salve from Babs. *What am I going to do without Babs?* She began to worry. For years, she depended upon the good witch to help heal her many injuries suffered at the hands of her husband. She found the small pot and lamented there was so little of it left. She made a mental note to have some of her serving women make discrete inquiries in order to locate another healing witch in Wycombe. *Perhaps, I can keep this a secret from Aaran.*

"Mom! Did dad hit you again?" Ally antagonistically asked. She'd come walking into her mother's chambers to complain about her own dire situation, but saw the swelling on Misty's face. "Here, let me rub the salve on it for you." She took the precious pot from her mother's hands and began to apply the healing ointment. "Damn dad anyway!"

"Dear, you must not be so hard on your father. Lord knows he's so much to handle these days, what with the war and now our own witch turning thief on us," Misty tried to dissuade her daughter from speaking ill of her husband. *Lord, knows I must've deserved this slap. I did speak out against him, and I ought not to have. What am I going to do without Babs? She delivered my four babies.*

"I just heard. News like that travels fast, mom, but I just don't believe it. Why would Babs steal from the COG? It doesn't make any sense. You and I both know the bishop hates the good witches around here and is doing his best to get rid of them. I wouldn't put it past the bishop to have framed poor Babs. She's very likely totally innocent," Ally declared forcefully. *Damn him anyway. Mom's going to have a big bruise on her face again. My god, Babs delivered all of us, and this is her reward for years of service to us? My own dad is the wickedest man I've ever heard of, but what can I do to stop him? Why don't the other men do something to stop him?*

"Well Ally, there's nothing we can do about that, dear. Babs ought not to have so riled up the COG, I suppose," Misty attempted to invent a reason for Babs to be guilty of something. After all, she knew the healer and witch was about to be executed. Well, at least, she had done that much for Babs. Being killed outright was certainly better than losing one's hands and being marked as a thief in everyone's eyes for the rest of their lives. "I was able to get your father to show Babs some mercy, dear." She thought, *Well, it'll be merciful. She'll have a quick death, that's something. No one can live without their hands, so I guess Aaran is being kind to her.*

Ally barked hostilely, "Mercy? You mean having her murdered instead of mutilated? Some mercy! There, you're all fixed up. Bad bruise, though. Why do you let dad hit you all the time, mom? He has broken both your arms and given you countless beatings." Her mind drifted back over the many years she'd witnessed her mother's frequent beatings and the two times her arm had been actually broken by her father, whom she now detested. *Why hasn't Norwood stepped in to put a stop to it? Or even Palmer?* She sighed and realized her brothers dare not defy their father either. She recalled something Norwood had told her in private just before he left to take command of their soldiers up by Wyth in the north. He'd said "Dad's a tyrant, but a powerful one. You watch yourself, Ally. One day he'll give his throne to me, and then I'll set things right." *Maybe you might, Norwood, but Babs will be long dead by then.*

"Dear, it's not as bad as you are making it out to be —

really it isn't. Besides, it's my own fault. I put him down in front of the other men, and so I deserved it, really I did," Queen Misty replied, again making light of the situation and finding a reason for Aaran to have struck her so hard. *I have to get Ally calmed down. It really isn't anything to get so worked up about, not really.*

Ally put her hands on her hips. "Mom! One of these days, he's going to go too far and kill you! I hope one day you will finally have had enough of his brutality towards you!" She pivoted on her heels and headed for the door, having forgotten entirely what she had come to ask her mother about. *Damn dad anyway!*

She sat in her room fuming, imagining all manner of "ends" for her father, but none of them by her own hands. Ally was a mere young woman, ripe now for marrying. She'd spent all her life cooped up in the castle. Well, that wasn't entirely true. She often went riding in the nearby fields and even once tried falconry. Most of her time had been spent learning to read and write and to perform wifely duties, sewing, cooking, and cleaning. "You must be prepared to care for your husband when you are married," her mother had often and patiently explained to her. Untold hours, she'd spent watching her brothers being trained by their father's sword master, all the while wishing she could be so trained as well, but King Aaran would never let her get near a blade. Often, she had wondered why? Of life beyond the stone walls of the castle, she knew next to nothing.

Now her thoughts drifted back to what she had originally gone to see her mother about — marriage. Her father had been increasingly talking of finding a suitable husband for her. She knew most of the women that worked here in the castle had married husbands who offered them either a higher social standing or a better position, though a few chose their mates for love alone. Strong willed, Ally wanted to marry for love, but more frequently now her father talked of arranging a marriage for her. So far, she'd been able to put him off by declaring each of his suggestions was a "fat pig" and that she'd have no part of the proposed man. The surprise invasion from the Kingdom of Rockton had been her temporary salvation. King Aaran was totally preoccupied with the ill-going war that began in the early spring.

An hour later, Ally was herself summoned to her dad's court. She dare not defy him and ignore an official summons. When she arrived, she found Palmer, April, and her mother were already there, along with the bishop and several guards. Plus, she saw a stranger was present and seated before her father. What's up, she wondered? The man had brown hair, and thus was not likely from Bettingham. In this kingdom, blonde hair was commonplace, not brown. *Can he be from Rockton?*

"Princess Ally," King Aaran used her formal title, "this is King Addam Chester's emissary. He comes with an offer of peace. If I hand over our northern town of Wyth to King Chester and marry you, Princess Ally, to his eldest son, Prince Orson, then King Chester will end this war. I've decided to accept his offer."

Ally's ire rose to a new height. "I will not marry Orson! He is a fat pig! You might as well go ahead and kill me right now! There's no way on Tierra I'll ever marry our enemy!" Ally's face tightened in anger; blood vessels in her neck throbbed visibly. Involuntarily, Queen Misty covered her face with her hands, as if to deflect the mighty blow that would *surely* follow. *Our enemy? Hideous! Kill me now. You can't be my father!*

King Aaran's face blazed; he clenched his fists. Only because the emissary was sitting across from him did he restrain himself from smashing his wayward daughter in her face. Between clenched teeth, he said to the emissary, "Ignore the bitch! Women are all bitches and must be put in their places. Orson will have his hands full with this one! She'll marry him or spend the rest of her days in our dungeon living with the rats while dining on bread and water. Come by tomorrow and pick her up. Of course, there'll be *no* dowry."

"King Chester has not requested a dowry. Consider Wyth her dowry. I'll relay the news to the king, and he'll send a carriage for the princess in the morning. Pleasure doing business with you King Aaran." He rose, bowed respectfully, and left.

Ally flew out of the room as fast as her legs could run. Once in her own room, she bolted the door and dove onto her bed, bawling like a injured child. *How dare he! How dare he!* A bit later, her mother knocked on her door, "Ally dear. It's mom. Surely, you can see the great benefits this will bring to us all. The war will be over. Think of the lives you will be saving. It's a woman's *place* to do as her Lord wishes. Ally? Ally dear?" Ally ignored her mother and continued to sob into her pillow. Her world was being crushed! Her mind now added images of stabbing both her father and the young enemy prince, whom she had never seen.

Sometime later, her sister, April knocked. Ally begrudgingly let her inside. "Are you okay, sis?" Ally nodded, her eyes were blood shot. "Mom's right, you know. Marrying that Orson prince will end the war and bring peace to Bettingham. That's something, isn't it?" she asked.

"Then you marry that fat slob!" Ally lashed out at meek April, but at once regretted her outburst. As April fought to keep from crying, Ally melted, "Come here, sis." She threw her arms around April. *God, now I am being like dad, hurting those closest to me!*

"What are you going to do?" April asked timidly. In her mind, ending the war might be reward enough to go through with the marriage. *Perhaps the prince will not be as bad as dad.*

"I don't know yet, but there is no way I am going to go through with it," Ally declared yet again.

"But dad will throw you in the dungeon. I know he will," April protested, fearing their father would do just that!

"How true! The bastard!" Ally spat on the floor. "You'd better go to mom and help her now. She'll be trying to get things ready for tomorrow." Ally couldn't take any more from her sister. She needed to think.

"You, you are going to do it then?" April asked hesitatingly.

Ally thought fast. *Whatever I say to April will surely find its way to mom and dad within minutes of April leaving my room. I need time.* "Yes, I'll do it. What choice do I have?" She shrugged her shoulders in a mock resignation.

15

April bought it, replying meekly, "None, really." She rose and left. Ally was certain her sister would report this to her mother. Meanwhile, Ally headed to Palmer's room. An idea slowly formed.

"Hi, tough break, sis," Palmer said sympathetically as she entered. Already, he had tried to imagine Ally married to a foreign prince, but couldn't accept it. However, he knew he could not defy his father on her behalf — certainly not on such an important decision as this one was, ending the war to boot. Still, he knew he too needed to get away from the castle and his father, just as Norwood had. Yet, the opportunity to do so continued to elude him. *I hope she doesn't take it too badly.*

"Wouldn't be *if* there was even *one* man in this family," Ally retorted. "Let me borrow some of your clothes, please."

"Huh? Why?" Palmer asked. His face flushed. *I know she thinks I ought to stand up for her with dad, but I can't! He'll punish me too. Why does she want my clothes?*

"I need a shirt, pants, and boots."

"I get it, you are running away!" Palmer glanced about, making sure no one was eavesdropping on them. He whispered, "Good thinking!" He rummaged through his trunks and found suitable clothes for her, wrapping them up in a bed sheet so that they would not be so obvious. *She's got more gumption than I ever imagined! Somehow, I have to follow her lead!* "Here, take this too; you might need it." He added a dagger. "And this too," he gave her his money pouch. "It's not a whole lot, you know dad, but it's something. Good luck. Where will you go?" The dagger was quite valuable in and of itself, considering how rare steel was on Tierra.

"Best that you don't know, Palmer. That way, you can't be forced to tell what you don't know. I don't want you facing dad's wrath. Thanks." *How can I tell him I have absolutely no idea where I can go?* She gave him a big hug, opened his door, and peered out. Seeing no one was around, she swiftly ran back to her bedroom and locked the door once more.

She changed into his clothes and looked at her appearance in her mirror. Her bosom and long hair gave her away. For a time, she considered cutting off her hair, which had never been cut before. While she was a bit vain about her golden locks, that wasn't the reason. If she did cut them, they'd find them and know she was fleeing disguised as a man. While Palmer may eventually be forced to tell their father she had borrowed some of his clothes, by then, she hoped to be far away, out of the city. *I need to buy myself some time,* she thought and rummaged around for an alternative. An old hat worked, she stuffed her locks up inside it, with enough dangling down to appear to be manlike. She then took off his shirt and wrapped her bosom tightly in part of an old blouse. Now with his shirt on, her youthful endowment was not quite so pronounced, and it would have to do. Strapping on the dagger, she again checked her appearance. She thought she'd likely pass perhaps as a slightly effeminate man. This was the best she could manage, and now she began to work on how to escape from the castle.

If I take a horse, that'll be noted at once. I go on foot, she reasoned. *If I go late at night, I have the best chance of sneaking away in the dark. Sure hope I don't run across any thieves in the dark streets, though.* Now she waited. A maid knocked to announce supper. She called out, "I'm not hungry. I'm trying to get everything packed before morning."

"Surely, you will let us help you. Can I send for Sally?" Sally was Ally's personal servant.

"No, I want to do this last thing myself. Thanks anyway." She listened, heard the woman's footsteps leaving, and relaxed. Now she waited. Her mind went uncommonly blank. *If I think about what I am about to do, my nerves will fail me. Think nothing, think nothing,* she told herself, and stared at her ceiling.

Around midnight, she finally ventured to open her door. The hall was clear. She gathered up a dirty sheet and stole down the hall. Ally knew the first floor would heavily manned by the night guards. However, the window of the king's study overlooked the outer walls. As she had imagined in her room, she looped the sheet around a chair and slipped the other end out of the window. Carefully lowering herself, her feet finally touched the walkway along the top of the outer walls. She pulled the sheet on through the chair and smiled. Thus far, it was working. Again, she wrapped the sheet around a parapet stone and slipped over the side of the wall. Hand over hand, she lowered herself to the ground, forced to drop the last three feet as the sheet gave out. She froze, hoping no one heard the slight noise. Hearing nothing, she wadded up the sheet and struck out for the streets of Wycombe, depositing the sheet behind a water barrel.

She was unnerved slightly by the near total darkness. Tierra's two moons, the bright and white Echador and the pale blue Palidez, had not yet risen. Her overactive imagination had thieves, soldiers, and assassins hiding in every dark recess. As she stealthily moved slowly down the first street, she gained a bit more confidence. Of course, she had not really thought she'd actually get this far. Now that she was out of the castle, where was she going to go?

I need to get as far away from here as possible, she thought and headed for the eastern outskirts of the city. Of course, there were the wooden outer walls to circumvent, and she had no idea about how to do that just yet. She continued walking towards the outer walls, several miles distant across the whole town. Soon the adrenaline rush was gone and she felt tired, but continued walking. Her mind drifted to the eventful day and somehow returned to the fate of Babs Wynne, the old woman who had delivered her and her siblings. She'd never failed to come when the queen asked, always helping her mother. She recalled how she'd come and set her mother's broken arm, twice actually, though she also told Queen Misty to leave Aaran before he killed her. Of course, her mother hadn't listened, only saying she deserved having her arm broken. For a time, Ally wondered what her mother had done that made her so feel like she had to have all manner of punishment inflicted upon herself. On that, she had no idea, but she must have done something bad. She had no idea her mother had slipped the poison into the Bettingham's heir to the throne, which had enabled Aaran to usurp the throne from the Bettingham clan. She had only heard rumors that somehow Aaran had stolen the throne from the founding Bettinghams.

Babs was now likely dead, a mercy killing. *Wait, her daughter!* Ally remembered she had a daughter about her own age, Aurora. Her father had ordered the removal of her hands; the poor woman would be totally helpless. The reality of that idea shocked Ally, and she immediately formed a new plan. She firmly decided. *I've got to get to Aurora, and see if I can help her somehow.* Babs had a small herb shop at the eastern edge of the city, close to the wooden walls. How to find it in the darkness was her problem. She'd only been there once, no twice, she corrected herself. The last time she'd gone to fetch Babs to help set her mother's second broken arm. *I am so worthless. I've hardly ever been out of the castle!*

After a frustrating hour, she finally found the place. Both Echador and Palidez had now risen. In the moonlight, the shop was plainly marked — Babs' dead body hung from a rope tied to one of her shop's outer support pillars that faced the street. *Damn dad to Hell!* Tears swelled up. She knew her father would leave the dead woman hanging there for several days as a reminder and warning to all thieves in Wycombe. *Aurora! Where's her daughter?* Stark reality hit her again.

The front door was ajar, and she crept into the darkened room. The smell of various herbs was overpowering, just as she remembered it. *Where is Aurora? Is she bleeding to death? Do I dare call out?* She decided against that, choosing to observe instead. Feeling her way along, she neared the back of the shop and found a light coming from under a crack of a door. Now she had to decide whether to open it or knock first. That decision was made for her. A soft female voice coming from beyond the door said, "Come on in, but be quiet though."

Ally jerked with surprise, but steeled herself and opened the door. She blinked, as her eyes shifted from night vision to the lantern-lit combination kitchen and dining room of the Wynne's. "Come on in. Best shut the door behind you. It is not safe around here." Ally saw an old woman dressed in a worn, black cotton dress sitting at a table. She looked haggard; her grey streaked blonde hair was disheveled from the bun atop her head. Drooping eyes suggested she was overly tired. "She's alive, if that's what you want to know," the woman added.

How does she know what I want? Oh, I'm about her age. She must think I am a girlfriend of Aurora's. "I'm so sorry this happened," Ally began, not knowing what she really could say. "You know the king and his violent temper. Who are you?"

"Best ask that of you first. You are a strange young man," the old woman said softly, then caught herself. "Say, you're not a young man, are you? Come, sit down. I am or was a dear friend of Babs. You look strangely familiar. I am Phyllis Roundtree."

Ally did as asked. "If — if you know who I am, then I would be putting you in grave danger, I'm afraid," she replied, uncertain whether to entirely trust this woman she had never seen.

Something she said struck a chord in the elderly woman, who cracked a smile, revealing several missing front teeth. Almost breaking into a cackle, Phyllis replied, "Child, I am already in grave danger just by staying in Wycombe! If I wanted safety, I would have already fled with the others. No, they'll get nothing useful out of me. I am old and dying, I'm afraid to say. You look quite familiar. I've seen you before. Somewhere around Wycombe. Take your hat off."

Ally hesitated. If she did, her long, curly blonde tresses would likely give her away. Still, she dare not refuse the woman. She took her hat off and allowed her long hair to slip down, tossing her head slightly. "You *are* Princess Ally!" Phyllis exclaimed, adding, "Well, I thought so. Dear, if your father finds you here, he'll go into a rage and beat you like he does his wife."

"Oh, I expect he'll do a whole lot more than that if he finds me now. I've run away," Ally sighed, glad to have at least spoken these words to another human being. She found herself telling Phyllis all about what had happened, ending with, "I'm so sorry about Babs and Aurora. I came here tonight to see if there was anything I might do to help her, Aurora, I mean. I don't know why I am doing this. I have to flee far from here myself. The hue and cry will go up in the morning. I'm sure of that."

Phyllis stared long into Ally's eyes and at last reached a decision. "Child, do you *really* want to help poor Aurora?"

"Well, yes, but I don't really know what I can do, but I

have to *try*. My despicable father did this to her and her mother. I owe it to Babs. She delivered all us children and helped mom countless times. I have to at least *try* to help Aurora, somehow," Ally tried to explain her feelings and rationale. Aurora's situation seemed to dwarf that of her own at this instant.

"Okay then. So be it." There was a strong hint of finality in her voice. "Come with me," she rose slowly; flickers of pain creased the old woman's face. Age was taking its toll on the woman. She opened the door to Aurora's bedroom, and Ally saw another young woman sitting beside the ill-sleeping Aurora. She looked up.

"This is my niece, Zoe Roundtree. Zoe. This is Princess Ally; she's come to help Aurora. Step outside, dear, we need to talk." Slowly, Phyllis made her way back to the table and sat down.

"Aunt Phyllis! What is *she* doing here?" Zoe said in an accusatory tone, glaring hatred at Ally.

"She's running away and has come to help Aurora. Babs delivered her and her siblings and always helped our queen. Princess Ally feels obligated to help her daughter. Ally, tell her what happened yesterday afternoon, please," Phyllis asked.

Ally complied and related the events. "I've got to get out of Wycombe soon. They'll discover I've escaped within hours now. All hell is going to break loose after that," Ally explained, growing more worried by the minute. "Maybe my being here is not such a good idea, if I bring more of dad's wrath on all of you."

Zoe's attitude softened a little. "Well, okay, if my aunt says to trust you, then I will too. Aunt Phyllis, are we ready?"

"Yes, here is the bag of psi-powder that I've prepared. You are to mix it in her drink, and see she gets a teaspoon of it three times a day. There ought to be enough to get her to the others. I've packed those saddlebags with food and other herbs. Unless you feel comfortable about it, I wouldn't change her bandages, unless they get wet or an emergency arises. Get her to the others as fast as you can manage, Zoe. Brad should be here with the horses shortly," Phyllis replied.

"I'm sorry. I don't have a horse. Where are we going?

How can we get out of the city gates?" Ally asked. "The guards will surely stop us."

Phyllis ignored her and continued sternly, "You and Zoe are charged with getting Aurora safely to Wyth, where many of the younger witches of Wycombe have fled. Zoe's younger brother, Brad, is bringing the horses, two of them," Phyllis answered.

"Won't we need three horses?" Ally asked. "I suppose I can walk."

"No, Brad is not going with Zoe. I anticipated another would be coming along with Zoe and Aurora. Zoe will ride double, holding Aurora. Ally, you will ride point and carry the supplies. I hear him now. Ally, lend Zoe a hand getting Aurora up and onto the horse. I'll meet with Brad out front and prepare the exit," Phyllis ordered.

How could she know I was coming? I only decided that a short while ago? A mystified Ally quickly followed Zoe into the bedroom. There lay Aurora, her arms wrapped in red-stained bandages. She fought from gagging herself. *This is more horrible than I'd imagined!*

Zoe and Ally lifted the semi-unconscious woman up, mostly walking her out of the bedroom and through the shop portion. Outside, it was still dark, but in the dual moonlight, Ally saw Phyllis standing beside two horses and a young man, perhaps but a boy still. He held the reins. "Sis, I wish I could come with you. Say, who is with you?" he asked as he noticed Ally.

Ally replied, "Best that you do not know. Give us a hand, please." The three lifted the handless woman up and into the saddle. While Ally steadied the poor woman and kept her from falling, Zoe climbed up behind her. Brad then ducked inside, brought out the stuffed saddlebags, and secured them to the other horse. Ally mounted wondering how they were going to get out of the walled city. *I'm supposed to lead the way, but how?*

Zoe saw Ally's confusion and whispered, "Aunt Phyllis will get us out. Watch." A note of extreme pride was in the young woman's voice. Ally heard Phyllis chanting and suddenly a gap appeared in the wooden walls beside the shop.

"Follow me. Be quick about it while she holds the gate open." Ally stared in disbelief at the mysterious gap that had just appeared in the walls. She swore it was not there before. *What is going on?* She looked back as she followed Zoe's mare through the gap and saw Phyllis collapsing, but Brad was there and caught her. He waved and the wooden wall reappeared. They were now on the other side and outside of the city. Ally had a million questions, but now was not the time. She followed Zoe, who seemed to know the proper direction to travel. In the dark, Ally did not.

Zoe decided she didn't fully trust the daughter of the man who had murdered Babs and mutilated Aurora. Hence, she didn't tell Ally that long ago, for just such a night as this, the witches cut that opening in the walls and hid it with a "believable illusion."

Before long, Ally saw they were on the northwest road, which led eventually to Wyth, some three hundred fifty miles ahead. She relaxed for the first time since she had heard of her proposed marriage to Prince Orsen Chester. Not long after that, the sun rose, and she moved up beside Zoe and Aurora. Zoe was twenty and blonde, as were most natives of Bettingham. She was also pretty, Ally observed. She now got a good look at Aurora. The woman's arms ended a pair of heavy, white bandage wraps, and her heart went out to the poor woman. *Perhaps dad was merciful to Babs,* she thought. *How can Aurora live like this?* Aurora was also pretty, but her white cotton dress was blood soaked, and her closed eyes were red and swollen.

Zoe saw her looking at them. "Our king is an evil, vicious, wicked man. I hope someone kills him soon. No one should have to live life like this! I'd kill him myself if I could! Hope you can live with this!" She was still antagonistic towards the king's daughter.

"I can't really. It's — it's more terrible than I imagined. I'm with you all the way, Zoe. He's beaten mom, broken her arms twice now. He has an awful temper. Did Babs really steal the COG's silver like the bishop claimed?"

"Don't be silly, princess! Babs never stole a thing in her life. The damnable COG is trying hard to kill off all of us witches. He simply made the whole thing up. Babs refused to abandon Wycombe when the others left. She ought to have gone; then this wouldn't have happened."

"Are you a witch too?" Ally asked, rather surprised the young woman might be. She didn't fit her imagined ideas of what witches ought to look like, namely Babs.

"Aunt Phyllis is, and she is training me. She's too old and feeble to make this long journey, and I stayed behind to both learn from her and to help her. I've had my bags packed for months now, planning to leave at the first opportunity. Well, this is not *quite* like I had imagined it. Brad is going to look after Aunt Phyllis now. I hope the bastard king doesn't hang her too!" Zoe replied, spitting on the ground. "Come on; we had best get off the main road now." She gently neck reined her mare to the right.

"Cross country?" Ally asked.

"Yes, safer this way. You do look like a young man, from a distance and as long as you don't speak," Zoe advised her. "Did you think of the disguise?"

"Yes, I'm doing the best I can to not get recognized. I'm sure dad's in a fit of rage about now. I'm hoping he'll spend hours scouring the city before he sends his soldiers out here looking for me."

"Another reason for us to be off the main road," Zoe agreed. "So what're you going to do now?" Zoe decided to chat with the princess. "This must be vastly different than your nice, orderly princess-world." She couldn't help tossing a dig at her.

"Well, yes, but I promise to keep up. I've a dagger and will do all I can to protect you and Aurora. Honestly, my planning hasn't even gotten this far. I expected to never be able to get as far as I did get. It's just as I was sneaking through the streets last night, I somehow thought of Aurora and knew I had to come and help her. After that, I don't have any ideas. Stay low and out of sight, I suppose. Perhaps I'll be able to stay with Aurora and help her with things. Honestly, I don't see how she's going to be able to do anything any longer. She's going to need me as long as she lives. Perhaps, if I cut my hair like a man's, I might be able to pass as one and get a job to support Aurora somehow. One thing is for sure, I am *not* going to abandon her now."

Zoe looked at her closely. "You're serious about this, aren't you?"

"Absolutely. It's the very least I can do for all Babs has done for me and mom."

After that, Zoe's view of Ally changed markedly, accepting her companionship. "Well, we're heading for the witches who recently moved to Wyth. They will help heal Aurora's arms. Right now, her lower arms are a god-awful mess. At least, Aunt Phyllis believes there are no infections, but that can easily change. The psi-powders are supposed to help her fight off any infections and the pain until we can get her to the witches. Honestly, though, I am more worried about her mental state," Zoe admitted.

"She watched her mother get hanged for a crime she wasn't guilty of and then endured the terror of the mad doctor's wicked machine. I can't imagine the pain she must have felt, first with the severing of her hands and then the searing heat that staunched the bleeding from her stumps. Couple that with what she must be feeling about being totally helpless for the rest of her life and I wouldn't be surprised if she tried to end her life somehow. Honestly, I can't blame her if she did. Ally, if she regains consciousness, we need to be alert for that."

"God, it's worse than I ever imagined. Dad's done this wicked thing to so many men and women now. I wish he'd have to experience what he has had done to them," Ally declared rather vehemently. Zoe chuckled. They rode on in silence for a time.

Later, Zoe explained, "We are going to have to make at least fifty miles each day if we are to get her there in seven days. We are lucky it is summertime. We've got long days. Pray it doesn't rain; that would soak into her bandages. Still, we don't dare even trot; the bouncing might reopen her wounds. I hope you don't get too saddle sore." Ally smiled and hoped so too. Already, she had ridden longer than she ever had in her life.

Around noon, they halted beneath the shade of an oak

thicket. A small creek trickled past them. In the distance, they could just barely see the main road. Here Zoe stopped. "Okay, Ally, hold her steady while I get off. Then, let's see if we can lift her down."

Mechanically, Aurora lifted her arms, and she was pulled off the horse. She came to a little, as they moved her to a soft patch of leaves, where she could sit and lean against a tree. She whined, "My arms are throbbing. I hurt so. Mom is dead; please kill me too, please. I can't live like this," Aurora moaned in pain, tears began flowing down her face once more.

"We have to get some lunch and psi-powders in you, Aurora. We're not going to let you die on us. Be brave," Zoe whispered. She and Ally fixed themselves a light lunch, rationing their meager food supplies. Water was plentiful, though, and Zoe carefully measured and mixed the powder. She held the mug up to Aurora's lips while Ally alternated holding a sandwich for her to eat. "Come on; you have to eat. Your body needs it," Zoe coaxed Aurora. By now, the woman was hungry, and her body ate mechanically, though her will to live was gone.

While they were eating, they heard galloping horses. In the distance, they spotted soldiers galloping up the main road. "Damn, they must be looking for me. If they find us, I'll lead them away from you two. Save Aurora, Zoe," Ally declared. Zoe nodded; her respect for Ally was steadily increasing.

They waited a while and then packed up. "Maybe I can get up," Aurora said as they led her to the horses. Zoe whispered to Ally that this was the psi-powders kicking in. She was weak but did manage much of the work mounting, though the two helped her keep her balance.

Once Zoe was safely mounted behind Aurora, Ally mounted herself, and Zoe led the way once more, much to Ally's relief. She had no idea where she was now at, save somewhere in Bettingham. *Damn my ignorance! My life has been a pathetic, worthless one, but I've got this **one** chance to really help, and I'm going to help Aurora or die trying!*

The frequency of the farmsteads began to dwindle steadily during the long afternoon. By dusk, they had put fifty miles behind them. For the next three hundred miles, they could expect to encounter only small towns, villages, and hamlets. The kingdom was sparsely populated out beyond the major two cities of Bettingham, as it was in all the kingdoms. Pioneering farmsteads still were present, but life in the wilds was dangerous.

Roving bandits, raids by the king's soldiers, and even attacks by enemy king's soldiers were a constant threat to those who chose to live far from the major cities. Yet wild animals were a much more serious threat. Wolves and bears raided human settlements with some frequency. However, the greatest threat of all was from the giant breed of lions found on Tierra, known as the Montaña Beasts. These carnivores grew to nearly ten feet tall with huge canines and claws, which could rip a man to shreds in mere seconds, a horse in three times that. Swift and sure hunters, they often tracked their prey for miles before striking at the most opportune time. Montaña Beasts were greatly feared throughout all Tierra.

Near the more heavily populated areas, the kings sent out regular patrols in hopes of driving the Montaña Beasts from those areas. Over these many years, such proved successful. Still, now the three had left Wycombe behind them, these Montaña Beasts would be a threat as well. Thus far, Zoe had not seen any signs of them on the ground. Their paw prints were hard to miss. Zoe didn't tell Ally this trip was full of danger. *No need to worry the princess needlessly.* Besides, if a Montaña Beast picked up their scent, the best they could hope to do would be to outrun it — the usual human reaction that often proved successful. Perhaps a very well-armed band of soldiers might have some slight chance of wounding this vicious hunter at the very top of the food chain.

Towards evening, Zoe explained, "We don't dare risk asking a farmer to spend the night in his barn, Ally. Aurora's wounds could easily get infected there. Besides, the soldiers are likely to start searching off-road for you as well. We'll make due over there by that creek. It is isolated enough, but no fires. We don't want to draw attention to ourselves," Zoe explained as they halted.

When Aurora was finally on the ground, she was in another bout of grief; the psi-powders had worn off. Still, Zoe had Ally put her arms around the woman and walk her some. "She needs to exercise a little. So do you; your legs look like they are going to collapse any second."

"No kidding, they feel like mush," Ally replied.

"You'll get your horse legs soon enough, Ally," Zoe answered, setting about fixing a light supper and Aurora's psi-powdered water. There was just enough light to barely see to do this.

While stretching their legs, Aurora again moaned from the pain and cried. "Mom is dead! I can't live like this. Please, kill me too or let me die," she wailed.

"Aurora, you can't. You must be *brave* and show everyone you can surmount this! If you die, then they win. You have to *live*, Aurora. I'll help you *always*," Ally promised, trying anything to get Aurora calmed down.

"How? How? How like this?" she raised her stumps up a little, though that only caused them to throb all the more. She quickly lowered them again.

"I don't know, Aurora, I really don't, but somehow we must manage. You can depend on me," she consoled her.

At last, Aurora began looking for the first time who she was with. "I know you, don't I?"

"I'm Ally, okay, Princess Ally Wycombe. I've run away from my despot dad and king who did this to you. Somehow, Aurora, Zoe and I are going to get you to safety and then, well, I don't know what, but I'm *always* going to look after you and help you. Together, we can overcome all this. I *know* it."

"Princess Ally? You look like a guy, but I know your voice. How? How can this *ever* be all right? If you want to show me mercy, use your dagger. Cut my throat or stab me in my heart. I'd do it myself, but now I can't even do that simple thing."

"Oh don't be silly. I'll do no such thing. We're going to survive, Aurora, you and I and Zoe; we're going to survive this *somehow*. Okay, I admit, I don't know how. Come on. Zoe has our food ready. I'm starving. How about you?"

"I am really hungry and thirsty. Can you wipe my face a little?" Once again, Aurora started bawling, as she suddenly realized she couldn't even do this simple thing.

"Sure, but once your arms have healed, I'm sure you can wipe your own face. Meantime, we have to keep the bandages dry." She wiped Aurora's tears, and they sat down to eat. First, Zoe had her drink all her potion, and then Ally slowly fed her their cold supper.

"One of us ought to stand guard while the rest sleeps," Ally suggested when they had finished. *I have to think like Norwood and Palmer now. What would they do? I wish I had paid more attention to them.*

"No need, I can at least handle that much," Zoe replied. She chanted a little and added, "There, if any trouble comes our way, I ought to be alerted and be awakened by my little spell. Come on; let's get some sleep. I'm dead tired." Ally wondered what Zoe had done and what she meant, but was too tired to ask.

The next morning, they rose at first light, hastily fixing a little to eat. Just then, they heard soldiers not far away. Ally drew her dagger and stood before Zoe and Aurora. Voices could just barely be heard, causing them to panic slightly. *I simply must defend these two. I have the dagger, and I simply must. Ally, try to remember all those fighting moves Palmer does on the practice field,* she told herself. After a worrisome few minutes, the riders drifted off in another direction. As quietly and as quickly as they could, they packed up and headed off once more.

As they headed out, Zoe whispered, "That was too close for comfort, Ally. You were right. The bastard king must be raving mad to have his soldiers searching *this* far afield. We best be more careful."

They rode for a few more miles when suddenly the three were taken by complete surprise. A dozen soldiers sprang out of the nearby trees, pointing crossbows at the three. One yelled, "Princess Ally! Stop where you are or we'll shoot you!"

Ally thought faster than she ever thought it was possible to think. In the blink of an eye, she'd analyzed what avenues she could take and then acted on the one that was the most promising. Jumping off her horse, she kicked Zoe's horse, startling it. The horse bolted. As Ally seemed to be falling off her horse in slow motion, she landed a kick on its rear as well, spooking her mare too. Somehow, she landed upright on her feet, as the two spooked horses galloped passed the surprised ring of soldiers! "Okay, I surrender," she called out, raising her hands in the air, further distracting the soldiers. With all her might, she hoped and prayed they wouldn't chase after Zoe and Aurora.

"Let them go; we don't have any orders about those thieves," the sergeant in charge barked, as several turned to find their horses and give chase. Ally realized Aurora's missing hands suggested to the sergeant that she was a tried and convicted thief. "We have what we came for. Bill, go alert Doctor Forrest now. Tie her up; lead her back to the road." Rough hands grabbed her, snatching her dagger out of its scabbard, then pinning her arms behind her. She felt the taut ropes as a man wrapped her wrists securely and tied them. Another poked her in the right direction, and Ally walked that way. She said nothing, and the soldiers merely joked over the rewards they fully expected to receive, when they brought the princess back to King Aaran tomorrow. Ally's thoughts all were on Zoe and Aurora. Had they gotten away? It looked that way now and then her mind went blank, accepting her fate. Soon, her life would be ended, but she'd at least saved those two from her father's wrath.

When they reached the road, they lifted her onto a horse and headed back down the road towards Wycombe, now some sixty miles distant. However, an hour later, they pulled into the hamlet of Whistlewaters and stopped at the small inn there. Ally was unceremoniously lifted down and forced inside the inn. Her heart raced, and she involuntarily gasped as she saw Doctor Corey Forrest was there along with his Amputator de la Mano. He grinned wickedly and said, "Well, well, the wayward princess herself. You've made your father angrier than anyone has ever seen before, to say nothing of jeopardizing his peace treaty. By King Aaran's orders, you're to be punished most severely such that you can never do this again, not to him or to your betrothed, if he'll still desire you. Untie her. Put her arms in there," he ordered.

Suddenly, she realized he was not going to kill her. No,

it was a far worse fate than that! Ally struggled, as did everyone who faced this awful machine of Doctor Corey's, but the men were far stronger than she was. Soon her arms were forced inside the machine. "Relax, Princess, you won't feel a thing, not at first. I am a humane doctor. I take the care of my patients and their health sincerely. I can't have you dying on me; the king would have my hide. You will feel this pin prick. It is numbing your lower arms and hands." She felt a bee sting in each arm.

"You'll pay for this, you butcher!" Ally screamed at him, wishing there was some way she could do just that.

After a few minutes, he asked her if she felt this. She felt nothing as he inserted a large needle into her right index finger nearly an inch. "Now you will feel a bit of pressure. That is normal; the machine is finding the precise location of where your hands join your arms at your wrists. Ah, there, feel it?" Ally nodded, biting her lip, bracing herself for intense pain. Doctor Corey pulled his lever down. The pressure seemed enormous, but suddenly it was gone, as were her hands, cleanly and surgically severed. She saw her own blood flowing out, and she passed out. Thus, she missed the huge blast of flames staunching her wounds. She also missed watching Doctor Corey tightly bandaging her two stumps, grinning all the while.

She awoke, she guessed, perhaps an hour later. She was still in the inn, sitting in the same chair as before. Ally looked down at her arms, her hands were gone; only bloody bandages marked where her wrists hand been. She screamed from both shock and the pain. The anesthesia had worn off. *How could my bastard father have done this to me? Now I've failed at the only thing I have ever chosen to do. I can't live up to my vow to help Aurora survive! God! The pain!*

31

Chapter 3 Repercussions Begin

"She's not in her bedroom. She's gone, Sire," Sally, Ally's personal servant, reported hesitantly.

"What? Gone? How's this possible? Speak woman?" King Aaran screamed at the poor woman.

"I don't know, honestly, I don't. She told me last night she was packing her things."

"You lie, bitch," he smacked her across her face; she screamed and continued to claim she didn't know anything. King Aaran didn't believe her yet and snapped her right arm in half. Amid her hideous screams, he now believed the woman and ordered a soldier to get her out of his throne room. "That's better. Okay, call out every damn soldier in the place. Search this castle first and then the entire city! Find that bitch of a daughter! Find Ally now!"

Never had Queen Misty seen him in such a terrible rage! Likewise, his soldiers who dashed out of the room. Before long, they reported what he suspected, that she was not in the castle and had somehow escaped during the night. He had the two night guards executed on the spot and ordered Wycombe be thoroughly searched. Not long after that, the soldiers dragged the sleeping night watchman of the city gates into his throne room. After beating the man half to death, he became convinced Ally had not exited through the gates.

However, as mid-morning approached, he got the sense she must have been clever enough to get over the outer wooden walls. He sent for his best trackers and ordered them to scour the grounds beyond the outer wall for signs of recent passage. A half hour later, they reported two sets of horses had been up close to the walls and then moved away from the walls, out onto the road heading for Wyth. That's all he needed to hear.

He called off his citywide search and ordered five hundred soldiers to follow her. "Five hundred silver pieces for whoever finds my bitch of a daughter!" With that as an added incentive, he knew his men would not fail. "Don't come back without her!" he yelled after them, as they cantered out of the castle grounds.

Turning to Doctor Corey, he said, "Pack up your Amputator de la Mano, good doctor. Go after them. If and when they find Ally, remove both of hers. I don't want her ever to pull a humiliating stunt like this ever again! Do it before you bring her back to me. If so, you get five hundred silver too, doctor!" King Aaran wanted the next sight of his daughter to be one of her utter humiliation.

"Aaran! No, she's our daughter! What're you doing? Prince Orson Chester will never want to marry her if she's a helpless invalid. You can't do such a thing to your own daughter," Queen Misty pleaded for her daughter. At long last, Misty was shocked at her husband's behavior.

"Bitch!" He slapped her hard, nearly knocking her over. "If you had borne me two more sons, we'd not be in this terrible mess! It's all your fault, bitch! Now get out of my sight! April, don't *you* try anything so stupid like your foolish older sister!" April nearly fainted; her mother caught her and led the white-faced teen out of the throne room, while holding her own swelling, bruised face.

"Mom! They're going to cut off her hands, both of them! How can she even live like that? She'll be totally helpless," April wailed. Misty pulled her youngest daughter into her bosom and held her tightly. Something Ally had said to her came back to haunt her, *One day he'll go too far and kill you, mom.* Misty began to wonder if that day had not come.

After that, April locked herself in her room and refused to come out at all. She feared her father would have her own hands chopped off like her older sister. She refused even to let Misty come inside. Standing in the hallway that night, Misty felt suddenly alienated, stripped of both of her two daughters. One son was off fighting the war somewhere in the north; all she had left was Palmer, but he always kept clear of his father's rage and had early this very morning joined the soldiers in their search.

Once well beyond Wycombe, Palmer struck out for the north, going in search of Norwood, hoping his older brother could do something, though it would likely be far too late for their sister. If nothing else, he was beyond his father's rage and wouldn't have to witness Ally's utter humiliation when she was caught. He had no doubts she'd be quickly apprehended. *She'll probably die from her wounds,* he thought. *That'll be a merciful death. Poor Ally.* Later, he got pulled into helping defend another town and decided against taking any further actions that might pull his father's rage onto himself.

Later that morning, the emissary from Chester arrived to consummate their bargain. However, he'd already heard the news that the princess had somehow fled the castle. He was not surprised, but he played his assigned role well. "This is outrageous, King Aaran! How can you control your kingdom if you cannot control one silly daughter? Well, the price will be doubled; we'll also take April as well. I will be staying at the Wessley Inn, notify me when you have your daughters ready to be taken to the Chester princes." He turned on his heels and left a raging king, whose face was brilliantly red.

He summoned Queen Misty, told her of the new demands, and ordered her to prepare April. He didn't bother summoning the pathetic excuse for a daughter to him to tell her to her face. Misty walked the halls but didn't tell April about this latest change in plans. Rather, she snapped. She'd been hit by King Aaran one time too many. She stole into Palmer's rooms and searched. At last, she found what she wanted and then went to her own room, brooding all the while.

When no soldiers returned that night, Misty took heart. Perhaps her daughter had somehow eluded the intense dragnet her father had cast. However, by evening word reached them that Ally had been found and captured. Her doom was about to be carried out, according to the soldier who was sent galloping back to the king with the news. He also said Doctor Corey predicted they'd arrive back at the castle in Wycombe in two days' time.

Queen Misty then heard King Aaran issue orders to send word to the Chester emissary that the women would be handed over to him in two days, just as soon as Doctor Corey arrived with Ally. Hearing that, Misty's ledger finally tipped the other way. In the past, she'd done far too many things which hurt others more than they helped others. Thus, for most of her married life, she'd been receiving harmful actions, reactively trying to get her ledger balanced. When one does regrettable actions, one feels he or she must have had proper justification. Misty's ledger had been entirely unbalance for many years. Now at long last, Misty felt entirely calm and collected; she'd received enough bad that she could outflow harm once more. She waited.

Later that night, King Aaran finally came to bed. As he undressed, he said, "Well, soon we'll see our errant daughter again, only this time she'll never, ever defy us again. I shall sleep much better tonight! I can't wait to see her face when Doctor Corey brings her before me! Oh, my victory will be delicious!"

"I do so hope you enjoy it, dear," Misty said politely, as she walked up to the bedside. She held one of Palmer's daggers in her right hand, hidden behind her back. As she stood over him, she added, "I've been waiting a long time to do this. I do so hope you enjoy your evil ways." He smiled, but failed to grasp her meaning. Before he could react, she plunged the dagger into his chest. Then, with a fit of wild abandon, she struck him again and again and again. The terror in his eyes spoke volumes to Misty. She finally ceased driving the dagger into his body after the twenty-third time.

King Aaran was quite dead. However, he was also quite confused. He was now viewing the bloody scene from the ceiling of the master bedroom. Below him lay his brutally stabbed and very bloody corpse. Standing over it was his wife, blood dripping from the very dagger he'd given to Palmer. She cackled and laughed. His rage was unparalleled, but he could do absolutely nothing. *What is happening to me? I'm a ghost?* A command appeared in his mind, *Go get a new baby body.* He thought, *Yes, that's what I must do! I'll show her, damnable bitch!* He flew through the stone walls and out over Wycombe, searching for a very pregnant woman.

Misty cackled to herself for a time. Then, she stuck the dagger one more time into his chest, blew out the lanterns, and crawled into bed as if nothing at all had happened. "I can't recall when I have ever felt this good!" she whispered to herself and soon fell asleep.

April heard the news that she too was to be given to the Chester prince. Her servant woman told her that through her locked door. She spent the night crying to herself and then spent the next day slowly packing her possessions. That fateful night, she went to bed dreading the confrontation what was sure to come in two days, but unwilling to do anything about it. She was only eighteen and powerless, she thought. *Maybe it won't be so bad. Poor Ally, I told her she'd get into bad trouble. Maybe dad will be merciful and kill her when she comes before him.* Finally, April cried herself to sleep.

The next morning, the castle steward came into the master bedroom to rouse King Aaran, as he had for the last dozen years. "Oh dear god! The King and Queen have been assassinated! Guards! Guards!" he screamed. His loud yelling woke Misty. "Thank the gods! Misty, you are still alive! Are you wounded? No, thank heavens! Did you see the assassin? I knew it was a bad idea sending out all our palace guards after Ally! A damnable assassin has snuck in right under our noses and assassinated the king! Guards! Guards!" He raced out of the room, rousing the few soldiers who were not out searching for Ally.

April heard his yelling and woke up. Unlocking her door, she wandered timidly to her parent's master bedroom. She screamed at the sight. Then she cried out, "Mom! Are you all right?"

"Why, yes, of course I am all right. Your father has finally got what was coming to him."

April timidly said, "I heard Tom yelling. An assassin got him in the night! My god, mom! You very nearly got murdered too!" Seeing her mother's gown caked in blood, her heart went out to her. "Come on; let's get you out of your bloody nightgown! Come on, mom." April pulled her mother out of the room with the corpse of her father. She helped her mother get bathed, get her hair washed, and finally helped her into a clean dress. By then, the commotion had died down and the body was removed.

Tom, the castle steward, found them and hastily explained, "Your Majesty, it is not safe for you in the castle. Is there somewhere you and your daughter can go for a few days?

Chaos is rampant here in the castle. There could well be further assassinations. I'm sure your sons will head here as soon as they are informed. I've sent out riders to find them."

April spoke up, "Yes, we will go stay with my aunt. Come on, mom; let's get out of here before the assassin returns to finish his job!" Misty followed her daughter, and they were escorted out of the castle, later arriving at her sister's home in Wycombe. By then, city criers were relaying the vitally important news up and down the many streets.

Aunt Agnus welcomed them both as soon as she answered their knock. "Come in, come in! This is so shocking. Misty, are you sure you are not hurt?" Her sister looked her over, up and down.

"I'm fine, Agnus, really I have never felt *better* in my life," Misty replied.

"Well, I say good riddance to Aaran. He beat you half to death. So many people have suffered his rage. I'm very happy he finally got what he deserved!" Agnes declared vehemently.

"Yes, he got what he deserved — long overdue. You heard he's had Ally's hands removed, just like a common thief? Well, he's not going to hurt anyone else anymore. No sir. I took care of that!" Misty replied.

"What? What do you mean?" her sister asked, not quite sure how to interpret what Misty was saying or implying.

"I did it, Agnus. Last night — when he climbed into bed. I used Palmer's dagger. Stabbed him lots of times. Had to make sure he died — that he was really and truly *quite* dead. Yes, I killed him, Agnus. I did it, though I am far too late to save my Ally." A strange glee sparkled in her eyes.

April and Agnus gasped, shocked beyond words. Both covered their mouths with their hands. April sank into the nearest chair; her legs gave out. At last, Agnus recovered. "Misty, does the steward know you did it — murdered the king?"

"No, for some idiotic reason, he thinks an assassin somehow got in last night and did it. Silly, stupid man," Misty answered her.

"Good. Don't tell another soul! We have to get you out of Wycombe. I've a brother-in-law who lives on a farm ten miles south of the city. I'm sending you there until all this blows over," Agnus declared. "April, you best go with your mother. Come on; we'd best make some arrangements."

"A farm? Yes, I do believe I would like to grow flowers now. Yes, splendid." Agnus began to think her sister had actually gone completely mad. *Well, that's what she gets for having put up with that vile man all these years!* An hour later, she arranged for a carriage to take her sister and niece out to the country farm. While April didn't want to have anything to do with her mother, fearing she really was insane, she also knew she dare not stay in Wycombe. The emissary from Chester might well simply kidnap her and take her away. Thus, she too accompanied Misty later that afternoon. Aunt Agnus promised to tell anyone who came asking about them that they had decided to go to Wyth instead. Agnus thus attempted to wipe her hands clean of the whole affair.

Zoe urged her mare into a full gallop. "My god! Ally was serious about making sure we got away, Aurora! They are not chasing us — I don't think. I'm going to try to see if I can get a hold of her horse. It has all our supplies on it." Zoe slowed down and prayed the other mare following them would also slow down. She did, thankfully. Then, she walked the lathered horses for a while, until she found a concealed glen and finally dismounted. "Come on, Aurora; you are going to have to help get yourself down. I don't think I can manage you all by myself." Aurora tried her best to help, but both women ended up hitting the ground hard.

"Damn! All that jostling has opened up your wounds," Zoe pointed out the obvious. Red soaked bandages covered both stumps. "Damn, this is going all wrong! Okay, you sit down and let me see what I can do. This is way over my skill level, Aurora."

"It hurts so," Aurora began crying again, which didn't help matters. Hastily, Zoe got out her psi-powders bag and mixed up a potion for Aurora. Once she helped her drink it, Aurora began calming down again. Now Zoe had time to think. She felt obligated to find a way to help Ally, but she also now needed help, urgent help. She sighed; there was only one thing she could do. She took a quadruple dose of the psi-powder and mixed it up, drinking it herself. She lay back and began to feel its effects on herself almost at once.

Focus, focus, focus, she told herself, trying to remember everything she'd been taught or had overheard. *Aunt Phyllis, Aunt Phyllis! Help!*

Zoe? Whatever is the matter? What's happened, dear child? The voice of her aunt appeared in her mind, much to her great relief.

Hastily, Zoe told her what had happened and what she knew was about to happen to Ally. *I've had to use a whole two days' of Aurora's psi-powders. There isn't going to be enough to get her to Wyth, and her wounds have opened up — all that mad galloping, and we sort of fell off the horse too. What do I do? Her bandages are blood soaked. Yes, I gave her some psi-powders.*

Aunt Phyllis told her what to do, step by step. *I'll get back to you, Zoe. I'll see what other arrangements can be made. You get her bleeding stopped. Stay where you are at now until you hear from me or have to flee.*

Aunt Phyllis broke the telepathic connection Zoe had formed with her. Grimacing, she ordered Brad bring her a stiff drink laced with six spoons of psi-powder. "Are you sure?" he asked worriedly. This was almost twice as much as she usually took.

"Yes, this is the worst emergency I've ever faced. Thanks, Brad." She drank it quickly and soon opened her own connections. An hour later, she relaxed and reconnected to Zoe. *How is it going now, Zoe?*

Not so good. I am having a hard time stopping the bleeding.

Okay, help is on the way. I had to pull in some long outstanding favors, but at my age, I might as well use them. They owed me big time, and they are the closest trustworthy folks I can find. Expect the Bettingham twins to find you in about three hours, maybe less. Aiden and Alford Bettingham. You can trust them with your life, Zoe. Now keep trying to arrest her bleeding. Here is another thing you can try. She outlined yet another witch's remedy.

Zoe agreed to try it and left Aurora dozing from the psi-powders, while she went in search of the herbs and that special kind of dirt. Later, she mixed them and dared to remove Aurora's bandages. She nearly gagged from the ghastly sight, but forced herself to apply the mixture and then re-wrapped them securely. *Now we wait,* she thought. *Either I'll see red seeping through or it'll hold,* she thought, but didn't say anything to Aurora, who was at least resting and not sobbing as she had been. *What do I do if I see red lines going up her arms?* Zoe knew poor Aurora was already far beyond her own healing training and skill. She needed a miracle. *If only the summer rains hold off a while longer. If we get caught out here in the open, the bandages will get soaked, and the wounds will become infected for sure!*

It struck her that probably right now Ally was like Aurora, handless and in great pain, suffering horribly without the benefit of a witch's care and the precious psi-powders to take the awful edge off the trauma. Ally had indeed kept her word; she'd kicked both horses, causing them to bolt before the soldiers could react. Zoe's respect for Ally rose to a new height, and she wondered if there was really anything she could do for Ally, assuming she even survived this ordeal. She drifted into a light sleep herself.

Warning! Her simple alarm charm activated, rousing her. She jumped up, her hand falling to her waist, but realizing it was Ally who had the dagger. If trouble came, she could only kick and strike with her fists. Zoe was not a fighter, but a beginning healer, a good witch to the locals. Two men on horseback came up to them; both were tracking her two mares. "Ah hail, Zoe? Aurora?" one called out as he spotted the two.

"Yes, and you are?" Zoe asked, placing her body before the sitting Aurora, who stirred a little.

"Aiden and Alford. Didn't Phyllis tell you to expect us?" one said. They were identical twins, with shoulder length blonde hair.

"Thank you for coming. Yes, she did. Which is which? How can I tell you apart?" she asked as the two dismounted.

"I'm Aiden, he's Alford. Probably can't. If mom

couldn't, you're not likely to either. Alford, have a look at Aurora. I'll get the facts from Zoe here," Aiden suggested.

Hastily, Zoe explained what had happened with Ally and how Phyllis had instructed her on stopping Aurora's bleeding. "Please, if there is any way you can get to Ally and save her, you have to try. She sacrificed everything to save us and help Aurora. She's not like the king, her father. Please," Zoe begged.

Alford stated, "Right, Aurora's bleeding has stopped. Let's give her another hour or two to stabilize. Meantime, let's see if we can get to Ally. Zoe, you should be safe enough here. You are well off all the tracks around here, and the soldiers have thinned out. See you in a little while." He and Aiden mounted up and galloped off.

Zoe laid back and relaxed, dozing for a time, but she could not stop imagining the horrid trauma Ally must be undergoing while she was here safe and resting. The returning men roused her again. "What news?" she asked even before they dismounted.

"We're going to try to rescue her tomorrow. The mad doctor has already done his dirty work long before we got there," Aiden replied, grimacing.

"Likely about five hours before we got there. They are at an inn and conveniently have sent most of the soldiers back to Wycombe. I think we stand a good chance of getting Ally from them," Alford added. "We brought more food supplies and a whole lot of your precious psi-powders, Zoe. If we can rescue Ally, you are going to need it. Let's rustle up some dinner. How's your patient doing?"

They set a campfire for the first time, and the brothers fixed the two women a nourishing hot meal. Aurora woke and began crying again. "My arms throb with pain. Can't you put me out of my misery, please," Aurora begged.

"My, you are the complaining type," Aiden teased her, though Zoe gave him an annoyed frown. "Here, try my stew and don't say you don't like it, 'cause I certainly like it." He began feeding her spoonfuls. She gobbled it up as fast as he scooped it up. "See, I told you this gorgeous woman would like my stew, Alford. She has taste, brother."

"She's awfully cute too," his twin replied.

"It *is* good. And no, I am not pretty anymore. Not like this," she moved her lower arms slightly, not daring to add to the constant throbbing in their ends.

"Oh I see, I am so terribly sorry, Aurora," Aiden continued his relentless teasing. "I didn't realize your hands contained all your beauty while the rest of you is positively ugly."

"What?" Aurora exclaimed. "That's not what I meant at all," she added defiantly.

"Well, according to you, a woman's beauty lies solely in her hands," Aiden continued in the same vein. "Take Ally, who we are going to have to rescue tomorrow. Take Ally, when we get her away from the mad doctor, she will now be totally ugly, since she lost her hands too. Right Aurora?"

"That's not what I meant at all!" she replied testily. Zoe noticed she wasn't in grief any longer and realized what he was doing. "Ally is very pretty."

"Well, then you are just going to have to accept the plain fact we think you are quite pretty and bright," Aiden then concluded. "You are a young witch, like your mother."

"But like this? I can't even take care of myself," Aurora countered quite testily.

"And you darn well better not even try right now! We need your body to heal itself well before you go back to cooking, eating, and all manner of witch things," Aiden admonished her in a teasing manner once more.

"But I can never do those things for myself ever again," she complained bitterly.

"Wanna bet? Okay, dear Aurora, I'll wager you a hundred silver you'll be cooking and eating by yourself in no less than a month after your stumps have fully healed."

"Are you kidding me?" she asked somewhat curious now, though still reserved.

"Look Aurora. You won't be doing it the same way you used to cook and eat, but I am sure you will figure something out — some way to do it. Either that or you are going to have to suffer eating my cooking for the rest of your life." She flashed him a momentary grin. "Now, we best get some sleep. Alford and I have a big day ahead of us. We're going to get going long before dawn. Got to be in that hamlet at sunrise. We have us a plan, don't we, Alford?"

"Yes, indeed. We have us a plan. Good one too. Hope it works out, though. Aurora, I assure you that you don't want to be stuck eating Aiden's meals all the time. I'll give you a big clue: you've just sampled the only meal he knows how to cook!" Aurora and Zoe both chuckled, and Zoe realized this was the first time Aurora had done so!

As the twins had said, Zoe woke to find them both long gone. She fixed Aurora's breakfast, fed her, and examined her two wounds. Neither had bled through the bandages. "He's kind of cute, isn't he?" Aurora chatted while Zoe cleaned up their things.

"Yes, very, but you can't tell them apart. Maybe we ought to tie a ribbon in one's hair so we can tell them apart," Zoe teased and both chuckled.

"I don't hurt so much today. Maybe we can ease off the psi-powder a little. Do you think he is right? Can I possibly live like this?" she asked, timidly.

"I think I got what he was hinting at last night, Aurora. Obviously, you are going to be finding other ways to do some things. I think that's what he meant." The two chatted and then lay back to await their return. Zoe hoped and prayed that Ally would be all right. Hastily, she amended her thought. *Obviously, she'll never be all right again, but I meant not dying,* she corrected herself, sighed, and relaxed.

"I make four soldiers. Counting the doctor, that's five. Can we take the four of them by surprise?" Alford asked.

"They'll likely come out to saddle up. Probably only a couple will do that. We'll take them first and then head inside the inn," Aiden replied. "Come on; let's ready our weapons and get into position. We want surprise on our side."

For some time, they waited on opposite sides of the entrance to the inn's small stables. Not long after sunup, two soldiers came walking into the stables, chatting about all the silver they were going to get just as soon as they returned with their prize. Uniformly, they intended to spend it on ale, wenches, and the gambling tables. Neither saw the twins' attack coming. Two broadswords came down upon their necks, ending their lives almost at once. Without a word, the twins dragged the bodies to the hay pile and covered them up. However, they did confiscate their weapons. Steel blades were highly valuable, and each would bring at least five hundred silver or more on this metal-poor planet.

After waiting a brief time, they decided the others were not coming out and that they would have to take the battle inside the inn, a far more risky proposition. Both brothers ambled inside the inn, their eyes surveying the layout and situation. The doctor's fancy machine sat prominently in one corner, where he'd left it from its prior use. When the soldiers brought the wagon around, Doctor Corey intended to have them load it for him, just as they had unloaded it and brought it inside yesterday.

The twins spotted the two soldiers just finishing their morning meal at a distant table. Doctor Corey was sitting near his machine, still spooning a hot porridge into Ally's mouth. Her lower arms were heavily bandaged, the deed long done, as far as the twins were concerned. For a minute, they discretely observed how Ally was doing. She had been crying that much was plain. Still, she was eating and not sobbing at the moment. Alford nodded to Aiden, who rose and ambled over in the direction of the soldiers. Alford did the same, but came at them from their other side.

Before either soldier knew what was happening, the twins struck with deadly accuracy. Here inside the inn, swordplay would be more difficult, far too many objects to interfere. Instead, their method of attack was more subtle. Each held a dagger behind their backs as they approached. In unison, they thrust their blades up and into the men's chests, giving the blade a powerful twist and lift, slicing the inner organs far more than a simple stab wound. The soldiers gasped and tried to react, but the twin's follow through was even more deadly. Two throats were slit almost at the same instant.

Doctor Corey called out a warning and rose, drawing his own short sword. "What the devil is going on here?"

"We've come for you, Doctor Corey Forrest. It's long since time you paid the piper for your brutality against the people of Bettingham," Aiden said softly. The innkeeper, spotting the two slain soldiers, hastily dashed out of his inn. No way was he going to get involved!

"We can do this the easy way or we can do this the hard way, doctor," Alford said menacingly.

"What, what do you mean?" Doctor Corey asked, his fear rising rapidly. "More soldiers will be coming in here soon."

"Idle threat. The others have met the same fate as those two over there. You are next, mad doctor. Some of us in Bettingham want you quite dead," Alford countered, while Aiden inched forward. When Aiden was in position, Alford make a fake lunge at the doctor, who valiantly but foolishly swung his sword, trying to hit him. Taking his attention off Aiden was all the man needed. Crack! His dagger's hilt struck the doctor solidly on his head. The man collapsed, and Aiden kicked his sword across the floor.

"Princess Ally, I presume," asked politely.

"Yes, please cut my throat too. I am ready now. You see what he's done to me. I'm useless to everyone now. Go ahead. No one will see you do it. Besides, I can't take the throbbing pain in my arms any longer," Ally pleaded with him, fighting to keep from crying from the pain.

"Don't be stupid; you are a gorgeous young woman. I've something for the pain. I'll help her with that; you take care of the good doctor," Alford said. He rapidly measured out a bit of the psi-powder and mixed it in a cup of tea. "Your majesty, care for a bit of tea?" he teased her a little, though he could tell she was fighting hard from breaking down from the intense pain. *Some woman to be able to handle this and not break down completely. Amazing woman.*

She gratefully took a sip and then another. It had a strange taste, and she soon finished it. "The pain is subsiding. Still throbbing, but less, thanks. What was in it?" she said, becoming a bit braver. "What are you going to do to him? He should be killed for all the damage he has done."

Aiden called out from several feet away, "My princess,

killing is *far* too good for him. Our plans are to give him a taste of his own medicine." Alford chuckled. Ally suddenly realized what he meant!

Soon, the doctor was secured in his own machine. Once they had it all set up, Aiden woke him up. "What? What are you doing? No, you can't! I'm a doctor for god's sake! You don't know what you are doing! Please, don't!" His scream was blood curling when Aiden brought the lever down hard, severing his hands.

"I think you forgot to prick him with something to deaden the pain," Ally called out. "He did that to me. I only felt a whole lot of pressure when he did that to me. Then, the blood gushed out, and I don't remember what happened after that. I think there is supposed to be a fire or something."

"We'd better tie his stumps off or he'll bleed to death. We can't have that, can we brother?" Aiden said jokingly.

"Oh no, that'll never do for the mad doctor," Alford added. Quickly, they tied off the circulation, but left him secured to his machine. The innkeeper could deal with him now. "Come on, Princess Ally. Time to leave. Zoe and Aurora await."

"Zoe! Aurora! Are they okay? Did they get away safely?" Ally asked.

Alford looked her squarely in her eyes. He did not expect such a reply. "Yes, thanks to your quick thinking, both got away safely. Zoe contacted a friend of ours, and we came to rescue them and you as well. Come on; can you walk?"

"I am really weak, but that potion is working. Can I lean on you a little?" Ally asked.

"Absolutely. I love having beautiful women hanging onto me, don't I, Aiden?"

"Well I am not so pretty any longer. Maybe your eyes are worn out," Ally suggested, as they moved slowly towards the door. Aiden took a quick glance outside. Finding nothing amiss, he headed off ahead of the two to get another horse ready. "I'm so weak," she felt a need to explain why she was leaning on him so heavily.

"Blood loss. Got to get more fluids in you, at least that's what the witches said. We'll get you fixed up in no time,"

Alford encouraged her, thankful she was not a sobbing basket case as Aurora apparently was. *Well, it's debilitating enough,* he thought, *but not the end of the world. She's damn pretty.*

"Is she going to be able to ride by herself?" Aiden asked as the two got to the stables. Aiden had already rounded up their two geldings and had one saddled for Ally. He stowed the additional steel weapons onto one horse. Thus far, they had twenty-five hundred silver profit from this little adventure.

"I have to try," Ally answered, surprising Aiden, who expected his brother to answer.

Alford grinned and added, "You heard the princess. Lift her up, and let's get out of here before we get into bigger trouble."

"I can manage," Ally tried to avoid being lifted up like a helpless sack, though images of how she and Zoe had to get Aurora up came unasked for in her mind. "And stop calling me princess. I am just Ally now." *I can't show them how weak and pathetic I am now. I simply can't!*

"Whoa there, we can't have you opening up your wounds, Ally. Let us lift you up for now. If you start bleeding like Aurora did, things could get really bad," Aiden interceded. "Time enough later to be independent again."

Seeing the wisdom in his warning, she allowed them to lift her up, all the while thinking to herself, *How the hell am I ever going to be independent again?* Although she tried valiantly to banish such negative thoughts from her mind, as they led her mare along after them, she simply sat like a sack of potatoes going to market. Ally fought hard to keep from crying. *I can't cry. I can't cry. I can't cry.* Somehow, she didn't. The psi-powders were doing their job, though she didn't know it.

By midmorning, Zoe was getting a bit worried. The men were not back yet, but at least Aurora was in better humor and had not gone into her usual despair as the psi-powders began to wear off. The two chatted about how nice the warm day promised to be. Zoe couldn't think of anything else to talk about that wouldn't cause either of them to worry.

Finally, Zoe heard horses coming and jumped up, once more realizing just how defenseless she was. "Maybe I need a dagger or something," she whispered to Aurora. "Whew, it's them. We can relax."

As the trailing horse came into better view, Zoe's heart sank. They had Ally, but she had bandages at the ends of her arms too. Now, she had two hopeless patients. For an instant, she had the thought perhaps they would have been better off dying. She found it hard to banish such notions.

"Oh Ally! How horrid! I tried to get help for you, but I was too late," Zoe gushed, as Alford helped Ally dismount, catching her as her legs gave out.

"She's weak from blood loss. Heat up some stew, and let's get some water in her now, Zoe," Aiden ordered. He got a fire started, and Zoe reheated the cold stew and made them all a pot of tea.

As Zoe fed Ally, she asked, "How did you find these men, Zoe? They rescued me from dad's insane doctor and soldiers thank god. You won't believe what they did to Doctor Corey! They cut his hands off and left him!"

"Serves the bastard right," Zoe declared then softened. "I used some Aurora's psi-powders on myself and was able to reach Phyllis. She contacted others and got Aiden and Alford Bettingham to rescue us all."

"But how? Phyllis is back in Wycombe," Ally protested. *She is a witch, but how can she do that?*

"I am a beginning witch — well, in training really. We have certain powers, that's all I can say," Zoe admitted, fearing she already revealed too much to a non-witch. *I wish I could tell her. Perhaps the witches in Wyth will tell her. I don't dare. Besides, I violated all the rules by using the psi-powders myself.*

"Don't let her fool you," Alford overheard them. "She used telepathy. The psi-powders increase a witch's mental strength, simple really."

Zoe wanted to burst out, "How do you know that?" but thought better of it. She merely nodded and continued to feed Ally.

Telepathy? Witches can do that? Psi-powders? I don't understand, Ally thought.

"We had better give Ally another day to recoup before

we hit the trail," Aiden discussed their situation with Alford. "Once her body regains her strength, we ought to be able to put some miles behind us." Aiden agreed, and they headed off to scrounge up more firewood, discussing whether or not it would rain and how they could keep the women's bandages dry. Though it was summer, the weather this close to the mountains to the west was always quite unpredictable.

Fed and with the men out of the immediate area, Ally asked, "Zoe, can you take off my shirt and undo the bindings around my chest? It is hurting me now, and obviously my disguise didn't work and isn't needed anymore."

"Sure, but let's just raise it up. I don't want anything to touch your wounds. They are likely very tender in spite of the potion." She lifted Palmer's old shirt up and untied the wrappings, allowing her small but perky breasts to gain their freedom once more.

"Thanks, that feels much better. What a relief. I'm glad I was able to get you and Aurora out of that ambush. I am so tired. Can I sleep a while?" Ally said. She needn't have asked, for she slumped into a deep sleep. Zoe lowered her to the ground, put a makeshift bedroll beneath her head, and covered her with a blanket. Then, she helped Aurora with her tea.

Late that afternoon, the three sat around their camp sipping tea, while the other two continued to doze or sleep, in the case of Ally. Alford had already decided they would spend several days here before hitting the trail. He wanted to give Ally the best chance for survival. Too much jostling and her wounds might open up, causing no end of potential problems that could be avoided if they just gave her body time to begin the long healing process.

As Aiden once more began making his stew for their supper, a rider approached them. Once again, Zoe's fears rose. Had the king's soldiers found them already? Aiden looked up. "Hey, it's sis."

Alford, who had been lying close to Ally, rose. "Good, she found us. Relax Zoe, it's Abby. She's brought along more horses and the supplies we're going to need. We came rushing to your rescue, leaving Abby to arrange the rest. Hi sis. Over here. We got two patients now." He got up and went to lend her a hand, as did Zoe.

Abby was twenty-two, tall and spindly. She'd not yet begun to fill out. Like her bothers, she had blonde hair and blue eyes. Her three foot long hair was tied back in a tight ponytail, and she wore leather armor. A longbow and quiver were strung across her back, and Zoe saw two more quivers of arrows strapped to one of the two packhorses she was leading. Both of them were heavily laden with supplies. She also had a short sword and dagger strapped to her waist.

"Did I miss all the action, Alford?" she called out. Ally awoke and heard her mellow alto voice calling out and propped herself up to see who had the angelic voice.

"Only a little. Not much. Most of the soldiers have likely headed back to Wycombe. Have any trouble finding us?" Alford asked cheerily.

"None at all. You two leave remarkably easy trails to follow. When have I or Adam *ever* failed to find you, eh?" she teased her older brother.

Both twins laughed, and Aiden called out from his cooking, "How's Adam anyway? Is he still trying to play soldier boy?"

"Yes, damn generals anyway. They simply refused to let me join up with Adam. Now if I were king," she answered.

Alford cut her off mid-sentence, "We know, we know, you'd let as many women fight as they desired. Come on; lend your older brother a hand with supper, unless you want his stew again."

"Men! Honestly, you'd think two grown men could cook something else besides just throwing everything into one pot!" Abby teased them, winking at Zoe, who smiled.

"It did taste pretty good," Zoe came to his defense.

"Hi, Abby Bettingham. You've met our two older brothers I see." The young woman was quite forward; nothing bashful about this woman, Zoe concluded.

"Hi, Zoe Roundtree. This is Ally Wycombe and that's Aurora Wynne."

"The Princess Ally Wycombe?" Abby asked both surprised and slightly awed.

"Ex-princess. Dad did this to me, and I am disowning

him," Ally replied, raising her two bandaged arms a little, though they throbbed just moving that much. "Sorry to have dragged all three of you into this mess. I was trying to get Zoe and Aurora safely to Wynn, but obviously, I failed utterly to do that. Sorry."

"Hey, it's a miracle you were able to get them safely this far. Is it true you got Zoe and Aurora safely away from the soldiers who ambushed you?" Abby asked.

"I was *not* about to break my promise to them. Yes, I kicked their horse and mine, as I dismounted, and they spooked as I intended. They were out of quarrel range before the solders could stop them," Ally answered honestly.

"Well done, Ally. I like your style," Abby complimented her. "We'll get you to safety so you can both heal up properly, Ally and Aurora. So Aiden, tell me about it. How many soldiers did you two get?" She was clearly interested in the skirmish.

"After you tell us about Adam. Where is your twin?" Aiden asked.

"He's with the garrison protecting Bettingham. They got word some of Chester's cavalry have broken through the northern lines and are heading toward Bettingham. Foolish general there wouldn't let me fight. Adam's okay. Now out with it," she replied a bit testily. Ally could tell she did not like being put off.

Aiden grinned. "Oh, Ally, Zoe, Aurora, Adam and Abby are twins too. Both are superb archers, but our foolish duo here wanted to play soldiers. We couldn't talk them out of it. Glad the general didn't let you join up. We need you here with us, sis."

"So you don't have to eat your own cooking? Bah!" Abby replied jokingly. Both men flushed, though. "Okay, I'll see what I can do with your pathetic stew, but you have to tell me all about the rescue."

They did and Aurora thought the stew was even better than the night before. Later, they stoked the fire and arranged for one to stand guard over the others, taking two hour watches during the night. Mostly, the men were concerned about wandering bears or perhaps wolves. They were too far from the hills and mountains really to expect to encounter a

Montaña Beast, though if one came, there would be little they could do but try to flee.

In the morning, Aiden and Alford decided, since Ally was much stronger and neither woman's bandages showed any significant bleeding, they could manage a light day of traveling. The four set about breaking camp, packing the eight horses. As they were just finishing up, they heard the sounds of many horses cantering their way. Hastily, Aiden doused their campfire. They spotted ten cavalrymen coming their way.

"Damn! Those are not our soldiers! Enemy cavalry!" Alford yelled, running for his swords. Aiden raced for his. Abby stepped back and grabbed her longbow and quiver. The riders wore bright red uniforms, and the three knew they must be from the Kingdom of Rockton.

"Zoe, we're not helpless. Wrap the reins around our arms. We can help hold the horses with our elbows," Ally ordered. "If we lose our horses, we will be doomed!" Zoe tried to protest, but saw she could not hold onto eight horses and wrapped the reins of two around each of Ally's arms. "Like this," Ally showed Aurora. She bent her arms and put pressure on the wrapped reins. "We can hold them, Aurora! We can't lose them." Aurora offered her arms, and Zoe wrapped another pair of reins around each of her arms too. That left Zoe trying to control four horses, still a bit more than she could safely manage. However, looking at the two women trying to hold a pair each with their arms bent tightly, she knew she had to manage at least this much.

The dozen enemy cavalry reined in some distance away, surveying what they had encountered, apparently surprised by them. One then raised his sword high in the air and brought it down sharply. The dozen kicked their horses and charged toward the two men, figuring they would have a little sport with the men and then some fun with the four women.

"All right! This is more like it!" Abby declared. She pulled back her bow and let an arrow fly. Ally watched as Abby's arrow flew true; a rider fell off his horse. Before they closed upon the two men, three of their lot had met an arrow from Abby, who finally had to drop her bow and draw her short sword. The riders swooped down on the men on foot; the advantage was all theirs.

Their horses spooked and whinnied, pulling Ally and Aurora in all directions, but they continued to squeeze their arms tightly shut, holding on to them while watching the battle play out. The two men carefully parried the incoming swings of the cavalrymen, avoiding their blades. Aiden managed to unseat one rider. For an instant, he toyed with the idea of joining combat with the fallen soldier, but two other riders wheeled and came galloping back at him. The fight was wholly lopsided in favor of the remaining nine.

The rider who had fallen rushed to regain his horse. Suddenly, he fell forward, landing face down on the ground. Ally saw an arrow sticking out from the middle of the back of the man's head. She looked up and saw another blonde man on a horse aiming a longbow. Twang. Another rider fell, catching the attention of the remaining seven. Seeing her brother distracting them, Abby grabbed her bow again and fired away. The seven soldiers found themselves in a crossfire of deadly arrows. These archers never seemed to miss! Four more went down in rapid succession. The remaining three kicked their horses and veered off to the left, abandoning the battle as fast as they could go. They were not fast enough for the archers. Twang! Abby was fast, lightning fast. She dropped two of the three while the mysterious other archer dropped the last one.

"Well, if it isn't little brother!" Aiden called out, as the blonde man rode up to them and dismounted.

"Hey, better make sure they are dead. And *do* try to save our arrows!" Abby yelled at them, stabbing the nearest soldier and then carefully pulling her shaft out of his head. "Damn, that one broke. Now I have to dig the valuable steel head out of his brain!"

Rapidly, Aiden and his three siblings went from fallen soldier to soldier, retrieving arrows and dispatching them, if they lived. Next, all were searched, while Adam and Abby rounded up their horses, adding another dozen to their collection. Aiden stowed the collected weapons and money pouches on several of the horses, while Alford tied them into a string. At last, they joined the women. The weapons alone would bring them at least six thousand silver, maybe more, while the trained horses might fetch a total of four hundred more.

"Well done, Ally, Aurora, and Zoe. I was really worried we'd lose the horses and our supplies. Great job, ladies," Alford praised them, knowing Ally and Aurora really needed to be validated for helping out, in spite of their horrible situation. "Oh yes, this is our younger brother, Adam, Abby's twin brother. Adam, this is Princess Ally Wycombe."

"Ex-princess!" Ally corrected him and he grinned.

"Aurora Wynne, Zoe Roundtree."

"Well, met, ex-princess. Aurora, Zoe. Say, we'd best hightail it out of here pronto," Adam broke in.

"Why?" Alford asked.

"The Chester cavalry has outflanked Prince Norwood's foot soldiers up at Wynn. A large bunch has been flooding this way. They've encircled our town, Bettingham. Prince Palmer is trying to keep the town from being overrun. My group got attacked and mostly wiped out. I trailed after some of them, knowing they were heading your way. Looks like I got here just in time. We've got to get moving, and Abby says you want to go northwest to Wynn. That right?" Adam asked. Aiden nodded.

Adam continued, "Well, that's out now! There are hundreds of Chester cavalry all along the main roads heading back towards Wynn. We'll never get through that way. We should go west by northwest to the Goza Mountains and follow the foothills north to Wynn, even if the weather should turn bad on us."

"Okay, little brother, lead the way," Aiden replied.

"Oh one more thing. It is really chaos out there right now. It seems our king has been assassinated in his bed. Word is spreading fast."

"What? Dad's dead?" Ally called out, taken by complete surprise.

"Er sorry. I forgot he's your dad," Adam said apologetically.

"A bastard dad! Look what he had done to me!" Ally raised her arms, ignoring the throbbing pain from the sudden movement. "I wish it had happened years ago! What about mom and April, my sister?"

"Really strange. The steward found her in bed with his corpse. She was covered in blood too, but unharmed. He suggested an assassin had struck in the night, but so far no one has found any trace of the assassin who had somehow got into the castle. Plus, Queen Misty and Princess April have also gone missing. The steward sent them to a place of safety, but they fled somewhere else from there. No one knows where they are. It is complete chaos. No one is on the throne at the moment, though I expect Norwood will claim it as soon as he hears about it. Of course, he's rather held up there in Wyth at the moment."

Ally listened carefully to what Adam said. Suddenly, it dawned on her what must have happened. "I bet anything mom finally snapped."

"What do you mean?" asked Alford.

"I think she killed dad. He beat her mercilessly for years, broke her arms twice. I think mom finally came to her senses and got rid of the bastard. I hope no one will go after her."

"I highly doubt that! If she did the deed, many of us will sing her praises!" Aiden replied. "No offense, princess."

"None taken. I'm glad he's dead. If ever there was a man who deserved death, it was him!" Ally replied. "Damn, will my arms ever stop throbbing?" She fought hard to keep tears from showing, though her eyes were watering.

"Hey, I'll fix her another potion; you get everything ready to go," Zoe offered.

A half hour later, the group was once more riding, westward this time. Ally, now freed from the pain via the potion, insisted on riding herself, though Alford led her horse behind his. Aurora, now feeling somewhat better, also tried to ride by herself, thinking if Ally can manage it, she had better too.

The day grew warm and the sun shone brightly. Not a cloud was in the sky, perfect for traveling, but would it remain so? Not likely. Slowly, the hills began to rise higher and higher, though the forest continued to dot the hills. They saw only a couple of remote farmsteads and steered clear of those. Three times, they had to hold up to allow a bear to lumber out of their way. By late afternoon, they were high in the foothills of the Goza range. The air chilled and clouds began streaking in from the far west. Suddenly, Adam pointed to the sky. Everyone stopped and stared upwards.

A huge, silver-colored object of enormous size, spewing flames from six openings underneath it, slowly descended from the sky! "What is that? Gods are coming to Tierra?" yelled Adam, shocked beyond belief.

"Good lord! What *is* that thing?" Aiden added his shock and awe to that of his brother's.

"It is enormous! It breathes fire! A dragon?" shouted Abby.

"It looks like a metal beast," Alford added.

"Is it gods coming?" asked Zoe. "Gods descending from the sky?"

"But it's got to be metal. See how it shines so!" Ally pointed out.

"Gods are coming to Tierra descending from their homes in the sky on a metal flaming beast," Aurora concluded.

"It is landing! That's what it has got to be doing. It's up there on the Plateau Grado, I'll wager," Adam added. "It can't be more than fifty miles from here. What say you? Let's go check it out. I'd like to meet gods firsthand!"

"I wonder what they look like?" Abby asked, growing curious. "We can get there by mid-afternoon tomorrow, if they don't leave before then."

"Will they be friendly gods?" asked Aurora.

"Only one way to find out," Aiden answered her. "Besides, it's not much out of our way anyhow. Come on."

Chapter 4 First Encounter

The Trail Blazer 5000 settled gently down on the plateau high in the southern Goza Mountains. The landing was gentle and by the book. After touchdown, the Drugi marched out of the ship and began setting up a nearby security perimeter, while Irena joined her work crew foremen. Together, they did a quick visual survey of the area and began making their construction plans. Base housing, landing ports, docks, and a refinery had to be fabricated rapidly, though the refinery had the lowest priority. It would not be needed until the first shipment of the precious psi-crystals came in from the mines, as yet to be found.

After the initial perimeter was activated with Groenin 200's, the very latest in alert-security barriers, the Drugi marched off to work on cordoning off the entire plateau, some hundred square miles. Irene's crews were efficient. Before evening came, the first of the housing units was up and running, providing its own power from huge banks of solar cells, which charged enormous batteries whose lifetimes were nearly a century. Only the latest and best technology had been sent with them, an indication of just how absolutely vital the psi-crystals were to the Imperium.

At dark, the Governor and his staff ministers moved their things into their new quarters. Doctor Zosia set up her hospital rooms, ready for the inevitable accidents. Meanwhile, Jurek and Kassia poured over the survey maps, indicating the most likely spots to open up first, though they would have to wait until the outer perimeter was secured. They needed Drugi to come with them and provide security, as they opened up the new mines. The survey reports had indicated there were some formidable local animals that lived in the mountainous regions. Plus, the primitives might pose some problems, though not likely. Besides, everyone was under orders to acclimatize themselves to Ashford-5's atmosphere, somewhat thin compared to what they were used to breathing. It was survivable here, once they got their bodies accustomed to the much thinner air and the dim light from the strange orange-red sun.

Late afternoon the next day, Governor Andrzej Bohater stood tall in his spotless green uniform of office, gazing at all the personnel who were busy at work on the basic construction activities. Thus far, everything was going precisely according to his overall plans, pleasing him.

Standing beside him and looking out over the distant peaks, Doctor Zosia mused, "It is rather pretty here."

"Pretty doesn't *count*, doctor. Psi-crystals *do*. Don't forget our *primary* purpose here," Andrzej pointed out didactically. No sense in waxing sentimental; they'd be stuck here on this backward planet for many months.

Just then, the Groenin 200 activated, sounding the intruder-alert alarm warning. "So soon? Intruders already?" he growled; this was not to his liking. He and the other ministers, along with twenty Drugi headed to the eastern edge of their inner perimeter. The governor now wished he'd had the Drugi set up the outer perimeters here on the eastern side of the huge plateau first, instead of the western side. They'd have had far more advanced warning, but then perhaps these were just some wandering primitives and nothing more serious.

"Wow! The gods live in big silver houses," Adam pointed out, as the group rode slowly across the high mountain plateau towards the huge silver machine they'd seen descending from the sky yesterday afternoon.

"That must be their flying bird," Aiden added, pointing to the Trail Blazer 5000.

"Look! There are the gods! Well, they look like people from a distance. I suppose that's so we are not so afraid of them," Zoe tossed in her opinion. Her eyes lighted upon the bodies first, not the buildings and the silver flying ship. People interested her far more than objects.

"Gosh, they are tall!" Ally whispered, though she wasn't sure why she did so.

"They must be seven feet tall!" Alford added. They reined in and began to dismount. Quickly, the two men helped Ally and Aurora get down, minimizing the threat of reopening their wounds.

Governor Andrzej and his group walked up to the primitives, and he spoke first. "Greetings. This is now Space Platform #1 of Ashford-5. Governor Andrzej Bohater. Who are you, and what do you want?" Zoe thought he sounded slightly annoyed. His voice seemed to be coming out of a box attached to his waist.

"Alford Bettingham, my brothers Aiden and Adam, our sister, Abby. Zoe Roundtree. Ally Wycombe, Aurora Wynne. You don't look like gods. We saw your flying machine coming down from the sky yesterday and came to see what was happening." He saw very tall and very thin people. Each had coal black hair and eyes, most striking. Their greyish, olive-colored skin looked strange to them, too. "How come you can speak our language?" he asked. Ally thought that was a very important question and wished she'd asked it.

"Luzia Lina, Native Relations Minister. It is our ULAT boxes on our waists. ULAT — Universal Language Translator device. Without it, you could not understand our language, nor could we understand yours. Clever device, most useful."

"I am Doctor Zosia Wiola. Say, you have two wounded women. We have a very advanced medical hospital with us. I would love to see what I can do to help your wounded. There is no need for such primitive wrappings. Why, I can have them healed up within minutes." She didn't add she could do this since the governor himself had vetoed the usual applications of Imperial Directive #5. At last, she saw an advantage of not having to follow that directive to the letter.

"Well, yes, doctor. I can see you are itching to ply your trade. Please, if you will accompany us, our good doctor here will have your wounded patched up in no time at all," Governor Andrzej replied, somewhat annoyed Zosia had been so forward about offering their medical services to these primitives. He vowed to speak with her about this later. Still, he realized, a gesture of goodwill would go a long way towards gathering local information from these primitives.

"Hi, I am Dita Ewa, our minister of Social-Anthropology. I'd love to chat with you about how you live, what your lives are like, what living on this planet is like. Say, what is your name for this world?"

"Tierra," Alford replied. "Well, I suppose we can gamble your doctor will not further harm our two women."

Dita gasped and replied, "Oh no! A doctor is sworn to render all possible aid and healing to her patients. Never would Doctor Zosia ever harm one of her patients. Come, let's chat, and you can watch her heal your injured women." She gave a knowing glance at the governor, who rightly picked up she would be pumping them for vital information.

Dita wouldn't take no for an answer, not with these being her first sample primitives! This was her day! Her enthusiasm affected the primitives, who relaxed a little and agreed, as long as they could watch the doctor. Doctor Zosia led them to her new hospital rooms, while several armed Drugi held on to their animal mounts, but only at the insistence of the governor. He was determined to put on a good display of hospitality, well at least this *once*. He rejected the notion of sharing some of their food with the primitives. First, it was a waste of very good food. Second, the primitives might not like it. This, he communicated to the others with his ULAT turned off.

"I am so sorry you both have met with such a bad accident. Both hands no less. Well, I will get them healed up in no time at all. Let me first numb them, there," Doctor Zosia said kindly. Ally felt nothing more than the tiniest of pinpricks. As the doctor unwrapped her stumps, Ally gagged! "Oh yes, I know it looks just awful and frankly, just between you and me, I wholly agree. Whoever did this has really made a complete mess of the whole thing. Well, you needn't worry, miss. I will have you fixed up perfectly in no time at all. You won't feel any pain at all. We have only the very best in Imperium medical equipment with us. Now then, just put your arm in there. Right, like that. It allows me to work on it." She inserted one stump into a strange looking machine, full of knobs, dials, and gauges.

Zosia mentally toyed with the notion of fitting the two women with the very latest in Imperium prosthesis, but decided she'd need the governor's permission to part with four of them. However, she decided to make that possible in the future, just in case she might get his permission later on.

Hence, she had the machine carve out a bit of bone. Carefully, she tapered the lower arm to a small cone. Satisfied, she pressed the Seal and Heal button, perhaps one of the greatest inventions to hit the Imperium. One button press and a surgical incision would be closed and fully healed up, all on automatic. "There you go, Ally. One arm done. How do you like it? Yes, it is fully healed. You should feel no further pain unless of course you bang your arm into something hard."

Ally could scarcely believe the difference. Her left arm looked aesthetic. Gone was the awful burned flesh, the ugly wound, and the awful looking shape that constantly reminded her of her missing wrist. Her arm ended in a nice conical shape. "This is a miracle, right? You are gods? It is fully healed! We expected it to take months. Look, I can touch things, and it doesn't hurt or throb anymore."

Doctor Zosia smiled, *Primitives think modern medicine is a miracle. Well, who am I to tell them otherwise.* She said, "We are not gods. I'm a good doctor, and you're getting the very best care any wealthy patient in the Imperium could get. Let's get your other arm done, shall we? You didn't feel any pain or discomfort while I was working on your left arm did you?"

"Oh no, none at all. I expected excruciating pain, but nothing, not even a tickle," Ally answered honestly. "Thank you for healing us."

Fifteen minutes later, both Aurora and Ally were pain-free and fully healed, showing off their rather amazing looking stumps. "My god, Aurora, your arms look attractive; no hideous scarring and strange looking bumps and all that!" Zoe exclaimed. "I've seen others in Wycombe who've lost a hand, and their stumps are dreadful looking, awful, even disgusting. Many wear a sock over it just to hide it. But yours — wow, they look pleasing, nothing disgusting at all. You have no need to hide them in socks." Her words pleased the two women, as she anticipated they might.

"Yes, our brilliant doctor has worked her magic on your two women," Dita Ewa said to the group, as they looked over the results. "In return, might I ask you for some information about your world?"

"Sure, what would you like to know, Dita?" Aiden replied, more than a little impressed with these aliens who claimed not to be some kind of gods.

"What are those huge cat-like beasts that stand ten feet tall? We've seen a couple of them. They appear quite dangerous," Dita began going down the page of questions she had been accumulating from the various ministers. This first one came from General Janek, who worried about such matters.

"It is the most ferocious and feared beast on Tierra," Alford answered her. "It is called a Montaña Beast. If it attacks us, it can tear us apart in seconds! If we encounter one, the creature usually stalks us for miles. The only defense we have against one is to flee on horseback as fast and as far as we can ride, hoping and praying it tires of the chase. You should be extremely careful of them. They tend to dwell primarily here in the Goza Mountains and the foothills."

"Duly noted. Thanks. We will be extra cautious. Next, I have here a map we were given. Can you draw in the country boundaries or kingdoms or fiefdoms or whatever you call your political boundaries? You do have such divisions? I should have asked that first," Dita corrected herself. *Well, this is my first actual anthropology interview, after all,* she thought.

"Kingdoms. This whole middle area is called Midlands. To the west of this mountain range is the Westerlings. These hills here separate the Midlands from the Easterlings. Okay, we all come from the Kingdom of Bettingham, which runs from these mountains we are in over to this huge river, the Wyndl River. It goes up two-thirds of the way to the far northern edge. Just beyond us is the Kingdom of Pinewood. Above them is the Kingdom of Bentwood. Above them is the Kingdom of Walsham. Just north of us is the Kingdom of Rockton, and they are currently at war with us, trying to steal a lot of our land. Here at the far north is the Kingdom of Haruk."

"The Easterlings have the Kingdom of Matruk next to the Buku Hills. Then up north is the Kingdom of Domi. Below them are the Kingdom of Arad and the Kingdom of Alba lies to the south. Now over here in the Westerlings, up north is the Kingdom of Zamora. Going on south, we have the Kingdoms of

Alavera and then Trujillo. I think I heard they are at war, but I am not too sure of that. You know how rumors go. To the far south lies the Kingdom of Almendia. That's all of them," Alford finished up, rather pleased with himself.

Dita jotted all this down rapidly, but her writing looked more like chicken scratches to the group. "Okay, next question. What do people and kingdoms accept for trading goods? Gold perhaps? Silver? Platinum? Cesium?"

Alford chuckled. "Sorry, I don't even know what the last two are. Here on Tierra, gold is very rare and extremely valuable. Hence, we use silver a lot, also gems, and some copper for smaller purchases. Why?"

"Interesting you should ask," Dita smiled. *These primitives were quite intuitive and intelligent, for primitives, that is,* she thought. "We are here to mine for something we use to fuel our spaceships, like the big one outside that you saw landing yesterday." She hastily thought for just the right words to explain this to the primitives, who likely had not the faintest notion of spaceship fuel. "We are going to be mining for some of these crystals; we call them psi-crystals. They are used to fuel our ships, you see."

"Oh, those are plentiful on Tierra," Alford suggested. "Some of our people use them for other purposes too."

"Well, we want to establish good relations with the kingdoms that border us and even perhaps hire some of your men to help us mine for these psi-crystals. In return, we will pay fair wages in gold. Do you believe that arrangement would be an acceptable one to those who run the kingdoms that abut these mountains?" Dita asked. Getting her key information from these primitives was extremely easy. Then, she realized that perhaps this was due to their gratitude for Doctor Zosia's healing of their two injured women. She reminded herself to compliment Doctor Zosia for her brilliant thinking and great timing.

"Sure, what king would not jump at such an offer?" Alford replied.

"I was *so* hoping that would be the case. We hate to use force when simple goodwill will suffice. Now then, by chance do you know the names of the rulers we need to contact. Let's see, those we need to see first are the ones in charge of Bettingham, Rockton, Zamora, Trujillo, and Almendia."

Rather bitterly, Ally laughed aloud. "What a joke! My wicked father was the king of Bettingham until he got assassinated a few days ago." She calmed down a little, adding, "I think my older brother is likely to be the king now. Norwood Wycombe. The last we heard, he was fighting against the invading Rockton forces of King Addam Chester there at Wyth," she tried to point to Wyth with her right index finger. Her face crimsoned, as she forgot she had no hand or fingers.

"Yes, I see the settlement indicated on the survey map. Thanks, Ally. It seems we will need to put an end to the war so we can get on with mining for psi-crystals. What about these three Easterlings kingdoms?" Dita asked, writing rapidly.

Aiden and Alford wondered what she meant about ending the war, but thought better of asking. Unfortunately, none knew who was in charge in those kingdoms. Dita thought, *Well, I rather expected these primitives would have somewhat limited information. They are primitives, after all.* That took care of her immediate questions. However, she was fascinated with the primitives and wanted to chat longer. Just then, she received a coded message from the governor who wanted the primitives to depart before dark. No way would General Janek tolerate primitives to stay the night in their secure buildings. Such would be a huge security breach, and he'd obviously complained to the governor.

Dita hastily said, "Well, I've kept you far too long. I bet you are anxious to get on your way. I won't delay you any longer. Please, though, if I want to visit with you again, where might I find you?"

"Wyth, for now. We are heading there. If we are not there, ask around for Aiden or Alford Bettingham. Someone will know where we have gone. We don't know how properly to thank your incredible doctor for healing Ally and Aurora so completely. To us, it is truly a miracle," Alford replied. *They may be aliens, but they are being extraordinarily kind to us. I wonder why?*

Dita smiled; what was to these primitives a miracle cure was a super-simple medical procedure, as far as she understood it. Healing someone who had taken a disintegrate beam through their head — now that was a tricky and miraculous medical procedure. She'd talked with Doctor Zosia about that one on their long trip here.

She led them back outside, where five heavily armed Drugi stood impatiently waiting with their horses. At Luzia's insistence, Governor Andrzej stepped outside and waved goodbye to the group, a mechanical smile on his face. He was only too glad to be rid of the primitives, and headed to Dita's office to learn what she'd discovered from her interrogation of the primitives, thankful he'd not had to do that dirty deed. *This is why I have a social-anthropologist along,* he thought.

The group walked their horses some distance before deciding to mount up. As they prepared to continue their northward portion of their trip, Alford prepared to Ally to lift her into the saddle.

"Hey, let me try it, Alford. I am not completely helpless, just mostly. If you tie the reins together, I might even be able to ride by myself," Ally suggested. "My arms don't hurt anymore, and they seem healed. Miraculous. They are almost gods, aren't they? Compared to us at least."

"But how, Ally?" Aurora complained.

"We still have our arms. Like this, hook the inside of our elbow around the horn." Ally did so and managed to mount successfully. "Aurora, they don't even hurt anymore. God, that alone is a huge relief. You would not believe the pain. Okay, try it, Aurora. You can do it," Ally coaxed her. Aurora emulated Ally and was surprised to see that she too could mount by herself.

"You are right; they don't hurt in the slightest! I keep expecting the throbbing pain to come back. This is a huge relief — that's putting it mildly," Aurora said with a broad grin, the first Zoe had seen on the young woman's face.

Alford was also smiling, but for different reasons. He tied Ally's reins, while Aiden did the same for Aurora. Ally was correct in her estimations. She was able to cradle the reins in her bent elbow and, by neck reining, control her mare. Far more timidly, Aurora emulated her. Soon, the group headed back down the side of Plateau Grado. They reached the rolling foothills shortly before dark on the warm summer evening. Thunder and lightning crackled off to the west of the plateau. It would rain soon.

Adam suggested, "Hey, we are not too far from out secret cavern hideout. Want to head there for the night?" Alford agreed, and Adam led the way, unerringly.

Ally focused on somehow controlling her mare. Going downhill was nerve wracking, but she managed to endure it without letting on how frightened she was. As they leveled out, the going was much easier. *The aliens sure do look weird. They all look so grey and such black hair. They're almost giants compared to us, but they're sure thin. I wonder why that is? Well, I do owe them much. It's incredible what she did for my arms. That awful pain is really gone now. I don't think I could have taken it much longer. Stiff upper lip, Ally. I have to be brave for a yet while longer.*

At last, the going became easier, and Ally could think more freely. *Well, I'm healed now, so I guess there's no excuse for my being so helpless. But how am I to do anything for myself now? I promised to help Aurora, but how can I? I'm as helpless as she is. Ally, you gave her your word. You have to help her somehow. Think.* Try as she might, she had no ideas on how she could do that. She fought hard to keep from plummeting into grief herself. *I can't cry, not in front of all these people, I can't.*

As they neared a narrow valley gorge, Alford pointed to a small rock cairn. "That's our marker. Our cave is a mile up the gorge. You are going to like it," he flashed her a smile.

A short while later, they dismounted and waited, while Adam and Alford went inside to light their lanterns and to make sure no bears or wolves were using it as their home. Ally guessed the entrance was too small for a Montaña Beast. Fortunately, their cave was not currently the home of any wild animals. As the lights came on, the others led their horses inside, just as a torrential rain began, drenching the stony hills. Ally insisted on leading hers, pulling at the reins crooked in her elbow. Aurora again tried to emulate what Ally was doing, feeling a bit more self-confident because of the day's ride. *Look, she's trying to do just as I'm doing. I have to lead us somehow, but how?* Ally thought.

Abby announced, "We women will make supper, but in return, we women get the four beds." The men laughed but went along with their sister. While the men handled the many horses, Abby and Zoe began to prepare another hot meal.

"I wonder what we can do to help," Ally said to Aurora. They were standing beside Abby and Zoe, watching them. "I feel so damn useless. I hate that feeling! But I guess I'll have to get used to being almost totally helpless now."

"Me too, but we are really useless. We're just going to have to accept having others do everything for us now, Ally," Aurora complained, fighting hard to keep from crying again.

"No, we are not!" Ally countered. *I have to do something to help Aurora. She's about to break down again. If she does, I will probably too!* "Hey, Abby, maybe I can stir that for you, if you can let me get the spoon between my arms," Ally suggested. Abby allowed Ally to try, and despite her awkwardness, Ally managed to stir. Zoe then found some little things Aurora could also do to help with the making their dinner. Both Alford and Aiden did watch the two women, as they made their brave attempts to help out, and the men smiled at each other.

As they sat down on the stone cave floor to eat, Ally admitted, "Okay, I haven't the faintest idea how I can possible feed myself. I guess someone is going to have to do it for me. Damn, damn, damn," she said.

"My pleasure," Alford hastily scooted over to her. "Don't get so frustrated. Give yourself time to work things out." Ally sighed, *Things will never really work out! Time isn't going to be of much help now. He can't use the excuse I'll reopen the wounds now.* She fought against saying such things. Deep down, she hoped and prayed he was right, though at the moment, she could not see how anything could ever really work out for her or for Aurora.

Later, as they sat around the lantern-illuminated cave sipping tea and chatting about the strangers from the sky, Ally asked, "So what's with the four of you? How come all your names start with the letter A? Who are you four anyway? Any relation to the Bettinghams who used to run our kingdom?"

"Dad's doing, Ally. He got it from grandpa, King Able Bettingham," Alford answered her, though he hated to mention that last fact. *As bright as Ally is, she'll soon work it out for herself anyway. Might as well let the cat out of the bag. The woman is sharp as a tack. Well, she is our princess.*

"Wow! Oh gosh! My wicked dad killed your dad and stole the throne of the kingdom!" Ally blurted out without thinking of the ramifications of her exclamation. "I'm terribly sorry about that!" Then it hit her, "Oh hell, now you are looking after the daughter of the man who killed your father! I'm sorry. I didn't know, Alford, really I didn't." Ally felt horrid. Although this happened before she was even born, still the irony and pain they must feel was real to her.

"It happened when we were barely three," Alford continued. "I hardly remember anything about dad, really. The twins were only one year old when it happened."

"But you should be our king now," Ally protested, "not my brother Norwood."

"Oh no way! We don't want it, not in the slightest! You could not pay us to be the king," Aiden spoke up.

"No, we are having too much fun living the life of roamers. We'd never survive being all cooped up in a castle every day. No, if you offer us the throne, then we'll simply run away," Alford added. "We want no part of that!"

Seeing her shocked face, Aiden added, "We like to go where we want and help whomever we choose — like you two. We *chose* to help the both of you. And yes, Ally, we knew you were the king's daughter before we agreed to lend you a hand. I'm truly sorry we couldn't get to you sooner than we did. We were up near Bettingham when the witches contacted us. We just couldn't get to you any faster."

Abby added her voice to the discussion, "He's right; they dashed off with hardly packing anything except the psi-powders. They had me take my time and pack the supplies we were going to need and then follow along later."

Ally spoke up, "I owe all of you my life. Thanks for risking yours to save me. I'll do my best to have made it worth your efforts. I've already pledged myself to doing everything I can to help Aurora, but. . ."

Aurora interrupted her, "But that was before you lost your hands too. You don't have to stick by your promise, Ally. You're in the same mess I'm in now. Both of our lives are now totally ruined." *There, I feel better. It's out in the open now. We're both going to be useless and helpless for the rest of our lives.*

"No, Aurora, my word is my bond. I don't have anything else that's *truly* mine, but my word. I promised to look after you and somehow I *will* do that, Aurora." Ally insisted.

"She's got a valid point. What do any of us have but our word?" Alford backed her up, very much impressed with Ally. *What a woman is Ally. Where has she been all my life?* They chatted a while longer and then turned in for the night. They were still three days out from Wyth.

Both women slept soundly for the first time since they had lost their hands. Pain free, their bodies now fell into a deep, recovering sleep.

Chapter 5 King Norwood Wycombe

Twenty-two year old Prince Norwood Wycombe continued to pace around his field commander's tent. The table, which he'd been circling for the last hour, contained toy soldiers, replicating what was currently known about the ongoing battle with the cavalry of King Addam Chester of Rockton. Months ago, for reasons best known to Chester, his mounted soldiers crossed the Wyndl River, the common boundary between their two kingdoms. The moment Norwood learned of this, he begged his father to allow him to take charge of their northern defenses.

Norwood had leapt at this chance for several reasons, not the least was to finally get out from beneath his father, who he'd grown to distrust and loath. The man was an angry brute, used to getting his way with absolutely everything. He'd witnessed Aaran breaking his mother's arms twice now. True men must be strong and unbending, his father drilled into him as a young lad. Norwood didn't think this applied to everything in life, certainly not to women. Worse, he began to suspect ulterior motives in the COG's bishop, who always now seemed to be offering Aaran advice, which the king usually accepted. The only way Bishop Gil Granville could possibly have such an influence over his father was because he held something over the king's head. Blackmail. Norwood could envision nothing else that would have so rapidly have gained his father's trust, if trust it actually was. However, he had few ideas what evil his father had done that he could be now be blackmailed by the COG. Until a few years ago, his father had nothing to do with religion and still didn't, for that matter.

The COG and the bishop suggested cutting off a thief's hand, and was eagerly implemented by King Aaran. Norwood protested and argued against such an over-reaction to seemingly petty crimes. There were far worse crimes in abundance, even in Wycombe, that were totally ignored by the king. The only conclusion young Norwood could come to was that in the past, Aaran had done something truly awful, something, which if known, might bring destruction upon him.

Bishop Gil must somehow know all about it and must have proof of said crime. That would account for his father's blind acceptance of this bishop into his confidence. Hence, Norwood wanted to get out from the court and away from this bishop.

That this was also a chance for him to prove himself worthy of inheriting the throne of Bettingham also played a factor in his hasty decision to personally command the northern defenses, here near Wyth. Now, young Norwood was facing true battlefield conditions, and they had not been pretty to say the least. The food, disgusting. Comforts, none. Worries, constant. Even disease had struck his forces until he abolished drinking the creek water without boiling the water first. At least he'd stopped the rampant disease, if little else. Well, it was actually one of the camp physicians who had suggested that might be the cause. He couldn't honestly take full credit for that, at least to himself.

The battles were a joke, only no one was laughing. He commanded some three thousand foot soldiers. Some who came from the wealthier families wore extremely expensive ring mail, but most had only leather armor to protect themselves. Swords of various types and even a few axes were no match for the saber wielding cavalrymen, who swept down from the neighboring hills, charging into his ranks, cutting this way and that before retreating, leaving dead, trampled, and mutilated men in their wake. It seemed to Norwood that the COG physicians only cure for a battle wound was to chop the appendage off, whenever possible, but allowing those with head or torso wounds to mend on their own; those seldom did.

"There is nothing we can do for them now. It is up to the higher power of the Lord God," the doctors always gave him the same line when he asked about those men. Yet with arm and leg wounds, the chop it off method yielded a higher survival rate. Nine out of ten who suffered chest or head wounds died within a week, but only five of ten who had the wounded appendages chopped off died within the week. He had no idea more died in the weeks they spent recovering far from the battlefield tents. Thus, he continued to support their decisions, though he wondered what good these discharged men would be with one or two arms missing or one or two legs missing or other combinations. By now, he'd seen all possible variations. Routinely, the wagons would cart these victims of war back towards Wyth and other nearby towns. Norwood did wonder what would become of them, but had no way of knowing. Rather, his task remained the same, find a way to defeat Chester's cavalrymen.

A week ago, he'd finally hit upon an idea that had actually worked. In desperation, he'd had his men fell young saplings and sharpen their points, turning them into twenty-foot long spear or pikes. He equipped his front line men with one each and set up a second row behind them. One old sergeant began to call them "pikemen," and the name caught on, especially after the tactic worked effectively. The idea was tested the very day he put his idea into operation.

Chester's cavalry had come sweeping down for yet another raid on his front lines. As the riders approached, a wall of pikes rose up at about a forty degree angle, sufficient to strike a horse in its chest or the rider. A wall of horses and men went down like a tide wiping out a simple sand castle. His soldiers, embolden by this first victory, dashed forward, hacking the cavalrymen to death. Chester lost three hundred men and an equal number of horses that day. Soldiers sung praises to Norwood that evening at the mess, celebrating their first real victory since the war began in the spring.

The next day, another two hundred fifty men and horses were lost, without Norwood's forces losing even a single man. Morale suddenly rose from the pits in which it had been buried for weeks. Then for several days, nothing more happened. Norwood prayed King Chester would abandon the war, pulling his forces back across the Wyndl River. Such was not to be. Two days ago, Norwood learned the cavalry had begun to flank his forces, driving deep into the heart of Bettingham, where the isolated towns and villages were largely unprotected.

Soon he learned just how bad it was going for these villagers. The cavalrymen, having dispatched what little local resistance there was, burned down the buildings, confiscated what was of any real value, raped the younger women, and murdered many younger men. Long lines of refugees began to walk the main roads that led northwest or southeast of their villages, hoping to find food and sanctuary in the next town or village. Today, many finally made it to Wyth, but they were in horrible condition. Beaten and bruised women, small boys and girls, many clutching broken arms, stumbled into Wyth. Most had been without food for days, though they had found water in the many creeks of Bettingham. Very few men made the walk, and they were uniformly older men.

What few mounted riders Norwood had, he sent out to gather news of the enemy. They too began returning along with the refugees; their reports were dismal indeed. If things were not bad enough, that very day a rider came from Wycombe with the news of his father's untimely death along with the disappearance of Queen Misty and Princess April. Also, he heard the devastating news of Ally, that his own father had Doctor Corey remove both of her hands. He also learned why Ally had fled and quietly backed her decision to flee. "Our king almost sold us out!" he yelled to his men. "The tyrant is dead! I am King Norwood Wycombe now! We will win this war!" His men cheered him, and he sent riders back to the castle in Wycombe with word of his ascension to the throne. Norwood doubted anyone would seriously challenge his birthright to the throne of Bettingham, and he was right about that if little else. In ordinary times, he would have dropped everything and gone in search of Ally, his mother, and young sister. These were not ordinary times. All around him, the war raged. It was his to win or lose. He pushed all but the war out of his mind for the moment.

What proved the most critical decision Norwood would make happened late that very afternoon. His men pulled his attention from his pacing within his tent to the southwestern sky. A huge, silver flying thing appeared in the sky, fire and smoke belching from its bottom side. He was less than a hundred miles from where it landed on Plateau Grado. Speculation ran rampant among the men. What was this? Had gods come to Tierra? Was this a new kind of terrible wild animal never seen before? Some claimed the end of the world was at hand.

"I will ride forth to discover what new thing this may

be. Perhaps it is the gods come to deliver us from the cavalrymen of Chester," he declared before his assembled majors. *My god, what devilry is this thing in the sky? I've no choice but to go see what it is. If I don't, I'll lose control of my entire army, if not my kingdom!*

"Sire, it is far too dangerous for you to do this!" one major advised him.

"I'll take six men with me. It's only a couple days there. Back in four or five days with news of this strange beast. With luck, I'll be able to harness its power to rid Bettingham of Chester's cavalrymen," he stated his final words on the matter, little knowing how correct his hopes would become.

Two days later, he and his escort arrived upon the Plateau Grado. Ahead off in the distance, they saw the strangest sights any of the seven had ever seen. "Sire, what manner of beasts or devils are out there?" one soldier asked.

"Steady on, soldier. I don't know, but I aim to find out. Come on; let's see what is out there." As they rode on, they spotted a number of tall, thin men scurrying about. Others seemed to be working on constructions, buildings perhaps, Norwood thought. *Devils have no need of homes, I hope.* The huge silver flying beast dominated the horizon, but to these men, the strange silver building, if that's what it was, became a close second. None realized they activated the silent sentinels, alerting the Drugi to their presence.

"Another batch of primitives has come up onto the plateau from the east, governor. Your orders?" a Drugi reported.

"Send Dita, Luzia, and General Janek to see who they are. If they are some of the kings Dita has listed, send for me. I've got these reports to oversee," Governor Andrzej ordered. He hated to be interrupted, especially when he was going over reports. Obviously, reports to the Imperium were vastly more important than mere primitives.

Minutes later, General Janek cautioned, "Okay ministers, stand behind me and my men. Are you wearing your deflector shields?"

"Yes, but surely we won't need them. They are only primitives, after all," Luzia declared, sounding a hopeful note.

King Norwood rode up to the encampment. *This looks as if it is more of a new village under construction. The silver colored building must be made from some kind of metal,* he concluded. Still, he could scarcely take his eyes off the huge silver flying ship. At last, he turned his attention to these "gods." He saw tall, thin men and women, not so unlike himself, save the shortest was at least seven feet tall. They looked unusual, he decided, because of their coal black hair and eyes along with their olive-colored skin. *So thin. How weird,* he thought. All looked very similar to each other, varying mostly in height.

Leading their horses, the six took King Norwood's horse and remained back a safe distance. He sensed his guards were terrified, and he set an example for them by boldly walking forward to meet these aliens. *Yes,* he thought, *they must be aliens or gods. I must find out which.* The tall man spoke first, startling Norwood as the man spoke his own language. Quite why that should have startled him, eluded him at the moment. "Welcome to Ashford-5 Spaceport and Refinery. I am General Janek Jerzy. This is Dita Ewa, our Minister of Social-Anthropology, and Luzia Lina, our Minister of Native Relations. May I inquire who you are?"

Norwood had no idea what their titles meant; he'd never heard those words before, except "relations." *Perhaps they're going to be friendly.* "Well met. I am King Norwood Wycombe, king of Bettingham. We saw your silver flying beast shooting flames, as it descended from the sky two days ago. I came to welcome you to the Kingdom of Bettingham." Something his father had drilled into him had resurfaced: *True men must be strong.* Hence, he took the approach that he did.

"He's the one we need to meet," Dita exclaimed, recognizing the name Alford had told her. "Send for Governor Andrzej at once. She held out her hand to Norwood. "Welcome King Norwood Wycombe. We're quite anxious to meet you. Two days ago, some of your countrymen paid us a visit and told us your name, King Norwood."

Norwood thought fast. *Two days ago? I've only become the king two days ago!* "How is that possible? Two days ago?

May I ask the names of those who were here before?"

Looking at her notes, Dita called them off. Norwood didn't recognize any of them until she called out the last one, Ally Wycombe. "My sister! Ally, she's my sister! She was here — two days ago?" he asked totally surprised and shocked. The last word he had of her was that their father had her hands cut off and she'd been abducted by persons unknown. He'd written her off as dead by now, probably having bled to death. He'd seen many men die within days of his physicians chopping off the wounded appendages of his soldiers.

"Yes, she was wounded, but our Doctor Zosia healed her up just fine, as well as the other equally wounded woman — what was her name?" Dita glanced at her notes. "One Aurora Wynne. They left here two days ago."

"Thank you; thank your doctor for healing her. I had assumed she perished from her wounds. They didn't say where they were going, did they?" he asked.

Consulting her notes, she answered, "A place called Wyth. I believe from the map that it is somewhere north of us."

"Yes, I just came from near there." He was interrupted by the hasty appearance of Governor Andrzej.

"Goodness, Dita. Why haven't you invited our king in for a visit? Governor Andrzej. I'm in charge of this installation. Come, come, we have much to discuss." He shook Norwood's hand like some long lost friend. Norwood didn't quite know what to make of this, but signaled his men to relax and followed them. As they walked to the base, Norwood watched Dita, fascinated by her appearance and looks. While she was easily a foot taller than himself, she was still attractive, an exotic beauty, he decided, since he had never seen anyone with such coal black hair and eyes.

Inside, he was taken to the main meeting room. There, after being introduced to the other ministers, the governor told him pretty much the same thing he'd told the first visitors. Norwood listened and attempted to grasp the situation. *They want to mine for the worthless psi-crystals? They'll pay miners to do some of the work, pay them in gold?* This sounded too good to be true. An ounce of gold was so rare and so valuable that it was worth nearly ten pounds of silver or even a good steel sword. When he heard they anticipated most of the mining to be done in the Goza mountains, he realized Bettingham had the greatest claim to the mountains than any other single kingdom, close to twelve hundred miles of the eastern side.

"We should form a close alliance, Governor Andrzej. Bettingham has many men who are already miners or who would love to mine and be paid in *gold*. We have teamsters who can haul your psi-crystals from the mines to your refinery here on the plateau. I can foresee many benefits for each of us, governor," Norwood began to bargain. "Besides, my kingdom encompasses more of these mountains than any other kingdom."

The more the two men talked, the stronger the proposed alliance became, especially in the mind of the governor, who was delighted to have the king, whose border with these mountains was the longest, allied with him. Having King Norwood on his side meant far less security would be needed.

King Norwood then said, "I've only got one small problem, though. At the moment, King Chester of Rockwood to our north has sent his cavalry into my kingdom attacking our defenseless villages, killing the able bodied men there, raping the women, and burning their homes. Would it be possible to get a little help getting these cavalrymen out of our country? If so, I can then get miners on the job within days. How many miners could you use?"

That he wanted at least a thousand men greatly appealed to Norwood. That meant sure gold for a thousand and, in return, they would be strongly supportive of their new king. General Janek said something to the governor in their own language, which was not translated. Norwood heard what sounded like gibberish. Seeing his confused look, Luzia hastily suggested, "Our language translators have a slight problem. Give me a second to fix it, please." She pretended to fiddle with hers and noticed the primitive seemed relieved.

"Governor, what about Imperial Directive #5? Do we dare directly interfere in the primitives' wars?" General Janek had asked, most concerned about such a direct violation of Imperial law.

"Psi-crystals, general, psi-crystals. Keep your focus. We are to be producing a vast quantity of fuel for this sector of the outer rim as soon as possible. If we need to quickly put an end to this conflict, then we do it. He can get us a thousand miners in short order. Think of the psi-crystal output, general. Now do it. Take care of this primitive's war immediately."

"Of course, governor," General Janek replied.

"Ah, there now, the translator is working again. We were just saying we would be delighted to help you remove these cavalrymen from your lands. How soon after that can you get the miners for us?" the governor asked what he most wanted to know.

"You say how many and where. I'll get them there as fast as we can. We use horses for fast transportation," Norwood answered, scarcely believing what he was hearing. These aliens were going to help him rid Bettingham of Chester's cavalrymen. It was too good to be true, he thought, but he could find no fault in their agreement thus far.

"Excellent, excellent. Dita, would you mind chatting with King Norwood here, while the general and his forces prepare themselves to come to King Norwood's aid?" the governor asked politely. Dita took this as he intended, a direct order to that effect. However, she was herself intrigued by this man. For a primitive, he showed little fear of them. All her studies suggested primitives would be terrified of them, especially if they were seen falling from the sky.

"So do you have social occasions among your people?" she asked.

"Social occasions?" he asked, not quite grasping what she was asking. Wisely, he added, "Perhaps we are having difficulties with words between our languages."

"Yes, that is likely my fault. I mean times where men and women get together and socialize, talk, drink, dance, watch movies, party."

"Oh, yes, now I get what you are asking about, sure we do. Musicians play for our dances. We have Royal Balls where we dance. Our people often visit our pubs, and drink and talk there. However, I am afraid that again I don't know the word movies, Dita. Do your people have such things too?"

"Yes, of course we do. All races do, but in various ways. I study these things, that's what I love to do. Perhaps I could come to one of these Royal Balls of yours," Dita asked. She had not cleared that with the governor, but this was a golden opportunity for field studies, and she was determined to take full advantage of it. Perhaps, there would be an Imperium paper or two on it as well. Such would not hurt her standing in her field.

"Certainly. I will send word to you when our next one will be held. How much notice will you need, a week?"

"Oh dear me no. I can be there later that very day, if that is okay with you, King Norwood."

"Great. That's settled then. I'll let you know when it will be held and where. I'd be honored to have you attend as my partner," Norwood suggested, imagining the impression he would make on all those in court.

In the next room, General Janek pointed out, "The fastest way is to simply disintegrate these primitive cavalrymen. Problem solved in less than a day. Now if we have to actually beam them into ships and transport them elsewhere, that is going to take several days, maybe longer."

"Make it one day. I don't want your men exposed to these primitives any longer than that," the governor ordered. He didn't say the alternative would add more days before the mining could begin.

"Ahem, might I use this opportunity to utilize our Mind Wipes on those whose bodies the general's men disintegrate?" suggested Cezar, the Psychman. "I can then program them to find new bodies and to be non-aggressive in their next lifetimes, as well as become miners for us."

"Oh perfect, perfect, Cezar! Make it so," a delighted governor replied. Non-aggressive in his book meant more miners, meaning more psi-crystals.

"Okay then, we'll take three runabouts and take the king along in one. That should impress him with our powers so he will never dream of crossing us," the general added. "We'll end this primitive war yet today. Let's get started."

An hour later, Cezar activated his electronic machinery in his laboratory on top of Plateau Grado. King Norwood had already ordered his six soldiers to take his horse back with them and make for their encampment. He would be personally taken back by the general.

Norwood gazed out of the glass windows, he assumed, at his countryside flying by at an incredible speed. To say he was awed would be a total understatement. Yet, he kept his focus and tried not to show his utter awe with each new development. Dita came along with them, insisting on further field study. Somehow, Norwood felt Dita would think less of him if he showed his utter awe like some silly child. Soon, they were over the fields, and he spotted a group of twenty-five of Chester's cavalrymen.

"There are some of them. You can tell the enemy soldiers, because they all wear the bright red coats. Our soldiers wear green uniforms. If you see other bright red uniforms like these, they are Chester's men," Norwood explained, hoping they would not harm his own people, only the invaders.

For security reasons, General Janek did not allow the ULATs to translate his orders and those among his crew as they armed and prepared the scout ship's weaponry. When the first volley was fired, Norwood simply could not help reacting. All twenty-five men and their horses simply vanished, though they had been cantering along. Not a single trace of them could he see. "Incredible! Where did they go?" he asked totally flabbergasted.

"Disintegrated into the very particles that once composed their physical bodies," General Janek answered, somewhat proud of his ship's armaments. *It is impressive,* he thought. The ship continued its sweeping path, darting here and there, pausing only long enough for the crew to get a positive id on the primitives on the ground and then fire their weapons.

Late that afternoon, General Janek landed the scout ship near the king's army headquarters. Some two thousand soldiers witnessed their own king departing from the god's flying ship, as well as some ten thousand plus inhabitants of nearby Wyth. After he rejoined his own awestruck majors, the ship rose into the sky and returned to the plateau, again at a tremendous speed, from their point of view at least.

King Norwood was besieged with questions and was treated with incredible awe and respect, for he had befriended the newly arrived gods of the plateau. This alone assured him of the throne of Bettingham. Word spread rapidly of this incredible encounter with the gods of the sky. By the next day, word also reached him of the sudden disappearance of all Chester's cavalrymen. He ordered his forces to march to the Wyndl River in a show of complete victory over King Chester's forces.

His messengers failed, however, to locate Ally within Wyth. There were just too many people there now and too many refugees. Confusion reigned. Plus, he was urgently needed back in Wycombe to solidify his ascension to the throne. Additionally, he needed to live up to his side of the bargain and get a thousand miners ready to assist the plateau gods. Regrettably, he headed back to Wycombe the next morning, vowing to return later on and look for his sister. He did leave messages for her with the small garrison force that remained at Wyth.

Prince Orson Chester, dressed in his finest red uniform, was not unduly disappointed the arranged marriage had fallen through, particularly so, when he learned King Aaran had her hands cut off for trying to flee. Instead, he continued to do what he most enjoyed, commanding his crack cavalrymen and raiding the local towns. He had his pick of the captured wenches, anyone of which, he felt, would be better suited for a bride than the king's daughter, as she was now. However, he dare not go against his father's wishes in such matters. He was heir to the throne and that meant all to him. She could still bear him sons, that was the bottom line in his book.

Late afternoon, they just finished destroying another small village and were riding back to their main encampment when this strange, silver flying object appeared overhead. "What devilry is this?" he called out. Those were the last words he uttered. A split second later, his body and horse vanished, disintegrated wholly. He was still there, a very confused spiritual being.

Stupefied, he blinked non-existent eyes. Then, he sensed a powerful energy flow coming his way. It was brilliantly white. Extraordinarily so. He was pulled towards this blinding light. Arriving at its source on the high plateau, he watched helplessly as all his memories of his twenty years of life flickered by and became totally scrambled, as if each memory was a card in some deck, which was then shuffled really well before the cards were dealt. A booming voice appeared, demanding his full, confused attention. "Find a new baby body. When you grow up, you will be totally non-aggressive in nature. No more fighting. You will want to mine for the aliens. Go now; find a new baby body." He did as instructed, having forgotten his own name entirely.

During the next few hours, some twenty-five hundred other men were similarly handled by Cezar, the Psychman. So successful was his operation he began to plot even larger scale psyche intervention. After all, the governor only wanted more psi-crystals. If he could ensure all future primitives were duly non-aggressive, why, there would be more mining done. QED, he thought, but he wisely kept his ideas to himself for the moment.

Across the Wyndl River, King Addam Chester lost his daily contact with his large army. He sent out scouts the next day. They returned with the most alarming news ever to befall a monarch. His entire cavalry force had simply vanished from the face of Tierra. They were gone, even his son and heir. Vanished without a single trace, including their horses. King Norwood's men found their main encampments and confiscated what was there, food and plunder. Thus, King Chester was the first ruler to grasp fully the incredible devastation potential that these aliens possessed. This war was over for now. His dreams of conquest abruptly ended.

Chapter 6 The Wyth Coven

"I tell you, times are changing. Something big is in the wind. I can feel it," Sheena Hilton complained to her fellow witches. The freckled thirty year old redhead, the most conservative of the five women who called themselves the Wyth Coven, was trying to explain and make sense of her intuitive visions she'd been having lately. Always the curious one, often her desire to know had gotten her into sometimes difficult messes out of which her four friends had to extricate her.

The latest had indeed been quite messy. She'd been spying on their enemy, Bishop Galen Heath, who ran the COG here in Wyth. She'd been entirely too curious about what he was planning, had snuck into his rectory, and overheard his plans to raid another "Evil Witch" shop, one Mary Hartwig. While relaying this information to her fellow witches, she'd been captured, and Bishop Galen reveled in his capture of the red headed witch. Her coven managed to get timely warning to Mary, who eluded the COG's raid quite nicely, but her coven had temporarily to charm the bishop to obtain Sheena's release. A forget potion took care of the rest. Sheena's curiosity and penchant for risk taking in satisfying her thirst to know often conflicted with her basic conservative outlook on life.

This duality also permeated her personal life as well. Her husband, Hector, owned and ran Hector's Inn in Wyth, a respected inn, though not the most elegant. Torn between helping him run his inn and the running of her own business, Sheena's Herbs, coupled with the raising of her son Len, who was ten, and her daughter Trish, now eight, Sheena could always be counted upon to be somewhat in a state of organized chaos, made all the more so with this damnable war with neighboring Rockton. She, with three of her coven, were awaiting the arrival of their coven's founder, who had summoned them to this late evening meeting, highly unusual because of the lateness, way past midnight.

"Oh stuff it, Sheena," her coven leader attempted to quiet Sheena down. Hearing her alluding to unknown things that might or might not be real always annoyed Wendy Lane.

Also a redhead, as were all five in this coven, Wendy tended to be abrasive and suspicious, especially since the death of her husband a couple of years ago. The fool had been a soldier and gotten himself killed; such was her attitude towards him now. Her son, Jordan, twenty-one, had rather taken after his father, becoming a respected weapon's maker, something that always annoyed Wendy. She ignored the fact a true metalworker was highly valued and highly paid. At least her blonde daughter, Tammy, now eighteen, was following in her footsteps and in training to be a witch as well. Tammy was fully versed in herb lore, and these days did most of the gathering of wild herbs Wendy used in her potions that she sold in her shop, Wendy's Herbs. Tammy often ran the store for her these past few months. Wendy's big concern at the moment was whether or not to allow Tammy into their inner circle and train her in their most powerful skills. Tammy was not a redhead, an aspect that Wendy thought was crucial to being a power witch.

"Well, Wendy, she does have a point. Strange things *are* happening. I'll admit much is from this stupid war. Men, anyway. You'd think they'd know better, but of course, they are men, and you can't expect anything but fighting from them. Still, you'd think with all the dead and limbless men being dumped on Wyth that they'd stop their silly battles, but of course they are men, and we can't expect more of them, I suppose, though I do wish they would learn from all this, but then. . ." the chatter box, Vivian Waters, thirty-eight, rattled away in Sheena's defense, only to be abruptly cut off by Wendy.

"Vivian! We *know* all about men," Wendy chopped her off mid-sentence. "My own Elmer was a prime example. Does anyone know *why* Holly called us together at three in the morning?"

Vivian was married to Finley who ran Fin's Teamsters, a small hauling company operating out of Wyth. Their seventeen year old son, Ken, was finishing up his stone mason apprenticeship. Their blonde daughter, fifteen year old Valerie, was also learning witchcraft and constantly hung around Tammy; the two were best friends. Vivian did not like to be cut off and gave Wendy a strong look of annoyance, but remained silent.

The fourth member of their coven was Sissy Skylar. The youngest at twenty-five, Sissy was also the prettiest of the five, but she was also the nervous type, quite paranoid, seeing conspiracies everywhere. Surprisingly, she was right more than she was wrong. Thus, her suspicions were given weight by her peers. She'd married Clay, a prominent blacksmith, a very good looking young man of twenty-six. They had two children, Curt, five, and Roni, four.

Sissy took advantage of the momentary silence. "It's midnight, not three in the morning. However, there *is* something stirring, something wholly *sinister*! I can *feel* it, but maybe it is more than *one* thing. I have a fear we are *all* going to be affected by this or these, perhaps."

Exasperated, Wendy exclaimed, "Oh don't you start in too, Sissy!" Thankfully, someone knocked on Wendy's door. Three times, one time, then twice. This was their secret knock, and they all knew it had to be their fifth member and founder, Holly Sprigs. Holly was the eldest of the coven at fifty. Widowed for many years now, her eldest son, Dalton, thirty, was married and had his own business. Likewise, Niel, twenty-eight, was married and had his own life. True, they got together at holidays, but they no longer factored significantly into her life. Her red headed daughters did. Roxane was twenty-five but had taken a life-partner, which was a polite way of saying she had a lesbian mate, since women were not allowed to marry other women, ditto with men. Sable Bighton, a blonde woman, was a year younger than Roxane. Together, they opened R & S Dressmaking. They made rather fine dresses and were doing well for themselves. However, twenty-two year old Sammi had taken after their mother and become a witch herself. Sammi was cute and a bit precocious. Holly was ready to allow Sammi into their inner circle and give her their advanced training.

Holly had formed this coven seventeen years ago with Wendy and Vivian as the first women in her circle. She was the quiet type, but extremely knowledgeable and wise. Holly was a teacher by nature and had taught the other four all what they considered their advanced training, which went far beyond mere healing of the sick and injured and the concoction of potions useful in life. Although Holly never said so, she had handpicked her coven members from all the other witches who lived in and around the Kingdom of Bettingham. Of course, the other four members believed a woman had to be a red head in order to be in this coven, since all five were just that. However, this was not the case; Holly had picked her members for their unique and special skills and insights. Wendy was a natural leader and had been appointed the leader of the coven from the very beginning seventeen years ago.

"Thank you all for coming at such a late hour. I would not have summoned you except for the gravity of the situation and of what may yet be coming," Holly said as she sat down and accepted a mug of green tea from Vivian.

"I've just been contacted by Phyllis of Wycombe. The COG has just connived to have Babs Wynne hanged, and her daughter, the promising witch Aurora, has had both her hands removed by the palace COG doctor."

Sheena burst out, "I knew it! Something horrid has happened. See, I was right! The COG has to be stopped before they have us all killed. Oh!" Sheena finally registered what had happened to Aurora. "Oh my god, not both of them!" She paled.

"I am afraid so, Sheena, both of them. Phyllis has asked for my aid and help. She believes she can arrange for someone to bring Aurora here to us, and I've promised to take her in and care for her needs."

Wendy frowned, "That is awful! Ruining that poor young woman's entire life! Well, I am sure we can find a place for her. But honestly, Holly, couldn't this have waited until morning?" Wendy saw yet another helpless cripple coming to Wyth. Already she'd seen and/or helped dozens of men who'd been brought to Wyth from the battlefields, missing one or more appendages. Some she was able to help heal, while others died from their "surgeries" in the battlefield medical tents. What was one more of them, save Aurora was originally one of them, a witch. Her thought emphasis was on the word *was*.

"Well, there is more, Wendy. I would not have asked

you here at this hour for only this. It seems our illustrious king has just tried to end this mad war of his by ceding Wyth to Rockton, along with his eldest daughter, Ally, who is supposed to be given to Orson Chester as part of the deal. Ally is something of a wildcard, as you all know by now. We've had our eye on her for some time, thanks to Babs. It seems our beliefs about her were correct. She has run away from the palace and has volunteered to help bring Aurora here to us. We have perhaps a week to work out just how we are going to proceed with Ally. However, more pressing is the king's ceding of Wyth to King Addam Chester. He's as much of a rouge and villain as King Aaran, though not as brutal, as far as we know."

"We can't allow Wyth to become part of Rockton; we don't have any influences in Rockton," Wendy stated the plain fact of the matter. Here in Bettingham, they had clever ties to a great many influential men and women. Through these contacts, they were able to juggle events to keep life on a fairly even keel, so to speak. If they became part of Rockton, their many years of work would go down the drain.

"True, we only have acquaintances there, fellow witches," Holly replied. "I don't expect any answers from you tonight. Think on it; we have perhaps a week to decide. If we become part of Rockton, then Ally may well be useless to us, unless she does marry Orson." She dismissed the women and headed back home.

"Whoa, there is a whole lot more going on. I just *know* it!" declared Sissy. "Why does King Chester want Ally in his control? Does he know about her? If so, how much? Well, I don't suppose he'll get his grubby hands on Ally now that she's finally flown the coop, so to speak. Honestly, I would have fled long ago. I wonder if there isn't more to all this than Holly is telling us. What do you think, Sheena?"

"You called it right again, Sissy. Why does King Addam Chester want to get his hands on Ally? Could it be that this whole war has been staged just to get King Aaran into a position where he would betroth his eldest to the Chester's heir?" Sheena asked.

"For once, I believe you have something here," Wendy had to agree. "This entire devastating war may have just been a pretext to force Aaran to hand over Ally to the Chester boy. It sure smells like it. That *is* something a *man* would dream up," she punched in.

"Yes, but what does he want with Wyth?" Sissy continued, tracing down her conspiracy lines. "There really isn't anything all that special about this town here, nothing at all. It isn't strategically placed. Wyth doesn't produce anything particularly valuable to others, you know, like a big gold or gem mine. There is a bit of precious iron ore from the nearby mines, but little else. So I ask you, why does Chester want Wyth? I think we need to find the answer to this larger question."

"Oh no more! My mind can't take any more of this, not this early morning. Get going; I am going to *try* and get *some* sleep," Wendy barked, signaling the others to leave in no uncertain terms. The other three departed, still chatting, especially Vivian.

Late the next morning, Wendy was still in an ill humor. She hated to be roused in the middle of the night. Holly wisely didn't drop by to chat. Had she, Wendy would have chewed her out. Her news could have waited until the morning. Her day only got worse. A soldier driving a wagon pulled up before her herb shop. "Tammy, go see what he wants, will you? I've a headache coming on."

"Sure mom. Try some elfin leaf tea. Val, coming with me?" the spirited eighteen year old asked her constant sidekick, Valerie Waters, Vivian's daughter. The two teens headed to the door to greet the young soldier in his bright green uniform.

Val giggled, "He's rather cute, don't you think?" Her cheery attitude soon changed.

"Hi, I have brought a wagon of soldiers who are in dire need of your best healing. I'm authorized to pay you what is fair for their treatment," the young lad announced. The two teens glanced at the wagon. Their attitude changed instantly upon seeing the six wounded men, crudely handled by the soldier's field COG doctor.

"Bring them around back. I'd better go get mom," Tammy said quickly. "Val, go with him and show him the entrance." She dashed off through the store to their living quarters to let her mother know.

Ten minutes later, the teens and the solider had gotten the six men inside the back room, where Wendy handled the worst cases first. *The army physician has been chopping again,* Wendy cursed silently to herself. Her opinion of men in general had been plummeting ever since her soldier husband had gotten himself killed.

She attended the first man. "How are you doing? Any pain?" She made pleasant conversation, though she knew the answer to both questions. The man had both his legs chopped off by the field doctor along with most of his right arm. Bloody bandages dripped onto the chair in which the man was sitting.

Barely conscious and in tremendous pain, the man whispered, "Please, good witch, give me something to finish this." She knew what he meant. Even if he healed up, without legs and one arm, his life would be nothing more than that of a street beggar, looking for a handout. Tammy watched as she poured a little vial of liquid into a cup of tea and handed it to the man. His last words were, "Thank you, good witch." He drank his tea and closed his eyes. Meanwhile, Wendy moved on to the next man, who had lost and arm and a leg.

Red lines ran up his two stumps and Wendy pointed this out to both Tammy and Val, blood poisoning. "I'm afraid he ought to have gotten to us sooner. If so, more of his arm and leg might have been cut off to save his life. Now it has gone beyond what's left of both." To the wounded soldier, she added, "There isn't anything more that can be done, sir."

"Please, some of that special tea of yours? I am ready; the pain is beyond bearable," he whispered very slowly, fighting to remain conscious. Wendy complied with his wishes.

The next man had barely three inches of his arms remaining. He too begged to be allowed to end his life. Once more, Wendy complied with his wishes. Finally, the remaining three men had only lost a single limb. She put Tammy and Val to work on a pair and took the third herself. After carefully removing their bandages, the raw wounds were washed in sterile water, and then packed with Wendy's special ointment and re-bandaged. She gave each man a pot of the healing salve with instructions on how to apply it along with several fresh bandages. The young soldier, now quite green, handed her the bag of silver coins and hastily helped the three back to the wagon, promising to return with a burial wagon for the other three.

"Well, three out of six isn't bad. Men! What they do to other men," Wendy swore. *At least, Tammy and Val got some very good experience treating such awful wounds,* she thought. "Both of you did very well today. Here, take a third of these coins each. You've earned them."

"Wow. Thanks, Mrs. Lane," Val exclaimed. Wendy smiled and continued to clean up the now messy room. What a day.

Around noon the following day, Wendy suddenly had Holly's voice in her mind. *Meeting immediately! My place! Emergency!* That was all; the connection broke. "Darn her anyway; she could at least tell us what the infernal emergency was," Wendy grumbled. "Tammy, I'm going over to Holly's for a few minutes. Mind the store, please." She headed out the door. It was a nice day, though it would likely rain soon. What possibly could be the dire emergency? All around her, Wyth seemed to be running normally, if one discounted the many soldiers coming and going and the many pathetic refugees walking into Wyth seeking sanctuary.

Before long, Sissy joined up with her. "What's the emergency?" Sissy asked. "She didn't say."

"Same here. We best hurry, you know Holly," Wendy answered rather curtly.

As they reached Holly's place, Vivian and Sheena joined them; they had been jogging to get here fast. Each looked questioningly at Wendy, who merely said, "I don't know either. Come on." They entered Holly's Herbs and More, ignoring the Closed sign in the window. They walked through the fragrant scented room to the living room where Holly sometimes held their meetings.

"Oh good. You are all together. Simpler this way. Sit down. We have to work extremely quickly. I just got an emergency contact from Zoe via Phyllis. It seems the soldiers have ambushed them. Ally managed to get Zoe and Aurora away from the soldiers, but she was captured. Doctor Corey is there with his infernal machine. By the king's orders, Ally is to lose both her hands. If we are going to save her and the other two, we must take immediate action. Phyllis is calling in her trump card that we owe her." She pointed out approximately where they were located and the likely location for the doctor, a small hamlet. "Who have we got near there?"

Wendy cursed, "Damn that Aaran. We ought to have slipped him hemlock long ago! No one, damn it. Not there, that's out in the wilds mostly. Hell, we've lost all three of them!"

"Hey, what about using the Bettinghams? They've helped us on numerous occasions," Sheena asked.

"They are the best we have," Vivian pointed out.

"I think Alford and Aiden are still somewhere in or around Bettingham at the moment. I talked to a friend of theirs on the street yesterday," Sissy pointed out. "He said they were there monitoring the situation down to the southeast, wisely avoiding the battles up here."

"Are we agreed we should ask the Bettinghams?" Holly asked, seeking agreement. All either nodded or said yes. "All right. I'll use the stone and contact them." She opened a pouch and brought out a bluish crystal, a psi-crystal. She placed it in her hand and closed her fingers over it, squeezing the stone. She closed her eyes and focused. *Alford. Holly here. Emergency. We need to talk with you immediately. Yes, Aiden too. Hurry. Life and death.*

Holly opened her eyes and fist. Sighing, she placed the psi-crystal back in its pouch before speaking. "Alford is getting Aiden. We'll all join together in a few minutes. Prepare your psi-crystals please."

Ten minutes later, the two young men sat down on their couch at their estate in Bettingham. "This is going to be strange," Alford said to Aiden. "A bunch of witches are about to enter our minds." Aiden laughed, but then his expression became serious, as he felt his mind joining with Holly's. *Ah, you witches are all here,* Alford thought teasingly.

What did you expect? Wendy barked. *This is an emergency after all. Are you both sitting down?*

I'll tell them, Holly interrupted her, for which Wendy was grateful. She rather hated having to deal directly with men these days. She rather envied Holly's daughter, Roxane whose mate was another woman, Sable.

Holly sighed and then launched into a lengthy explanation. *If you can't get to Ally Wycombe soon, Doctor Corey will be carrying out the king's orders, and Ally will lose both of her hands. Aurora already has lost hers and was forced to watch her mother, Babs, hanged in front of her own store. Right now, Zoe has Aurora safe, thanks to some fast action on Ally's part. We need the three of them rescued and brought here to us in Wyth. You will need more psi-powders, since Zoe had to use half of Aurora's supply to contact Phyllis.*

Well, we still have some you gave us a while back, Alford thought back to Holly. *Can you see my image of how much we have? Is it going to be enough?* He focused his mind on the small pouch in Aiden's hand.

Holly added, *Yes, that's enough for Ally as well, if you can't get to her in time. Yes, I know it was her father who killed your father and stole the throne of Bettingham. I'm begging you to do this for us. We need Ally here at all costs. She isn't her father, Alford.*

You have to remind us of old wounds, eh, witch? Alford replied. *Don't worry. We know Princess Ally isn't her father. We'll do it. All these years, Holly, you and your witches have never been wrong and have helped us. We'll do it. See you in a few days.* He rose along with Aiden, who had been silent.

Thank you, both. If you succeed in this mission, be it known we witches owe you a very large debt that you may call upon one day when your need is great, as ours is now, Holly sent. Alford nodded, thinking such a debt would be a very great asset for the future. After all, these particular witches were the most powerful ones the brothers had encountered in their wide travels. Holly then broke her telepathic connection to the two men.

"We best get Abby too; might need her arrows," Aiden suggested, as the two headed down the street towards where their sister was checking on new longbows.

"We can have her acquire the supplies we're going to

need and join us. She can follow our trail. Do you think we could possible ride hard and fast enough to get to Ally in time?" Alford asked.

"Doubt it, but what the hell, we have to try. Losing one hand is bad enough, but both is almost a death warrant," Aiden replied. They broke into a jog.

"Now we wait," Holly said after breaking contact with the two men. "There's nothing more we can do."

"But if they can't get to Ally in time," Sissy started to ask.

"I know, I know. We'll just have to wait and see," Holly advised.

"Holly, she's got a point," Wendy insisted they follow Sissy's path. "If Ally loses both her hands, then that ruins everything we've planned. We can't use her sister, April; she's not much better than a mouse!"

"I told you all there was *far* more to *all* this than we thought at first!" Sissy declared. "I think we are going to see *many* more things happening too. I can feel it. Something huge is coming, really *big*."

Wendy cut her off. "Oh you see something huge in everything, Sissy! Give it a rest until Ally gets here."

"Okay, you may go back to whatever you were doing," Holly said softly. "I will contact the men periodically, and let you know what has happened. As we know more, we can prepare."

"I say, *prepare* for the worst!" Sissy refused to be silenced. "A *monster* storm is coming! I can feel it coming." With that, she turned on her heels and left, followed shortly by the other witches. Holly watched them go and then sighed to herself. Things were going all wrong, at least from their point of view. Still, there might be a way to salvage all this. Would the men get to Ally in time to save her and their future plans for the princess? She didn't know.

Around noon the next day, Holly sent the four a sad, short message. *Ally lost both her hands. Our men are bringing the three here.*

Late that afternoon, Holly sent them another message. *Phyllis just told me that King Aaran Wycombe is dead!*

Assassinated in his bed. Probably Queen Misty did the deed. She and April have fled Wycombe. They're sending riders to let Prince Norwood know. He'll probably claim the throne when he hears of this, likely a couple of days. We should meet tonight after supper.

"See, I told you something *huge* was going to happen!" Sissy declared as the five witches met at Wendy's around six that night. "But I don't think it is *over!*"

"What do you mean, Sissy?" asked Sheena, convinced Sissy could see the future.

"This *is* a huge event, one we've worked on bringing about for years, *but,*" her voice trailed off.

"All right, Sissy, but what?" Wendy gave in, curious to know what Sissy truly intended to convey to them.

"Well, this is huge; the king is dead, no dismissing that, but it is *not* what I have been feeling is huge. I don't know how else to say this, but this doesn't feel like the huge change that is coming. There is something vastly huger, but I can't tell what yet." Sissy sighed deeply. She hated when she couldn't state her gift well to others. "I've held the crystals for hours, but I can't get a good grasp on it. I get strange, impossible images, like silver things in the sky. You know — things that can't possibly be. I tell you, something *really* huge is coming soon."

All five witches sat silent for a moment; Sissy's pronouncement was unnerving, primarily because they all knew she was a seer and seldom wrong. If Sissy didn't think these momentous events were not what she was sensing, then there must be something more coming, but what?

"We ought to get handling what we *do* know has happened," Holly broke the silence. *Be practical,* she thought, *deal with what is in the present here and now.* "We have two women who have undergone massive traumas and who have lost both their hands. Worse, Babs was one of us; we owe it to her to assist her daughter, Aurora, who has completed her basic training and is a witch herself."

"*Was* a witch," Wendy corrected Holly. "Without hands, she and Ally are just two more totally helpless women, just like all the damnable men we've been handling."

94

"*Is* a witch, Wendy. I agree, life will be incredibly hard for both women, but Aurora's knowledge was not in her hands, but her mind," Holly pointed out.

"But how can Aurora do anything at all?" asked Sissy.

"She and Ally will need someone to be with them at all times, being their hands," Sheena pointed out. "We take so many things for granted. How will they eat, brush their hair, dress themselves, or even handle their personal needs? I guess we can arrange for a couple of women to stay with them at all times, being their hands, but that might be rather expensive in the long run. Still we *owe* it to Babs to help Aurora."

"Yes, we do," Wendy agreed. "Unlike the men, when such disasters happen to women, we look after our own. I pity the poor soldiers who have undergone their COG physician's mad chopping substitute for true healing. After that, they are routed out of their army and left to get by on their own. Yet, they can blame no one but themselves for having agreed to play soldier. Men! We women would never *do* such despicable things. Okay, ladies, we can set aside a little bit of our profits each week and pool the funds to support Aurora and Ally with permanent assistants so they can at least live like women."

Holly, who had been silent finally spoke up, "You are all forgetting one key point. By the time both women get here, each will have consumed sufficient psi-powders to make the transformation. Do we deny these women the chance that so few witches ever get?"

"Well, no, Holly, *but*," Wendy began and stopped.

"But what, Wendy? That they have no hands?" Holly asked softly.

"Right. How are they going to be able to even use the precious gift the psi-crystals may give them?" Wendy finally said what she was thinking.

"You forget, Wendy, we cannot predict what the psi-crystals will give anyone of us witches," Holly pointed out. "Perhaps their gifts will not require the use of their hands. If so, we owe it to them, because such a gift will help give them new purposes for their lives, replacing all their many lost purposes, lost with their hands."

"True, Holly. Yet, what if the gift they receive requires

the use of their hands? Now they'd have to experience a second, even greater loss," Wendy pointed out. "Are we willing to chance making them have yet another traumatic loss?"

That was sobering. "You are assuming their gifts will require their hands," Holly finally broke the ensuing silence. "I believe we owe it to Babs to try. Let us cross that second loss if it occurs. Let's not presume such will occur." They agreed on this point.

"But Ally is not a witch. Surely, you don't plan to have her receive such a priceless gift without any training whatsoever?" Wendy raised her next objection.

Several nodded their agreement. "She's not a redhead," Vivian added.

"Ally's life is destroyed. Perhaps the psi-crystal's gift will restore some purpose for her to continue to live," Holly stated dryly, ignoring Wendy's protest.

Miffed, Wendy then asked, "It's in your hands, but where are we going to house the two? With all the refugees coming into Wyth and with more coming in each day, housing here is at a premium. The inns are full. Sheena's husband is kindly operating at a loss so many of the homeless and husband-less women and children at least have a room and something to eat."

"Should we consider moving from Wyth?" Vivian suggested. "We all know Norwood is unable to stop Chester's cavalrymen, who are raiding the center towns of Bettingham. Soon, Wyth may well be encircled and forced to surrender to King Chester. Perhaps bringing them here is now is not such a good idea. Should we consider moving elsewhere and taking the two women with us?"

"Where would we go? This is our land, the land that we know. I won't leave," Sheena answered. The others agreed; they really had no place to go. Doing so would force them to start over completely, assuming they could even get their husbands and families to agree.

The witches then spent their time trying to work out a safe place to house, care, and train the two women. They presumed they would have three or four days to get these details worked out. Late in the afternoon, the five headed outside to see what the confusion and yelling was all about. Had the cavalrymen broken through the city gates? Everywhere, people were yelling and pointing to the sky.

The five witches stared at the silver beast spewing fires from its belly slowly descending to the earth somewhere to the south of Wyth. "I *told* you something *really huge* was coming!" Sissy whispered, awed by the spectacular sight she was witnessing.

"What is it? Some new *monster* that breathes fire?" asked Sheena.

"My place! Tonight!" Holly yelled to her friends over the noise of the city dwellers swarming the streets, staring skyward, yelling all manner of ideas.

After dark, the five met at Wendy's, sharing the various opinions about what they'd heard others suggest this strange silver beast actually was. The ideas ran the gamut from descending gods to a mythical dragon. "Well, they are supposed to fly and breathe fire," Sissy defended that idea.

"Let's cease speculations. Witches, take out your psi-crystals, and let us see what we can determine about this silver beast thing," Holly brought them all back to the present. Dutifully, the five retrieved their precious psi-crystals. Each held theirs in their hand and squeezed them, making good contact. Some were bluish, some greenish. They closed their eyes and opened their respective senses, which differed from witch to witch.

Sometime passed before one by one, they opened their hand, replacing their psi-crystals in their pouches. "Well, as your master telepath, I sensed many minds, but they are foreign. I cannot understand their language; thus their thoughts are unknown to me," Holly spoke first. "I sense a great intelligence and mastery of machines. Some images I did capture from a few minds make no sense to me as yet. Perhaps some of you can impart greater wisdom than I can," Holly said humbly.

"Well, I sensed a great malignancy and disgust towards we inhabitants of Tierra in general. Nothing specific, I am afraid," Vivian spoke next. "Not too helpful yet." Her gift was the ability to sense when danger was imminent though unseen and otherwise undetected. "I think we need to be very, very careful with this thing, whatever it is."

"They are some kind of people," Sheena added her observations. "Terrible and powerful people. If we try to fight them, the odds are a ten thousand to one, with us being the one! Perhaps they are gods after all." Her gift was to always know the odds in any given situation, as well as whether or not she ought to pursue her innate curiosity, and what the odds of her succeeding might be, though she often ignored bad odds when her curiosity was roused.

"I agree, some strange kind of people, but they want to use us for their own purposes. They are here to get something, a whole lot of something. They do not respect us and will destroy us if needed," Sissy added her take. Her gift was to be able to glimpse the hidden motives people had, which only fueled her conspiracy theories.

Wendy added her observations last. Her gift was to sense the right action to be taken in any given situation. "Extreme danger to all the people of Tierra, not just us. We should not go against their requests, at least not overtly. I sense they could wipe us out in a blink. Witches, we are facing the most powerful opponents imaginable. Exercise extreme caution! Gather more information. Sissy, you were more than right. This is beyond huge!"

"Hang on a second. Zoe is using some of her psi-powders to contact me," Holly interrupted them. A bit later, she opened her eyes. "Yes, they have seen the ship too, a flying ship. They are very close to where it landed. Alford believes it landed on the Plateau Grado. I asked her to see if they can go check it out. I know that is very risky, but I am willing to take the gamble. Aurora and Ally's situation pales compared to this new threat. We need to know more." They discussed this surprising turn for some time before adjourning for the night.

Two days later, they still had not found a suitable location for the two women. Wyth was still getting more and more refugees, mostly women and children. All were in the most desperate need of food, clothing, and shelter. The raiders of Chester had destroyed their homes and villages, murdering most of the able-bodied men who were there. They had no choice but to walk to the nearest town or village, which had yet to be raided and beg for help. Wyth, being the largest town in the northwestern portion of Bettingham, naturally took in all who walked through its gates. Now nearly every house had accepted at least one refugee, and some had accepted the wounded and maimed soldiers, giving them a place to recover from their wounds or amputations that saved their lives.

These past two days, the witches had been swamped with those in need coming to their herb shops looking for cures for all manner of ills, the least of which were bad foot blisters. Some women wanted help with recovering from their rapes.

Just after lunch, Vivian very nearly freaked out. Her gift triggered so massively that her legs gave out, and she slumped to the floor of her shop. Fortunately, Val was with her today, helping with the massive numbers visiting the witches seeking help. Val frantically sent word to Sissy, who came running, followed shortly by the others in her coven.

Vivian was rolling on the floor, holding her head as if it were about to burst, moaning in pain. Sissy was about to administer a bit of psi-powders when Wendy grabbed her hand. "No, that will make it much worse. Let's join with her and calm her down." Quickly, the four held on to their psi-crystals and focused. Wham! All four were hit with Vivian's full torment: the utter annihilation of many humans. Vivian was hearing their death screams and intense, but brief pain — a pain none had ever experience before, pain from every cell in the person's body delivered at nearly the same instant in time, an overwhelming pain. The four also collapsed onto the floor. Val panicked and raced to get Tammy and Sammi. Whatever was occurring was way beyond her experience, probably theirs too, but she could think of no one else to fetch.

By the time that Sammi, Tammy, and Val returned, out of breath from running, Holly had managed to break her connection. She was pale and in shock. Seeing the three, she whispered, "Remove their psi-crystals." Her own voice sounded distant, as if speaking from some mountaintop. The three girls obeyed, bringing the three out of their overwhelming torment, though poor Vivian was still writhing in pain even though she was not holding her psi-crystal.

Wendy now knew what to do. She dashed around Vivian's shop, found what she needed, an herb that would dampen out, at least temporarily, the psi-crystal's effects. She brewed a bit of green tea and mixed the juice of a *bacal* leaf in it. With Sissy's help, she forced it into Vivian, who rapidly calmed down. A few minutes later, her special gift fully blocked by the herb, she was a "normal" person once more.

"Dear god! So many people, men, I believe, totally destroyed, dead. I never dreamed such horrors could exist. Utter annihilation of bodies!" Vivian exclaimed. "Did you. . ." She didn't finish her sentence. One glance at her fellow witches told her they had.

"I told you it was ten thousand to one. I think it may be far higher, incredibly awful," Sissy whispered, as if even saying so would bring this catastrophe down upon them!

"Well, at least we will know when these aliens are attacking us," Vivian commented. "Just watch for me to have a fit." She tried to bring a bit of levity into the room, but failed utterly.

"We are facing an opponent who is vastly more powerful than we," Holly concluded. "I wonder who they are slaying?"

"I aim to find out, give me back my crystal," Sissy looked about to see who had hers.

"No, you could get killed too," Vivian gushed.

"No, I think that is a right action to take," Wendy spoke up. She had no idea why she said that, only it came from her heightened intuitiveness.

"See, Wendy says so too. Okay, thanks," Sissy said as Tammy handed her the psi-crystal. Sissy, still sitting on the floor, decided sitting was a wise idea and merely closed her hand and focused. Since she didn't go into a fit as Vivian had, the others finally relaxed a little. Val dashed off to make them all some tea, strong black tea this time.

The other four remained silent, allowing Sissy to work her magic. After a time, Sissy opened her hand. Her eyes then opened, and Vivian helped her to her feet, but didn't press her for instant information. Instead, Val called out that the tea was ready. Vivian pushed Sissy off toward her dining room, and the others followed. Tammy and Sammi were silent, but intensely curious. What was and had happened to these powerful witches?

Over tea, Sissy finally had her nerve back. "Well, they were soldiers, I think. I got the impression they were Chester's cavalrymen. Our aliens somehow completely killed every cell in their bodies. I've no idea how. I did see them, the spiritual beings, floating above where their previous bodies had been located. Then, there was this terrible white light. For some reason, none of them was able to resist it, and they were sucked into it, like water up a hollow straw. I believe they were taken to the Plateau Grado. I decided not to risk going any further and seeing what happened to them after that. It is still going on right now. Hundreds if not more are being murdered by our new aliens! I told you this would be huge, but now I think it is *huger* than huge," Sissy related.

Holly grinned at her expression, "Indeed, Sissy, thank you. This is the worst threat we've ever faced. Chester's war pales compared to this."

"Yes, we need to rethink absolutely everything," Wendy pronounced, "but not tonight, I think. My nerves are shot after that experience. We should keep Vivian under the herb for tonight, until we are sure the aliens are done murdering people."

"Mom, what is going on with you and the others? What is with these psi-crystals? We ought to know," Val hounded her mother. She had received the worst shock of her life and, as a witch, wanted to know answers. Vivian looked at Wendy and then Holly; it was not her place to reveal their closely guarded secret.

Holly looked at Wendy, who didn't disapprove, and thus began, "Girls, there is more to the psi-crystals than mere healing properties. Yes, the psi-powder does all we've told you it does, but there is something more. I am not going to tell you how to make this work, mind you, so don't go getting any wild notions. When we believe you are ready, we will initiate you three. When a witch gets attuned to her psi-crystal, it unlocks some hither to fore unsuspected abilities in her. Vivian is always alerted to unknown, unsuspected dangers. That's what triggered her collapse. She sensed what was happening to the soldiers not far from here, though distances have little meaning with these special powers. Each of us has unlocked special abilities in ourselves. None of us have the same abilities, and we know of no way to predict what abilities might or might not be unlocked in a witch undergoing the initiation. Trust us; learn your craft well. One day when Wendy feels it is right — that's her special skill: to know intuitively the right thing to do, we will initiate you and invite you to join our special coven."

"How many of you are there? I mean with these special skills?" Sammi asked, very curious now.

"We've discovered when another is initiated, all of us who have already have been initiated, also know about it. There are some fifty of us witches scattered over Tierra who are attuned to psi-crystals. We are very cautious in initiating others. It is a most precious gift, not one to be flaunted or given to the unworthy or untrained. You must be able to control and use your powers. Trust us to know when that time comes," Wendy answered her.

Val, Tammy, and Sammi accepted this. They had just heard more inside information than they ever had before and were very excited about it. They headed off to Val's room to chat about all this.

The next day, town criers began circulating through Wyth relaying the news King Norwood wanted disseminated. "Hear yea, hear yea. King Norwood has met with the aliens, who landed on Plateau Grado, and has formed an alliance with them. The war with King Chester of Rockton is over. Our alien allies have destroyed all Chester's cavalrymen on our side of the Wyndl River. You may begin returning to your normal lives now. The war is over. King Norwood needs a thousand able bodied miners to go to work for our alien friends, who will be paying the miners in gold!" He provided brief instructions about where miners were to report and moved on down the street, repeating his terrific news. Celebrations broke out spontaneously throughout Wyth.

Upon hearing this, the five witches again congregated at

Wendy's place. "This is unbelievable! Norwood has made an alliance with the aliens? We sure didn't see this coming!" Wendy exclaimed. "And *gold* no less!"

"Well, he used the aliens to end the war. I can see his reasoning. Now, no one will dare challenge his right to the throne of Bettingham," Sissy proclaimed.

"Jobs, a thousand miners — paid in gold? That will be a hit with the men of Bettingham as well," Sheena decided. "Hundred to one in favor of Norwood's actions being considered extremely beneficial to Bettingham. Well, this sure changes the picture entirely!"

"But we dare not trust these aliens! They are following their own plans, which have little to do with us. We must use *extreme* care!" Sissy pronounced.

"My god, after all these seventeen years of planning, everything must be tossed aside. Everything on Tierra pales compared to the threat these aliens pose," Holly proclaimed with a very heavy sigh. "Perhaps I am getting too old for this."

They were sitting in Wendy's living room, back of her shop, when Wendy heard someone knocking on her backdoor, the one which led directly to her emergency services room. They knocked three times, paused, knocked once, paused, and knocked twice.

"Well, that must be Alford! Who else knows our secret knock?" Wendy announced. All five got up to answer the door. As always, Wendy was right. Alford had finally gotten his group safely to Wyth, as promised, though he had gotten much more than he'd bargained for initially.

Chapter 7 New Beginnings

"Come on in, all of you. Welcome, welcome. We are so glad that you made it!" Wendy said enthusiastically as the group filed in, leaving their many horses tied to Wendy's back hitching posts. "Ally, we're all so sorry we couldn't get to you in time," she apologized without even thinking about it. "Come in, come in." She led them all into her living room, while Tammy and Sammi dashed about finding more chairs.

That done, Sammi quickly sat down beside Adam, and Wendy's son, Jordan joined them and sat beside Abby. Sammi and Jordan were trying hard to win the love of the two younger Bettingham twins. "Well, let's look at your wounds, Aurora, Ally. After we get you fixed up, we can introduce everyone and have a long talk and dinner," Wendy declared. Healing always came first in her book.

"But we don't need it. Look," Ally spoke before Aurora, who was still very shy around strangers, particularly now that she was so helpless. Ally used her teeth to pull up her sleeves, while Aurora held out her arms. All five witches stood up and examined them closely.

"Well, I never . . ." Wendy couldn't finish her thought. "It's not possible!"

Holly recovered first. "We'd best sit down and introduce everyone. I am Holly Sprigs." One by one, the five introduced themselves. Ally couldn't help notice all had flaming red hair, usually quite long, though some were curly as well. Next, Wendy introduced her two children, Jordan and Tammy. Vivian introduced her daughter Valerie. Her son Ken was back home, as were the children of Sissy and Sheena. Holly introduced her youngest daughter, Sammi. Then, Holly asked, "Are you hungry? Should we fix you something before we talk?" Since none had eaten supper, that was a wise question.

An hour later, they all sat around Wendy's dining room table, sipping tea. The five witches were pleased that Aiden and Alford helped the two women with their meals, and the five relaxed a bit. "Okay, momentous things have been happening around here, but we'd like to hear your stories first," Holly began. "Spare us *no* details." Aiden grinned; for once, he had the witches' full attention!

For an hour, they talked. First, Ally told about her flight from the castle until she joined with Aurora and Zoe. Zoe told of their trip until the soldiers ambushed them. She was most detailed about how Ally managed to get her and Aurora away from the soldiers. Alford took up the story from there. He knew the five craved the knowledge they'd gained from their encounter with the aliens on Plateau Grado. He was as specific as he could be relating that to the five.

When he finally finished, Wendy told them what had been happening around Wyth, particularly about what King Norwood had done. Ally said, "So my brother is now the King of Bettingham. He's ended the war and made deals with these people. So far, it sounds okay to me. They seemed nice enough to us; just look at how their doctor fixed up my stumps. I mean they are fully healed, no ugly scars; and they have this kind of pleasing shape too. No pain, none at all. Though at times, it still feels like I can feel my fingers. Isn't that really weird?"

"She's right, look at mine; they are at least pleasing and not the horrible, ugly mess Doctor Corey left them in when he bandaged me up," Aurora decided to finally say a bit more. "I still sort of feel my fingers too, even though they aren't there anymore. Maybe these aliens are okay. They treated us with respect, I think."

"Yes, but they also *murdered* several thousand of King Chester's cavalrymen," Sissy pointed out. "True, it ended the war, but they killed them. They could have, well I don't know, maybe picked them up and plopped them on their side of the Wyndl. They didn't have to kill them. Oh, those are called ghost fingers. Many have them just like you do. I'm told the effect diminishes with time, though I don't know that first hand, of course." She tried to be helpful.

Wendy added, "But they truly did heal Ally and Aurora. We must not discount their medical knowledge, skill, and machines far surpass us. Honestly, you two, your stumps are very pleasing. You've nothing to be ashamed of. Please don't go around wearing socks on them to hide them. They're nothing at all like what we've been seeing around here. Alford, you wouldn't believe the sheer number of soldiers who have been coming here seeking healing of their bodies. The field COG physicians do a horrible job of chopping off limbs. Those that survive have the ugliest stumps I can possibly imagine. They're frightful even to look at. No, yours are a marvel to behold. I wonder how their doctor does it? And with no pain at all? Amazing. We could learn enormously from her."

"Well, they may be pleasing, but we are helpless now," Aurora countered. "Well, mostly helpless. Ally did show me how we can mount by ourselves and ride. We hold the reins pinched in our elbows. Uncomfortable, but it works."

"That's amazing, Aurora, Ally. Well done. In time, I'm sure you both will find new ways to adapt. We all promise to do everything possible to help you recover and be able to live fruitful lives once more," Holly promised the two.

"It's getting late. What are we going to do for tonight? The inns are overflowing, and none of us has enough space for them?" Sissy asked.

"Hey, if it's all right with you, we'd like to take them to our place, just outside Wyth," Alford said. "The refugees must come first; they have lost everything. We can take care of Ally and Aurora very nicely at our place."

"Well, okay then, Alford. Tammy, you and Sammi go along with them and help the women with whatever they need for tonight. Give poor Zoe a break. Tomorrow, let's get together again and see what more permanent arrangements can be made for you. Again, Alford, Aiden, Adam, Abby, Zoe, we can't thank you enough for all you've done for us and for the women," Holly said.

Jordan spoke up, "Mom, I'll go with Abby, just in case there are more of Chester's cavalry about. I can help protect them." Abby flushed; she didn't need protecting, but enjoyed Jordan's company. She also saw Sammi was extremely pleased to go; she could be with her twin, Adam, for the night.

Wendy looked at Alford, who nodded. "Okay son, you can go too. Just don't make a pest of yourself."

Once outside, Sammi and Tammy were prepared to help the two women mount their horses, but the two women had the teens merely hold the reins for them. Ally hooked her arm over the saddle horn and climbed up. "Reins, please," she said. Aurora emulated her, leaving the two wide eyed.

"Wow, I thought you were teasing them," Sammi exclaimed, "but you really do this yourselves. Great!"

Sammi mounted and moved beside Adam, while Jordan rode beside Abby. He said, "Well, Abby, how did my new arrows work out? I see your quiver is missing a couple."

"Perfect, Jordan. They fly true. I'll take a whole lot more, if you don't mind," Abby replied. "I saved the steel heads from the shafts that broke, of course."

"Great! Nothing is too good for you," he said.

Ally glanced at Aurora. In the twilight, she saw that Aurora also noticed the two young pairs. Abby and Jordan were very close, as were Sammi and Adam. Ally smiled at Aurora, who smiled back.

Alford commented, "Well, that went well. It's good to be on their good sides."

Aiden added, "And to have them greatly in your debt — which we now have!"

"How come or why?" asked Ally, a little confused.

"Oh you never know when you might have great need for a witch. At such times, it's wise to have some that owe you a really *big* favor," Alford attempted a simple explanation. "These are especially powerful witches."

"Exceptionally!" Aiden added, leaving Ally wondering just what he meant by that. She knew so little about witches. They rode out of Wyth's northern gates. A mile later, they veered towards the mountains, and then a mile further on, they rode up a long cobblestone driveway, halting at a stable and manor house. "One of our two family estates," he announced for the two women's benefit.

Although it was getting dark, they could see a stately brown stone building, rather large, though the grounds sorely needed tending. Ally suspected these four might not be found here often, or didn't have the time or funds to hire someone to look after the grounds. Abby spoke up, "Guys, we women could all use a nice hot bath. Will you fellows be nice boys and take care of the horses and stuff and fire up the water heater for us? We women will bathe and join you for tea after a while."

"Absolutely!" Jordan replied first.

Alford chuckled and teased the young man, "Speak for yourself, love struck!" He added, "Okay, seriously, we'll do it, sis. You get our two guests cleaned up properly. Aiden, stoke the hot water heater right away or Abby will be complaining there isn't enough."

As the women walked inside, Abby moved from lantern to lantern, lighting them as they went. She went straight for their large bathroom. "We have a really good bath, Ally. Come on; this will be wonderful."

"It sure is, better than we have at the castle, I think," Ally replied, impressed.

"I've never seen such a fancy bath before!" Aurora added. "Incredible." *They must be rich or their parents were. Oh, I remember, their grandfather was once the king of Bettingham. These are his grandchildren.*

"Come on; let's get you two undressed and into the hot, warm waters," Abby suggested. "I'll join you. Zoe, Sammi, Tammy, you can join us or not." The three decided to join them; a luxurious bath was a welcome event for all.

"This is so pathetic," Ally said, waving her stubs, as the women entered the huge tub. Once more, she saw how dependent she now was and cursed her father once more. *Damn him. I hope he rots in Hell, if there is one.*

Aurora fought back tears again, "I know."

"Well, let's at least make some attempts to bathe ourselves," Ally steeled herself.

"But we're supposed to be your hands," Sammi protested a little.

"Yes, but let us see if we can do any of this ourselves. It's so utterly humiliating to be wholly unable to do much of anything," Ally stated what she thought was obvious. She and Aurora did manage to hold a washrag and wash each other's bodies somewhat, though they were unable to do themselves. Later, the two helpers washed out their long hair, but allowed Ally and Aurora to experiment with ways of drying themselves off. Once more, they discovered they could more or less dry each other, but not themselves. Still, they had participated some and felt a little better about it.

Abby dug out some of her clean dresses, which mostly fit the two women. About two hours later, they joined the men, who were sitting around the dining room table drinking ale, chewing on some bread, while chatting about their adventures and the aliens.

"Wow, Ally, you sure do clean up very nicely. You look beautiful," Alford complimented her.

"Same goes for you, Aurora; you look very nice indeed. Come, have a seat. Ale? It's a good, dark ale," Aiden suggested.

Abby, Jordan, Adam, and Sammi quietly stole off to the living room. Alford whispered to Ally, "Young lovers." Both smiled knowingly at each other.

"They are pretty serious about each other, aren't they?" Aurora asked.

"Yes, for the last couple of years," Aiden replied. "One of these days, I expect there'll be two weddings around here." They grinned.

"So what about you, Aiden? Don't you have a girlfriend yet?" Aurora asked.

"Nah, too busy traveling and seeing the world," Aiden replied.

Ally nodded to Alford. He added, "Well, okay, okay. Perceptive women here, brother. No, we have not found any women who can keep up with us. We want pretty, intelligent, sharp, loving, kind, honest women, and oh did I mention pretty too?" All five laughed.

Later, Ally and Aurora shared a guest bedroom, though they allowed Sammi and Tammy to help them into a pair of Abby's nightgowns and to tuck them in for the night, promising to help them dress in the morning. Sammi added, "Tomorrow, maybe we can take you to my sister's dress shop. Roxane and her mate Sable make the best dresses in Wyth. I know, sis is unusual, so is Sable, but they really do love each other, and I guess that's what counts. I hope one day to win Adam's heart," she admitted, as she left them.

In the dark, Aurora asked, "Ally, do you really think we can somehow live a proper life like we are now? Hopeless cripples?"

"Somehow, Aurora, we must; we just must find ways. I don't know how, but we must. I don't want to be so utterly dependent on others for everything. It's so demeaning."

The next morning, the two returned, dressed the pair, and all headed to the dining room for breakfast. Abby again did the cooking, helped by Jordan, who almost never left her side. Ally guessed he was taking full advantage of this opportunity to spend as much time with her as he could. After eating, Alford asked Ally if she wanted a guided tour of their estate; Aiden did the same with Aurora. Naturally, both did. Hence, Jordan and Abby headed off arm in arm, followed quickly by Adam and Sammi. "I'll do the dishes," Tammy volunteered, grinning at her friend Sammi. She knew just how much Sammi was in love with Adam. The two shared their deepest feelings as best friends are wont to do. Zoe also helped her, chatting about the two young couples.

"Miss Ally, will you care to join me," Alford said formally and in a slightly teasing manner, holding his arm out as if she were a dressed for a formal ball. She stuck her arm out, forgetting for a moment she had no hand. They locked arms and began to stroll. "Here we have the living room by daylight. Yes, that's our parent's portraits hanging there and our grandfather, the king before dad."

Aiden followed suit, offering Aurora his arm. She saw Ally gave him her arm, as if there was nothing wrong with them physically and emulated her. She found Aiden's light touch very comforting. They trailed along after the other two. She was attracted to Aiden. *If only I were whole and not a mutilated freak,* she thought. As the two couples walked around the large manor house, two things struck both women. First, dust was everywhere. Obviously, the four seldom lived here. Second, their parents and/or grandparents had spent a considerable sum building this luxury manor house.

Around ten, as promised, Alford brought the group over to Wendy's place. This time, they used the family carriage, though Abby and Jordan chose to ride their horses so they could chat privately. Wendy asked, "Well, you two look splendid this morning. I take it you've gotten cleaned up and had breakfast. These two haven't taken advantage of you, have they?"

Ally laughed, "No, the perfect hosts. You needn't worry so." *No one's going to want to take advantage of me, not anymore, excepting maybe some drunkard.*

"Excuse me," Zoe said. "I'm supposed to get back to Phyllis as soon as possible. She really needs me." Wendy agreed, and sent Jordan off to fetch her a carriage. Zoe said farewell to her new friends and was heartily thanked by Aurora in particular. A short time later, Zoe was riding back to Wycombe in royal style. All her expenses were paid in full, and she stayed at the better inns, which pleased her considerably.

Wendy then took charge once more. "Good, good. Now then, that's handled. Come, we have much to discuss. You too, Alford, Aiden. Oh, okay, you too, Adam and Abby. This concerns your futures too, I suppose." Again, her intuition told her not to separate them.

The five witches sat around Wendy's dining room table, opposite the six. Holly began, "Welcome again, Aurora, Ally. We are about to tell you all some things *very* few people know. I hope you will keep what we say here private."

"Are you sure you want us here?" Alford interrupted her. "We four are not witches."

Holly looked at Wendy, who answered, "Stay, Bettinghams. All of you. It's the *right* thing to do. Holly, continue." Wendy was a take charge type person, Ally noted, strong willed for sure.

"Aurora here already is a healing witch. Her mother, Babs, did a good job training her in all the basics, just as Tammy and Sammi have been trained. Ally, of course, knows nothing about such things. We understand that. However, what none of you know is, while all witches know more or less the same things — which plants to use for which potion, how best to heal others — not all witches are the same. A very few of us have gone way, way beyond that level. I suspect you suspect such might be the case. After all Ally, how could Zoe have made contact with us or how could Phyllis contact us that early morning? We five and a very select few other witches scattered around Tierra possess telepathy. Yes, we can talk to each other and others via our minds."

"So that's how Zoe did it!" Aurora exclaimed. "I know she did something, but I couldn't figure out how she could know help was coming and all that. But then, I was pretty out of it most of the time. I often thought mom was doing something like that."

"Yes, we five here along with Babs and Phyllis, all use telepathy. Indeed, your mother, Babs, let Phyllis know what was going on the moment the soldiers came to her shop to hang her. That's why she was there so quickly to help you. When Ally was abducted, the situation was so critical that Zoe took a gamble and did what she had to do to be able to temporarily use telepathy to contact Phyllis, who contacted us. After that, we stayed in contact with Zoe. Later, Alford, we contacted you for daily reports on the women's well-being."

"But how is it you can use telepathy? Is it because all of you are redheads?" Ally asked, feeling rather silly after saying it.

"An excellent point, Ally. Very astute question, in fact," Holly answered her. "We get our ability to use telepathy from these." She took out her psi-crystal.

"Say, isn't that one of those psi-crystals, which you grind into powder and give to the wounded to help ease their pain and help healing?" asked Alford.

"The very same, Alford. Yes, the smaller crystals are ground into powder for just those very purposes. Zoe also knew if she ingested a large quantity, it would temporarily allow her to make telepathic contact with Phyllis. Now then, this is only the smallest of our powers."

Holly continued; she had their full attention. "When one of we witches becomes first attuned to her own psi-crystal, it activates some of her native abilities, magnifying them tremendously. Each witch has different things re-activated. No two of us are alike. There are now over fifty of us, and none has received the same exact gift. The special powers are always unique to the witch."

"Take myself, for example. I possess great wisdom and a telepathic ability far beyond all the others. Wendy has the intuition to always know or sense just the right action to take in any situation, whether or not danger is involved. Vivian here is always alerted to unknown or unseen danger. She was instantly aware of the aliens murdering all those cavalrymen. Sheena always seems to know the odds associated with some proposed action. She's always right about them. Sissy is able to see hidden motives in people, though you may think she just sees conspiracies everywhere. However, she's always correct about them. Uncanny. So you see, we five are very special witches indeed."

"Amazing. I knew there was something unique about you five," Alford spoke up. He flashed back to something that his grandfather had once said to him when he was three. *You note these special witches, Babs and Phyllis. They possess true power, grandsons.* Well, the twins had spent long hours watching those two and the five here in Wyth, and knew there was something uncanny and special about them. Now so much began to make sense to him and his siblings.

"Ditto," Aiden added. He had identical thoughts. They were interlocked twins.

"But what has this to do with us?" asked Ally.

"Plenty. All along, Aurora, your mother, Babs, was planning to one day attune you to a psi-crystal, which will give you not only telepathy, but also some other incredible gift. We promise to do that for you; it is the very least we can do for Babs. She was one of us. Hence, we took the liberty to get your body fully prepared for this very special gift."

"Prepared? How? I don't understand. I'm mostly helpless now. Surely, you should give this priceless gift to others who can make use of it. I can hardly do a thing for myself anymore," Aurora replied, fighting back watering eyes. *I never knew. I suspected mom of hiding something from me.*

"We prepared you for the gift by infusing your body with all the psi-powder. Helpless or not, we are giving you the gift that Babs so greatly wanted to give you," Holly answered.

"Ally, we also decided to give the gift to you as well. You too have been primed, so to speak, with psi-powder."

"But why me? I'm not a witch. I know nothing about all these things," Ally protested slightly. Then, she flushed; her cheeks seemed terribly hot all of a sudden. *Is she doing this because of my hands?* She added, "Because of this?" She held up her arms.

Holly flushed. *Amazing intuition. We were not wrong about her.* "Yes and no. Yes, in that we feel something good may yet come from such a great gift. And no, we had other reasons, but those are now null and void. You see, Ally, for years, we were working on a way to remove King Aaran from his throne. No offence meant to you, but your father was an evil tyrant. He stole the throne from the Bettingham's grandfather and killed him, though we've no proof of how it was done. Babs suspected poison, but we couldn't prove it. I admit we fully intended to one day use you to help us overthrow your father. Now that purpose isn't needed. So far, Norwood is doing an acceptable job running our kingdom, we think, though there is no telling, what with this alien alliance he's formed. So we've talked it over and have agreed; this is the right thing to do. Wendy is never wrong. When she says something is the right thing to do, it always turns out to be true. We've all learned that fact the hard way." All four glanced at Wendy, who smiled.

Wendy spoke up, "Giving you the gift at this time *is* the right thing to do, so we *will* do it. Period."

"But," Ally replied.

Sheena spoke up, interrupting her protest, "Ally, it's three hundred to one odds against us if we do not give you the gift, just terrible odds. I feel it's a thousand to one in your favor for you to personally to receive the gift."

"We need all of you to help us fight this awful alien conspiracy!" Sissy added her viewpoint. "Look, you know they are going to mine and take away our psi-crystals to make their fuel. For us, the psi-crystals have incredible healing properties. As important as the psi-crystals are to us who live on Tierra, this is definitely a great cause for concern, don't you see?"

"I can see troubles ahead," Alford spoke up. "It's simple. We need psi-crystals for proper healing of our wounded, and they need it for their fuel. Sooner or later, conflict is going to occur. It doesn't take any gift to see that one coming."

"Precisely. We need all of you, if we are going to have any chance against these aliens. Look what they did to Chester's cavalrymen," Holly continued.

"Are you suggesting we also ingest this psi-powder?" Abby asked, feeling a bit nauseated about doing that.

"No, just these two for now — well, some of our daughters are old enough now to get this gift as well. We must do it soon," Wendy answered her. Abby visibly relaxed.

"It only is for women?" asked Ally.

"Yes, only women," Wendy replied sternly.

"Okay, then let's do it, and get it over with," Ally decided. "We have so much to figure out, Aurora and I, if we're ever to be independent again. I aim to be, mind you. Gift or no gift, I simply can't live my life as a helpless invalid, not like this."

"Thank you for accepting our gift. The process is a simple one. We take you out to the creek where we found ours, and let your psi-crystal choose you."

"Huh? What do you mean? These rocks choose us?" asked Ally, in disbelief. "How can a rock choose anything? It is just a rock."

"It seems a psi-crystal knows to whom it is destined to belong. The odds are thousand fifty to one on that detail," Sheena answered her. "We haven't the foggiest idea why this is, only that it is."

"Since we'll have to wander around, and with all these soldiers about, we think it prudent if you Bettinghams accompany us for our protection," Wendy added.

"Sammi is ready to get hers," Holly spoke up. "Wendy, do you suppose now is also the time Sammi should get her gift too, since we're all going out to the creek for these two?"

Wendy took out her psi-crystal, closed her palm over it and then her eyes. A moment later, she opened them, placing her psi-crystal in her bag. "Sometimes, Holly, I think you are psychic or something. Yes, the right course of action is to have Sammi tag along and find hers as well. It is very important the Bettinghams come along. Perhaps we'll meet with some danger while searching."

"I'll need five days to get Sammi ready. Meantime, we should get the two women properly settled in, new clothes and such," Holly suggested. "Plus, we should continue to see these two get their daily dose of psi-powders too."

Sissy spoke up, "Alford, Aiden, I think it is very important Ally and Aurora stay at your estate for now. I don't know why, just that they should. Do you mind terribly?"

Alford laughed, "Are you kidding? We are honored to have two beautiful women staying with us, but they do need clothing. They're wearing Abby's dresses now. Sammi promised to take them to Roxane and Sable's to get new dresses."

"But we don't have any money to pay for them," Aurora pointed out.

"Nonsense, child. Babs has a fortune stashed away. She told us where it is hidden, and Zoe and Phyllis will retrieve it when Zoe gets back to her. They'll send it along to us here, child. As far as Ally goes, it's not safe for Norwood to know of her whereabouts just yet. We will cover her costs for now," Wendy countered.

"I'm so used to having everything provided by my folks," Ally spoke up. "Now I need to find a way to support myself. I promise I'll find a way to repay you."

Wendy gave her a motherly smile. "I know one day you will, Ally. For now, accept our generosity, and pay us back when you are able to do so. Now then, we best get back to our shops. Refugees are still wandering into Wyth, and many need our healing potions and salves."

As they left, Sammi was elated that finally she would be receiving the precious gift. "Adam! Once I get the gift, then I'll be one of the power witches of Tierra, and then I'll be truly worthy of you!"

"Silly woman, you're already more than worthy of me. It's I who am unworthy of you," he replied.

"No you're not!" Sammi declared.

Later, they entered R & S Dressmakers. Sammi insisted the men stay outside, that this was women's business. She and Abby escorted the two inside. "Sis, I'd like you to meet Ally and Aurora. This is my big sister, Roxane. Oh, this is her mate, Sable." Both women were quite pretty. Roxane had her mother's flaming red hair and freckles, while Sable was a few inches taller with long blonde hair.

"Oh my god! What happened to you two?" Roxane

exclaimed after withdrawing her offered hand.

"You can't be thieves. Who did such a horrid thing to you? I hope he gets what's coming to him!" Sable declared angrily.

Ally laughed, "No, we are not thieves. We do need new dresses. We've just come to Wyth with nothing at all. Sammi has the funds for them, but we really don't know how much we have to spend or the prices." Just now, she didn't feel like going into her nightmare; neither did Aurora, especially to total strangers, even if one was Sammi's sister.

"Well, you've come to the best dressmakers in Wyth! We like to think so anyway. Come on; let us show you around. I think Ally would look exceptional in a red dress. What do you think, dear?"

Sable agreed, "Yes, most definitely. Aurora would have her best features brought out by a light blue, don't you think, love?" So it went. They left with four new day dresses with all the needed undergarments. Sable insisted they also take one fancier gown, for special occasions, she had hinted. Neither Ally nor Aurora thought they would ever have a special occasion, not ever again, but Sable insisted.

The five days passed altogether too swiftly for the young adults. Ally had never experienced such happiness, as she did for those five days. Even Aurora came out of her depression, smiling frequently and cracking jokes with Aiden and Alford. Sammi stayed with them so Abby was not overworked, caring for the two's many needs, though always Ally tried to do it herself first, before giving up and letting Abby do it for her.

Both she and Aurora did figure out how to drink for themselves; this they could manage. However, the two men continued to be their hands for them at their meals. Of course, when Sammi wasn't actually needed, she hovered around Adam. Each evening, Jordan came by, and he and Abby always managed to "disappear" for a while. More than once, Ally or Aurora caught sight of the two young couples passionately kissing, though they were careful to avoid interrupting them.

The last night, while Sammi was off helping with the dishes after supper, Ally overheard Abby and Adam talking, whispering rather animatedly. Abby said firmly, "Adam, you *have* to ask her to marry you. I know it and *so* do you. So *why* don't you just go do it?"

"What about *you*? You know you and I always know what and how each other is feeling. How are *you* going to manage if she and I are — well you know what I mean?" he whispered back.

Abby blushed, "Well, maybe Jordan will hurry up and ask me."

"Okay, maybe if I ask Sammi, Jordan will ask you, but what if he doesn't?" Adam whispered back, still hesitant.

Abby put her hands on her hips, "Then, I will ask *him*. How's that? Now go ahead. I know Sammi is nuts about you. Go on. Ask her."

Ally grinned; she rather wanted to hear what would come next, but Alford spotted her and came over, "Want to go for a stroll around the estate grounds? We've been lax in keeping up the gardens, but you can still get the idea." He offered her his arm and she, hers, though she still felt a little uneasy about slipping her stump into his arm.

They had barely gotten to the front doors, when they heard Sammi's squeal followed by an enthusiastic, "Yes, oh yes, yes I will!"

Alford looked puzzled. Ally grinned and whispered, "I think Adam has just asked Sammi to marry him."

"What? Oh, well, I should've seen that one coming! They've been close for years now. Come on; we should go congratulate my little brother."

"And Sammi," Ally added.

"And Sammi," he added. "I wonder how Abby is going to take this. They are really close, like Aiden and me. We always know what each other is thinking. Kind of spooky at times, terrific at other times."

When they got to them, Abby had her hands on her hips once again, staring at Jordan this time. Sammi and Adam were holding each other tightly. "Well?" Abby said to Jordan.

"Abby, will you marry me?" Jordan asked, his face flushed.

"Well, it is *about* time, Jordan. Yes, of course I will. Now come here, silly," Abby threw herself into the arms of her longtime boyfriend.

"Congratulations, all four of you," Aiden said, entering with Aurora on his arm. "I wondered when this day would come. Alford and I've been expecting it for the last couple of years now." Abby pulled her older brother into her and Jordan, giving him a big hug, then Aurora too. A mutual hugs followed among all eight of them.

As they split up to go get some privacy, Abby teased Alford and Aiden, "So when are you two getting hitched? Looks like your younger twins have to show you older twins how it's done." She and Adam laughed, enjoying the mutual flushes on the older twins' faces.

A bit later, back on their evening stroll on the warm summer night, Ally asked, "So how come you and Aiden haven't gotten married yet? I know you both said that you wanted — oh how did you put it? Oh, you two want pretty, intelligent, sharp, loving, kind, honest women — no, make that double pretty women." She laughed and flashed him a teasing, coy grin.

"If you persist, I am going to have to, well, tickle you, Princess Ally Wycombe," Alford teased her back.

"Then, I'll have to bat you on your face with my stumps," she teased him in turn, raising her right arm, as if she were just about to do that.

Alford caught her arm gently and pulled her close. He leaned over a little and gave her a loving kiss instead. Ally, caught off guard a little, found herself throwing her arms around him, returning it in kind. When they separated, she flushed and said, "Oh my."

"I'm sorry. I didn't mean to offend you, Ally, but I'm sure that finally I've found the right woman for me. You're going to have a hard time getting rid of me," he admitted. She answered him with another kiss.

Later that night when Ally and Aurora were tucked into bed, Aurora whispered to her, "Ally, guess what? Aiden kissed me tonight. Passionately. I think he is in love with me, but I don't know why he should be. What do I do?"

"Alford kissed me too, Aurora. Do you like him, Aiden, I mean?"

"Well, yes, in spite of everything that has happened to me, I do. He's kind, gentle, and, well, really cute. Of course, so is Alford; it is so hard to tell them apart," Aurora found it easier to admit such things to Ally while the darkness of their room hid her from view.

"Me too. I've never been happier in my life than these past days, Aurora, but then considering what my life was like back in my dad's castle, that's not saying much. I just feel so alive and happy around Alford. I've never felt this way before, and I like it."

Aurora sighed, "Me too, but Ally, what can they possibly see in two hopeless cripples like us?"

"I can't get that same thought out of my mind either, Aurora, but maybe they don't see us that way. Well, you and I, we must show them we aren't a pair of useless cripples, Aurora. I don't know how, but we must."

"Okay, but I don't know how either," Aurora admitted. "Did you see how terrible some of those soldiers who were wounded in the battles look? Awful." The two chatted a bit more before they fell asleep.

A few miles away inside the wooden walls of Wyth, Holly wrestled with another interesting development. She'd been in contact with others of her gifted witches in Benito, Trujillo. Amazingly, she'd found a way to help the two learn to live independent lives once more. However, did she want to allow them to make such a long journey and spend a half year learning alternate ways just now or should she wait and see how the young women managed on their own? It was crucial they receive their gifts right now, no question of that, but then after that, should she allow them to depart for a half year or more, considering the incredible magnitude of this new alien invasion? Surely, their gifts would assist them somehow, but then her friend offered her a certainty in Benito. Personal daily life versus the safety of all Tierra — that was the underlying question Holly faced this fifth night.

Six months to a year in Benito and the two ought to be able to live independently once more, but a whole lot of bad could also happen to Tierra in that same time, perhaps preventable somehow by the witches and their gifts. Two versus the many — Holly had a tough choice and decided to confide in Wendy and go with her decision.

Wendy was a bit surprised to see Holly at her door, just as she had risen to fix breakfast. "Come in; you are way early," Wendy said sleepily.

"We need to talk. I must have your gift," Holly answered. The two women worked together making breakfast, and Holly explained what she'd learned last evening. After eating, Wendy used her psi-crystal and sat back a bit perplexed. "Well?" Holly asked.

"How strange, dear. I got nothing this time, nothing at all, one way or the other. Now that doesn't happen very often," Wendy replied. "So what are we going to do about it?"

Holly sighed, "I was hoping your gift would make the decision for me, Wendy. I guess this one I'll have to make myself. Come on. I better go get myself ready to go psi-crystal hunting."

Chapter 8 Psi-crystals

The summer's day proved to be a hot one, as the large carriage rolled along the rutted dirt road, heading north by northwest. The five witches, along with Ally, Aurora, and Sammi sweated inside the stuffy coach. Conversation was at a minimum because of the heat and apprehension. Outside, Alford, Aiden, Adam, and Abby rode their horses, providing security for them, while Jordan drove the carriage.

Twice now, they had to stop and wait for a large bear to decide to leave them alone and wander off their path. The farmsteads had already dropped away, as the foothills of the mountains rose. A few talus slopes indicated the presence of mines, but these they avoided. Their destination was the headwaters of the Wyndl River, where it came dashing off the snowy Goza Mountains flowing southeast across the entire Midlands, dumping into the Southern Ocean at Madya, Bashir, some four thousand miles distant.

What bothered the two sets of twins the most was overhead. They'd spotted several of the small flying machines of the aliens moving further north of them and hoped they were not noticed. All they wanted right now was to be wholly ignored by the aliens. The use of unlimited weapons tends to do that to a people.

The pairs of twins had been to the headwaters area before. Actually, they had explored nearly all their kingdom at one time or another, along with the neighboring kingdoms of Pinewood and Bentwood to the east. They'd even traveled around the southern edge of the Goza Mountains, where they reached the Southern Ocean, though they'd not gone into Bashir proper. That trip, they had gone into a bit of the Westerlings, following the coastline of Almendia to that kingdom's capital and port city of Arabella. During that trip, the four had learned somewhat to speak the Westerlings dialect. That excursion was two years ago to the day, Alford recalled as he rode along this hot day.

This was their third day out from Wyth, and they hoped journey's end. Camping out with the five witches was proving to be quite an experience. The women insisted on having a comfortable camp, quite unlike the "roughing it way" the Bettinghams loved. All four were outdoors people, that is partly why they had roamed so far and wide. Alford and Aiden were a bit bothered, because this trip was noticeably hard on Ally and Aurora, who had to rely upon others heavily out here in the wilds. Both detected a subtle change in the women's attitudes that first night out.

"Well, looks like we can't take the carriage much farther," Abby called out to her brothers who were on point. "I'll let them know. Let's stop and see if this is where they want to start their search." It was.

"Oh, this is a perfect spot!" Wendy assured them, as she stepped out and looked at the rugged hills with the tall mountains hovering behind them. "What a view. It's almost like you could reach out and touch the mountains from here."

"Actually, they are many miles distant, rough ground, but passable partway on horseback," Aiden explained, dismounting and starting to care for the carriage team.

Holly walked over to the small stream, which was the mighty Wyndl here at its beginnings. Small pieces of the blue and green psi-crystals lay strewn all over the rocky ground, interspersed with tufts of a hardy grass and several wild plants, some of which Holly absentmindedly began collecting for her herb shop.

"Will the psi-crystals harm us if we touch them?" asked Abby, just a little concerned after seeing how the witches held them in their hands to activate their "gifts."

Wendy chuckled, "No dear. Unless your body has been primed with a lot of psi-powder, they will just be ordinary, inert, green or blue rocks to you, pretty, yes. Okay, ladies. Here's where you'll find your personal psi-crystal. Remember, the psi-crystal chooses you. You'll feel especially drawn to it. See here, these are what they look like in the raw, greenish or bluish crystals, something like clear quartz crystals. You three merely wander around the hills and even wade in the creek there. Open your senses and feel your psi-crystal calling out to you, pulling you towards it. You'll know it when you have found yours. Ally, Aurora, you will have to somehow touch yours. When you think you have found yours, let us know, and we'll help you somehow touch and activate it." She didn't mention the five had yet to figure out just how the two would be able to "squeeze" their psi-crystals to activate its power. Holly suggested they might do so by squeezing it in their bent arms.

"The rest of us will stay alert. We are out in the wilderness — the domain of the wild animals, so stay vigilant while the three search," she added.

Sheena added, "Yes, she's right. There's a three to one chance some danger will happen to us."

Great! thought Alford. *Bringing the women out here in the wilds seems a trifle foolish. Couldn't they just bring back a pile of the pretty green and blue rocks, and let the women chose from them? Far safer that way.* He felt overly protective of Ally, more so than any other woman, save perhaps his late mother. Aiden felt the same way towards Aurora, and he could sense how his brother felt about Ally.

The four plus Jordan took up positions around the area. Adam and Abby had their longbows at the ready as well. The five witches took turns leading Sammi, Ally, and Aurora about the hilly, stony ground, going back and forth, slowly moving on upstream. "I'm not getting anything, mom," Sammi complained, worrying this wasn't going to work.

"Take your time, dear. There is no rushing the finding of your very special psi-crystal. We can spend days here if necessary," Holly answered her daughter's worry.

Hours passed, dulling the senses of those on guard duty. Suddenly, Vivian called out, "Sammi, don't move! Freeze! There is a viper just in front of you!" Sammi froze; her heart started beating rapidly as her eyes spotted the diamond head and fangs looking at her exposed legs, barely two feet from the coiled reptile. She desperately wanted to scream and flee, but forced herself to remain motionless. Abby circled around, trying to get a clear shot at the reptile.

Sheena held her back, "Wait, there's a five to one chance the viper will back off and go its own way. There, see it's uncoiling. Good, it has decided to yield its sunny spot to Sammi."

As they watched the viper move away from the area, Abby noticed Vivian and the other witches all held their own psi-crystals in their hands. Apparently, Vivian did have the gift of knowing when unseen danger arose, she decided. The women continued their searching.

Aiden concluded as late as it was getting, they would have to make camp here. Accordingly, he and Alford began collecting firewood for the night. Abby moved over to Jordan's side. "It is kind of a shame you can't get one of these psi-crystals yourself, love."

Jordan replied, "Nah, I don't want to be a witch like mom. All those smelly herbs and yucky stuff she brews up — no way. I like making arrow heads. Anything made out of metal, now that's the real thing," he replied.

Wendy overheard them and added, "Only women can become witches, not men. Men just don't have a *nurturing* bone in their bodies. That's what it takes, a strong desire to nurture others, not kill them like men do." Wendy's bias came to the fore once again.

"I know mom, I know. Just because dad was a soldier doesn't mean all men are butchers," Jordan countered her.

"Well, some are, but not all," Abby defended Jordan.

Sammi had taken off her shoes and was now wading in the creek, relieving her hot, sore feet in the cool waters. She'd given up the search, figuring this was fruitless. How good the waters felt, she mused as she carefully avoided the rocks, staying on the sandier bottoms. She didn't even realize she had bent over and picked up a large psi-crystal.

Rather, she found herself somehow high above looking down upon all these tiny bodies, seemingly wandering aimlessly about the hills and creek. She looked off in the distance. The world looked so bright, so beautiful. The craggy mountains beckoned. She moved over to them, admiring their beauty and form. One peak got her attention. Fascinated with its particular form, she rose even higher and stood over its top, looking down upon its rugged features. An eagle soared past her. How magnificent the graceful bird seemed to her, soaring on the thermal currents that she could also feel. For a moment, she wondered what it would be like to be an eagle.

She found herself flying along with the soaring, graceful bird. She was the eagle. Looking down, there was the Wyndl River, a sparkling line cutting across the rolling green patches of forest and hills, breathtakingly beautiful. Wyth! She saw Wyth way down there. It seemed so small, so insignificant to her.

Wendy called out, "Holly! It's Sammi. Look, I think she's found hers!" At once, all eyes turned to see Sammi, who was perfectly motionless, standing in the middle of the creek. Her hand held a very large psi-crystal. Holly kicked off her shoes and waded out to her daughter, a little concerned that she was so motionless.

"Sammi. Sammi, it's mom. Can you hear me? What's happening, dear," Holly tried hard to conceal her worry. Always the obtaining of the gift was nerve wracking. One never knew just what form the gift would take. Somehow, her daughter was simply "not here," though her body most definitely was. Try as she might, Holly could not get the slightest recognition from her daughter. At last, she squeezed her own crystal in her right palm and focused, making mental contact with Sammi. *Hello dear. It's mom. What's happening? Oh my goodness!* Holly began to see what her daughter was seeing.

Dear, it is time for supper. Let's return to your body now, shall we? You can always go soaring in the morning. At last, Sammi found her body way, way down there and moved to it, reluctantly, though. The world around her was so beautiful. At last, she found her body, and with Holly's help, loosened her grip on her large psi-crystal. She blinked and stared at the stone, and then looked up at everyone else who were staring back at her.

"Why is everyone staring at me? What's going on?" Sammi asked, slightly confused.

"You have found your psi-crystal, dear. Let's get out of the stream and fix some supper shall we?" Holly spoke very softly, but forcefully. Sammi did as her mother asked, though she still acted as though she were in some kind of a trance. However, after eating supper, she came out of it fully.

"Gosh, mom, mine is twice as large as yours," Sammi declared, comparing hers to her mothers.

"I don't know if size has anything to do with it, dear."

"So what is my gift supposed to be?" Sammi asked. Of course, everyone else want to know this very same thing, but they had been kind enough to allow Sammi to recover from her experience before questioning her about it. As far as the others had seen, she had been in perhaps a trance.

"What did you experience, dear?" Holly asked gently. Sammi responded by describing in detail what she had seen and felt. Slowly, Sammi and the others began to realize what her gift was. She could "be" anywhere in the world she desired and see what was there, what was going on, though her preferred viewpoint ever afterwards was from that of an eagle. Alford and Aiden realized that Sammi's gift was far more powerful than those possessed by the five witches. They found that interesting, especially when the next morning Sammi took a "brief flight" over the Plateau Grado, spying on the aliens there who were setting up a new mining operation.

Embolden by Sammi's success, after breakfast, Ally and Aurora eagerly continued their search. Both decided to go wading as Sammi had. Besides, their feet were tired of walking on the sharp rocks of the stony ground. Occasionally, each bent over and touched their right stump to a psi-crystal lying beneath the clear waters, though nothing happened as a result. Slowly, the pair wandered further upstream from their camp. Dutifully, Alford and Aiden followed them from the shore. Abby and Adam kept back, watching over the six witches, Sammi now being considered one of them.

As the sun reached its zenith, the bored watchers suddenly got a huge, surprising shock. All eyes, excepting those of Ally and Aurora, saw a huge psi-crystal seemingly rising up from the stream waters of its own accord! Sparking in the sun with drops of glistening water dripping back into the stream, the hovering psi-crystal seemed to split into two halves. If that was not startling enough, each half moved into the foreheads of Ally and Aurora! From the witches' point of view, this should not, could not, and ought not be happening. Psi-crystals didn't move of their own accord, nor could they split, nor could they move into one's body!

Aurora found herself suddenly seeing a stream of future

events. A Montaña Beast was about to attack them, but she took no action, seeing Ally was easily handling this threat. She pushed on into the future time. Slowly, she realized what she was seeing and observing. She knew what she had to do now. Everything on Tierra depended upon her. She swore she would make it happen, but she also knew Ally had spoken truthfully when they had first met: that Ally would always be there to protect her. With a supreme confidence she'd never known, she opened her eyes, forcing herself into the present time once more.

She was just in time to hear Vivian's warning screams, "Montaña Beast! Montaña Beast! It's picked up our scent! Flee! Flee for your very lives!" Almost in slow motion, she saw happening what she'd just seen! Abby's arrow flew true, striking the monstrous beast. Adam's arrow struck it a moment afterwards. Neither arrow seemed to phase the huge carnivore. She saw Aiden and Alford moving to get their bodies in front of hers and Ally's in a useless attempt to defend the two women who were directly in the cat's path, which had wandered down from the more distant hills in search of food — human flesh, in this case.

Aurora found her voice. "Relax everyone. Ally will handle the Montaña Beast for us." Her voice sounded strange, and she realized she was still partly in the future and blinked a few times, trying to focus more on the present. *There, that's better.* She repeated her words, "Relax everyone. Ally will handle the Montaña Beast for us."

Ally found herself feeling incredibly strange. She could see everyone plainly, but she could also "feel" their bodies, and it dawned on her that she could somehow manipulate them. Then, she heard Vivian's warning screams of Montaña Beast! She looked up and saw the huge cat slowly positioning itself to jump down upon her and Aurora. She saw the twin's arrows strike and do nothing to the cat. She felt the cat, sensed its powerful muscles, contracting, ready to explode in a mighty jump. She felt its razor sharp claws twitching, ready to pierce into flesh, holding prey tightly. She felt its hungry stomach growling.

Ally acted, taking over for a moment the Montaña

Beast's body. *I should go away. These humans are too small to eat. A bear will be far tastier. Now where is one? Sniff, sniff.* She relaxed her powerful muscles, rose up to her full height, stretched, yawned once, and sniffed. The powerful cat moved off to the south, completely ignoring the humans. Still somehow out of her physical body, Ally followed it briefly to make sure the cat was leaving. Satisfied, she returned to her own body. She found her eyes had closed, so she opened them, and saw she was still in the middle of the stream, a foot from Aurora. "I had the weirdest dream, Aurora, just now. A Montaña Beast was coming after us, but now it's gone. Weird, eh?"

"No, it was here, and you got rid of it for us, Ally. You're still and always will be my protector. Thank you, Ally," Aurora explained.

The others were shocked utterly. Alford came to his senses first, "Ally! Aurora! Get out of the stream fast. Get over here to us! There's a Montaña Beast after us! Quick!"

Although only seconds had past so far, he and Aiden dashed into the waters, taking a hold of the women's arms, helping them move to dry land more quickly. Both also held their swords, heads glancing in all directions, looking for the springing cat. Adam and Abby had gotten the others all together in a tight circle. They too had their swords drawn, prepared to defend against the overwhelmingly powerful cat, whose body dwarfed theirs. Even their horses were far smaller than this fierce-some beast.

Aurora had to stay alert to avoid stepping on sharp rocks, since Aiden was pulling her swiftly to shore. Once there, she called out, "It's safe. Ally sent the cat on its way elsewhere. It's all right now, really it is."

Of course, they didn't believe a word of what she said, but then Aurora knew they wouldn't, not for a while yet. She'd already seen their reactions and merely waited for the events to unfold. *How strange,* she thought, *to be living what I've already seen happening!*

The others clustered together; all eyes searching for the monstrous cat. Time passed but no cat appeared, and slowly the men began to relax. "That was the proverbial close call!"

Aiden finally ventured to say.

"No kidding. We were goners for sure. My arrow did nothing to it!" Abby added.

Hearing them speak the words that Aurora already heard them saying caused her to laugh. Just as Alford was about to speak, she spoke in unison with him. Everyone heard them both say, "That Montaña Beast ought to have eaten us all! How come it left?" That did the trick, as Aurora had already seen it would do so.

Holly spoke up, "The psi-crystals?"

"Yes, that's it, Holly, the psi-crystals. They have their gifts now, whatever they are," Wendy confirmed what her intuition told her.

"Huh?" Alford and Aiden said simultaneously.

"I can explain," Aurora said quietly, just as she'd seen a bit before. "I am able to see the future now. I saw the cat coming, and I saw my protector would save me, Ally. She promised always to protect me, and she is doing that. I've seen a whole lot of future already."

Jaws dropped. Never had anyone received such a gift! Slowly, the sheer magnitude of Aurora's precious gift dawned upon Holly. Alford spoke up, "Ally, how? How could you get rid of that monstrous Montaña Beast? The twins' arrows didn't even bother it!"

"I don't know. I can just take over a body and make it do what I want it to do. I made it go in search of a bear instead of eating us. I wonder what else I can do?" She picked up Alford's sword arm and swung it around.

"Hey! What's happening to my arm?" Alford cried out, shocked his own arm was acting on its own.

Ally stopped and laughed. "Oh boy, Alford! Now you are in big trouble! I can make your body do what I want it to do. How about a little jumping?" She teased him. Everyone saw his body jumping up and down. The shocked expression on his face told them he wasn't making his body jump.

"I hope I didn't spook you too badly, dear," Ally said, realizing she was indeed doing just that.

Aurora spoke again, just as she'd seen happening. "Yes, that's Ally's gift. She'll be my protector from now on. She'll be able to prevent any harm coming to me and to you, if you allow her to do so."

"This, this, this is incredible, unbelievable," Wendy tried to vocalize her shock over the magnitude of the two women's gifts.

Squeezing her psi-crystal in one hand, Sheena exclaimed, "Wow! Aurora! You are right! When Ally is around you, the odds of someone or something harming you is about ten thousand five hundred sixty-three to one against them succeeding! Unreal!" She loosened her grip on her psi-crystal, as everyone now stared at her. She smiled, knowing she was correct.

Aurora then said, "We are done here. Shall we return to Wyth now, please?"

Still afraid of the Montaña Beast, Alford insisted they put some miles between them and this place before camping for the night. Later, as Ally sat beside Alford who was carefully feeding her supper, she said, "I hope I didn't freak you out or embarrass you too badly, Alford. I really don't quite know what this psi-crystal has done to me or what I can really do."

"I admit, dear, you really spooked me back there. However, I did say I wanted a pretty, intelligent, and sharp woman. You are that and then some. All is forgiven, but please don't make me do something I would regret having done."

"Never. I promise. Thanks for feeding me. How the devil am I ever going to do this for myself, Alford?"

"I wish I knew, dear, I truly do. We'll just have to figure it out soon. I'm sure there must be a way."

The next day as the carriage began rolling back towards Wyth, Holly asked, "Okay, Aurora, what can you tell us about the future that we critically need to know? Yours is perhaps the most vital of any gift any of us has ever received."

"I knew already you would be asking me this and at this time, Holly. It is so weird knowing in advance what is going to happen, what someone is going to ask! I haven't seen too far into the future yet. I have seen it is supposed to be we all who takes a stand against the aliens, though that won't happen for several years yet. I believe we must make a lot of preparations before that occurs. Somehow, someway, I think it will come down to Ally, you all, and me who will stand against the aliens, preserving life here on Tierra. But we have lots of time before that happens, lots. There are some others who will be joining us down the road, so we won't be alone."

"So there is time? We do not have to rush?" Holly asked.

"Yes, a lot of time. Though there'll be much to do, still we don't have to rush. We've years to prepare. Events move slowly," Aurora added.

"Okay, I'll abide by your visions, Aurora. In that case, I've some good news for you. A fellow witch in Benito, Trujillo has offered me a way to show you and Ally how you can do everything for yourselves. She has made arrangements for you both to go and spend many months learning special ways from a friend of hers. She has assured me if you spend enough time with this woman, you'll be able to live quite independently. We owe you both this opportunity. I'll make the arrangements when we get back, if you are willing to go there and learn new ways."

"That would be a holy miracle," Ally replied. "We simply can't live like we are now. I refuse to be a helpless invalid for the rest of my life, gift or no gift. Right, Aurora?"

"Yes, we simply can't. I think Holly's right, Ally, we'll learn how to do things for ourselves again," Aurora agreed. This part, she had not yet seen; her focus had been pulled towards the aliens, probably because everyone had aliens on their minds for obvious reasons.

"Of course, you'll need to learn their language," Holly pointed out. "Then of course, there is the question of whom we send along with you."

"It should be the Bettinghams," Aurora answered up without any hesitation. "We'll ask them tonight."

"Say," Sammi asked, "what happened to your psi-crystals? I have mine in my new pouch, like mom's, but where's yours?"

"Dunno," Ally replied honestly. She had no idea.

"They have merged with us," Aurora answered. "They are always a part of us now. I have a feeling there might be more to these psi-crystals than we know. Anyway, that's a good thing, since we can't pick them up or squeeze them like you can, Sammi."

Around their campfire that night, Aurora explained to Aiden and Alford what Holly had worked out for them. "Yes, she honestly believes if we go to this person in Benito, she can teach us how to live again. So we're going. Aiden, I really want you to come with me. Alford too. Abby and Adam, if they will too. Please?"

"Are you still you? I mean after today, are you still the Aurora I knew and loved yesterday?" Aiden asked.

"He's right," Alford interjected. "Are you still you, Ally? Or have you both become something different?"

"I'm still me, honey. I just can do something I couldn't do before, that's all. I'd really, really like you to come with me," Ally begged. Somehow, living life without Alford seemed completely hopeless. It wasn't because she needed his help for so many things, rather it was how happy he made her feel. Suddenly, Ally sat up straight. It dawned on her what these feelings she had were. "I love you, Alford! I've never loved anyone else before, so it's taken me forever to realize it. I love you. There, I said it. It is okay, though, if you don't feel the same. After all, I'm certainly not a fine catch, not like this," she waved her arms a little.

Alford didn't reply with words. He leaned over and gave her a loving kiss. He whispered, "I've longed to hear those words from your lips! I've fallen hopelessly in love with you too, Ally."

Nearby, Aurora took a deep breath and plunged in herself. "Aiden, I feel the same way. I've fallen in love with you too, but I can understand if you don't want to love a partial woman. I'm only a partial woman now. I'm sure you can do a whole lot better than me, but I at least want you to know how I feel about you." He too replied by giving her a loving kiss.

A bit later, Alford whispered, "We should get married before we go on the long journey. It'll be like our honeymoon. I love to travel, and we could finally have some time for ourselves. What say you, will you marry me?"

"Of course I will!" She gave him a passionate kiss.

A bit later, Alford and Aiden made their surprise

announcement. Abby commented, "What took you two so long?" To Ally, she added, "Men are so slow to figure these things out, aren't they?"

Ally laughed, but added, "It took me forever to figure it out, Abby. Until now, my life has been pretty much devoid of such things as love. Being around your brother these past days have been the happiest days of my entire life."

"It's been very obvious to me. I'm glad to have you and Aurora as sisters. I've been surrounded with these three boys all my life. Now it's going to be great having three sisters, so to speak," Abby said gaily.

When they announced their plans, Holly was a little concerned for the well-being of the two. They had only known the men for such a short while. On the quiet, she asked Wendy for her opinion. After using her gift, Wendy put Holly at ease. "Yes, that is another right action, though I simply don't see what those young women see in Aiden and Alford! I do hope they are not too terribly disappointed in their choices. You know how fickle men can be."

Holly smiled, thinking, *Wendy just picked the wrong man, who got himself killed.* She felt a little sorry for her dear friend, having to carry that on her shoulders all these years. *Perhaps some of it rubbed off onto Roxane.*

They kept the weddings small. Only the five witches and their families attended the ceremonies. Little Trisha and Roni were the flower girls, while Tammy and Val were the bridesmaids for Abby and Sammi. Ally and Aurora asked Roxane and Sable to be theirs. After the simple ceremony, Holly arranged a reception and party for all their families, which was a big hit for all, a nice change of pace from the grueling months of the nearby war.

The next day, Aurora's funds arrived. Phyllis and Zoe had recovered Babs' secret stash, and Aurora now had the equivalent of several thousand gold, which pleased her. Only then did Ally and Aurora learn the Bettinghams each had inherited some ten thousand gold from their parents, along with two estates — one in Bettingham and this one, just outside Wyth. Ally relaxed, money was not going to be a problem, and she understood now how the Bettinghams were free to have done so much traveling.

Three days later, with their few possessions packed, the four couples set off on the long journey to Benito, Trujillo. They had over three thousand five hundred miles to cover, but they were in no hurry.

The three months of travel was a welcome relief to all. Besides getting to know each other far better, the Bettinghams also taught their spouses the Westerlings language. Two thirds of the distance was through that land. Sammi, Jordan, Ally, and Aurora became fairly fluent by the time they reached Benito. In essence, the four couples had a three month honeymoon.

Chapter 9 Benito Days

The war between the Kingdom of Alavera and its southern neighbor, the Kingdom of Trujillo had ended in a stalemate, with both sides withdrawing their forces under somewhat mysterious circumstances, it was said by the locals. By the time the four couples rolled into Benito, the capital and port city of Trujillo, thousands of men were also returning home from the battle. Just as in Bettingham, the awful casualties of war were plainly visible. As they entered the large city, they saw soldiers hobbling along with a leg missing or an arm. A few poor souls rolled along on little wagon-like devices; both of their legs were long gone. "Looks like their field COG physicians had a grand old time chopping off limbs here too," Aurora said snidely.

"I can see why Wendy feels as she does about men," Ally added.

"It is not a pretty sight," Alford commented. Aiden was currently driving their carriage, while Alford consulted the hand-drawn map that Holly provided. "Okay gang, keep an eye out for Alcalde Calle." Their directions would take them to the witch Alita Cruz who was expecting them. After getting lost twice and turned around once, the men finally asked for directions, while the women laughed their heads off.

"Just like a man to not do the simple thing and ask," Sammi teased them. Abby roared; she was often their navigator in years past when the four had roamed into the Westerlings. Near dusk on the fifteenth of October, they finally pulled up to the right place: Cruz Herbs and More.

An old woman with white-streaked hair greeted them. "Welcome, welcome to Benito. Holly speaks highly of you. My, your arms, they are so perfectly done. Is it true the Rigels healed you so perfectly?" Alita Cruz asked.

"Rigels?" asked Ally.

"Oh, yes, that is the name of the aliens who landed in the mountains."

"Yes, we met them not long after our hands were cut off. Their doctor healed us. At least, they look much better than the soldiers who lost limbs in the war," Ally answered.

"I am afraid the effects of a war last through a whole generation, though men seldom take that into consideration. Come on in. I have crude quarters prepared for you tonight. Tomorrow, I'll introduce you to the others and more permanent accommodations. If you don't mind, let's wait on the many questions and answers until tomorrow, when my coven can meet all of you at one time. I hope you don't mind the fish smell. We are not too far from the docks."

Alita had supper waiting, though it had been steaming for a while. As always, they found the local food rather hot and spicy. Fish was the dominate meat along the coast, and they were a little tired of eating it for the last two months. After dining, they divided up and headed for makeshift beds. Alita's home was quite small, but she'd managed to find a space for each couple for the night, apologizing for the cramped quarters.

The next morning, they followed their hostess out into the street. "Most all the witches shops lie along this stretch of Alcalde Calle," Alita explained as the group walked down the bustling street. Women wearing very fancy cotton dresses caught everyone's attention. They were colorful and embellished with large amounts of embroidery. Hair color was predominately a rich black or a deep brown. Most of the women wore theirs long and straight, though a few curls were sometimes in evidence. A surprising number of recovering soldiers were also making their way to the witches shops, in a last ditch attempt to somehow salvage their lives, hoping for miracle cures, which were not to be found, of course. This, Alita explained as she walked the two blocks.

"These two shops here, Anacleto's Herbs and Bolivar and Camila's, belong to three of my coven. Their shops are closed, and they are awaiting us at our destination, Esteban's. See, there is her sign. We all run small healing and herb shops, rather profitable, I might add. I should warn you not to be shocked when you meet Drina and her children. You see, Drina was born without any arms at all. They simply were not there, and no one knows why. She found a loving and devoted husband, Ernesto, a stonemason. They have three children,

Elena, ten, Felipa, eight. Her two girls were also born without arms, most distressing. Still, they did not give up, guessing this deformity was only affecting the female line. Then, they had Emilano, their little boy who is seven now. He too was born without arms. After he came, they decided not to have any more children. This is rather a touchy point for poor Ernesto. Please say nothing about that. Ah, here we are now. This is Drina's shop and home. As you will soon see, it has been set up around Drina and the children so they can live a normal life."

They stopped at a grey stone building with the common Westerlings red tiled roof. A wooden trellis marked the entryway, hung with the last flowers of the season. A sign on the door said Closed, but Alita knocked anyway. A tall, well-muscled man opened the door. He had black hair and a large moustache to match. Ernesto, thirty-three, cut a handsome figure, Ally noted. "Welcome once again, Alita. Ah, these must be our honored guests from the Midlands. Come in, come in."

Just inside was the herb shop. Unlike the ones they'd seen before, here everything was displayed on low shelves. Nothing was above about four feet off the ground. Just inside, they saw Drina, thirty-one, and their three children all standing in a line, from tallest and oldest to the youngest. She too had rich, long black hair falling to her waist, the most common hairstyle seen in the Westerlings. Her dress was rather unusual in that it had no sleeves. Where sleeves would normally be inserted, hers were sewn shut as if sleeves were never part of the design, which in this case was correct. Still, her white dress was colorfully done with volumes of needlepoint. Her slightly olive skin contrasted with her hair and dress. Her oval face was captivating, and she was blessed with a mouth that always seemed to have a smile upon it.

Ernesto proudly introduced his family. "This is the most beautiful woman in all Benito, smartest too, my Drina. Our wonderful children, Elena, Felipa, and little Emilano." The girls' dresses mirrored their mother's dress, and Emilano's shirt also had no sleeves in it.

Drina stepped forward, pressed her body into Ally's and threw a leg around her in a little squeeze, which Ally recognized as a welcome hug. She returned the hug. "So very glad to meet you, Drina." And so the introductions began. Once that was done, Ernesto excused himself and left for work. Drina told her children to run and play kick ball, which they gladly did, calling out who was "it" first.

"If you will follow me, the others are waiting to meet all of you. I am so glad you could come here, all the way from the Midlands," Drina said, leading them through her shop. At the back door, she used her foot to slide a latch over and pushed on into their main living quarters. They found a spacious living room. Rows of high windows allowed plenty of sunlight into the room. On low stands around the room, Drina had many potted plants. Six other women were already here and rose as they entered.

"This is Inez Anacleto and her daughter Benita." She was thirty and Benita was ten, both had long brown hair, slightly curly. Drina explained, "Her husband was a sailor. Three years ago he ran off with their son and abandoned her. This is Isabel Bolivar, her daughter, Marisol." She and her daughter both had lustrous black hair, long and full. She was forty and Marisol was twenty-one. Both women were very attractive. "This is Luisa Camila and her daughter, Ria." They had brown hair, long, as was the style. Luisa was thirty-nine and Ria, eighteen. Again, both were attractive women.

Drina then added, "Isabel and Luisa are mates. Here in Trujillo, a woman cannot officially marry another woman, but they can be mates."

Isabel grinned and smiled coyly at Ally. "My, you look ravishing!" Turning to Alford, she added, "Alford, is it? Well, you'd better be careful sir; we might steal her away from you."

"Isabel! You know we want to snatch up Aurora too," Luisa added with a flirting smile.

Ally and Aurora didn't quite know what to make of this. Their statements were so believable. Drina grinned and explained, "Don't pay them any mind. Their gift is that of creating totally believable illusions. Isabel only has eyes for Luisa and vice versa. They've been together for nearly twenty years now. Honestly, you two. Showing off and we've only just met them!" Drina was a little annoyed with her fellow witches.

"Can one of you serve up the tea please?" Drina asked.

"Our guests probably have lots of questions, and I know we certainly have lots to ask them! Oh, that's my seat there with the low table. I have to use my feet as hands, you see. Well, you probably don't see, but you soon will. Come on, sit please. We've heard so much about you and have loads of questions. Is it true you weren't thieves before you lost your hands? Is it true they cut off the hands of thieves in the Midlands?" Obviously, Drina could not wait on the tea that Inez went to fetch.

"No, we were never thieves," Ally decided to speak for Aurora. She related what had happened to them four months ago, including their visit with the Rigels and how their doctor had healed them so miraculously. She figured they might as well get as much explained as possible to avoid many questions. She stopped to watch Drina, partway through her lengthy explanation, however.

Inez brought in their tea and placed a cup with a large handle on the low table before Drina. She used her toes to lift it up and began sipping her tea, causing Ally to stop and watch. "Incredible!"

Drina chuckled. "What else have I got to use to lift it up, eh? Don't worry. I've promised to teach you both all I know, and it is quite a lot actually. Please, continue. This is most intriguing!" Ally went on with her narration, but she did keep an eye on Drina, fascinated with the utter ease with which she drank her tea.

A bit later, Drina interrupted her again. "The COG is very active here in Benito too," she explained. "They are trying to run all of us witches out of the city. Already, they have forced five to abandon their shops and flee. We won't be bullied by them, though."

"Funny, I was just about to ask about the COG," Ally replied.

The four witches laughed. Drina explained, "That is my gift. I always know what someone else wants to know. Sorry, I just do that all the time around here. Please, continue."

Isabel broke in, "Yes, she does that all the time, and it can be a bit spooky or unnerving."

Ally then told them about their "gifts" and that of

Sammi, who had been rather quiet. Now, Sammi was a bit flustered by all the attention being thrown her way. All four witches were extremely impressed by the magnitude of their gifts. "Sammi, you are so powerful!" Drina exclaimed.

Marisol noticed that and changed the topic. "Ria and I are about ready to get our gifts too. We've learned all the basics now, right mom?" Isabel nodded.

Alita said, "Yes, Marisol, you and Ria will get yours soon. You've heard what Drina's gift is and that of Isabela and Luisa. I am sure you'll soon see just how real their illusions can seem to be. Sometimes, even I am fooled by them. Oh yes, Inez has a special gift. She can tell when a person is telling the truth or is lying. That has been very useful in our coven over these many years."

"Now then, we best get everyone settled properly, and let Drina begin teaching these two ladies, who have come so far to learn. Jordan and Abby will be staying with Inez. Adam and Sammi, you will stay with Luisa. Aiden and Alford, you will stay with Isabel. Actually, you four will have rooms in the backs of their shops. They live in separate homes in the street behind their shops. So Ally and Aurora, you don't have to worry about your husband's being tempted." Everyone chuckled at her jest.

"Ah, where's the fun in that?" Isabel teased, adding to the humor. Her retort was totally believable.

Sammi added, "My sister is mated to Sable; they run a fancy dress shop."

"Terrific! It is comforting to know there are other women out there who are not afraid to live their lives as they desire, Luisa," Isabel commented, pleased to hear of another similar relationship. "I'd very much like to meet your sister and her mate, wouldn't we?" Luisa agreed wholeheartedly.

Alita retook control. "That means Ally and Aurora will be staying here with Drina. That way, they can get the maximum amount of learning done each day. The rest of you, why don't you tour the city? Now, I am getting tired again. All these pitiful soldiers keep knocking on my door begging for me to restore their lost limbs. What do they think we are, magicians? Gods? I'll talk more with you tomorrow. Drina, do your best, as you always do, dear." She rose and left them.

Inez, always stern, rose, "Come on, the rest of you. Let's get you settled in, and let Drina get on with it. I'm afraid they have an awful lot to learn. I will say this, ladies, Drina and her children are able to do just about anything that we can do. So do pay attention." She and her daughter led the others out of the room.

"Okay, let's start in the kitchen, making lunch. We have to allow ourselves far more time than others do," Drina began. Thus began weeks of intensive training and practicing for the two, who were continually amazed at just what Drina and her children could actually do for themselves. However, they quickly saw that Ernesto had made special arrangements for them, which greatly assisted their ability to accomplish the things they needed to get done. Bit by bit, the two women had Alford and Aiden make sketches and draw up plans for similar items for them when they got back home. Everything had to be low to the ground to make it easier for Drina to manage.

Some miles away, King Arturo Bajardo's comfortable world was gone, forever lost to him. He paced his private study, worried and nervous. Fear — he'd never tasted this before in his life, but now that it arrived, he knew that he didn't like it. Better let others fear him had been his motto all his adult life. Now that was gone, utterly gone. Arturo was fifty and had ruled Trujillo for almost a quarter of a century. Until two weeks ago, his word was law. Even his generals feared his wrath, but no more.

Two weeks ago, his generals and his army of four thousand men were steadily gaining ground against King Emilio Perez of the Kingdom of Abvera just across the Brozas River, which formed a natural, centuries-old, boundary between their two kingdoms. No one was sure just which kingdom had actually started this five-year war, but King Emilio's army of four thousand men had made significant headway into Trujillo on a heading that led straight from Malaca, Abvera, to Benito, Trujillo. King Emilio wasn't stupid, his forces moved in a straight line from his capital city to King Arturo's. However, during this past summer, King Arturo's generals had finally begun to push them back towards the river and Abvera, giving Arturo a strong hope he would eventually win this war, but not now.

Two weeks ago, a dozen small flying ships made of a silver-colored metal appeared over the current battle lines. Miraculously, the ships spoke their Westerlings dialect! "Cease your fighting immediately and withdraw to your homes or die." That was the message his generals had later told him was heard by all the men. His generals, though awed by the sight of these strange flying beasts, as they thought they must be, refused to do so. Instead, both sides marched five hundred men against each other. As the two groups met in the valley between the two hilltops on which most of the remainder of the armies were encamped, the dozen flying beasts let loose a barrage of strange light. All thousand men simply vanished from sight, though their clothing and weapons remained, falling into a heap where the men had stood a second before.

Shocked utterly, all the generals backed off from the attacks. Had they not, their remaining soldiers would have simply routed. The "gods" had struck their fellow soldiers down, everyone had heard the god ships speak and saw the results with their own eyes. Only the strong wills of the generals kept the remaining men from an utter panicked rout, though rout they did. Strategic withdrawal was the term the generals called the mass movement of their men that same afternoon.

As the two opposing sides struggled to control their retreating men, some of the flying ships landed. Tall, thin olive-skinned men came out onto the grassland battlefield. Speaking in very loud voices and in the Westerlings dialect, they said, "Generals, send one of your men to speak to us immediately!" Thus, eventually, one general from each of the two kingdoms reported back to their king the "Divine Orders" from the gods, who called themselves Rigels.

"You are hereby ordered to cease your fighting. All those who persist in this conflict will be disintegrated, as the thousand who are now gone. We Rigels have taken over the mountains you call the Goza Mountains. Any attempts to interfere with us will be summarily handled. Send us a thousand miners, and we will pay them in gold to work for us. Send them to the place that called Plateau Grado. Tell this to your kings."

While the wording was a little rough, their meaning was quite clear. King Arturo's generals had reported all this to him just two weeks ago. At first, he could not believe what his generals were saying. Yet, they all reported having seen and heard the same thing. Besides, his five hundred men were gone.

His first reaction was, "What the hell do I care about the Goza? It's over two thousand miles from here?" The eastern portion of his kingdom was very sparsely populated anyway, though the southern bordering kingdom of Almendia did have its second largest city not far from there, Valen, at the headwaters of the Alcantara River, which divided Trujillo from Almendia. In fact, for a quarter of a century now, settlers from Almendia had been steadily moving into his hilly lands there, drawn by the forests and rolling grasslands most suited to raising horses. Still what happened two thousand miles from here meant little to King Arturo.

He had complied and issued a formal proclamation that able bodied miners could seek profitable work with the Rigels. Many days later and upon much reflection and discussions, he began to rethink his whole point of view on his far eastern territory. What did these aliens really want with worthless mountain lands? Rolling grasslands, forests, farmlands, even ports were more valuable than rugged peaks. What were they mining for and why? True, he had a few ore mines in the foothills and even a couple gold mines. If they mined for gold, why pay the miners in the very gold that they dug up?

Strategic position. His generals began thinking along another line of thought. Suppose, one said, that the Rigels' plans were to conquer all Tierra. What better place to establish themselves than in unassailable mountain strongholds? From such positions, they could fly their flying beasts out over the lower lands and conquer whatever they chose. King Arturo began to believe the ultimate objective of these Rigels was indeed controlling all the lands of Tierra, as a "super king." What else could they possibly have in mind? He rationally could think of no other real possibility. Hence, fear began to seep into the back of his mind, slowly at first, but it rapidly began festering.

He stopped pacing around his study and looked at his map of Tierra on his wall. Of course, Trujillo was drawn in the most prominent color of all the kingdoms. Then, it struck him that neighboring Almendia's claim to the Goza Mountains covered eleven hundred miles up from the southern seacoast to his. However, Trujillo's claim was barely three hundred miles at most, and some of that was in dispute with Abvera. Abvera's claim was at least six hundred miles, while the Kingdom of Zamora in the far north claim amounted to eight or nine hundred miles. Trujillo's claim was the smallest of any of the Westerlings.

Worse, he looked at the Midlands, which he had seldom, if ever, given much thought to before now. "Good god! Bettingham has almost a two thousand mile claim to the Goza!" Rockton, north of them had nearly the same amount, though perhaps a little less. Its boundary with the far northern kingdom of Haruk was rather vague. Perhaps Haruk could claim a couple hundred of it from Rockton. "These two kingdoms will have a vastly larger claim and say in matters, if the Rigels do indeed attempt to control all Tierra! Trujillo will have the lesser say." He didn't mention that all the other kingdoms would have none at all.

If these Rigels made pacts with their immediate neighbors, Trujillo would get the least of any deals made! That bothered King Arturo immensely, who had never entertained any idea other than Trujillo being the center of the world. Indeed, only the Midland kingdom of Bashir was larger in size than Trujillo. "We will become a second class kingdom!" he barked to his advisors. "We cannot allow that to happen!"

What to do? That became the overriding thought in King Arturo's mind for days on end. Attacking these Rigels directly seemed out of the question, considering how easily they wiped out a thousand men on the battlefield. He tended to believe his generals in this regard. Still, what to do?

What were they mining for? That, he decided, ought to be answered first, mostly because it could be answered. He sent a dozen of his soldiers, disguised as miners off to seek employment with the Rigels. After they learned all they could about the mining operations, they would return and report to him. That seemed plausible, though the one-way travel time alone from Benito to the Plateau Grado was forty days, assuming they made good on fifty miles each day. King Arturo guessed he might have that answer come the start of the New Year.

Arturo also reasoned if the king of Bettingham, by virtue of having the longest stretch of the Goza Mountains under his domain, ended up with the most influence with these Rigels, then it would be in Arturo's best interests to be on good terms with this king. Nay, perhaps even an alliance would be better. Hence, he ordered his aides to setup a diplomatic mission to Wycombe, Bettingham. Six trusted men would make the three month journey there, bearing gifts for the king and do what they could to establish close ties with this king or work out an alliance, if such was even possible.

Gifts? He decided upon a five hundred gold coins, a pair of the finest blades to be found in Benito, and six of Benito's finest bailarines populares tradicionales, accompanied by five competent musicians to play their traditional music for the dancers. What Trujillo man could possibly resist the exotic charm of these exciting women dancers? Impress the king — that was his charge to the six men in charge of this diplomatic mission.

Finally, having at least taken two positive steps, he was forced to return to the problems of Benito. He'd put Bishop Ethan Findlay off for nearly two weeks, and at last, he agreed to see the COG leader. King Arturo was not an overly religious man, but the COG was highly supportive of him, both financially and politically. He valued the former more than the latter, of course.

"Ah welcome at last Bishop Findlay. You must forgive the long delay. These alien Rigels have caused quite a problem for us, as you probably have heard," King Arturo attempted to provide an acceptable reason for not having seen the man for the last two weeks.

"Rumors, Sire. Is it true these aliens killed many of our

soldiers?" he asked point blank. No sense beating around the bush. Rumors were running wild in the streets.

King Arturo saw his opening and took it. "Yes, we lost five hundred brave soldiers, gone in a flash; their bodies totally vaporized, it seems." He saw a look of disbelief on the bishop's face and took this opportunity to go over all that had happened. Of course, he had it all secondhand, but he relayed it as if he'd witnessed it personally. He watched the bishop's reactions closely and saw he'd achieved his desired effect. That is, the bishop's viewpoint changed from one of annoyance of having been put off for two weeks to one of utter shock and surprise. Bishop Ethan began to realize the rumors had been partially true.

"Dear God! Who are these aliens who can murder a thousand men without the slightest provocation? They must be incarnations of the very devil himself or else servants of Lucifer. I assure you I will dispatch the Archbishop yet today, relaying this most awful and unimaginable news. King Arturo, I will request his Holy Guidance in this matter and will advise you on what our Most Holiest Leader suggests."

With the potential flap with the top religious leader of Trujillo nullified, King Arturo then brought the bishop back to what the man wanted. "So you can see now why I was unable to see you for the past two weeks. This alien problem is of enormous proportions and had to be dealt with at once. Now that I've begun my countermoves, it is time I return to the welfare of our great city. What can I do for our illustrious Church of God this day, Bishop Findlay?"

"As you know, the COG has been trying to remove the unholy, devil-influenced members of our wonderful kingdom so the honest, god-fearing citizens may live lives of purity and holiness that they may attain the Heaven of God when he thus calls them," Bishop Ethan began using his more formal speech.

Arturo hated all this flowery language and enormously, over long sentences. Why didn't the man just come right out and say what he meant? Arturo fought to keep from showing his complete annoyance with the man. That wouldn't do at all. He said politely, "Yes?" He hoped that the bishop would hurry up and say what he wanted.

"Sire, it is these devil-spawn witches who ply their unholy trade down on Alcalde Calle. Many of your returning wounded soldiers are spending their last coins on the evil potions and salves the witches there are foisting off on them. Men who have suffered greatly in the Great Battles and have lost an arm or leg are going to see these witches, hoping to have them bring back their lost arms or legs. Surely, Sire, you will not stand for such blatant theft and trickery of the very men who fought so bravely for you and gave their all for your victories."

King Arturo knew the bishop was greatly exaggerating what was going on. No reasonable man would expect a witch, no matter how powerful, to regrow a missing arm or leg. He suspected they were after balms or salves to ease their pains perhaps. Still, he didn't want to start an argument with the bishop. He valued the funds that the COG regularly donated to his war chest. He thus relied, "No, of course not."

"I thought as much. We would like to at least run all these witches out of Benito once and for all."

"How do you propose to do that? Surely, you don't want my soldiers to go around and execute every witch on Alcalde Calle."

"No, no, that would upset a great many of our citizens, who are still trusting of their unholy witches. Rather, Sire, we would like to set an example. Pick one of their leaders and hang her before her unholy store. Let her body rot there in public for all to see for say a week. Cast the righteous fear of God in all the other witches. Many will flee the city for their lives. Other bishops have taken this course in other kingdoms with great success, eliminating their devil-spawn witches."

"That makes good sense, Bishop Findlay. Let's follow that path, then. Have you determined who their leader might be? I must admit I don't know much about the witches of Alcalde Calle." He spoke the truth, he didn't. However, from time to time, he sent aides in search of a healing salve or potion, but had never himself set foot in one of their shops. Well, he had once in his youth and left quickly. The heady odors he found nauseating. How anyone could stand to be inside such a odorous shop was beyond him.

"Yes, we have identified one. With your permission, she will be hanged later today."

"Excellent. On your way out, see Captain Hermes. He will lead the execution detail, though someone from the COG ought to accompany him to make sure they hang the right witch," King Arturo advised. The bishop bowed and thanked him, making a hasty exit. He'd achieved precisely what he'd desired, though he'd had to wait two weeks to get it. Well, what was two weeks? In days now, witches will be fleeing Benito in droves! If they didn't, well, he could deal with another witch in say a week's time. A few dead witches and they'll get the message quickly, he coldly calculated. "All in the name of our Holy Father," he whispered to himself as he walked up to Captain Hermes.

"What is all that commotion?" Alford asked. He and his siblings along with Sammi and Jordan were out strolling the streets of Benito. Already, they'd visited several shops, adding a few high quality weapons to their arsenal. Both younger twins had acquired new longbows as well. As always, the streets were swarming with people, many carrying recent purchases. Gaily colored dresses contrasted with the browns and greens of the men's various shirts and pants, creating a rainbow pattern along the streets. The shops and buildings were quaint, quite different from the purely functional wooden structures of Wyth. Nearly every building had a trellised flower garden section, contrasting with the red tiles of the rooftops. Abby rather wished she could have seen these many gardens in their full summer blooms. However, as they entered Alcalde Calle heading for home, a large crowd of common folks yelling protests blocked the street ahead of them. Soldiers were shoving people aside or back. No, these had to be palace guards; their red uniforms gave the men away. Many folks were yelling and shouting.

The six pressed closer. "Hey, they are outside Cruz Herbs!" Aiden yelled above the din. They spotted the crimson robes and skullcap of Bishop Ethan Findlay and several other purple robed COG officials as well.

Above the shouting, Bishop Ethan yelled, "Heathen witches, spawn of the devil, we cast thee out of our hearts, minds, and Benito." His voice was shrill and loud above the protestors' counter-cries. Alford and Aiden began to press and shove their way through the crowd. If these fiends were going to harm the old witch, they intended to try to prevent it.

Almost as if they thought the identical thought at the same time, Abby and Adam gave up trying to push their way through the throng. Instead, they pivoted and retreated across the street. Abby pointed to a side stairs in an ally, and the two dashed there and raced up the steps two at a time. At the top, they stretched out their arms just reaching the side of the roof. They pulled themselves up on top. From here, they had a clear vantage point. Below, their older twins were still struggling to get to the front of the crowd. Already, Abby and Adam knew they were too late.

"Last words, witch?" Bishop Ethan asked.

Alita, her hands tied behind her back with a rope around her neck hanging over a beam in front of her shop, said calmly, "Thank you for this kindness."

Bishop Ethan looked dumbfounded. The witch was thanking him? This made no sense whatsoever to the priest. He mechanically moved his raised arm downward, and the captain signaled his men. Alita felt the rope go taught and heard her neck snap; she had a smile on her face; she was at last released from the pains of her aged body. The crowd gasped and some screamed. Alford and Aiden finally got to the front only to see Alita's body hanging from her shop. Already Bishop Ethan had hung a sign over her dead body.

From the rooftop across the street, Abby fumed. "God damn bishop! Well, he's going to pay!" Twang! She fired an arrow. Twang! Adam's bow snapped as well. Both twins had the good sense to get off the roof immediately, ducking down the alley and returning to the chaos in the street a block from the scene. Neither had to see the results of their shots to know their results. They were completely competent and certain of their skill with their bows.

Alford and Aiden watched as two arrows thudded into the head of Bishop Ethan. Both men automatically smiled, recognizing the feathers, their younger twins. Chaos erupted. The captain of the guards and his men pushed and shoved against the crowd, trying to get free and see who had shot the bishop. Many in the crowd resisted them, cheering the murder of the bishop, though none had any idea from where the archers had shot. Soon, the dozen guards cleared the throng and looked in all directions, but only saw more and more people coming over to see what was going on. Wisely, the men headed on up the street back towards the palace. Their work was done; no sense in getting themselves killed. Besides, mob control was going to need a whole lot more guards.

Alford and Aiden rejoined Sammi and Jordan, who both looked rather pale. They knew their spouses had undoubtedly shot the bishop and feared for the twins' safety. "Come on; back to our houses. Twins will be heading there now," Alford told them, grabbing Sammi's arm and leading her away from the steadily growing crowd.

By the time they got to Isabel and Luisa's shop, Inez, Izabel, Marisol, Luisa, and Ria were already just outside, looking up the street with frightened looks on their faces. Adam and Abby walked up from the other direction, waving to their spouses and their brothers, satisfied smiles on their faces. "What's going on down at Alita's?" Inez called out worriedly.

"The bishop has had her hung as a warning to all witches. It seems the COG wants all witches to leave Benito soon," Alford hastily explained.

"We took care of the bishop though," Abby declared. "Sorry, we were too late to save Alita."

"Oh dear god! It's finally *really* happening," Inez cried out, her hands holding her head as if in disbelief that this could actually be happening.

"I suggest we all get together at one place, in case more trouble comes," Alford suggested. The three witches decided that was a good idea. Hastily, they put a closed sign in their shops and headed on down to Drina's Herbs. Her three children were standing on the porch looking at the confusion on up the street.

"What's going on up there?" asked a worried Elena.

Inez suspect the ten year old probably already had a good idea.

"They've hung Alita. The damnable COG bishop actually hung her, Elena. We best get inside and close up the shop for today. It isn't safe out here on the streets right now, honey. I brought Benita to play with you today," Inez replied.

Her daughter was good friends with Elena and Benita said, "This is really bad, Elena. Come on. I'll tell you what I saw!" Naturally, Felipa and Emilano also wanted to know too, and they followed behind the two ten year old girls, as they dashed inside.

"We'll stand guard," Alford suggested. He and Aiden took up positions around the front door, while the rest headed into the back living quarters in search of Drina, Ally, and Aurora. "This is going to get pretty ugly, I think," he added to his twin when they were alone.

"Yes, COG supporters are flooding in from side streets now, as well as more witch supporters. I think tempers are going to flare soon. Too bad those palace guards fled, but they probably were wise. That crowd got awfully riled up after the bishop got it," Aiden pointed out.

"Yes, it emboldened the witch supporters and enraged the COG supporters. Look, fist fights have already broken out," Alford indicated a scuffle not more than a block away. "Brawl time on Alcalde Calle. Sad, really," he added.

Inside in Drina's living room, Aurora apologized, "I am so sorry. I ought to have used my gift and foreseen this happening. I've been focused only on learning from Drina. I'd best use it now." She closed her eyes and drifted a little towards the future.

A while later, Aurora returned to the present. Sometime must have passed, for it seemed a little darker than it had been. Aiden and Alford were sitting close to her. "It's not going to be safe for all of you and all the other witches to stay here much longer."

Inez interrupted her. "How do we know what she says will be the future? Isn't this sort of making your own ideas of the future come true? I mean, she tells us it isn't safe and that we should leave. So we do, but how do we know that things might be different if we stayed? Can the future she sees be changed or is her future absolute? What do we know about her gift?"

Aiden wanted to jump to her defense, but restrained himself. He knew nothing about such things. He only said, "We make our own futures."

"I don't know the answers to all of those, Inez," Aurora replied. "I know what I have seen before has come to pass. I don't know if anything I see can be changed or not. I did foresee you would ask me this. So I've decided to tell you about several separate 'events.' We can see if they come true and perhaps if what I saw could be altered."

Inez grinned, "Aurora, I like your answer. I half expected you to say something like 'I am never wrong.' She is speaking the truth. Okay, challenge accepted. What have you seen?"

Aurora smiled; she'd already seen Inez would accept this. "First, later tonight, someone is going to take Alita's body down and bury it. After that is discovered, COG supporters are going to set fire to her shop. It burns down, and the shops on either side get damaged. A week from now, the bishop is going to finally be laid to rest in a lavish ceremony, lavish from my point of view. I don't know how funerals are done here in Trujillo. After that, the angry COG supporters are going to rampage down Alcalde Calle and try to bust into another witch's shop and hang her as well."

"We must prevent another of us from being murdered," interrupted Drina, knowing her three fellow witches wanted to know, which witch would be threatened. "Can you see who it is? Identify the shop someway? Maybe we can figure out who will be in danger."

Aurora complied, and the four worked out who she was. Inez vowed to see that future got changed! She then continued. "I looked at two possible futures because of something else I saw long before we even came to this kingdom." Aiden looked up; she'd not mentioned this before. Inez also noticed his surprise.

"I wanted to see if such a thing was even possible. It is. I decided I wanted to see what would happen if we did nothing, if you did nothing. You know, stay here in Benito. It is grim.

The COG supporters and your supporters fight it out; the COG ends up burning down this whole section of town, and so many witches are hanged that I couldn't keep them all straight, but all four of you were hanged, that I did see. That won't happen for at least two more weeks."

"Second, when I had my first visions, we were all terribly worried about the aliens, the Rigels, now they have a name. I saw the COG had pretty well eliminated all the witches in Bettingham and many other kingdoms as well. However, I saw our group forming a new group that will stand up against the Rigels, the kings, and the COG, and somehow win, to save all the people on Tierra. I am not sure saved from what, though. That part is very confused. Anyway, in that vision, I saw our group had many other new members, who I did not know or recognize back then. I was a little surprised when I met all of you. You four are part of that group. I think you four are supposed to be returning to Bettingham with us to help fight against tyrant kings, the COG, and the aliens."

"Okay, we best hurry up and eat. Supper is getting cold," Drina said when she finished. "We can talk about this over diner."

"What? How did it get so late?" Aurora asked.

"Dear, you were 'gone' for almost four hours," Aiden teased.

"Gosh! I thought it was mere minutes," she said, flushing slightly.

The others discussed what she'd seen while they ate. Alford was all for cutting Alita's body down and giving her a proper funeral, making that part come true.

"We should go to Alita's place and get what is valuable out of there before it gets burned down," Inez suggested.

Thus, Aiden, Alford, Inez, and Isabel headed off to see what could be done at Alita's shop and home. Adam, Jordan, and Abby took up defensive positions, protecting the other three shops. Meanwhile, Drina and Ernesto began serious discussions about what they should do.

"I love you Drina — you and the kids. If the COG is intent on wiping out you witches, we have to get you somewhere that's safe," he pleaded.

"But this place you've fixed up for us, me and the kids — we can live properly here. If we go to a normal home, you know we four are going to be so helpless. I can't put such a huge burden on you. I love you too, Ernesto, more than anything. I'd cry constantly if the kids and I had to have you do everything for us. Surely, we can find some other way. Maybe her visions are not always true. Maybe they can be altered," Drina suggested. She wanted this to be so, and also knew Ernesto wanted it as well.

"Everyone we know is here. Where could we go?" she added.

"I've a cousin who lives about fifty miles north of here on a farm. We could go there. I can build you and the kids a new house. There's your aging parents too, but they are in the city. Best not go to them. What about your uncle in Carcacion? Maybe he'd take us in, until I can build us a new place," he suggested.

"We've been married eleven years, honey. It took you nearly two to get this place fixed up properly," she countered.

While they were discussing their plight, the four reached Alita's shop. Even on the dark street illuminated slightly by the oil lanterns some distance away, they could see Alita's body was gone. Someone had beaten them to it. Somewhat surprised, Inez led them to the rear and unlocked her mentor's door. "Pull all the shades. Keep lanterns low. We don't want to arouse suspicions," Inez ordered. The two women knew precisely where Alita kept her valuables. Inez quickly found her precious psi-crystal, still in its bag, where she'd purposely dropped it when the soldiers came for her. Inez tucked it away and continued searching. Before long, the two men were loaded up with a number of sacks. Then, the two headed into her shop and returned with another pair of bulging bags. "Okay, we're done. There is nothing of any great value left in here."

Outside, she locked the door, and the four headed back to Drina's. There, the men discovered the bags contained nearly four thousand silver coins, which Inez divided up four ways among Alita's coven members. All were very pleased with the inheritance.

The next day, Aiden and Alford spent their time out on the streets, seeing if they could prevent Aurora's vision of the devastating fire at Alita's shop. They moved firefighting water barrels closer to her shop. They checked on the availability of men to respond to fires and so on.

Later that afternoon, the expected fights broke out once more, and someone torched Alita's Herbs shop. The fire had been set. Immediately, Alford and Aiden called everyone's attention to the blaze, literally forcing the men to stop fighting each other and to pitch in to put the flames out. When the fire was finally extinguished, only the front part of the store had been damaged. The heavy fire damage, which Aurora had seen, had been prevented. Around the supper table, everyone was excited about this aspect. What she foresaw could be altered; that gave them all some comfort.

Inez visited the witch who was supposed to be hanged next and tried to convince her to leave or stay elsewhere until things cooled down. The woman refused, "This is my home, my city too. I won't be driven out by ignorant COG supporters!" Inez begged and pleaded with the stubborn woman who refused to budge.

"Well, how about coming by for dinner with us?" Inez tried a different tack with the forty-five year old widow.

"As long as you don't serve fish," she answered. Inez grinned and settled for keeping the witch from her shop-home around the predicted time.

While they were all eating and chatting, they heard a wild commotion from the street outside. All rushed to take a peek. A large mob had congregated several doors down at the very woman's shop. After the ruckus died down, they all went to see what had happened. Her shop had been ransacked. Someone had made an effigy of her, and it hung from the front of her shop. A placard around its neck urged all witches to leave Benito or be hanged. Shocked, the woman decided to flee to her sister's in the country.

Back inside, the group took tea to discuss this event. "Well, it looks like what I see can be changed," Aurora declared. "That is something; it's not absolute. What a relief. Now what are we going to do next?"

Many ideas were floated about, but no real decision was reached, save all planned to leave the city before the end of the week. There were the children to consider, as Inez pointed out. The next day, many other witches dropped by to ask Inez, Isabel, and Luisa what they planned to do. Exodus became the rule, and some even packed up that very day, leaving Benito by the north road.

At last, Ernesto put his foot down. "Okay, Drina, I, and our children want to live. We aren't going to stay here any longer. I've thought long and hard about this. I don't care what happens to me, but Drina has a hard life to lead, harder than any of us. If there's a chance she can live in safety with our guests in their kingdom, I aim to take that chance. We're going to pack up and go to this Bettingham place."

He added, "It doesn't make sense for us to pull up stakes and move say fifty miles out of town. Sooner or later, the COG is going to find us and force us to move again, at the very least. If Aurora's visions are accurate, then, with them, my Drina has the best chance to live. I've made up my mind, Drina. We're going to this Bettingham, though I have no idea where it is." He sat down and crossed his arms. Drina had seen that expression before and knew he had made up his mind. No matter what else was said, he'd not budge, not ever. He was like that, a stone mason, solid as the very stone he worked. It just took him a long time to make such decisions.

"We will need a lot of wagons," he admitted. "Might I beg you men to lend me a hand driving some wagons?"

"Absolutely, Ernesto. Count on us," Alford replied, looking at the pleading man and his family. How could they not assist him?

"Okay, okay. We'll go too," Isabel sighed. "Besides Luisa and I want to meet your sister and her lover too."

Sammy grinned. "I think they would like to meet you as well." The two mates chuckled. "So when do we go?"

"We have a week, if Aurora's predictions hold. We should obtain the wagons and teams, and get what you want to take with you packed into crates," Alford took charge. "How many of you have ever driven a team of horses?" The answer was what he'd expected. Other than Ernesto and a surprising

Sammi, none of the others had. "Okay then, we have to get everything into six wagons plus our carriage. Thanks Sammi," he gave her a nod.

"Well, I have to, since I'm married to a hot traveler," she teased Adam, who grinned, proud of his new wife.

"We women will take care of the camping duties, cooking, washing, and such. We have to do our fair share, Alford," Inez said sternly. "We can donate funds for the purchase of the wagons, teams, and crates, but can we leave the getting of them to you men?"

Thus, the division of labors began. While the women set about packing crates with the possessions they most desired to bring with them, the men helped Ernesto begin to dismantle his specially built kitchen. Obviously, Drina and the kids would need this setup once they arrived at their new home, wherever that may be.

Interestingly enough, more and more wagons began appearing near other witch's shops. Inez soon realized most all the witches on Alcalde Calle were getting out. The situation was too fraught with danger to remain, though their customers began showing up and begging them to stay. "Who will help us when we get sick or break an arm?" For days, the four heard similar pleadings at least five times a day. They did at least sell off most of their normal supplies, though. Inez figured her loyal customers would have enough to get them by for a while. She also urged them to seek out other witches, perhaps in nearby towns and villages.

A month after they arrived in Benito, the group made their exodus. Sammi drove the carriage bringing up the rear. Alford drove the lead wagon, followed by Aiden with the next. In case of trouble, Ally insisted on sitting beside Alford. "Look, if we get accosted, I can handle it for us. We have to get everyone safely back, and there are over three thousand miles to go."

"Well, I admit, I'm going to enjoy this, having you by my side to chat. So do you like to dance? I've heard all courtly women are into royal balls and all that finery," he replied, as they left the wide gates of Benito behind them, heading east along the coast road.

158

She laughed, "Well, if you must know, yes. Those few times, I was actually somewhat happy. Honestly, living in the castle with my sadistic father was awful. Only at the rare dances could I relax a little. He couldn't beat up on mom or us kids during those public times, you see."

Chapter 10 The COG Makes a Play

The forty-three year old Archbishop Mata Hatta bowed before his Golden God statue in his private rectory, his Planning Room. He felt having a statue of his god watching over his decisions would help him make the right ones. He'd put on a little weight since his attainment of the COG's highest, most holy position, some ten years ago. Already, he'd been able to get many of his Holy Pronouncements implemented worldwide.

Backing him was the simple fact perhaps half of the people of Tierra were followers of the COG. That there were virtually no other gods to worship never factored into his thinking. Parishioners gave him power, and he fully intended to use it, for the betterment of the people — at least his concepts of betterment.

Witches. Until now, Archbishop Mata saw them as the antithesis of his COG. They believed in the forces and powers of Nature, not those of the divine God. Worse, they had the following and backing of a large number of people, second now only to the COG. Why? They cured people. That they also did other actions were of little consequence as far as the Archbishop Mata was concerned.

Early on, he saw for the COG to continue to grow and prosper, they had to take on the single action their competitor did: healing. Hence, he founded the Medical Academy here in Valcia. After studying for two years, a man would then be certified as a COG doctor. That their methods of treatment worked poorly, if at all, was of no consequence. Besides, by their own statistics, one in five was fully healed as a result of the treatment. No one ever took the time or had the curiosity to study the interesting fact that one in five would get well no matter what the treatment actually was. Bloodletting, bleeding out the illness, was one of their pat solutions. If a limb was severely wounded, chop it off. Crude methods. At this point in time, the year 1000, over two hundred COG certified doctors plied their trade among the kingdoms.

Now, it was time to make the big push to remove all the

unholy witches from Tierra. Hence, he'd issued orders to his fifteen Bishops to begin to request their kings take overt actions against them. Wisely, he suggested they go after the older, more powerful and influential witches first. Thus far, the results seemed promising. He had the results from Bashir first, since his Holy City was in south-central Bashir. Now, word reached him from neighboring Bettingham and Pinewood. He was most pleased to hear their kings had begun to drive out all the witches in their capital cities. His grand plan was working to perfection, and he waited patiently to hear from the other dozen kingdoms, though it would be months before he got word from the northern kingdoms. It took nearly that long just to get his dispatches through.

His next phase involved setting up free schools for the male children, where they would learn from priests the word of God, along with the ability to read and write. Of course, the priests would only teach them what was officially sanctioned by the Archbishop. None of this freethinking, no blind experimentation. No, the young minds would learn to pray properly, to work hard, and to support their local church with undying devotion. By doing only this would their precious souls be granted the right to enter God's Kingdom of Heaven, when their mud body died.

Then came the bad news. King Aaran Wycombe had been assassinated in his own bed! After reviewing all the information at hand, namely next to nothing, the Archbishop issued a Holy Proclamation, declaring the king had been assassinated by unknown witch or witches in retaliation for his driving them out of Wycombe. He had their local Bishop Gil Granville and Bishop Galen Heath of Wyth post copies of said proclamation, and to preach for three Sunday Services on this topic. He also issued private orders for Bishop Gil to get close to Norwood, as he would be the logical successor.

No sooner had he sent out these orders than word reached him of the landing of the aliens! Suddenly, his methodical, orderly world, his voluminous plans — all were being tossed out of the window! Who were these aliens? He prayed to his Golden God, thanking him that the locals had not begun to call these aliens from the sky "gods!" He at least felt he'd received a huge break on that point. However, the power possessed by these aliens was almost incomprehensible. He knew half of the population of Tierra would be looking to the COG for guidance and explanations of these aliens.

Thus, he had little choice but to make the two thousand mile trip northwest to meet with these aliens personally. Mata Hatta was a shrewd judge of people. He had not gotten to his position without that skill. He knew he needed to speak personally with the aliens. Hence, in late June, he began his long trip, thankful it was at least summertime, when such a long trip was bearable. Still by Holy Coach, it took him fifty days to reach them, arriving in the last week of August.

Now, it was a day later, and he was beginning his fifty-day homeward trek, the meeting had lasted but perhaps an hour! Still, he had an excellent memory and the time to reflect upon his meeting with the aliens, who called themselves Rigels.

It had not started off on the right foot. After barely being able to get the heavy carriage to the top of the plateau, they had encountered some kind of force screen, which sounded an alarm and prevented them from entering the relatively flat plateau area proper. He, the Archbishop of the entire worldwide COG had to wait, like some common courtesan! A soldier in a dark green uniform eventually came, and he'd had to identify himself. Well, he'd done that satisfactorily.

"I am Archbishop Mata Hatta of the Church of God, which is the largest worldwide organized religion on Tierra. I represent nearly half of all the people on our world," he said both a little pompously and somewhat didactically. He added, "I demand to see your leader or, if you have none, whoever is in charge." That had done the trick.

"I wonder now how they could understand our language," he said to the air beside him in his carriage, as they rolled along going back down the mountainside. "I missed that detail. The soldier understood me and I understood him. Interesting."

The soldier did speak in some utterly unintelligible language before he replied, "The governor will see you. If you will follow me." Argh! The archbishop actually had to walk over a mile to get to the silver buildings! He was not allowed to bring his coach or other personnel with him. While he'd been a bit unnerved about it, he walked as upright as he could, having no intention of showing these aliens that he was weak.

At least, he was able to get a good look at these strange facilities. He saw what must be their mother ship, a huge silver flying machine. There were dozens of smaller flying machines, a few taking off and a few arriving during his long walk. In addition to the silver buildings that he was taken to, there was another facility, quite unlike this one. Pipes and cylindrical tubes ran in several directions into and out of the strange shaped, silver building. Currently, some kind of light ash was drifting out over the plateau, though it didn't seem to bother his breathing as smoke might have done. Perhaps, he thought, as he reflected on those images as he was returning home, this was their form of smoke from their "fires."

"Ah welcome Archbishop. I am Governor Andrzej Bohater. My assistant, Cezar Gerwazy. My Ministers of Native Relations and Social-Anthropology, Luiza Lina and Dita Ewa. Come, this way to my meeting room," the tall, thin man said, shaking his hand. All these aliens looked similar to him. Seven feet or more in height with almost emaciated bodies, they had olive colored skin and the strangest coal black, yet shiny, hair and eyes. Well, they are aliens, he justified.

After being seated at the large chrome-plated table and offered a glass of water, which he accepted, Governor Andrzej asked, "So tell me, what exactly is this Church of God of yours, and why have you chosen to visit us?" The governor was once more a little annoyed that he was being interrupted from his afternoon nap at this time. The thin air of Ashford-5 took some time getting used to, he felt. Still, the man across from him was probably an important one, based on Dita's suggestions.

"The Lord God created all of us, and he looks over our souls. We of the COG preach and teach the Holy Words of God to all our people on Tierra that they may purify themselves of evil, wicked thoughts and actions. By following the Holy Laws of God, their most precious souls can then go the God's Holy Realm of Heaven when their fleshly, earthly bodies die. It is the duty of the COG to teach the heathens the Holy Word of God and to help them to prepare and organize their lives so that their most precious souls can be received unto Heaven when their bodies perish. Surely, you also worship the Lord God," the Archbishop hinted.

The governor didn't. He thought, *Ah, more of this religious mumbo jumbo. Superstitious primitives.* He asked, "So when you observe something you cannot understand, you assign that to God's Will?" he asked, remembering something Dita had once tried to explain to him about what to expect from primitive cultures. They'd had this discussion while en route here; the briefing was a requirement of the Imperium.

"Yes, governor. Many things happen that can only be the action of our Lord God above. It is not ours to decide whether such is good or bad, only to accept Lord God's Divine Holy Will. Is this not the case with your people?" he'd answered and probed a little.

Governor Andrzej bit his lip. He wanted to reply, *We fly among all the millions of stars in the galaxy. There is no such thing as God. No one has ever seen such a being. It is all merely the Laws of the Universe at work. Man's task is to learn those laws and to make full use of them as we spread civilization far and wide among the galaxy.* Recalling Dita's strong admonition not to say such a thing, he did not. Instead, he asked, "What is it that you wish of me? My time is precious, and I have much work to be done."

Archbishop Mata didn't like his non-answer to a direct and fundamental question. However, he stifled his rising anger and replied. "As the worlds most revered Holy Messenger and Servant of the Lord God, I came to find out your purpose in being here on Tierra. All people everywhere want to know that. Are you also God-fearing people, honest and faithful, or are you spawn of Lucifer, the devil? Are you here to enslave us or help the COG rescue the souls of men? Already the COG under my direction has nearly wiped out the wicked, evil witches, the Lucifer spawn, who use the disguise of healing people as a means to spread their insidious ways among the common man. We have highly trained doctors from our Medical Academy, who are now going forth throughout Tierra, healing the sick and injured properly. I am about to embark on a huge mission to provide free schools for all our male children, that they may learn to read and write the Holy Word of the Lord God, that they may learn right from wrong so that their precious souls may earn the right to enter Lord God's Holy Heaven."

The governor had heard enough dribble. "Yes, yes, all that sounds fine. I am an administrator. My job is to run this facility and see it produces the proper quota of fuel. Nothing more. That's why I have others here with me who are trained and most competent to deal with the kinds of issues that most concern you. Cezar, Dita, I believe this is in your areas of specialties. I will leave the Archbishop Mata Hatta in your care. If you will excuse me, I have a spaceport to run." He rose and unceremoniously left the room.

Dita saw that the man was becoming both alarmed and angry over the governor's seemingly callous ignoring of his questions and purposes. She jumped in to smooth the archbishop's emotions. "You must forgive our governor. He really is a bit overworked these days, what with getting this new facility here up and running. He is under a crucial deadline. Now then, I am sure I can help you with your many questions, and Cezar and I can find ways that you and we Rigels can work best together to achieve our common, yet different goals."

As the Archbishop reflected on the conversation, he realized that this Dita was very competent and quite understanding, something in which the governor was entirely lacking. Dita continued, "Let me begin by explaining our purpose here on your world. It has a valuable mineral known as psi-crystal, which for us and our advanced technology can be refined into fuel, which we use to power our many spaceships. We will soon be turning this plateau into a refueling port and a refinery for turning the raw psi-crystals into our fuel. The governor is paying local miners in gold in return for their mining the raw psi-crystals for us, though in time, we will have automated mining machines going as well to ramp up production of the most needed fuel."

"We are members of the mighty and vast Imperium,

which now controls thousands of planets throughout the entire galaxy. However, other than the obtaining and refining of these psi-crystals, we have no other interests in Tierra. None with your people. We do not intend to interfere in your society or the ways in which you chose to operate."

Cezar interrupted her, "Unless your people interfere with our production of the fuel, mind you. That is the only thing we cannot allow to happen. You can understand that right?"

The Archbishop acknowledged that point. It seemed harmless enough. Dita then went on with her explanations. "You asked about our religious beliefs. I put it to you this way, Archbishop Mata, but we believe a person's religious beliefs are a very private matter to each person. Thus, we do not impose upon one another to even ask about them." She thought this was a polite way of saying there really wasn't any such person as the Lord God, that this was just a superstitious being to which and upon which primitive man could assign all his travails and life's seeming unsolvable mysteries.

The archbishop accepted her explanation. Cezar, however, asked, "That being said, perhaps there may be some ways in which we Rigels here may be able to assist you, Archbishop Mata Hatta." Cezar looked at Dita and Luzia. To his two fellow ministers, he said, "I believe you are both finished with the Archbishop Mata, since you've answered all his questions. If you two will excuse us, I would like some private words with the good archbishop here, religious matters, you see."

Dita knew she was being summarily dismissed and didn't like it. However, as the governor's second in command, she had no choice but to obey him. Her status was only one step above the lowest, that of Luzia, Minister of Native Relations. Luzia wanted to protest, but caught Dita's frown and desisted. Both women rose, shook the man's hand, and left the two men alone.

"What's Cezar want with him?" asked Luzia. Dita shrugged her shoulders; she had no idea. "Well, I am going to see Andrzej about this! After all, the Minister of Native Relations ought to be present at all times, just in case my

166

services are needed." She stormed off to find the governor.

Cezar, embolden by his many mind wipes of the enemy soldiers, wanted more subjects on which to experiment. "Now then, perhaps there may be ways in which we Rigels may be able to help you achieve your most honorable goals for your people of Tierra. Let's take these unholy witches. Tell me about them. What is it that they do that is so wicked?"

Finally, the archbishop thought he was getting somewhere with these aliens. Dita had indeed calmed him down. He launched into a lengthy explanation of their wicked conduct. Cezar reasoned this man did wield considerable worldwide power, and it would be ideal to have him firmly in their camp, so to speak. Secondly, this offered him a great research opportunity. He had many theories of the human psyche he would like to test, though he knew he'd never be allowed to experiment on Imperium citizens. Primitives, well that was an entirely different manner, especially since the governor had abolished the prime directives of the Imperial Directive #5.

Cezar listened to the archbishop's explanation of the witches. This seemed a perfect situation for his experiments. "I believe I may be able to help you with this problem of yours. Rather than simply killing them, which, as you have pointed out, often makes martyrs of them, inciting others to riot, I believe I may be able fundamentally to alter their behavior to that of which you would be proud. Tell me, what ought to be the ideal way you believe your women should think and act?"

Archbishop rapidly rattled off various opinions, which Cezar jotted down, though Archbishop Mata thought it looked more like chicken scratches than proper writing. Apparently satisfied, Cezar then coyly said, "Would you allow me the chance to show you what is possible for us to do for you?"

"Of course, of course, but I don't quite know how this may be possible," the archbishop recalled his response. Here riding back to his Holy City in the comfort of his Holy Carriage, in hindsight, he realized this had been the most critical of his all responses to the aliens. True, what happened after that was terribly frightening, awesome, and nearly beyond belief. Yet, the results! The results! This had to be Lord

God's Divine Will in action!

Cezar took Archbishop Mata outside to his private flying ship. Before long, the church leader was flying over the countryside, watching the kingdom of Bettingham moving rapidly past the strange viewing screen, some kind of window, he'd assumed. They quickly arrived over the town of Wyth. Why this town? Bishop Galen Heath had sent in his monthly reports on the witches of Wyth. Many had moved here from Wycombe, when King Aaran had begun driving them out by having the most influential witches hung. Setting that example had worked. Many fled to Wyth, the second largest city in Bettingham. One of those who fled was Barb Weston. She'd been quite outspoken against the king and the COG. In his report, he identified just where she'd resettled, opening up another herb shop.

It took a little time for Cezar to locate the woman and her shop. Just how he managed to do this, the archbishop had no idea. Fifteen minutes later, Cezar found the woman's shop and her as well. "I will transport her into my ship and use our technology on her. Then, you may take her back with you to see fully just how effective our alterations of behavior actually are. Or after you examine her, I can return her to this town." He activated his machine, and the thirty year old woman was teleported from her herb shop into the bowels of his ship, confined to a metal chamber which apparently had no exits at all. Inside her shop, her customer merely saw the woman vanish completely!

Cezar then adjusted numerous controls, and Barb was immersed in a powerful, white energy field. Her mind was flooded with intense pain, and she wasn't aware that a robotic arm came out of a concealed compartment and injected her with a drug. Barb only sensed a huge, overwhelming mental mass of grey filled with an almost unendurable pain. Above all this, a bellowing voice began speaking. The words were Cezar's best guess at what was needed to make the proper behavioral modifications Archbishop Mata desired.

"A woman should always be subservient to a man. A woman should always do what a man asks of her. A woman exists to bear and raise a man's children. A woman exists to take care of a man's needs, always putting her needs behind those of men and children. A woman should obey the Holy Laws of Lord God and of the COG. You will repeat these words many times a day."

Over and over, those words were repeated, lodging them solidly within the massive combined pain and drug mental mass within her mind. At first, Barb tried to fight it, but quickly her will was totally overcome, for the pain, the drugs were far too powerful. She finally slumped, accepting the words. Cezar had no actual idea just how long he needed to subject the witch to his therapy. She was his first experimental subject, after all. He left the woman have it for fifteen minutes, before he ended the spoken words and injected the counteracting drug. Satisfied the drug had been neutralized, he turned off the energy field. Barb slumped down, holding her head in her hands.

She moaned a little, "Who am I? What's happened to me? Where am I?" Before she could even begin to think of answers, she found herself saying, "A woman should always be subservient to a man. A woman should always do what a man asks of her. A woman exists to bear and raise a man's children. A woman exists to take care of a man's needs, always putting her needs behind those of men and children. A woman should obey the Holy Laws of Lord God and of the COG. You will repeat these words many times a day."

Barb then cried out, "I am, I am! I will, I will! A woman should always be subservient to a man. A woman should always do what a man asks of her. A woman exists to bear and raise a man's children. A woman exists to take care of a man's needs, always putting her needs behind those of men and children. A woman should obey the Holy Laws of Lord God and of the COG."

Cezar then said, "Shall we go see how effective this has been? Let us see how well she now satisfies your criteria." He led the archbishop the short distance to a concealed door and opened it. There was Barb, sitting on the metal floor holding her head and chanting the words that Cezar had installed in her. She looked up and saw the archbishop. Although she had never met the COG leader, she recognized his purple robes, which meant that he was at least a bishop in the Church of God.

"My Lord! How may I serve you?" Barb found herself saying, bending down and kissing his feet.

Archbishop Mata was shocked at the change in her behavior. He made numerous requests of her, from licking his feet clean to other actions, including those of a sexual nature. At last, he was completely satisfied. She was now behaving like his idea of a model Holy Woman. "Cezar, this is indeed a Holy Miracle. You are definitely sent here to do our Lord God's Holy Work!"

They decided to return her to Wyth. Archbishop Mata would soon be sending Bishop Galen a critical message asking him to watch Barb Weston and report on her behavior each week. After depositing the confused Barb back in her shop, they returned to Plateau Grado.

"Okay, archbishop, I will give you time to monitor the subject's long term behavior. If it meets wholly with your satisfaction, then we can begin to implement this more broadly. Now all I ask of you is this: let's keep this between you and me, shall we? I don't want to bother our governor with such matters that are best left to men such as ourselves."

"I wholly agree. The governor appeared to care less about such things. I am humbled to be in the presence of one of Lord God's Holy Servants, which you surely must be, Cezar." Even reflecting as his carriage rolled on downhill, Mata Hatta agreed with Cezar's view and fingered the small device in his hands.

"Here, take this signal device, Archbishop Mata. See this button here? After you are satisfied our methods do indeed work, or if you find that you wish additional alterations, then simply press the button once. It will send me a private signal, and I will come to you as soon as I am free. I look forward to working with you, Your Holiness, in making Tierra a Divine Planet, filled with those worthy of reaching Lord God's Holy Heaven," Cezar tried to recall all the special words the overly plump man had used, hoping he put them in the right order and context. *Primitives and their superstitions,* he thought to himself. This had been nothing but a simple mental implant that he'd done on Barb Weston, though its effects would be neither simple nor transient, he sincerely hoped. Well, she was his first test subject. In time, he felt confident he could improve the treatment.

The archbishop wrote out a very lengthy dispatch for Bishop Galen Heath of Wyth, Bettingham that evening and had it sent off immediately. By the time that he finally entered his rectory in Valcia, he ought to have some of the reports there waiting for him, since official messengers traveled far faster than his lumbering Royal Coach. Now, he began to reflect upon just how he could proceed with this wholly unexpected avenue to turn the heathens of Tierra into Holy Children of Lord God. His mind raced down many paths.

After the archbishop left, Dita confronted Cezar. "Just what did you two do? As your Social-Anthropologist, I need to know, if I am to ever be effective at my job."

"I am the Psychman. What I do is none of your concern. He is one of the more powerful primitives, even if he is so utterly ignorant. I merely am ensuring he will not only give us no trouble, but will support us, as the governor wishes. Nothing must interrupt our refueling station."

"Well, I won't argue against our prime orders, Cezar, but anthropologically speaking, I do need to know what you did with him." Dita refused to give up. She disliked the man and distrusted him, but perhaps the two went together.

"Well, if you must know, I took him for a short ride in my ship, showing him a bird's eye view of the lands around here. He was most impressed, I might add," Cezar replied a bit sarcastically, as if even deigning to speak to Dita was somehow beneath him. He turned on his heels and left her standing just outside the barracks doors. *I do like how she looks when she is frustrated,* he thought to himself, a mischievous grin on his face, which she could not see.

Dita thought, *Well, he's lying about something. He's only told me a partial truth.* After she'd seen them take off in his ship, she had gone to the ship tracking station. She'd monitored their flight and knew they'd hovered for nearly a half hour over the Bettingham town called Wyth. What had they been doing there for that long, she wondered? Wyth was just another non-descript, primitive town with little to call attention to it.

Dita decided to do a little investigation of her own. After all, if Cezar did *more* than just give the archbishop a little flight tour, then whatever he did might seriously impact the Social-Anthropology of the primitive civilization here on Tierra, something she was dead set against, in spite of Governor Andrzej's abandoning of the Imperial Directive #5. *I'm going to have to do some fieldwork among these primitives; I can see that now,* she said to herself and entered their residence complex of silver buildings.

The middle of September, Archbishop Mata Hatta's ornate carriage finally rolled into his Holy City, Valcia, Bashir. Home at last, after over a hundred days on the road, the archbishop was tired and more than ready to stop traveling! If he never took another long trip like that, he would be a happy man. He hated to leave behind the comforts of his beloved Valcia. His carriage rolled up to his rectory, and he gladly climbed down, waving off the many priests and servants who came scurrying out to greet him with their well wishes and welcome backs. At last, he graciously accepted them and then headed to his chambers.

After a long overdue bath, he sat down at his business desk and looked through the mountains of accumulated dispatches, documents, and letters that had accumulated during his three month absence. He collected together those from Bishop Galen Heath of Wyth, Bettingham. Travel by dispatch rider was significantly faster than by Royal Coach, primarily because he had to stop at acceptable inns along the way. His dispatch riders rode long and hard days, covering many more miles each day. He spotted two recent dispatches from Bishop Galen, one was dated a week after his experience with the witch Barb Weston. The second came a week later. Judging by the dates on the dispatches, he also suspected another one would be arriving within a few days.

He hastily tore the first one open and read Bishop Galen's report. He found the news to his liking. Barb Weston had closed her Weston's Herb store. Apparently, she had forgotten all about her witch skills, and she no longer even knew one plant from another. Bishop Galen wrote, "She now spends her days walking the streets of Wyth, speaking out loud to everyone she sees. Over and over, I've heard her tell others, 'A woman should always be subservient to a man. A woman should always do what a man asks of her. A woman exists to bear and raise a man's children. A woman exists to take care of a man's needs, always putting her needs behind those of men and children. A woman should obey the Holy Laws of Lord God and of the COG.' She also stops nearly every man she encounters and who will listen, asking him if there is something that he needs or something that she can do for him. If they say no, I swear that her face becomes incredibly downcast. Further, she comes to every mass now. This is truly a Divine Miracle."

Archbishop Mata smiled and opened the second dispatch. The following week's report was quite similar. She continued to beg men to let her help them in any way possible. More than once, Bishop Galen had seen her perform sexual acts on a man just to please him. Well, thought the archbishop, that might not be quite the right thing to do; yet she was pleasing men and doing right by them. He read on.

"This week, a number of her fellow witches caught up to her and took her away. I followed them discretely. I believe they attempted to figure out what caused this Divine Miracle in Barb Weston. Later, Barb left them, and I caught a glimpse of the other witches. They seemed horrified, if that is the proper facial expression. Barb was un-phased by whatever the witches did or said to her. Clearly, Lord God's Holy Work cannot be undone by mere Lucifer-spawned witches, Your Holiness."

Archbishop Mata laid the dispatch down and smiled broadly. The results were beyond his wildest expectations. He'd anticipated hearing the witch was slowly returning to her wicked ways. So far, there was not the slightest indication that would happen. "Well, it has only been a couple of weeks. I ought to withhold my final opinion for a while longer."

It took Dita a few days to make the necessary preparations for her first field trips out among the primitives.

First, she needed to fabricate a few of the silver coins the primitives used as a means of exchange. That done, using the cover story that she needed to acquire the proper apparel to be worn to the Royal Ball that King Norwood had promised to invite her to attend, Dita took off in her private shuttle craft. No sense in hiding her destination. Anyone could track her ship's path on the security monitor back at the base. She went directly to Wyth and did an aerial survey, trying to locate the spot where Cezar had hovered for a half hour. She had little luck; the town layout seemed random and yet uniform in its randomness somehow. She landed her ship just outside the town. After disembarking, she pressed her security button, and the ship's entrance was sealed. Only she could get back inside. She then activated her personal defense shield, otherwise known as the PDS. Confident now that none of these primitives could physically harm her, she waved at the small crowd who saw her ship landing and had come to have a look.

Dita found the men, women, and children were quite curious about her. More than one remarked about her height and weight. They seemed friendly enough, and she headed into Wyth proper, strolling along the main streets, looking at the various shops. How quaint, she thought, impressed with the wide variety of items that could be purchased here. True, she was frequently stopped and asked many questions. "Are you really an alien? How come you are so tall?" Those were the most frequent questions, and she answered them as best she could. In turn, she asked about where Cezar's ship had hovered. Slowly, she focused in on her destination. The closer she got, the more specific the men and women were about the location of Cezar's ship overhead.

At last, she approached Barb's Herbs and More. Several women were trying to obtain some of the witch's cures, she noted. However, Barb seemed distant and confused. "I'm sorry. I don't know which herbs do what. I don't think I can help you women. You see, a woman should always be subservient to a man. A woman should always do what a man asks of her. A woman exists to bear and raise a man's children. A woman exists to take care of a man's needs, always putting her needs behind those of men and children. A woman should obey the Holy Laws of Lord God and of the COG."

Dita thought her speech a little strange and was surprised to see the other women reacting as she did. A middle aged woman in a rather nice cotton dress walked up to her. "Excuse me, but what have you aliens done to poor Barb Weston here? Oh, mind my manners, I'm Vivian Waters, a friend of Barb's — well I used to be a friend, at least I was last week. Something has come over her. She is, well, I don't know how to put it. She's totally a different person now. She keeps going on about how women are subservient to men and all that Church of God crap. Honestly, how those COG men could ever dream up such dribble is beyond me. They must be off their rockers."

"Off their rockers? I'm sorry; I am not familiar with that expression. I am Dita Ewa, by the way."

"Oh mad, insane. Please to meet you Dita. My, you are as tall as they say you aliens are," Vivian replied, eager to chat with Dita herself.

"Rigels. We call ourselves Rigels, not aliens. I suppose I should say how come all you on Tierra are so short." Both women chuckled at that.

Dita asked, "When did Barb begin acting so strangely?"

"Well, that's not totally clear to me. So many things are not clear to me, you see. But I do believe it was that day when one of your flying machines was above her shop over there for some minutes. Now, I cannot honestly say for sure your people had anything to do with poor Barb's insanity. You are not connected to the Church of God. No, I cannot see you could possibly be connected with them. Dear me, something awful really has happened to Barb. She was a witch, you see."

"Oh my. Say, I am afraid I know so very little about your people. Pray tell, what is a witch? What does she do? Cast spells and such?" Dita inquired, gaining valuable insight into the primitives whom she was studying.

Vivian laughed. "So like the men and the COG. Cast spells, ha. Far from it, Dita. A witch merely knows the forces of Nature. Which plant can help cure which disease, which rash. She knows how to make potions to aid healing. She knows how to set broken bones and to heal terrible wounds, quite unlike those so called doctors that the COG is foisting off on the kings. Why, do you know those doctors have only one cure for everything? Bloodletting. Make the patient bleed, and the infection comes out with their blood. How utterly ridiculous. Now, any witch worthy of her name can actually heal their patients. I bet you have marvelous doctors too, right?" Vivian carefully avoided any hint she knew how they had healed Ally and Aurora.

"Yes, we certainly do at that. Bloodletting? How awful! Such barbaric methods," Dita replied, honestly. She was shocked at the primitive methods being used by these so called doctors. Well, that fit with what she'd seen during her first encounter with the primitives and their two women whose hands had been cut off. She recalled just how nicely their arms looked after Doctor Zosia finished healing them. Too bad the governor could not be convinced to give them prosthetic hands. Understandable, though. They were expensive and might well be needed for themselves. Mining accidents were commonplace.

"Say, is this your first time in Wyth? Perhaps I can help you with something," Vivian suggested, eager to pump Dita for more information.

"Well, perhaps you can at that. You see, King Norwood of Wycombe has promised to invite me to one of his Royal Balls, and I don't have a clue what apparel I ought to wear to such an affair," Dita replied.

"Well, you've certainly asked the right person. Come on. I'll take you to a pair of the finest dressmakers in Wyth. They are friends of mine and about your age, I expect, if you look your age. I can't tell with Rigels, never having met one before. Now Roxane and Sable will certainly know how to doll you up for a king's ball, if anyone does. This way." She led Dita on down the street while continuing to chat. She sensed no danger whatsoever from the alien woman.

"Roxane and Sable are mates, you see," Vivian explained, not wanting Dita to discover this later and become alarmed about it. "For reasons only known to men, women are not allowed to 'marry' women, only men. Silly rather, don't you think. A person ought to be with the person they love.

Well, men don't allow other men to marry men either, so I do guess that part balances out. Anyway, the two women, Roxane and Sable, are just about the best dressmakers in Wyth. When they get done with you, why, you will be a knockout at the ball."

"Excuse me, knockout? I don't want to be harmed," Dita said, a little confused by the unknown expression.

"I'm sorry, a smashing success, the prettiest woman at the ball, the woman that everyone wishes she could be like, you know, the greatest, a knockout," Vivian explained. "How do your people view women mating with women?"

"Oh, we are quite tolerant of one's sexual preferences. As long as they love each other, no one minds at all, though same sex unions are rather rare. Obviously, they cannot procreate."

"How true! Anyway, here we are," Vivian replied. Dita had to duck slightly to enter, for she was taller than the door. Inside, she had a little headroom, thankfully. Vivian introduced her to the long haired women, the redheaded Roxane and the blonde Sable. Both young women were elated to have Dita visiting their shop. Now they could boast that the aliens visited here. When they learned what she wanted, they were extraordinarily pleased! That they had made dresses for the aliens would double their business — both anticipated. For an hour, the two fussed over Dita, trying to match her perfectly with just the right colors. Her olive colored skin and coal black, yet shiny long hair and intensely black eyes required just the proper selection of colors to bring out Dita's inherent beauty, or so Sable claimed. At last, they decided on a bright red satin-like gown.

Next, they took Dita's measurements and were a little dismayed at the smallness of her bosom. Nevertheless, they guaranteed Dita that her dress and outfit would be ready within a week, but she would need to return for a final fitting and adjustments. "We want you to look absolutely perfect at the king's ball. It is *the* event of the year in Bettingham," Sable explained. "Everyone who is anybody will be there. When they see you, wow! They will be very much impressed, Dita." Her enthusiasm began to rub off on Dita, who enjoyed the two women hovering over her appearance. She sensed they wanted nothing more than to make her look good.

After promising to return in a week, Dita finally left, and Vivian accompanied her to her ship, still chatting. However, Vivian had the good sense to back away as the ship lifted upwards into the sky.

Dita now had many field notes to jot down and analyze. While much was very pleasurable, this secret business of Cezar's was not. Barb Weston had all the signs of having been altered somehow by the Psychman. Had the Imperial Directive #5 been in force, she could have had him up on charges and, at the very least, sent home. Now, her hands were tied. What had he done? Why? Would he do this to others? If so, why? What had the archbishop to do with all this? Why was a witch chosen? Poor Dita had so many unresolved questions that her mind spun that night.

She knew one thing. More field research was definitely needed if she were to obtain answers. Dita resolved to leave no stone unturned in her quest to find out. She trusted Cezar even less than before.

At the base, she simply could not gain access to Cezar's lab, though even if she could sneak a look, she doubted much of his equipment would mean anything to her. He was the Psychman, not she. A Social-Anthropologist just didn't have this kind of training. Then, she got a bright idea. The cargo manifest. This was available to her, and she spent hours each day going over the extremely lengthy list, copying off items, which she thought might possibly belong to or be assigned to the Psychman or his assistant and wife, Jolanta. Eventually, one item caught her attention, asylic acid. "What's this?" she whispered. "It's a psycho tropic drug. He's got a huge quantity of it. Curious indeed. Wait, in this liquid concentrated form, he'd need to inject it. Ah, a vast supply of needles. What is he doing with this large an amount? I am on to something, but what?" She continued her search.

Days later, she found a retrofit order. Cezar had his private shuttle in for a "retrofit." The order didn't specify what was done or what was requested, only that the request and work had been done back on Rigel-3 before they left to come to Ashford-5. What was he planning on doing? He had enough of the asylic acid to turn half of Tierra's inhabitants into mindless zombies. Why? Had he suspect that the primitives here would pose a serious threat to the mining of the psi-crystals? How absurd, she thought; their personal shields would stop any weapon the primitives possessed from even scratching them. The Drugi had the latest in Imperium weapons. The more she learned, the less any of this made sense. Still, there was nothing illegal about any of the supplies he had brought with him.

The week was up, and Dita decided she'd about exhausted all avenues here at the base. It was time to go back to Wyth for her new dress and undergarments. Perhaps, she could learn more of what Cezar's plans were by examining the field, that is, the primitives. She landed her personal ship where she had before and headed into Wyth. As before, she was greeted by friendly, if curious, faces. A few recognized her from her previous visit, and they waved and said hello as she passed them. Dita found this rather pleasant — to have people whom she really didn't know giving her a friendly greeting. That was never done on Rigel-3, where, when out in public, people kept their feelings to themselves. Here, life was so open, she noted.

"Ah, good afternoon Dita!" Roxane exclaimed, genuinely glad to see her again. Dita's heart raced a little; she didn't know why. "Your dress and outfit are ready for your final fitting. Let me get Sable, and we'll get you fixed up."

"All these parts?" asked Dita, rather amazed at all the pieces of clothing that somehow would form her final look. Roxane giggled and began to educate Dita on the details. Of course, Dita had to strip first, giving a curious Roxane and Sable a look at her body. Dita suddenly realized these women were looking to see if her female body differed in significant ways from theirs. All three women were pleased that it didn't. It took Dita nearly an hour to get properly dressed in her new Royal Ball gown. Twirling around in her hoop skirt before the dual full-length mirrors, Dita was quite pleased at how she did look.

"Amazing, simply amazing. I do look good, don't I?"

Dita admired her new look.

"Like we said, you'll be a knockout at the ball. All eyes will be on you, that's for sure," Roxane replied.

"Wait a minute! I don't know how your dances are performed!" Dita suddenly realized the fatal flaw in her plans. She'd look elegant on the dance floor, but then would ruin it by not having a clue of how their dances were done.

Sable laughed, "Well, that is easily fixed. We know a couple local musicians. Roxi and I can teach you, if you can be here evenings."

Later, Dita approached the Minister of Native Relations about her plan to spend a week off-site with the dressmakers in Wyth, reputedly to learn the forms of native dance. "I need to be prepared when King Norwood sends me his invite to their formal dance," she explained.

"Oh, I agree. We must take that opportunity to blend in with the primitives, gaining more of their trust. I back you one hundred percent. Come on; let's clear it with the governor," Luzia enthusiastically supported her idea. Luzia did most of the talking to Governor Andrzej, convincing him of the vital nature of maintaining good relations with their nearest king, and he agreed, allowing Dita to remain off-site for a week, though he did ask her to check in daily.

Late that afternoon with bags in hand, Dita walked into R & S Dressmakers. "Ta da. I'm yours for a week. Where should I stay at night? I supposed I should stay where visitors would normally stay." Dita wanted to appear as much as a native would. She had been taught an anthropologist must blend in with the local culture as much as possible.

"If you want to blend in, you ought to wear one of our cotton day dresses, like most women of Wyth wear," Sable suggested.

"Dear, the inns are filled to overflowing with all the war refugee women and children who were displaced," Roxane pointed out to Sable. "Perhaps, Dita ought to stay with us."

"Hey, terrific idea. Yes, you simply must. Getting a room right now is going to be tough. We've plenty of room, a spare bedroom no less. Plus, after the dancing lessons, you can just hit the sack."

"Why would I want to hit a bag?" Dita asked, again slightly confused.

"Sorry, slang for going to right to bed," Sable replied. "While we are working during the day, you can wander the town and visit the many shops. If you get too bored doing that, why we can give you sewing lessons."

"We'd better get her a cotton day dress whipped up fast," Roxane teased.

Around ten the next morning, dressed in a white cotton dress with flowers embroidered on it, Dita stepped out of the back of R & S Dressmaking shop, where the two women lived. She noticed she did blend in much better. She began strolling, but headed more or less to the witch's shop, Barb's Herbs. She fully intended to meet with Barb and see if she could work out what had happened to the woman to cause her apparent huge personality shift.

As she approached, she noticed another of the COG men idling around just across the street. He was definitely watching Barb Weston, Dita noted. Further, he was not very good at disguising his purpose. From his robes, she made the connection to the archbishop. For some reason the COG was plainly interested in this woman. That pricked Dita's interest. She strolled up to him.

"Hello. Forgive me, sir, but are you with the Church of God?" Dita started the conversation.

Evidently, he was most pleased to talk with her, an alien, she guessed. "Why yes, yes I am. I am Bishop Galen Heath. I've heard much about you Rigels. Pleased to meet you, miss."

"I'm Dita Ewa. I thought so. A few weeks back, I met with an Archbishop Mata Hatta, who came to visit us."

"Ah yes. I must say our COG leader has been most impressed with all of you. I see you are now wearing our women's dress. It does look far better on you than the green uniforms we've seen before."

"Yes, and more comfortable too. Say, isn't that woman one of the witches I've heard mentioned who live here?"

"Yes and no. Yes, she was most definitely one of those wicked women who had made so much trouble that she had to leave Wycombe and come here. Now, however, she has totally changed. Look there at her shop. It is empty; she no longer practices her vile witchcraft. Now she is a model COG woman, doing her best to serve man."

"That is good, then, that she has changed her ways?" Dita suggested, probing for more information. Naturally, the bishop definitely agreed. "Please, I am not too familiar with your ways and culture here. What exactly is a model COG woman? What is it she should do?" Dita figured this might cause the bishop to talk more freely and it certainly did.

Bishop Galen simply could not resist her request to know more about his religion and the roles of men and women. Once started, he chatted for quite some time. "Men, naturally being the stronger and brighter and wiser, lead in all areas of life, you see. The role of a woman is to be a silent, ardent supporter of man and his endeavors. She should think not of herself but of men and our society and how that she may best serve them. For does not the man provide for her support, her care, her home, her food, her clothes? In return, the woman maintains the man's domicile, bears his children, cares for them, cooks his meals, washes his clothes, cleans his house, and provides for his every sexual need. A woman should always be subservient to a man, you see, doing always whatever a man might ask of her. A woman exists to take care of a man's needs, always putting her needs behind those of men and children. Further, it is our belief that a woman should obey the Holy Laws of Lord God and of the COG as well."

He was about to elaborate further, when he stopped to point out, "Look there, Barb is now doing what a good woman who is not married ought to be doing for men, though she ought to be doing that inside her home and not in public. Excuse me, I ought to really go insist that she take him inside. Children should not be seeing this." He nodded to her and stepped across the street moving rapidly. As Dita watched, he carefully moved the two inside her shop out of sight from the street.

That's utter rubbish and totally disgusting! The witches are far better than these supposedly holy COG men and bishops, Dita thought. *It's just like men to think they are the center of the universe. I wonder if the basic nature of all men in all societies is the same? Governor Andrzej is much like this primitive in his views of women. No, wait a second, some men are and some are not. Trouble arises when the wrong men obtain power as the COG are doing here. So why would Cezar be wanting to give the wrong men more power here on Tierra? I need more data. I'm going to have to talk with Barb. Best wait until she is done with that man, though. Disgusting.* She waited. The bishop left the area after shooing the couple inside, and Dita strolled the street, though keeping an eye on Barb's door.

"Hello," Barb said very politely. The man had left, and Dita quietly entered. Barb's eyes looked a bit glazed, but her facial expression suddenly changed; her hopeful look replaced by a more somber one. "Oh, you are not a man. We women are supposed to serve men, to help them, and to satisfy their needs. Are you one of us Holy Women too?"

"Not exactly, Barb. How come you stopped helping others with your herbs and potions? This used to be your shop. At least the sign says so," Dita probed gently hoping for more clues. The asylic acid might cause huge behavioral changes, but its use would have to be continuous, probably on a daily basis. She saw no signs of its use, no needle injection points. Cezar had only brought the concentrated liquid form of the psychotropic drug, not the usual daily pill form.

"Women don't help other women, silly. We are here on Lord God's Tierra to serve and help men in any way that we can, in any way that a man needs us. They have strong sexual needs, you know, that only we women can fulfill. I try to do my very best so my precious soul can go to God's Heaven when I die. Do you do that too — strive to be your best for men?" Barb asked genuinely interested in her reply.

"Oh yes, I always try to do my best," Dita answered, but didn't quite finish her sentence on purpose. Hence, she had not lied to the woman.

"Then, that is good, very good. We women must serve our men, always you know. They come first above all else. Well, then so do children, if we have any. I don't have any yet, which makes it easier for me to serve men. Do you have any children to serve?"

"No, I am not yet married," Dita replied truthfully. Just now, she certainly didn't want to either.

"Well, then that's good too. You can help me serve the men. There are an awful lot of men on the streets. Have you noticed all of them? It is hard for me to help all of them; there are so many of them, and we must serve them at all times, though I wish I could get some sleep once in a while."

"Haven't you gone to bed at night?" Dita began to wonder if Barb was up all the time.

"Well a little, usually after midnight. No men are on the streets that late, but then I have to be up at the crack of dawn to be on the streets here to help any of the men who may need assistance," Barb replied cheerily. She had heavy bags under her eyes, and Dita could easily see she was considerably behind on her sleep.

"Well, you know Barb, if we women don't get our full sleep, then we are not at our best to help the men. I think maybe you should get more sleep so you can do a better job helping the men," Dita played to her aberration hoping to make small dent in it.

"I suppose that's true, but then my own needs are totally secondary to those of the men, you see. It will just be my cross to bear in life. Oh, there goes another man. He looks like he may need some help. I simply must check on that. I don't want to fail in my duties as a woman of the COG. You can come with me if you like," Barb suggested.

"Oh, I am afraid I must go help another man just now. Been nice talking to you, Barb. See you later on," Dita replied and headed the opposite way as Barb, who rushed up to a stranger and began begging him to let her help him in some way.

As she walked along, Dita felt disgusted and repulsed. What had Cezar done to this poor woman? It was as if he had somehow brainwashed her completely. The Mind Wipe machine would not account for her behavior modification, Dita estimated. Its purpose was to erase memories. Criminals often underwent that procedure as part of their rehabilitation.

Also, those in top secret positions also were Mind Wiped when they left that post. Hence, there could be no security breaches. Since Barb clearly had many of her memories intact, Dita ruled that device out.

Suddenly, Dita recalled something Governor Andrzej had said at their first meeting, just before touchdown: *bring them to Cezar for Behavioral Modification or a full Mind Wipe, if needed. Behavioral Modification! That has to be it!* Unfortunately, Dita knew next to nothing about this branch of psych-medicine. She couldn't discuss this outright with Cezar, but she could take a backdoor approach and chat with his wife, Jolanta. She was his assistant and certainly would be well versed on Behavioral Modification. Now she had a plan.

The seven evenings spent with Roxane and Sable learning to dance well were the happiest times in her life. Dita was accepted by the two young women as an equal and not as the outsider, the alien that she was. Never before had she so thoroughly relaxed and just enjoyed herself and the company of these two women. Certainly, she had never ever felt this way on her home planet Rigel-3, not even as a little girl. *How peculiar and strange,* Dita thought as she headed back to the base.

When she arrived, she found huge signs saying Anastazy. Carrying a large bag with her two new dresses in them, she asked, "What?" as a security man came over to latch down her ship.

"Governor Andrzej's orders. He's decided our spaceport and refinery here needs a name. It's called Anastazy now. Get used to it, Minister," he chuckled. Dita didn't see what was so funny, though. Why call this place Resurrection?

After stowing her dresses, she reported to the governor, who plainly didn't want to hear her report. "Just write it up, and send me a *short* memo on it, please." Dita turned on her heels and left. She did just that, filling her week's report. It read: Spent a week in the primitive's town. Met natives, talked a lot. Lots of goodwill established. Dita. "Well, I hope that is short enough for him!" she thought as she filed it from her computer. Now to find Jolanta.

As she joined the woman for lunch in the cafeteria, she

had the awful notion, *What if Cezar has used his Behavioral Modifications on her? That would be blatantly illegal,* she countered. Still she could not get that notion out of her head. She sat down beside the young woman who was four years older than she was. Jolanta had filled out, something Dita's body would be doing soon. Rigel-3 women's reproductive systems were not fully developed until around twenty-six years old. Their breasts were the last to develop, and Jolanta's had definitely developed. Dita realized she was particularly flat compared to Jolanta.

"Hi, I heard you had to spend a whole week out among the primitives. How awful that must have been for you, Dita. Bet you are glad to be back here among intelligent folks once more," Jolanta suggested.

"Well, it is my job. Have to take the good with the bad," Dita replied, sizing up Jolanta. How could she tell if Jolanta had undergone Behavioral Modification?

"Yes, I suppose that is so. You'll never catch me out there among the filthy primitives."

"Say, the primitives do have so many strange behavior patterns. They make an interesting Social-Anthropology study, but I got to thinking about your area of expertise. Since the governor has relaxed the Imperial Directive #5, could we use Behavioral Modification on the primitives?"

"Oh sure we can do that. If the primitives pose any real threat to our mining operations, then we are authorized to use it."

"I'm sorry. I don't know a thing about your area. Is such a thing permanent? Or does the effect wear off in time? I do know mental cases have to take their meds daily or their unwanted or undesired behavioral patterns return," Dita probed a bit.

"Oh, you are confusing med-suppressants with Behavioral Modification. Most people do have them completely confused and mixed up. No, we don't have any of the med-suppressants with us. If troubles arise, there's no way we could see each patient got and took their daily meds to keep it at bay. That's out here on Anastazy. Say, don't you just love the name Andrzej picked out for this place? Anyway, we'll use true Behavioral Modification here if something comes up. Its results are permanent."

"Oh, so it is like when a primitive culture discovers fire or the wheel. After that discovery, there is no going back?" Dita asked.

"Rather similar I suppose. Your wheel thing — that would affect their analytical thinking, which would keep them from retrogressing back. Without Behavioral Modification, we don't have any way to analytically change their notions of proper behavior," Jolanta explained, taking another long sip of her strong coffee. "Take a child molester, for example. You can talk until doomsday telling him how wrong and devastating his perverted actions are on the child and the society, but it will accomplish nothing."

"Oh, I see. How can you then change his behavior?" Dita asked, having perfectly manipulated Jolanta into telling her what she wanted to know.

"We implant the proper conduct modes into the other mind, the person's reactive, stimulus-response mind. This mind is wholly beyond the person's control and is probably what is driving him to do his perverted actions with children, you see. The science of Behavioral Modification then attempts to lay in the correct behavior patterns into the person's reactive portion of his mind. Of course, the real trick is to lay in an implanted behavior, which has more force and control over the person than the reactive behavior that we want him to cease doing. Now that is the real trick, you see," Jolanta smiled, satisfied with her layman's explanation.

"Oh, I see, I think anyway," Dita feigned a bit of confusion. "So how can one possibly do this to the child molester? How can anything be so powerful as to override his drive to harm the children and prevent him from doing it?"

"That's the trick all Psychmen have been trying to solve, you see. Behavioral Modification is still in its infancy. Now you take my brilliant husband, Cezar, for example. He's already worked out a really effective way to administer an effective modification. Of course, it's still in the experimental stage, but I expect he'll publish a paper on his findings once we all get back to civilization. He's the most brilliant man I've ever known, intelligent, kind, generous, thoughtful, considerate, honest, thrifty, and brave. He really is all that and more!"

Dita noticed her eyes glazed over briefly as she rattled off this absurd bit about her husband. That look was the same as she'd seen in Barb Weston's eyes. Dita suppressed her shock and gag reflex, smiling instead. "I'm sure he is, Jolanta. You are lucky to have him for a husband." Jolanta looked very pleased by her comment.

"I must admit, all this reactive mind stuff is beyond my area of study. If one is not aware of it, how can you implant something there, if you can't see it? Sounds like an impossibility to me," Dita attempted to set Jolanta up to feed her more details.

"Yes, that is the trick, since you can't see what's there, you have to estimate how powerful it is and design the implant to be even stronger."

"So you have to hit them really hard, like with a hammer or wrench?" Dita asked.

Jolanta laughed, "No silly. That's barbaric. No, we use a combination of electronics to deliver the pain and asylic acid to form the base upon which to lay in the proper behavior that we seek. Perfectly harmless to the patient. That's important. We certainly don't want to physically harm our patients, now do we?"

"Oh I see. How humane! Forgive my ignorance, Jolanta. You certainly are in a most interesting field."

"I should say so, well, I have to get back to my duties. Catch you later on, dear." Jolanta left, and Dita remained, sipping her coffee. She'd been without any brew for a week now. The primitives had not yet discovered coffee but drank tea instead. Dita missed her strong black coffee.

She thought, *Pain and drugs. So that's what he's done to Barb Weston. I wonder how something like that can be undone?* She had no answers to that one.

Later that day, she ran into Jolanta in the hall. "Say one quick question about what we were talking about at lunch. Can you erase one of your implants if it doesn't work quite right, like you wanted? You know, the child molester now begins to molest young women instead?" Dita asked.

Jolanta laughed, "Don't be silly. If it could be undone, it wouldn't be an implant, now would it? No, if it doesn't work quite right, we just have to lay in another one, more powerful than the last and get the wording said properly, that's all."

Dita went her way, rather depressed. Then, there was no hope for Barb Weston, unless somehow Cezar gave her another implant more powerful than the first one. How could he possibly restore the woman to her previous personality and mental state? Dita began to see how insidiously awful this Behavioral Modification actually was. Yet, there was nothing she could do about it. The governor had ordered its use here on Ashford-5 on an as needed basis. Perhaps, she thought, this was merely an isolated test case Cezar had done. If so, perhaps she could ignore it. She hoped so anyway.

The first of October, Archbishop Mata Hatta pressed the signal button, summoning Cezar to Valcia, Bashir.

Chapter 11 Fall Events

"I take it the Behavioral Modifications are to your liking?" Cezar asked. He began with his verification question. *Always a good place to begin,* he thought, *get them agreeing with you.* He'd just arrived at the Archbishop's Rectory in his Holy City, Valcia. The homing beacon he'd installed in the hand-held signaling device he'd given Archbishop Mata Hatta worked perfectly. He was a little impressed with the magnificent marble columns and architecture of this giant complex. Perhaps someone around here was not so primitive after all. He'd been warmly greeted by the slightly pudgy man and taken into his private chambers. Plush. That was Cezar's opinion as he stepped inside. All manner of personal comforts were here, including super-soft, sofa-style chairs. For a minute, he admired this man's lifestyle, but that was only a fleeting notion.

"Yes, my oh my, yes! Brilliant, Cezar, positively perfect! Every report from my bishop has been stellar. She has had no regressions, just an absolute perfect model of a truly Holy Woman of the Church of God. Now then, you mentioned the possibility of — how should I put this?"

"Ah, you would like far more recalcitrant women handled as this one has been?" Cezar interrupted him, in the form of a question, though spelling out exactly what was wanted. Cezar hated to waste time, especially on primitives. His work was far too important to squander precious hours bandying words around.

"Yes, to be quite blunt. As you may know, these evil witches are found all over our world. I would like to setup a routine conversion of all of them to Holy Women. Of course, if we can come to some amicable terms," Archbishop Mata hinted. All this would be fruitless if Cezar demanded too high a price.

Cezar wanted people on which to experiment and perfect his technique. However, he realized the archbishop would get suspicious if he charged nothing for his miracle cures. Besides, there was always the damnable governor hovering in the background. He'd already worked out his price. "For each woman I cure for you, I only ask you send an able-bodied miner to Anastazy to help us mine for the psi-crystals. He will work for a year, but you must provide his pay. Oh, Anastazy is our name for our installation there on Plateau Grado. How does that sound to you?"

Archbishop Mata could not believe this magnanimous offer! Total cures for the COG's worst enemies and all the man wanted was a simple laborer for a year's service. "I accept wholeheartedly, what a grand gesture on your part. I am truly humbled." The two men shook hands and got down to the details of how this project could be handled.

The witches were fairly uniformly scattered across the fifteen kingdoms of Tierra. This created a logistical mess for Cezar. He was unfamiliar with the primitive's towns and kings, for the most part. He made the suggestion, "Look. Why don't you have one of your bishops round up say two dozen of your witches and hold them at a known location. Once they are all there, then signal me. I will provide you with fifteen of these signaling devices. I can handle no more than two dozen in one day. When the devices are activated, I will come and perform the miracle cures, but I may be delayed a few days because there is no guarantee five of your bishops might signal me on the same day. Of course, the bishops should have the two dozen miners ready to be sent to Anastazy at the time they signal me."

"That is easily arranged. When I send these devices and my orders to the various bishops, I can assign them a specific day to signal you. I'll try to space them out every other day. Expect then a batch from each kingdom every month until at last all the wicked, devil-spawn witches are no more," the pontiff replied quickly analyzing the situation.

"That would be most satisfactory. I assume your messages may take several months to reach the more distant kingdoms?" Cezar asked.

"Yes, unfortunately that is true. The dispatch riders will take two and a half months to reach the most distant kingdoms. This will spread out the workload for you. Again, I am eternally in your debt, Cezar. Such miracles you create.

Lord God must certainly grant your soul into Heaven one day."

Cezar wanted to laugh his head off. He knew very well there was no such thing as a soul, only these bodies and their minds. Minds, he could now control utterly and via their minds, their bodies. All this was just superstitious rubbish, but he forced himself to keep a serious mien. They talked further, and then Cezar took his leave, laughing wildly for five minutes, as he flew his private shuttle back to Anastazy.

Hastily, Archbishop Mata began writing the most important fifteen dispatches of his career. He spelled out precisely what each bishop was to do, utilizing whatever means they could pull together to abduct these witches and hold them for their miracle cures, and then returning them to their homes. They were to ensure any families they might have that the witches would be return to them wholly unharmed. Once he was satisfied with the letters, he summoned the dispatch riders and gave them their orders and packages to be delivered into the respective bishop's hands only.

Next, he issued another COG order, demanding another five hundred men be found and admitted into their Medical Academy. He needed to begin supplying the much needed doctors to replace the pagan cures foisted off on the people by the witches. While it would take time to train these new doctors, it would also take time to rehabilitate all the witches. His goal was to have doctors ready to take their positions by the time all the witches had undergone their miracle cures. Finally, satisfied his planning was complete in this arena, he started work on his COG School project.

Back in Wycombe, Bettingham, King Norwood finally got his rule firmly established. He cast aside all those whom his hated father had hired, from aides to guards, forcing them all to reapply for positions. He refused to take back on any of the aides, however. His brother, Palmer, became his top advisor. At this time, Palmer was the only person in the castle he trusted, besides his childhood friend Captain Able. Together, they handled the massive reorganization.

It had not been hard to find the thousand men to begin mining operations for the Rigels. That had been easy; many soldiers wanted that job, terrific pay and no danger. Other soldiers, he formed up into two new armies. One would be composed of pike men and archers. The other would become cavalry, once sufficient horses could be acquired. Each would have a thousand men in them.

The remainder of his soldiers he formed into work groups and sent them to rebuild the destroyed hamlets and villages of north central Bettingham. Estimates suggested nearly five thousand were homeless and being cared for by relatives in unaffected towns or by the common folks of neighboring villages. Wyth alone was busting at its seams with well over a thousand staying there, homeless and jobless. So many were women and children that King Norwood had to take swift action to rebuild the hamlets and villages, and certainly before the late fall came. His objective was to have these displaced people in new homes by the first frost. If not, he would have to oversee a vastly different distribution of the fall harvests, sending much more into the towns that were supporting them from their own stores. Palmer pointed out that by doing this, even more people would be solidly behind their new king who was demonstrably different from their previous tyrant King Aaran.

He had not forgotten his sisters and mother. His messengers to Wyth failed to locate Ally, and he resigned to wait until she contacted him. Surely, she would soon see conditions were vastly different now and that it would be safe for her to reappear. In August, his messengers finally located Misty and April on a distant farm. Misty refused to return to Wycombe; she was quite content to merely plant and raise flowers, which her relatives sold in Wycombe. April, on the other hand, had undergone many changes.

At first, she was terrified of her mother, who had admitted to murdering her father. April thought Misty had really gone mad. Yet, she dare not defy her mother and meekly accompanied her to the farm. During the long summer, she gradually got accustomed to farm life, free from the rigid court life she had known. She also met a young neighboring farm boy and had struck up a budding romance. When the messengers finally located them, April decided she was going to marry the lad and never again return to the palace or the court. In truth, she was still afraid one day down the line, she too would be forced to marry against her will, much as Ally had been. April wisely decided to leave the whole princess lifestyle behind her.

When the messengers returned with the news, King Norwood and Palmer accepted their decisions and left them alone to live their own lives. However, without women in the castle, the two brothers felt their distinct absence. Nevertheless, as the days passed, the two slowly got law and order restored to Wycombe.

Of note, Bishop Gil Granville didn't press his witch issues with the new king. Why? With all the war and bloodshed and the assassination of the king, he knew his new King Norwood was preoccupied with far more serious matters. Besides, he was not his father. Blackmail was out, and he had no real leverage to coerce King Norwood into going along with his proposed hanging of more witches. Rather, he visited Bishop Galen Heath in Wyth and personally observed Barb Weston. Like Galen, he was very impressed with the total behavior changes in the former witch. He began to suspect the Archbishop Mata Hatta might have a far better way to deal with the evil witches. Thus, biding his time, he merely continued to preach against the wicked witches. Many more did quietly depart the capital city, though. The hanging message came through rather plainly to many witches.

The last week of October, the fall harvest was pretty much finished. and King Norwood scheduled the Royal Harvest Dance for the evening of the 31st. He sent word to Dita, asking her politely to be his date at the ball. He left all the dance arrangements to Palmer, who truly enjoyed this task. A great dance had not been held for quite some time. His father's balls were always tense affairs; few truly enjoyed them. This time, things would be very different, Palmer promised. Indeed, many of the young women saw this as a golden opportunity to ply their charms on the two very eligible bachelors, hoping that one of them would get lucky and become a queen. He hired the largest band ever to play their traditional dance tunes. The Great Hall of the castle was decorated in fall colors with streamers and banners. Corn shocks and pumpkin displays added more color. While their father had been stingy on using their best ales and food stocks, Palmer wanted the best to flow freely that night. Again, he was thinking ahead: show the people times have indeed changed for the better.

At four, Dita carried her dress bags to her private shuttle craft. She wore her normal uniform. She felt too self-conscious to get fully dressed here on their base. The others would certainly raze her about going native on them. Still, her heart beat faster as she anticipated the ball. Within a few minutes, she landed her craft outside the castle. After she stepped out and secured it, King Norwood came running out to greet her. "Hi Dita. I am so glad that you accepted my offer! Come on, this way. I've set aside a room for you to change. Then, I would love it if you would dine with us before the dance. It will be just Palmer and us, nothing fancy."

"Sure, love to," Dita replied, her heart racing. Why was she so excited? She thought, *Perhaps it is because this anthropologist is actually going to be a part of this dance ritual of the natives. Could be a whole paper on it.* Somehow, that notion didn't seem to be it at all.

When Dita made her appearance in the Royal Dining Hall, both men gawked. "Wow! Dita, you look incredible!" Norwood was totally enthralled with her, and again, Dita felt emotions, she never knew she had, flowing through her whole body. She was pleased and enjoyed Norwood helping her get seated between the two brothers. They chatted and dined on roast duck. Around six, King Norwood, took Dita's arm in his. Although she was nearly a foot taller than he, it didn't seem to matter. "Time for us to make our formal entrance and get the dance started." Proudly, Palmer walked ahead of his brother, making sure the musicians were cued on the arrival of their king.

Over a thousand attended the ball. Men and women wore their finest and Dita noted that her bright red dress did fit in with all the other women's dresses, except that hers, perhaps, was just a bit finer looking. The place erupted into a loud round of applause as they entered, arm in arm, though the clapping didn't drown out the fanfare of the musicians. King Norwood spoke his prepared opening words, "Welcome one and all to our Harvest Ball. Tonight, we celebrate. The kingdom is at peace at last. Homes have been rebuilt for those whose establishments were ransacked and burned by our enemies. The harvest has been a good one. Finally, it is my great honor to have one of our Rigel allies with me tonight as my date. Let's give Miss Dita Ewa a warm welcome." She flushed as they did just that. "Let the dance begin."

"Wow, Dita, you are an amazing woman. You dance far better than I do," Norwood whispered towards her ear. He was simply too short to reach her ear without standing on his toes. She beamed with pride, but didn't tell him that she'd spent a week learning how to dance. As the evening progressed, she discovered she was often the center of many women's envious looks, as Norwood hung on to her arm, passing up the many opportunities to dance with other young available women. They latched onto Palmer instead. "I don't want to let you go," he added a bit later. She flushed, but knew that this must be heaven. She'd never experienced such happiness before and certainly didn't want it to end.

When midnight came and the dance came to a close, Norwood asked her, "How about a little snack? You are welcome to spend the night and fly back in the morning. It is awfully late and quite dark outside."

Palmer headed off with two young women, one on each arm, while Norwood and Dita, still holding onto his arms, headed for the pantry. "That was incredible fun, Norwood. I loved every minute of it."

"I bet you have even fancier dances where you come from," he replied.

"Honestly, no. Nothing we have can compare to tonight's dance. I've never had so much fun. Thank you for asking me, Norwood."

"Great. I loved it too. I'll let you know when the next one will be. How about a spring dance?" She smiled. As they snacked, he asked, "Say, among your people, do couples show affection for each other by kissing?"

"Of course," Dita replied, "do your people show affection for each other with a kiss as well?"

"You bet we do. Like this," he stretched up on his toes

and gave her a brief, but passionate kiss. Dita felt electrified; she'd been hoping for this most of the evening. She put her arms around Norwood and returned his kiss.

"I really am growing very fond of you, Dita. You are quite a woman," he whispered.

"Thanks, you are good yourself."

"I'd sure like to see you long before spring," he tossed out the idea.

"Same here. I will see if I can drop by more often. You don't mind if I just come by to see you, Norwood?"

"Not at all! Please, come anytime that you can. During the winter season, there isn't much going on around here. I'd love your company, Dita. You were the prettiest woman at the ball tonight."

"Well, certainly the tallest," she teased him.

"That too," he chuckled. "I suppose you are tired and need to have me show you to your room now."

Dita made an instant decision. Smiling, she said, "Sure, but it is a little chilly. I would love to have a warm body beside me tonight."

"You don't have to ask twice." He led her down the halls and up the stairs to the spare bedroom where she'd changed earlier. She then began passionately kissing him, and soon they laid down together.

Around ten the next morning, Dita gave Norwood a farewell kiss and stepped into her shuttle, momentarily lifting up into the sky. She punched her destination into the ship's controls, but adjusted the speed to Slow. She felt incredibly happy, peaceful, and satisfied, something she'd never felt before, and she liked it, not wanting it to end. As Anastazy came into view, once more, her cold, hard life began to replace the warm, comfortable feeling and she didn't like it.

On the fourth of November, Bishop Gil Granville of Wycombe met with Bishop Galen Heath of Wyth. He had to share the incredibly exciting news from their archbishop. Both men were well aware of just how well Barb Weston had changed into the perfect COG woman. Now, their leader had given them direct orders to gather up all the witches they could find and have them converted from Satan-spawn into well-behaved churchwomen. Their date to signal Cezar was the twenty-fourth of November and the same day each month after that, as long as they could round up more witches. That they also had to send off an equal number of men to become miners for a year was only of slight concern.

"Look, we can ask our congregation for volunteers. I'm sure we can assemble the men, especially since our church will guarantee them their pay at the end of their year's work," Bishop Gil pointed out. "Our real problem is one of taking and holding the witches until Cezar comes to work his Holy Miracles on them."

Bishop Galen asked, "We can't ask for soldiers from the king, can we?"

"No, I haven't any leverage, not like I had with his father, but I have another thought. If we can at least get the king's okay for us to take this action on our own, that is, to sanction it, then perhaps we can form up our own militia from our parishioners," Bishop Gil suggested.

"We can probably get enough strong men. Some really hate the witches and will be glad to lend a hand capturing and holding them, but how are we going to get King Norwood to not take action against us or even to sanction it?" asked Bishop Galen. "Is there something the king desires that we could give him?"

"I believe so. Look, he's had to dig deep into the kingdom's treasury to rebuild all the destroyed villages. Money. Let's offer him a thousand gold not to interfere in our efforts to reform the witches. We'll present it as a new church sanctioned reform program that will not harm the women physically in any way and that they will be returned on the twenty-fourth as well. I think he'll at least not give us any trouble over it. I've arranged to meet with him in two hours. Let's count out the gold and take it with us," Bishop Gil suggested.

"Welcome bishops. I haven't seen you for a while," King Norwood addressed the pair in their purple robes as they entered the throne room. "What can I do for you today?"

"Sire, we want to make a generous contribution to your

treasury for having so selfishly rebuilt all the villages destroyed by the cavalrymen from Rockton. We've gathered a thousand gold for you, our way of saying thanks," Bishop Gil replied.

Norwood wasn't stupid; he'd seen this man manipulate his father time and time again, often wondering what the bishop held over his father's head. Rather than accepting it, he asked, "And what am I to do in return for your generous gift?"

Shrewd man, not like his father, Bishop Gil thought. "We are about to embark on a new church sanctioned reform program in which we are going to reform the Satan-spawn, evil witches that plague our lands as well as all the other kingdoms. Our reform program will turn the witch from her evil ways into wonderful examples of Holy Church Women, women you and I can be proud of. We regret we did not have our reform program created months earlier and were forced to hang some of the witches. Now we have realized the errors of our ways and have created a way to do this without harming a single hair on their head. They will not be physically harmed in any way and will be returned the day their program is completed. However, we both know the witches will not come with us to be reformed willingly. We'll have to abduct them with a little force, but we'll not harm them in doing so, if at all possible. Rather the opposite, we want them to reform and become highly respected members of our society once more."

"So you want me to look the other way when you abduct these women, is that it?" Norwood asked.

"Yes, Sire. We don't want to cause trouble, just get these witches reformed so that we all can work toward the betterment of our kingdom," Bishop Gil replied, wondering if he might be pouring it on too heavy. Norwood was very astute and quick on the uptake, wholly unlike his father.

"Conditional approval, gentlemen. If I get too many protests from my people, I'll be forced to put an end to their abductions. If I don't get too many protests, then you may continue your holy works. That's the best I can offer. I have to report to my people. I can't rule effectively if they hate me, like my father did. His rule was that of a dictatorial tyrant. No one was sad to see him assassinated, and a good many cheered his death. Thus, I will pay attention the level of protests. Too many, and I'll have no choice but to put an end to it," King Norwood stated in no uncertain terms his view.

"That is only fair, Sire. We will be as judicious as possible about it. Again, you have our word they will not be harmed by the reformation process," Bishop Gil replied. Though they chatted a bit longer, only pleasantries were exchanged. It was clear to both bishops that King Norwood would be a tough one to get around, unlike his father.

Back at Bishop Gil's rectory, the two men worked out their first collection of women to be reformed. Both men realized the situation was troublesome. Their target was to remove as many of the witches from both Wycombe and Wyth as possible. However, already many had moved out of Wycombe. In time, the men expected to learn where the witches had now setup their shops, possibly in remote villages, they suspected. At this time, there were far more in Wyth than in Wycombe, at least as far as they knew from their parishioners' reported sightings.

They agreed to take Wycombe's few remaining witches up to Wyth and combine the two batches for this first reformation. After that, they would focus on Wyth and then the outlying towns and villages.

On the twenty-fourth of November, Holly Sprigs headed across town to help out her son, Dalton. His wife Sally was giving birth to their third child. She noticed a number of COG members on the streets, but paid them no mind. Soon, she was engrossed in the delivery. Dalton and Sally later had a little boy.

Wendy Lane decided that today was the right day to take Tammy to R & S Dressmakers to get her a new fancy dress. Tammy had turned nineteen and was filling out, perhaps a little too much for her current dresses. "Yes Tammy, today, the right thing is for us to go get you a couple new day dresses, a winter outfit, and that fancy party dress you've had your heart set upon for months now. Come on; we'll just leave the closed sign in the shop. It's nearly winter, folks can wait a while for their herbs."

"Really mom! Okay! Thanks!" Tammy gushed, excited

about the fancy dress. Ever since she saw how fabulous Dita Ewa had looked in hers, she wanted to have a similar dress. For weeks, she had been dropping hints and even outright begging for just such a dress. Now the boys would really notice her. Off they went, spending all morning getting Tammy properly fitted. She too wanted a red dress, but Sable pointed out it would clash with flaming hair. A light blue blended far better.

Sissy Skylar brought Clay's breakfast out to him in his blacksmith shop this early morning. He had a rush job to complete and had gotten up earlier than normal to get it done. Curt and Roni had just finished theirs and were off playing around the house. "Here you go big man," Sissy teased him.

He gave her a quick peck. "Thanks, lots of early travelers up and about this morning."

Curious as was her nature, Sissy took a short stroll to see for herself. "Those are COG members, I recognized five of them. I smell a conspiracy! I wonder what they are up so early for? It cannot be good, it never is. *Something* must be going on. I wonder what?" she talked to herself, pulling her hooded cloak over her head. Covered as she was, no one would really recognize her. Suspecting a big conspiracy of some sort, Sissy squeezed her psi-crystal in her pocket.

"My god! This *is* a conspiracy! They are after the witches of Wyth!" she gushed to the air around her. "Oh no, they are going to my place!" She followed them at a safe distance. One man, upon seeing her herb shop was closed, moved on around the corner to the blacksmith shop, which abutted the back of their home. The front was her herb shop. She followed behind them and crept to the corner so that she could overhear the men.

"Morning, Clay. Is Sissy around? There is an emergency out at the Brigs farm and they sent me to fetch her and her healing herbs," the man asked.

That can't be true, Sissy thought.

"Sissy? She was just here a while ago. Probably headed back to the house to open up her shop."

"No, the closed sign is still in the shop and no lanterns are on. Can you help?"

"Oh all right. I'm rather busy with this order. Come on inside. I'll fetch her," Clay replied, slightly annoyed at being interrupted. He and the man headed inside. Sissy slipped around to the other side and hid behind their rain barrel, which collected fresh water off their roof. Currently, it was empty, ready for the winter freeze. "Well, I really don't know where Sissy has gone. I'm sure she is just out on a quick errand. She'll be back shortly. Why don't you wait?" Clay suggested, returning to his hearth.

"No matter. I'll try another witch. Thanks, Clay." The man definitely looked annoyed Sissy was nowhere to be found. He left, joining several other men; all looked miffed and headed on down the street. Sissy snuck around the other side of their street and soon spotted one of them entering Vivian's shop!

The Waters family was just finishing their breakfast. Vivian and Finley Waters were discussing his having to haul a load of stone from the quarry to Randal's Polishing, where their son Ken worked as an apprentice stonemason. Valerie said, "Mom and I will watch the shop today." She was interrupted by a knock. "I'll get it mom."

The COG member asked the young teen who answered the door, "Is Vivian Waters here?"

"Yes, mom, some stranger is here asking for you," Val called out.

"Typical teenager, yelling instead of minding proper manners," Vivian said to Finley, who merely smiled. "Oh bring him back here. I'm right in the middle of something." She touched her psi-crystal. Why, probably it was Val's use of the word stranger. Vivian got a strong sense of immediate danger!

"Finley, something is very wrong here." She didn't get any further when Val brought the COG man into their dining room.

"Excuse me, but I was sent by Mr. Brigs. There has been an emergency there, a bad accident and I requested I fetch you to help," the man said politely.

"I don't know any Mr. Brigs. I recognize you; you are one of those COG fanatics," Vivian declared hostilely. The man whistled and five more men came barging into the home.

"What's going on here?" Finley rose, clenching his fists.

"Vivian, you are coming with us to be reformed. We will bring her back later this afternoon, unharmed," the man said.

"I'll do no such thing! Get out of my house!" Vivian hollered.

Finley and Ken tried to prevent the six men from snatching Vivian, but were overpowered and knocked out. Val jumped into the fray and received a solid back jack thump on her head as well, falling unconscious to the floor. They carried Vivian bodily out of her house, kicking and screaming.

Sissy saw them come out and realized they were abducting Vivian! She grabbed her psi-crystal and focused. *Holly! Emergency! Six COG members are carrying a screaming Vivian out of her house! No, I don't see Finley, Ken, or Val.*

I'm right in the middle of delivering a baby. Contact the others, get Clay and check on Finley and the others. Contact Wendy and Sheena too. Keep me posted. Holly broke the connection and continued helping Sally.

Sissy raced back to her place, being careful not to be visible to the men on the main street. A minute later, Clay picked up his heavy hammer, and the two dashed back over to the Waters' home. They found the three unconscious on the floor. While Clay carried them to couches and beds, Sissy tried to contact the others. Wendy was at the dressmakers and agreed to come over at once, then thought better of it. *Stay out of sight, Sissy, until these men are gone. Then we'll meet and see what we can do to rescue Vivian.*

Help, I've been abducted! They tricked me, Sheena responded to Sissy's telepathic connection. *We are in a carriage, tied up at the moment. Vivian's here too and several other witches. Now we are rolling. Contact me in a while, and I maybe can tell you where we are being taken. It's these despicable COG members, the fanatical ones!*

"They have Sheena too and a bunch more of us, Clay. I'd best see to their wounds. Thanks for getting them comfortable. Looks like they took a blow to the head," Sissy replied, having pocketed her psi-crystal for the moment. She dashed about the house preparing cold compresses. Then, she found the right herb and hastily ground it up. After mixing it with a little hot water, she held it before each person's nose, rousing them.

"My head!" Finley said as he came around, holding his head with his hands. "Vivian! They took her! We must get her back!" He sat up and the pain in his head throbbed wildly, forcing him to sit back down.

"You took a bad knock, Finley. Sit for a while and recover a bit. They took Sheena too and several other witches. Got to wake Ken and Val yet," Sissy ordered.

Clay said, "I'll go check on the Hilton's and see if they are okay. It's not safe for you to be out in the street, Sissy."

He returned a half hour later. "Well, the Hilton's are all fine. A man came to ask Sheena for aid, and she went off with him. The COG man said she'd be back later this afternoon. Hector is furious his wife has been abducted. He said if Sheena is harmed in anyway, he'd make the COG pay dearly. I've never seen him so angry. He's an innkeeper after all! Besides, he's been running at a loss since the summer, keeping all those women and children refugees housed and fed these many months, until they could move back to their new homes last week. Damn that church anyway."

"Well, they did say they'd bring mom back later this afternoon," Val muttered, holding her head too. "Then they hit me too. I wish I could hit them back!"

Clay added, "They are gone now. No sign of them on the streets."

"I'll make contact with Sheena and Vivian and see if they are still okay. Perhaps Sheena knows where they have been taken," Sissy said, getting her psi-crystal out once more.

Clay said, "Okay, while you are doing that, I am going to round up some friends. Perhaps, we can bust them out of wherever they are being held prisoner." He left to do just that. Once on the street, he saw one of the small alien flying ships descending just outside Wyth, close to the fancy new Church of God and Holy Rectory buildings.

When Sissy made contact with Sheena, she learned indeed an alien was with them. She could not learn more, because the alien took Sheena away, and she abruptly lost contact with her. *That shouldn't have happened,* she thought.

Sissy focused again and made contact with Vivian. Hastily, she broke the contact. Overwhelming pain and unconsciousness came flooding down her initial telepathic connection. Sissy was barely able to break it before getting slammed herself.

Clay, Hector, and a dozen other men, all armed with hammers, axes, knives, pitchforks, whatever they had at hand, returned. He said, "We saw one of those alien flying machines landing over beyond the new COG and Rectory buildings. This doesn't sound good."

"I know. I think they are being harmed, but I can't get through to either one of them. Sheena thinks they are at the rectory," Sissy replied, white with worry and a growing awful fear.

"If the aliens have them, we had best take a wait and see approach. The aliens could vaporize us in an instant," Clay pointed out. While none liked this idea, they all knew what had happened to the thousands of Rockton cavalrymen and their horses this past summer. A very tense bunch waited as the hours passed. Around noon, Holly and Wendy joined the worried crowd. Hector and some of the other men had gone home, hoping that their wives would be brought back to them unharmed as the abductors had stated.

Meanwhile, Dita had spotted Cezar taking off. She checked the sign out log. He had not listed he was taking his ship out. Only the governor and Cezar could get away with this flagrant violation of Security Protocols! She hastily signed herself out and raced to her shuttle. A few minutes later, she was hovering above the snow clad mountains out of sight of Anastazy. She checked her instruments and found his ship. Theirs were the only two shuttles currently airborne. She then trailed his from a safe distance. Before long, Cezar landed his just outside Wyth.

Dita made a decision. She had friends down there in Wyth, good ones. If Cezar was harming them, she'd raise hell with him. Meantime, she wanted to know what he was doing. Carefully, she landed hers on the other side of Wyth, close to the Bettingham Estate. From there, she headed into Wyth, shivering a little from the cold. She'd been so hasty in her departure that she forgot to grab a winter coat. Soon, she knocked on R & S Dressmakers.

"Hi, come on in. Something awful is happening. They took Vivian and Sheena and a whole bunch of other witches!" Roxane gushed out rapidly, as Dita stepped into her shop. Obviously, she was worried, Dita observed. Tammy was too; she had wanted to go to her best friend, Val, and help her, but Wendy insisted she stay here, out of sight.

Vivian was standing in a basement room of the rectory along with twenty other witches, some of whom she didn't know. The next instant, she was inside a metallic room, gold in color with no sign of any way to get in or out. She pounded on the walls; they sounded hollow. Suddenly, Vivian was immersed in a powerful, white energy field. Her mind was flooded with intense pain, and she wasn't aware that a robotic arm came out of a concealed compartment and injected her with a drug. Vivian only sensed a huge, overwhelming mental mass of grey, filled with an almost unendurable pain. Above all this, a bellowing voice began speaking the words designed to make the proper behavioral modifications.

"A woman should always be subservient to a man. A woman should always do what a man asks of her. A woman exists to bear and raise a man's children. A woman exists to take care of a man's needs, always putting her needs behind those of men and children. A woman should obey the Holy Laws of Lord God and of the COG. You will repeat these words many times a day."

Over and over, those words were repeated, lodging them solidly within the massive mental combined pain and drug mass in her mind. At first, Vivian tried to fight it, but quickly her will was totally overcome; the pain, the drugs were far too powerful. She finally slumped, accepting the words. Only barely conscious, she found herself back in the basement, but was unable to keep herself from slumping onto the floor. Sheena was looking at Vivian and saw her simply vanish from sight. A half hour later, Vivian reappeared, slumping onto the floor. Sheena moved to help her and found herself instead in the gold, metallic room.

When Sheena reappeared in the basement, Vivian was

sitting on the floor, her legs tucked up, her knees touching her chest, her arms around her legs, rocking a little back and forth saying over and over, "A woman should always be subservient to a man. A woman should always do what a man asks of her. A woman exists to bear and raise a man's children. A woman exists to take care of a man's needs, always putting her needs behind those of men and children. A woman should obey the Holy Laws of Lord God and of the COG. You will repeat these words many times a day." Other witches were also speaking the same words as well. Not long after that, Sheena too began reciting their new litany.

Late that afternoon, a COG carriage pulled up at the Waters' home. One of the religious fanatics helped her down and led her to her front door. "Please, there must be something that you need me to do, sir! A woman must always take care of a man's needs."

"Inside, take care of the men inside, woman," the gruff voice said, ushering her inside her home.

"Mom! You're back! Are you okay? What happened to you?" a worried, but relieved Val called out, the first of her family to reach her. She'd heard the door opening.

"I don't matter. We must take care of our men. Where are they?" Vivian said. Val noticed that her voice sounded rather funny, and her eyes were glazed.

"Vivian! You are okay?" Finley exclaimed, as he entered their front room and spotted Vivian.

"I don't matter. I must take care of you. What do you need me to do for you right now?" she asked, adding, "A good woman should always do what a man asked of her. Please, tell me what you need or want me to do for you?"

She spotted her son coming into the room behind Finley. "I must take care of you, too. What do you need me to do for you right now?"

"You can start by telling us what happened to you, Vivian," Finley said. "Come, sit down, and tell us. We've been frantic with worry!"

"Sit down, yes, I can do that for you," she promptly sat down. "Nothing happened to me. I really don't matter. A woman should always be subservient to a man. A woman should always do what a man asks of her. A woman exists to bear and raise a man's children. A woman exists to take care of a man's needs, always putting her needs behind those of men and children. A woman should obey the Holy Laws of Lord God and of the COG. You will repeat these words many times a day. We should go to church tomorrow."

"Dad! What's happened to mom?" Val nearly screamed.

"Val, you should not speak to a man that way! You are almost a grown woman and should always be subservient to a man. A woman should always do what a man asks of her. You should be asking Ken and Finley what you can do for them. A woman exists to bear and raise a man's children. We should find you a man soon, so you can bear him some children. A woman exists to take care of a man's needs, always putting her needs behind those of men and children. That's your purpose in life, Val. I will help you find a man to bear his children tomorrow. We must always help the men," Vivian replied.

Meanwhile at the Hilton Inn, Sheena was dropped off, much to the relief of Hector and their two young children. That relief lasted only briefly as Sheen began begging for Hector to give her things to do for him, reciting her litany just as Vivian was doing. "Hector, I know that a woman should always be subservient to a man. We women should always do what any man asks of us. A woman exists to bear and raise a man's children. We need to make more children, Hector. We only have two. A woman exists to take care of a man's needs, always putting her needs behind those of men and children. A woman should obey the Holy Laws of Lord God and of the COG. Don't you think we should be taking our children to hear the Holy Words at church tomorrow? I certainly do. Please, what can I do for you right now?"

After listening to this for a few minutes, he said, "Sheena, you can take care of our children and watch the inn for a few minutes while I go out. Can you do that for me?"

"Oh yes, yes, thank you for giving me something to do for you." Sheena replied with a smile and then began reciting her litany once more. Hector didn't stay to hear it; he was out the door. Soon he met with Finley. Then, both men headed over to meet with Clay, who led them over to Holly's place, where Sissy and Wendy were waiting with Holly for news of their two dear friends and companions. Also, Roxane, Sable, and Dita were there.

Quickly, the men reported the awful state their wives were in and begged them for help. All six women rushed over to the Hilton Inn, while Finley returned home to bring Vivian there as well. With all the women hovering over the two, both began trying their best to convince these women always to do what any man asked of them. Both continued to repeat their litany, much to the dismay of everyone else.

Dita's heart sank; she now realized what had happened. "They've undergone Cezar's Behavior Modification. I am so sorry for them. He should not be doing this, not ever."

"Will they recover soon?" asked Hector.

"I am perfectly fine, Hector. You need to tell me what you need me to do for you. You too, Ken. Please, tell me what you want me to do. We need to make more children tonight, Hector. Two are not enough. I exist to bear and raise your children."

Dita shook her head no, "Sadly, the whole point of Behavior Modification is that a person's behavior is permanently modified.

Hector declared, "They will pay for this! I swear, Finley, they will pay dearly for doing this to our wives!" He stormed out of his inn, ignoring the others. He thought, *Time to call in many favors owed to me.*

He visited the general store owner, Hank, and had him make a special trip to his store. Night had already fallen, but this suited Hector. An hour later, he had all he wanted, a horse and wagon loaded with his supplies. Under the canopy of the nighttime sky, Hector went about making the COG pay dearly for what they'd just done to twenty women. Before long, he arrived at the relatively new and very fancy Church of God and Holy Rectory complex. Methodically, he went about his tasks, carrying the heavy casks from the wagon to key locations. Using a rag to muffle the sounds of his axe hacking holes in the casks, he prepared each one. Gallons of lantern oil gushed out over the wooden outer walls of the two huge buildings. Finally satisfied and having dumped nearly two hundred gallons of lantern oil over the walls, windows, and doors, he sat back and lighted his cigar. With a determined arm motion, he tossed the burning match into the oil.

Within five minutes, the huge church and rectory were totally engulfed in flames. While fire was one of the greatest fears in these towns, the COG had purposely built their fancy new complex quite some distance from the nearest other buildings. Hence, they had planned for a town fire. However, they had not planned for their buildings to be the targets!

Lying in his bed totally satisfied with how terrific this day had gone, Bishop Galen Heath smelled smoke. Had he left a lantern burning? He got up and walked out of his plush bedroom. Smoke was rapidly filling the halls. Panicking, he headed for the front doors. They were completely engulfed in flames. He hastily backed away, coughing from the acrid smoke. He felt his way along the hall to the back door, but it was also burning. In desperation, he tried to get out of some windows, but was once more driven back from the heat of the flames. He backed into several other priests who had awakened to find their Holy Rectory engulfed in flames.

Outside, townsfolk were roused by the fire gong. Many rushed out of their homes to help extinguish the fire. None more so than the frantic COG members, who were appalled at the sight. Their revered new church was entirely engulfed in flames, which were racing up all four sides — likewise their rectory. All that could be done was to prevent the flames from spreading to buildings across the street. Because of the distance factor, this action was successful. Two days later, the charred remains of six priests and their bishop were found together in the rectory's main hallway.

Holly had to act. Dita's information seemed crushing. Others needed to be warned about this latest hideous action taken by the COG against the witches. Dutifully, she focused and began making contact with all the other advanced witches on Tierra, beginning with Aurora. She was pleased to learn they were a week out of Benito, on their way home. Aurora insisted she continue to do what she'd already begun. That is, alert all her contacts and have them alert the other normal witches. She also suggested any of these fifty advanced witches, who wanted to, could come to Wyth and join up with Aurora's group. Aurora also told Holly to take the two modified women to the Bettingham estate just outside of Wyth. *Hold up there, all of you,* Aurora sent.

By the next day, Holly learned ten of her group of advanced witches had already undergone Behavior Modification. They resided in Pinewood, Matruk, and Bashir. She had at least alerted all the others about this new threat, far worse than just hanging a single witch.

While many others stepped outside to watch the burning church, Sissy and Wendy with the assistance of Tammy and Val, worked with Vivian and Sheena. First, they tried getting the women to hold and squeeze their psi-crystals. Over many protests that they were not helping the men fight the fires, the two finally did so, but they were no longer in tune with their psi-crystals, very disheartening to Sissy and Wendy. At last, they decided the best thing they could do would be to sedate the two and allow them to get some rest. Tammy and Val whipped up the potion and mixed it into their tea.

A half hour later, the two women were asleep. Val whined, "I never ever thought I would be drugging my own mother. Can't we do something for them?" She'd used a bit of the juice from a *bacal* leaf which deadened the nerve pathways, shorting out the effects of psi-crystal enhanced telepathy and allowed the body to relax into a deep sleep. In a larger quantity, it was a deadly poison.

Wendy ran her hands through her red hair, frustrated. "Nothing we've tried has had any affect upon them. Dita might be right; this might be permanent." Val looked crushed.

Wendy and Sissy looked stumped. Sissy asked, "Dita, do you have any idea what kind of drug he used? If so, could we possibly get a sample of it?"

"I believe it is a highly concentrated asylic acid. I will see if I can steal some from Cezar when I get back. I don't know if I can, but I will try," Dita agreed. She felt awful; these were her friends, and it was her own people doing this to them.

"Okay, we should move everyone to the Bettingham

estate. We are supposed to hide out there for now," Holly reported what she'd heard from Aurora.

Hector replied, "That is probably best. I don't want Sheena around men. Lord knows what she will do with them. I can watch over the kids; I've lots of women refugees here who can help. How about you, Finley? Did you like the payback?" He was referring to the massive fires blazing during this night.

"Yes! Val, close the herb shop for now. You go with your mother. Payback can be a bitch," Finley added. He gave Hector a big grin. He never suspected the mild mannered innkeeper of doing such a thing.

Clay added, "Sissy, you and the kids go with them. Stay out of sight of the townsfolk. I'll come by each late evening, if I am not being followed. I don't trust these COG men any longer, if I ever did."

"Tammy and I will close my shop too," Wendy spoke up. "We'll spend all our time trying to come up with a cure." Dita sighed; she didn't think would ever be happening.

The next day, while the group packed up to leave town, Holly visited the other witches who had not yet been modified, warning them to leave town and hide out somewhere. Once done, she too headed over to the Bettingham estate.

Dita stuck around to lend the others a hand with packing. Once they were on the move, she hopped into her ship and headed for Wycombe. "Hi Norwood," she greeted the king.

"Hello! I like nice surprises, like seeing you so soon!"

"You won't like the reason for this visit," Dita said solemnly. She told him what had happened in Wyth and how ruined the lives of these women now were. Plus, she told him witch supporters were so angry about what was done to them that they burned down the COG church there.

"Well, I will put a total stop on this in Bettingham! I best send some soldiers to Wyth in case the two fractions start fighting each other. Can you stay a while?"

"No, I have to see if I can put a stop to this on our side. I will come when I can, I promise." Dita then gave him a passionate kiss and left him, though she really would have preferred simply to stay there with him.

"Look, I understand your concern," Governor Andrzej said to Dita. She'd just reported what Cezar had been doing behind his back. "Normally, the Imperial Directive #5 does take precedence, but Cezar has gotten us even more miners, and we don't even have to pay them for their work. This is definitely forwarding our basic purpose here, to get the fuel flowing in quantity. I have to side with Cezar on this one. Look, it is just a simple Behavioral Modification. It's not as if he's harmed them physically in any way. Besides, they are just primitives, Dita. I understand your concern, but stick with your anthropology studies, please." He summarily dismissed her formal protest and charge.

As Dita left the room, she had expected this would happen. She'd been blindsided by the free miners. *Oh, Cezar is clever,* she thought. *Okay, how do I get my hands on some of the asylic acid?* The Psychman's drugs were stored in a secure bin, locked, and video monitored. A key card was required, and only Cezar and his wife had the cards to gain entry. Well, she'd have to be more inventive.

Sitting in her room, she pulled up the plans of their base on her computer screen. She'd had training in archaeology as well, the digging for ancient treasures. For an hour she stared at the plans and then it hit her. She had no way to gain access from the secure bin's door, but she could tunnel underneath it and cut a hole in the bin's floor. She smiled and headed for her store of archaeology tools. While she never expected to have a situation where she'd need to dig, she'd brought them along as any good Social-Anthropologist would.

She took her equipment to her shuttle and filed a short flight, labeled Archaeology Dig. She landed just to the west of the plateau and set up. Her digging robot was remote controlled. The machine would dig a round hole barely six inches in diameter. Following the printout of the plans from her computer, she punched in the coordinates and powered it up. Soon, the robot began drilling speedily through the stone, burrowing beneath the stone upon which the base rested. A half hour later, the robot returned to her, and she stowed it,

213

retrieving her exploration tool. Again, it was fully automated, and she drove it into the hole and parked it below the metal base of the security bin. She activated the remote cutter and in a minute had a one inch hole bored in the bottom of the bin.

She activated the light and looked at her small portable monitor. *Rats, I am beneath a crate of the liquid drug.* She carefully activated the cutter once more and removed a piece of the base. Now she extended the retrieval arm and gently latched onto one of the liquid vials. Gently, she retrieved the vial back out of the hole. Next, she sent her robotic filler into the hole and backfilled six inches of the hole. She figured if someone discovered the hole in the base of the crate and security bin and looked beneath them, they'd see a solid surface and believe the bin always had that hole it its bottom. She packed up her gear, stowing it in her ship. As she flew off towards Wyth, she mused about how the ancient archaeologists used to have to dig with shovels and trowels. *How crude,* she thought.

With some pride, she presented Wendy with the vial of an ounce of the concentrated asylic acid. She cautioned them on just how potent this stuff was and then hastily returned to her base. She forgot and left her digging bag in her ship.

Chapter 12 A Long Winter

The five witches and their children moved into the Bettingham estate quietly, without drawing any attention to themselves. Three husbands and their sons brought in food supplies on the sly as well. Wendy and Sissy spent most of their days analyzing the asylic acid sample that Dita had procured for them. That it was so concentrated aided them, since they could make a much diluted volume to analyze. Holly spent her time keeping track of the COG's Behavior Modification program. She began to see a two day pattern to it. Every other day, Cezar went to one of the kingdoms to modify another batch of abducted witches.

Fortunately, most all the forty remaining advanced witches had taken her advice seriously and quietly left their towns and villages, going into seclusion wherever they could hide. They had delivered their dire warnings to the other normal witches. As Holly suspected, many of these kindhearted women just could not believe the COG would do this to them. Of course, once it happened to them, they could no longer remember anything about their former skills as healers. Since they were unharmed, perhaps this was acceptable to them, Holly thought. At least they still had their families, though they would be rather insane afterwards.

By the first of December, around one hundred witches were no longer witches, but insanely begging to be the slaves of men. During December, the numbers increased to nearly a hundred eighty more. During January, the number dropped to only a hundred more and by February, only forty-three were wiped out. After that, the number dropped to five, and then the project seemed to have ended. Others retaliated and another six of the COG's main churches were torched. By the spring of the year 1001, all active witches had disappeared from Tierra. Hundreds of other witches simply vanished into smaller hamlets and villages and no longer openly plied their trade, save perhaps to their own families and close, trusted friends. The long history of the healing witches on Tierra had come to an end.

Still Wendy and Sissy didn't give up on their dear friends, Vivian and Sheena. While those two worked on developing a way to help the two, Holly worked with the two to see if she could find a way somehow to undo their Behavior Modification. Vivian continued to reply to Holly, "Look, I keep telling you a woman should always be subservient to men. A woman should always do what a man asks of her. A woman exists to bear and raise a man's children. I need to bear more children. Please get me a man so I can do what I am supposed to do. Besides, a woman exists to take care of a man's needs. How can I do that if there are no men around here? How can I always put my needs behind those of men and children, if there are no men here? You won't even let me help the children. I am trying hard to obey the Holy Laws of Lord God and of the COG. I just keep repeating this to you. How many times must I keep telling you all these things?"

Holly wanted to reply, "Until it deactivates," but withheld it. Finally, exasperated with the two patients, she sent them to their bedrooms. She needed to think this through. If Dita was right, Cezar had somehow caused them to experience a terrific head pain and then buried it deeply with a heavy drug overdose. Obviously, right in the middle of this, he'd carefully spoken these sentences. The combination of pain, drugs, and the suggestions then took control over both women's minds, overpowering all their analytical reasoning. Neither were being logical or even rational.

Holly began to draw out a sketch of what the two women must be like. After drawing a circle and putting eyes and ears and a nose on it, representing Vivian's head, she then drew a greyish mass around the head. She added some lightning bolts representing the pain associated with it and wrote the word man in the middle of it. Holly then stared at her drawing; it seemed to be accurate. Sissy wandered by and innocently asked, "Where does time fit in there?"

Suddenly, it struck Holly! "Sissy! Brilliant, time! That's what we are missing here. Look, I think I have it worked out. This whole Pain-Drug-Suggestion, or PDS as I am now going to call this thing, sits right here in the present time. As long as Vivian obeys the commands, she is comfortable. The moment she fights it or is forced to be unable to obey it, this pain and drug dopiness moves in on her to inflict pain and grogginess on her, trying to force her to obey the commands. So time is the answer. We are going about this all wrong. The more we force them to face this, the more we are pulling in their pain, and the more they fight us."

"So let's try doing nothing; allow them complete rest, and leave them totally alone. No men, of course. Let's put some time between the PDS incident and the present. If we can keep them from activating the incident and acting it out, perhaps it will move off of them enough for us to come up with a more permanent cure."

As December rolled around, the area was blanketed with a heavy snow. Holly showed this to the two patients. "See, all travel is impossible. Why don't you both just sit back and relax. Play with the children who now have to stay indoors." Vivian and Sheena agreed to that, and thus the pressure on them to fight the PDS incident dropped off dramatically. That very day, they saw the two finally relaxing, a good sign.

Mid-December, both Vivian and Sheena were relaxed and calm. No longer were they reciting their litany; they just went about caring for the children and dealing with household chores. Holly did a bit of experimenting on Vivian only. She reminded Vivian her husband had not been by to see her for a while. Boom! Holly could almost see the PDS mass moving in on Vivian, who began chanting the sentences that had been laid in by Cezar. Curious about this effect, Holly wisely allowed her to vent and suggested the snow was too deep for him to come. "See, it is way too deep." Vivian relaxed and calmed down again.

Later, when the two women were asleep, Holly discussed her finding with Sissy and Wendy. "If we can just keep them calm and relaxed with no pressure on them, time comes to their aid, moving the PDS mass off of them. When that happens, they are rather back to some degree of normalcy. Yet, the instant anything happens in the present that reminds them of that incident, such as reminding them men are not here, boom, the PDS mass moves back into control of them, and they become highly reactive once more."

"So what do we do?" asked Sissy.

"We keep them calm and quiet with little or no real responsibilities all winter. Perhaps by spring, they will be more able to keep this PDS thing at bay," Holly replied. That then became their operating basis.

Meantime, Wendy and Sissy continued their experiments with the drug that Dita had stolen for them. In January, they discovered the right mixture of psi-powder in an alkaline base actually neutralized the chemical. The trick was getting the right dosage. As Wendy pointed out, surely neither woman still had the asylic acid still in their systems. At last, the two gave up their experimentation. At least, if another got injected with the drug, they could attempt to rapidly counter it and perhaps lessen its effects on the victim.

In Wycombe, Bishop Gil Granville was furious. First, King Norwood refused to even search for those who set fire to their beautiful new Church of God and their Holy Rectory in Wyth, killing Bishop Galen and his fellow priests, thus wiping out his entire COG leadership in the town. He was forced to send some of his own priests there just to conduct Sunday Services after Wyth had none for three weeks. Second, the king ordered him to cease abducting witches and forcing them to undergo the Behavior Modification process. He even sent soldiers to make sure Bishop Gil obeyed that order, making the bishop roaring mad. Third, he offered the COG no recompense for their lost church or any assistance to rebuild it.

Thus, Bishop Gil waited a few weeks and then in secret rounded up another five witches and met with Cezar personally when he came. "Sir, I have a really big problem here that perhaps you can help me with," Bishop Gil began. "Can your Behavior Modification be done on men or is it only for women?"

Cezar's eyebrows rose. *Now this **is** interesting,* he thought. "Of course, it can be done to men, only we'll need to work out the proper behavior desired for the man. What have you in mind, bishop?"

"It is the infernal King Norwood. He is totally

interfering with the COG and our beneficent goals for Bettingham. I'd like to get him modified somehow."

"Ah, well, then, after we finish here, let's have a discussion about this, shall we?" Cezar replied, scarcely believing his good luck. Now, he could expand his control and methods to these primitive men, gaining more valuable experimental data on his new methods.

Captain Able Smith spotted the flying ship landing not far from the Church of God and headed off to see if the bishop might be violating King Norwood's orders. He saw five women undergoing Behavioral Modification, but they were so quickly handled that he knew he would not have time to summon help and stop them. Instead, since he had not been spotted yet, he decided to spy on them. Although he didn't know it at the time, his actions would become a pivotal one.

He saw the two men going inside the Rectory, and he slipped around to a side window. Although the snow was deep, he managed to get up close. The bishop had the window opened a crack, allowing some fresh air inside and their pipe smoke to go outside. Captain Able was able to hear the two talking clearly. When the meeting broke up, he raced to the castle to find King Norwood.

"Sire! Your life is in jeopardy!" Captain Able exclaimed, out of breath from running through the cold and deep snow. He explained what he had overheard. Bishop Gil arranged for Cezar to come by and use his flying machine to abduct Norwood from inside the castle. Worse, they were planning what kind of Behavioral Modifications to make in Norwood. At very least, they were going to make him do everything that Bishop Gil asked of him!

Norwood and Palmer had a quick meeting. "Look, there isn't a damn thing you or I could do if Cezar brings his flying machine here. He can abduct us at will. We've seen what that Behavior Modification stuff does to the witches. I sure as hell don't want to be a puppet slave to the bishop or their damn church," Palmer declared.

"Neither do I. Promise me, if they get me and change me, you will kill me as quick and as painless as possible, Palmer. Promise me, please," Norwood begged his younger brother.

"I don't know if I could do that, Norwood. You are my brother, after all," Palmer squirmed. He knew if it came down to that, he would not be able to murder his brother, brainwashed or not.

"Hell, what are we going to do?" Norwood asked frustrated. *I know I couldn't kill Palmer either.*

"We can flee. Give the bishop the throne and get the hell out of Wycombe. Probably the bishop will make a complete mess of running the kingdom, and we can later come back and try to pick up the pieces," Palmer suggested.

Norwood threw his arms around his younger brother, giving him a surprise hug. "Brilliant, positively brilliant. Come on; let's grab all the kingdom's remaining funds, our stuff, and get out of Wycombe. I'll send a message to Bishop Gil telling him that he wins. He's now the king. I doubt if he will come after us after that."

Norwood asked Captain Able Smith, one of his trusted guards, if he wanted to flee with him. He didn't have to ask twice. The guard headed off to round up a carriage and his own few possessions. Meanwhile, the two men packed their possessions and then began sacking up the Royal Treasury, what was left of it. Norwood had spent the vast majority of it rebuilding the many destroyed towns and villages and seeing the soldiers were well taken care of after their lengthy campaign against the cavalrymen of Rockton. Around midnight, the three men loaded their many sacks into the carriage. After an hour, they then stored a goodly supply of food, blankets, and lanterns, figuring they would likely not stay at village inns. Finally, Norwood wrote the letter to Bishop Gil, leaving it on the dispatch table, where the morning runner would come to pick up the dispatches and deliver them or see to their delivery if they were out of the city. He added many other dispatches as well.

Around two in the morning, Captain Able drove the carriage out of the main castle gates into Wycombe proper. A half hour later, they headed up the northwest road toward Wyth. Norwood decided first to go to Wyth. Once there, he hoped to contact Dita and make further plans. None of the three had any real destination in mind, only that they had to disappear from sight for the time being. The threat posed by Cezar and his mind altering methods were far too real, far too powerful for them to ignore.

On the fifteenth of December, they pulled into Wyth and headed for the R & S Dressmakers, where Dita had her ball gown made. She'd told Norwood about them, and he thought this would make an ideal location where he could meet with Dita. Neutral ground. Since neither Roxane nor Sable had ever met King Norwood, they would not like recognize him.

Leaving Palmer and Captain Able with the carriage, Norwood entered. "Can we help you sir?" asked Roxane, somewhat surprised to see a young man entering their shop.

"I am meeting a young woman here. Perhaps she will find a dress she likes," Norwood replied, wondering if this would be sufficient to satisfy Roxane's curiosity. He pressed the button in his pocket and hoped Dita would not be too long in answering his signal.

Norwood had never been in a woman's dressmaking shop before and was rather nervous and self-conscious about it. Roxane and Sable picked up on this; their keen eyes seldom missed a thing. Roxane hinted, "Well, we do sometimes have men drop by to have us make them a dress."

Norwood flushed. *Does she think that I want to wear a dress?* His embarrassment rose a little higher. "No, I really am waiting for a woman to meet me here."

"Yes, of course, you said so," Roxane replied. "How soon will she be here?" Roxane refused to give up and kept hounding him.

"Okay, okay you win. You made her a fancy ball gown recently."

"Oh, we did? I sure hope she liked it. What color was it?" Sable asked, truly enjoying this man's frustration and embarrassment. *He is really squirming,* she thought, rather amused.

"Red, bright red," he admitted, figuring they probably made quite a few of that color.

Sable looked at Roxane and winked. She asked, "And

does this mystery woman have black eyes?"

"Well, as a matter of fact, she does. Why? Is that important?" he grew more defensive.

"Only if her name is Dita Ewa. We've only made one bright red ball gown in the last six months and that was for her." She lied. "So out with it. Who are you? Are you after her? Why? If you are not straight with us, we'll go get the local sheriff," Roxane challenged him, both her hands on her hips, as if she'd tolerate no funny business in her shop. Sable moved quietly towards their door. Norwood noticed her movement.

"Okay, okay, yes, it is Dita Ewa. I have asked her to meet me, and I need to stay here until she gets here or she may get confused about where I am at. I don't quite know how this signaling device of hers works. Now, please can I stay here until she arrives?" Norwood finally burst out.

"Now that wasn't so bad was it? You can stay. Who are you anyway? No more lying or half-truths, buster," Roxane declared firmly.

"Norwood Wycombe."

It was Roxane's turn to flush and be embarrassed, "Our king? Your Majesty? Oh my goodness! We're sorry; we didn't know it was you."

"Please, just Norwood. I am no longer the king. Bishop Gil Granville has just stolen the throne from me. I am on the run for my life. Not a word or you could get yourselves in deep trouble!"

At last, Norwood calmed down, but both Roxane and Sable were stunned with the news. While both wanted to hear about what happened, Roxane thought better of pressing her king, well, ex-king. "Would you care for a tea? Are others out in the cold waiting too?"

For an hour, Palmer, Norwood, and Able sat around the couple's dining room sipping hot tea and biscuits dipped in honey. There was very little business here in the middle of the winter, and Roxane and Sable kept the men company, but were careful not to press them on what was really going on. An hour passed before Dita arrived.

Dita was quite startled to find Norwood signaling her from R & S Dressmakers. "What on earth are you doing here,

Norwood? Oh, hi Palmer. Captain is it?" Dita asked, a little annoyed she could not rush over and plant a loving kiss on Norwood right away, as she had anticipated.

"Really bad news, actually, I'm afraid. I've had to abandon my position as king and flee," Norwood replied. She sat down, and Norwood began a detailed explanation. Roxane and Sable were all ears, listening quietly, excited they were not being told to leave.

"Oh this has gone too far! Cezar has to stop this interference with your people on Tierra! What are you going to do now?" she asked.

"Hide somewhere we won't be so easily recognized. I suppose we could migrate to another kingdom if worse comes to worse," he suggested.

"If you can lay low, I'll see if I can get this madness of Cezar's stopped. If so, you can reclaim the throne," Dita suggested.

It just so happened that Holly made telepathic contact with Roxane once each day just to check on how her daughter was doing. It wasn't safe for her physically to appear in Wyth. Some COG member might spot her, and they might attempt to abduct her in their mad attempts to rid the town of witches. Silently, Roxane relayed the incredible news to Holly. The wise woman made a decision she hoped was the right one.

Roxane looked up and said, "Mom says you three are to come and stay with them on the old Bettingham Estate north of town. They are treating two of the Behavior Modified witches there, so you'll have to stay in the guest house, and under no conditions are you to enter the main mansion building."

"That's a good offer," Dita spoke first. "This way, I know where to find you. I think I'd best take my signaling device back with me. Anyone in security can also track it and that would lead them to you. If you're with Holly, I know where to find you, Norwood. I'm going to see if I can't put a stop to Cezar's madness. I'll come visit you when it is safe."

They agreed, and Dita gave Norwood a goodbye kiss in spite of all those present. She left, but her mind was seething. Cezar was blatantly violating every major rule of the Imperium with respect to more primitive cultures that they encountered as they expanded their domain ever outwards in the galaxy. Taking sides was verboten. Going so far as to use Behavior Modification on a ruler to get that ruler to obey another faction, who wanted to control the country, or kingdom in this case, was a violation of at least five major rules! Even one of these infractions would normally get Cezar arrested and his Psychman license to practice revoked, along with substantial prison time. With five broken, he'd more likely get Mind Wiped and sent to do menial labor for the rest of his lifetime.

The problem Dita faced was that the Imperial Directive #5 had been laid aside here on Ashford-5. Still, she couldn't see how Governor Andrzej could continue to support such blatant violations of the directive. He would have to rein in Cezar! The more she thought about the governor, the more she worried. He continued to support Cezar's actions, because each time they somehow seemed to aid the mining of the psi-crystals, which was the only thing the governor was interested in achieving here on Ashford-5.

Well, there is still one avenue open to me. She though, *As Minister of Social-Anthropology, I can bypass the governor and file a formal protest with the Imperium of Social-Anthropology. They'll have to send an investigatory team here. They can't miss the flagrant violations and probably will sack Cezar and Andrzej both!* She decided would be her last resort action, because it would certainly alienate her from everyone on the base. Of course, she might also get transferred elsewhere. That sent a pang of deep regret through her whole body. "Last resort!" she declared flatly, biting her lip. Ahead the base appeared, and she punched in the landing codes.

She headed straight for the governor's office. He was pouring over the latest mining figures. He looked up and seemed annoyed to be interrupted. Dita suspect he was having a difficult time understanding the figures. Such was not his strong suit, she knew. "We need to increase production rates. We just are not making the grade yet. Have you found something we can use to increase our rates, Minister?"

Dita realized now was not the time to present her case.

"No, I was just checking on how you are doing, boss."

"I'm doing better thanks to Cezar's little pick-me-ups. I'm afraid we just are not making the progress I'd anticipated. So hectic. If we don't get this fuel resupply depot going at a hundred percent soon, we could be stuck here for a whole damn year! See if you can use your skills to find a way to get more production out of the primitive miners. Use your social skills. Make it happen, please." Dita nodded and left.

Back in her room, something he said bothered her. *Cezar's little pick-me-ups. What was that? Why had he not gone to Doctor Zosia if he felt poorly?* Dita became suspicious. Was something going on behind the scenes between the two men? The more she thought about this, the more paranoid she became. Dita began seeing conspiracies everywhere. *Perhaps Sissy is rubbing off on me!*

Finally, exasperated with herself and totally frustrated, Dita sat back and decided she simply had to have more evidence. If she were going to bypass the governor and go straight to the Imperium with charges, she'd need indisputable facts. What better facts than video evidence? She went to her own secure storage bin and rummaged through her work tools. "Ah, here they are," she said satisfied. Part of her field toolkit consisted of spy-cams so she could listen and observe primitive cultures without their knowing she was observing them, thereby eliminating observer influence in the primitives. She grinned mischievously.

She could not get inside Cezar's shuttle, but she could place one on the exterior of his ship. Late one night, she did just that. Next, she cleverly installed two in the governor's quarters. One would monitor his study area and the other his kitchen. The latter placement merely occurred to her as she was planting the first one. She just followed her intuition this time. She also put one in the storage area, aligning it to watch over whoever entered the Psychman's secure bin.

Back in her room, she checked the feeds. All worked perfectly, and she activated them, recording all video onto her computer. "The cat is now watching the mice," she said with a big grin.

Bishop Gil Granville received the dispatch from the

carrier. He had not been expecting to hear directly from King Norwood, and he opened it carefully, suspecting all manner of treachery. Poison on the envelop or perhaps inside. No, just a short note.

20 December 1000
Bishop,
You win. The kingdom is yours to run. I've abdicated my throne to you. Bettingham is all yours to run.
Norwood Wycombe

This was too good to be true! He had not even anticipated this! Here he was working out how he could control Bettingham via using Norwood. This was vastly simpler. He was the ruler now! Incredible. "But how?" he questioned. Always a suspicious man, Gil speculated, "Damn, Norwood must have been far cleverer than I ever gave him credit for. How could he possibly have known I was working on a perfect way to gain control of Bettingham? He must have had spies watching me! I bet he did just that, after that fiasco in Wyth came to his attention. He must have spied upon Cezar and me. Either that or he figured if Cezar could use Behavior Modification on the witches, why not himself? Well, that would be enough to frighten any sane man. Really, it is scary, but Cezar is on my side in this. I have nothing to worry about now."

He sent for his fellow aides and priests. After showing them the abdication letter, the men headed to the castle and palace. It was deserted. Norwood had already disbanded the entire army, sending the men back to their homes. One of the other dispatches did just that. Likewise, the palace guards had been disbanded. All palace staff including the cooks were nowhere to be seen. He did find a short note addressed to him. It said simply, "You have a fresh start. N. W."

Well, that he did. He now controlled Bettingham, but had no treasury, no soldiers, no staff, no nothing. "Well, this is just as well," he declared to the empty throne room. "I wouldn't trust any of Norwood's staff."

As he sat on the throne, it occurred to him his fellow bishops in the other fourteen countries could use this very scheme to take control of those kingdoms as well. His first action as King of Bettingham was to send a lengthy dispatch to each of the other bishops. In it he outlined what he had done here in Bettingham. He suggested they employ similar methods, hinting they drop a hint about the possibility of using Cezar's Behavior Modification on their kings. That alone might inspire other kings simply to abdicate their thrones to the bishops. After those were prepared, he then sent a lengthy report to Archbishop Mata Hatta, knowing the archbishop would be incredibly pleased with his action. In short, Gil suspected one day he might become the archbishop, overseeing the running of the entire world!

Lacking any substantial staff with which to run the kingdom, Bishop Gil pressed his more faithful COG followers into service. His first act was to send them out to all the towns and villages announcing the change in leadership of Bettingham. Once they finished visiting those, they were then to visit all the smaller hamlets, before returning to Wycombe. Lacking any palace guards let alone soldiers, he installed many of his church faithful men as the Wycombe Holy Militia, as the WHM as they later became known, charged with maintaining law and order in the palace, castle, and the city of Wycombe. Of course, this only further alienated those who were not COG members. Slowly but surely, the population became quite divided between the religious fanatics and the average citizens of the Kingdom of Bettingham.

At a local tavern, a regular patron exclaimed, "How could this have happened? Norwood was a fine king. Look how he saved us from the cavalry of Rockton and rebuilt the towns and villages that were destroyed by those soldiers. He was good for Bettingham."

"Hey, Ben, you'd better watch your tongue. There are plenty of them COG men around. If you aren't careful, they'll arrest you and hand you over to the aliens to be modified like those witches were and turned into a slave miner for the aliens!" Ben guzzled his ale and shut up, looking wildly around for spying eyes.

Slowly paranoia crept into daily life in Wycombe and the other larger towns of Bettingham. All this the bishop ignored; he was in control now. Here at the start of a new year, he would run the kingdom as he saw fit. He'd make

Bettingham a model that the COG could be proud of!

Chapter 13 Dita Goes Native

Every other day, Dita watched Cezar leave on yet another Behavior Modification run. By watching her video feed in conjunction with their survey map of Tierra, she could tell to which kingdom he went. The second of December, it was Alba. The fourth, it was Trujillo. Then came Rockton, Bentwood, Arad, Abvera, Zamora, Haruk, Walsham, Bashir, Pinewood, Bettingham, Matruk, Almendia, and finally Domi. Each trip was about two days from each other and now quite predictable. She did see many witches being handled by Cezar. Each time, she felt utterly frustrated that she could do nothing to prevent these innocent women from having their lives destroyed by Cezar.

On the twenty-fifth of December, Dita spotted something on her video recordings that sent a chill down her spine! She backtracked the video on her other spy-cam and fast forwarded it. Yes, there was Cezar making another withdrawal from his asylic acid supplies. Minutes later, there he was using a syringe injecting an unknown amount into Governor Andrzej's wine bottle through the cork! She went to her next feed. There, she saw him and his wife drinking from the bottle. She watched them doze off in bed. Fuming, she had a hunch, put on her headset, and turned up the volume from her feed. The sounds of two deep sleeping people filled her ears. She frowned; she'd hoped that there was more.

"Governor, you will always do what Cezar says to do. He is wise and brilliant. You trust him with your life and this station." Dita nearly fell out of her chair, as she heard the words of Cezar coming through loud and clear. After repeating it several times, she heard a click and realized it was some playback machine turning off.

"My god! He's got the governor and his wife under his control!" Dita exclaimed. True fear crept into Dita's mind! Cezar controlled the governor and through him, this whole base! "My god, who else has he gotten to?" she exclaimed. The next most important person was General Janek Jerzy, who controlled their base security operations. Should she take these videos to him? Surely, he would take the appropriate actions at once, ending this charade of Cezar's.

"Wait! What if he's under Cezar's control too?" she exclaimed. Dita knew she needed to find out. Once more, she used her tool kit and bugged the general's private quarters. To do so, she bored a small hole in the metal ceiling and inserted her spy-cam, adjusting it to automatically record as well. She waited. All she needed was to hear the automated voice of Cezar speaking to the general sometime during the night. She didn't need to see how Cezar was managing to get the asylic acid into the man's system.

The following morning, Dita rose. She'd slept ill. Nightmares of being Behavior Modified herself kept her in cold sweats all night long. The first thing she did upon rising was to don her headphones and listen to the tape of the sleeping general. Her face whitened. "My god! Not the general too!" Cezar controlled this man as well! Now Dita was really spooked! What could she do?

At breakfast, Doctor Zosia joined her at the chrome-plated table. "Morning Dita. Say, you don't look too well. Perhaps you should drop by my office after we eat. Let me give you a checkup."

Dita tried to protest, but Doctor Zosia was insistent. She agreed, if only to get the ugly doctor to be quiet and let her think. As she followed Doctor Zosia back to her medical treatment room, Dita's mind went into overdrive. She had to do something. *Who else is under Cezar's control? My god, if the doctor was too, she might inject me if I let on what I know to her!* Dita broke into a cold sweat as Doctor Zosia began her examination. Then, an idea flashed in her mind.

"Doctor, I think I have been exposed to one of the primitive's diseases that I have no immunity too. If so, I have probably spread it to everyone on the base," Dita suggested.

Doctor Zosia laughed, "Dear, you can't possibly have infected everyone here, only those whom you have come in contact with recently."

"Oh, well, in that case, it would be the governor, yourself, and all the ministers. Oh, and General Janek too. Say, could you possibly draw a small amount of blood from all of them and check for an infection us Rigels are not immune to, or perhaps it is a virus or some bacteria," Dita suggested.

"Sure, that's the proper protocol to be followed. That's why you have me along. I'll get them today. Routine action. I won't raise anyone's suspicions, until I confirm the presence of an alien virus or bacteria," Doctor Zosia suggested. "Now then, take one of these pills every four hours, and I order you confined to the base today. Try to avoid contact with others who you haven't had contact with, say in the last four days. I'll let you know what I find out."

"Thanks. I am probably being paranoid. It is my line of work, you know, to be out there in the field with all these unknown viruses and bacteria. Occupational risk and all that," Dita properly justified.

"I know. Anthropologists. Your kind do so often come up with the most unusual diseases. Keeps we doctors happy though. Something to do," Doctor Zosia replied cheerily.

Back at her quarters, Dita didn't take the pills. Instead, she rummaged in her tool kit once more. She used her computer to search her field medical database. What was that test for asylic acid? Ah, she thought, finding it. Now she used her portable field test kit, adjusting its settings per the database settings. She pressed Analyze and waited, holding her breath. Had the doctor tried to slip asylic acid into her? Negative flashed in red letters, and Dita relaxed a little. Then paranoia struck once more. Had she already been injected with it? She rinsed out the test vial and spat in it. A minute later, the red Negative flashed on her small screen, and Dita breathed a huge sigh of relief. She realized Cezar probably figured there was no point in modifying a lowly Social-Anthropologist, since the Imperial Directive #5 was null and void here on Ashford-5.

Dita grinned. Her plan might just work yet. Doctor Zosia would be collecting blood from everyone. All she had to do was to slip into her lab and test each one for the presence of asylic acid in their blood. In one fell swoop, she would know who was and who wasn't under Cezar's control and influence.

Late that night, Dita carried her portable field testing kit with her as she crept to the doctor's lab. Then, she discovered the fatal flaw in her plan. Because of the expensive machinery in there, Doctor Zosia had her own private security locks. Dita peered inside through the window in the door. In the dim emergency lighting, she spotted a tray with the blood vials just begging to her to be tested. Yet, she could not gain entrance. Disappointed, she had to return to her room and come up with another way.

At breakfast, Doctor Zosia again joined her. "How's my patient feeling today? I have good news. I could find no foreign bacteria or virus in your blood or that of any of the other ministers. You probably just have a cold, nothing more serious. You can relax, Dita. You didn't spread a new and awful virus among us." Zosia grinned, guessing that was what was so worrying Dita.

"Say, would you mind terribly if I drop by this morning and use my field test kit on some of those samples? I want to check for a rare virus that sometimes grows on mummies that we dig up and study. I did find one the other day. I took the proper precautions, of course, but I have the time, and it would make me feel lots better just to be doubly sure, if you don't mind."

"No, of course not. Come by anytime, and you can run your checks. Isn't it great how the medical detection kits are now so portable and simple that even you anthropologists can use them to ward off potential medical emergencies before they become real emergencies?"

Dita had to agree. A half hour later, she joined Doctor Zosia in her medical lab. "Go ahead, dear. Test away. There they are — properly labeled," Doctor Zosia said. "I've got some forms to fill out. Holler if you need me."

Dita set to work. She already knew the governor, his wife, the general and Cezar's wife had been given asylic acid. No need to test them. She started with Doctor Zosia's blood, not trusting the good doctor. A minute later, the red Negative flashed, and she cleaned off the probe. Next, she tried Jurek Kacper's blood, their Mining Minister. She waited impatiently. Then, the green Positive flashed. Dita's breath inhaled slightly; not him too, she thought.

"Ah, you *have* found something?" Doctor Zosia said

from just behind her. She'd also seen the green Positive led lights flashing. "What's old Jurek gotten himself infected with?"

Dita didn't quite know what to do. Should she confide in the doctor? She was negative at this time. While she was trying to figure out what to say, the doctor looked over her shoulder and exclaimed, "Asylic acid? What's that doing in his blood? That's illegal. I've no report he's on a mind altering drug! I'll have to report this to the governor at once. Jurek will have to be relieved of his post."

"Wait, doctor. Let's look a bit further, shall we?" Dita replied. *The doctor now knows. I can't change that*. However, she had to get the doctor apprised of the true situation. Hastily, she cleaned the probes and inserted them into the governor's blood. A minute later, the green Positive flashed once more. The doctor gasped and held her breath. "There is a whole lot more. Watch." Dita cleaned the probes and tested the general's blood.

"Not him too? Oh my god! What's going on here and right under my own nose?" Doctor Zosia exclaimed, clearly both very nervous and frightened of the consequences of this wide spread use of the illegal mind altering drug. Dita mechanically tested their wives, all positive too. Next, she tested Luzia Lina's blood, their Minister of Native Relations. Positive. She also tested her own blood and the doctors, both Negative.

Doctor Zosia collapsed onto a chair, nearly falling off it. "Oh my god! They are all on it — all but us two! How about Cezar?" Dita complied. While his wife was positive, he was negative.

"I've got some damming video that my spy-cams have recorded. They show Cezar injecting the asylic acid into the governor's wine, and I have a recording of Cezar's mind altering words spoken while he and the general were asleep. Cezar is behind this and is running this whole operation covertly!" Dita felt relieved finally to say this openly to another of her race, one who fully understood the ramifications of it all.

"What — what are we going to do about this?" asked a

crushed doctor. "If we bypass the governor and report it, the moment that we do, Cezar will drug us, and the game will be up long before they send anyone to investigate. Worse, he might just Mind Wipe us both! My god, Dita, what are we going to do? I'm so scared now; I can't possibly eat in our mess hall any longer. He could be slipping it into our food at any time. My god, he has a huge supply of it on this base. I saw the manifest before we left. My god, I'm scared, Dita, *really* scared!"

"Me too, Zosia, me too. If you report it, what will happen? What are the protocols the Imperium follows in this kind of a case?" Dita asked.

"That I can answer, come." She led Dita to her main computer station and typed away. Soon, both women viewed the official rules. While it looked very hopeful at first, soon both women were crushed. "Oh my god! Look! If the base is classified at Critical Level 5, then the use of drugs is of no great concern. Ashford-5 is classified as Critical Level 5 because of the highly vital nature of the fuel manufacturing. Dita! If we report this, nothing is going to be done about it! I feel sick!"

Dita slumped into a nearby chair, her last hope totally dashed. She'd hoped having their base doctor report the widespread illegal drug usage would bring the hammer down on Cezar, but no, the report would be ignored by the Imperium, which only wanted to obtain critically needed fuel and at any and all costs. Nothing would be done, and obviously, Cezar would find out that they had sent in the report and likely Mind Wipe them. He had no need of a Social-Anthropologist at all. Dita was completely useless baggage. The doctor might fare better. She would be probably merely Behavior Modified to go along with whatever Cezar told her to do.

Dita realized Doctor Zosia had already realized this and was scared to death over the prospect. "We're *never* going to get off of Ashford-5 unaltered, are we?" Zosia whimpered.

"Not in the foreseeable future we aren't, but I refuse to be Mind Wiped, Zosia," Dita declared.

"But what can we possibly do? They are all under his control?" Zosia nearly sobbed.

"Chin up, Zosia. There is one thing that we can do."

"What? Tell me," Zosia begged, looking hopefully at Dita for a miracle cure, as though she was dying from some mystery illness.

"We can disappear out there among the inhabitants of Tierra. Sooner or later, all manner of spaceships will start docking here for refueling. Perhaps at that time, we can find a way to sneak aboard one and get off this planet," Dita suggested, though she now knew she had no intention ever of leaving. She wanted to join Norwood and spend her life with the only man who ever made her feel totally happy, free, and a woman.

"Can we really do that? Don't they have ways of finding us?" Zosia asked.

"We can disable the tracking devices on our shuttles before we leave. As long as we remove our id chips in our shoulders, they cannot ever track us by using our medical tags either. If we don't take along anything that has an RFI tag embedded in it, they can't track those either. Zosia, if we do this right, we can simply disappear on Tierra." Dita sounded as hopeful as she dared. Abandoning their base and people was fraught with risks.

"But where will we go? How will we live? What will we eat? It is winter out there, cold and snow everywhere," Zosia complained.

"I have made some good friends out there, and they will be glad to put us up and keep us safe from Cezar. Trust me on this one, Zosia. We will be just fine, as long as we are careful not to bring along anything they can use to track us once they have discovered we've gone native on them."

"Okay, we best do it soon. I don't know how I can possibly eat anything on this base. The acid could be in nearly anything!"

"Okay, first, let's pack what we need into our shuttles. Say, can you do me a really big favor and bring along four of our prosthetic hands for the two women you healed when we first came here? If we can fix them up with hands, that will go a long way with the locals greatly desiring to help hide us."

"Sure, I can remove the RFI tags. No problem. I need to

remove ours too."

"Yes, but let's do that when we are about to leave. Otherwise, it will draw undo attention to us. I think we will only get one chance to flee this base," Dita explained. "Once we have everything we need packed, let's each check over the other's stuff to make sure we've disabled all the RFI tags and id markers. We might overlook one, and that's all it would take for them to find us," Dita urged.

"What do we take?"

"Anything you might find really useful. We'll be on our own on a relatively primitive world."

"I need a lot of my doctor's equipment then."

"True, but make sure what you take can't be identified by Cezar."

Dita left her and headed off to pack her own things. She had her side blaster. However, ideally she would have liked to take along a bunch of their weapons. Norwood could use them to fight against the Rigels, but they were under lock and key. Only General Janek had access to the armory. "I guess my blaster will have to do," she said to herself. Once she had all her things packed, she fetched her archaeology tool kit from her shuttle. "Ah, here you are," she said, lifting out her small portable RFI tag identifier, which was used in the field when trying to identify or date artifacts. One first checked to see if there was a tag in the object. If it were Imperium-made within the last thousand years, it would likely have such a tag. This technology greatly improved archaeology digs. Now it served an entirely different purpose!

She spent the entire day going from article to article, removing their RFI tags. At last satisfied, she carried her stuff to her shuttle. There, she checked the shuttle over for more such tags and id markers. These, she carefully removed and stored for disposal the moment she took off. Finally satisfied that she was as ready as she could be, she headed off to see how the doctor was faring.

"I've just got to bring along my field med kit. Without it, I can't heal anything at all," Doctor Zosia insisted. "I know it has limited battery power. Nevertheless. . ." Dita agreed and began helping her remove the many RFI tags. Then, they lifted it onto a wheeled cart and began the long push to get it out to her shuttle. Unfortunately, General Janek came by as they were pushing it down the hall.

"Say, what are you doing, doctor?" he asked accusatively.

Zosia froze, Dita replied, "Hi. I am helping Doctor Zosia here move this unit to her shuttle. She wants to be prepared for field injuries. She says you now have so many miners working that an accident is statistically likely to happen at any time, and she wants to be prepared to go to the accident site just as soon as you tell her about it, sir."

He bought it. "*Very* good idea doctor. Hasn't happened yet, but you know primitives. It *will* happen. Good thinking, be prepared. You'd make a good soldier, doctor," he grinned and continued on his way. Zosia breathed a sigh of relief and whispered thanks.

By nightfall, both women had their things stored in their shuttles. Dita explained tomorrow they would RFI check each other's stuff to make darn sure that none were missed. Zosia was still frightened. "Can I stay with you tonight? I am really scared of them all now."

Shortly after breakfast, Cezar took off on another one of his Behavior Modification runs. The two women headed for their shuttles. Dita was very thorough. She knew she must not miss a single tag or id. If she did, the general would sooner or later find them. He was thorough, if not bright. She found one she'd missed and three that Zosia had overlooked. Next, they went over their shuttles proper. All Imperium ships had a locator beacon in them, which identified the ship and provided its location. Anyone with any security clearance could access the devices and activate the beacons. These had to be removed and left behind. Fortunately, those were the only id devices in their shuttle crafts. Such beacons were never removed, so why bother with other tags — that was the Imperium logic. Saved money too.

"Once we are discovered missing, they will change all the security codes and make our cards null and void," Dita explained. "So we dump them along with the beacons when we take off."

"When are we going?" Zosia asked, glancing around making sure no one was watching them. She was now quite paranoid and frightened.

"Let's sit back and see if we have overlooked anything at all. Be prepared, you know. Once we take off, there will never *ever* be any coming back, not unless you want to be Mind Wiped or Behavior Modified," Dita replied, growing excited. Soon, she would be with Norwood, who strangely was also in exile. *Yes,* she thought, *we both are now exiles.*

At last, Doctor Zosia said, "I'm ready. There are a million more things I'd like to bring, but the shuttle can't hold them. I hope they don't shoot us down."

"They won't. Trust me. I'll go file a flight plan with security. You get ready to dump your id card and the beacon when I get back." Dita walked into security and logged onto to a computer. She typed in her message. Taking Doctor Zosia to see my archaeology dig. Back by nightfall. She looked at her entry. *Perfectly harmless.* Taking a deep breath, she hit enter and the computer logged their flight. She walked back outside to her shuttle. Two minutes later, she tossed her id card out on the ground, followed by the locator beacon assemblage. Zosia saw her doing it and dumped hers too. Dita lifted off and saw Zosia was right behind her. She headed out westward over the Westerlings.

After flying a thousand miles to the west and north, she then gained altitude and crossed as low as she dared over the Goza Mountains, and quickly descended to nearly ground level. This low, they would be completely off any base radar. A few minutes later she set her ship down near the guest house on the Bettingham Estate. Doctor Zosia followed her, landing beside her ship.

As Dita powered down the craft, she saw Norwood coming running out of the guest house, tromping through the deep snow, a huge grin awaiting her. She smiled while still inside her ship, watching him struggling in the deep snow.

"Hi my lovely Dita. Nice cold day for a visit. Who's with you?" Norwood said, overjoyed to see her again.

"Hi Norwood. I am here to stay. This is Doctor Zosia Wiola. She's here to stay too. Long story, but we are now exiles

238

too. We've blown the base. If they find us, they'll Mind Wipe us both for sure. Now handsome, you are truly stuck with me always." Norwood gave her a passionate welcome kiss, and then Palmer came to see what was happening. Two flying ships were unusual, he thought.

After introductions, the men and their captain helped both women unload their shuttle crafts. "Now we have to hide them from sight," Dita requested. After some discussion and inspection, they parked them in the nearly empty barn, stacked one on top of the other, which proved to be a tricky maneuver for the top craft. Then, the men covered them with loose hay. When they were done, they all stood back and admired their concealment. Dita commented, "Well, no one is going to see them at all. Thanks."

After they all got inside, Norwood brewed some hot tea, and the five sat down at the crowded table. Dita explained what had happened and what the two women were doing, abandoning their own base and kind, becoming renegades in the process. "As of now, the fifteenth of January 1001 on your calendar, we are now fugitives from Rigel-3," Dita said solemnly.

"Yes, but you are alive and well. I aim to keep you that way. You too, doctor. Now here's the situation here," Norwood began to bring her up to date on the latest news.

Later, the two women headed up to the manor house. Dita and Doctor Zosia wanted to explain their presence to the witches, and the doctor wanted to examine the two women who had been Behavior Modified by Cezar. Holly and the others were shocked to hear all Dita knew about what Cezar was doing across the whole of Tierra. While they were chatting, Doctor Zosia examined both women and then joined Holly.

"Well, I must say you have worked out the best treatment for someone who has undergone this new treatment of Cezar's. While we don't know actually what all he did to them, we know he used asylic acid and electronic pain stimulation, and then laid in his command sentences on top of that. You are doing the best treatment I know of — complete rest with nothing around them to restimulate the control words, men in this case. In time, they ought to pull more out of it, but it'll always be there, unfortunately, just waiting for a trigger to go into action one more. I am sorry modern medicine does not have a permanent cure for such things the Psychmen can do to people. I'm truly sorry about that." Zosia was quite sincere.

She added, "If it acts up again, I can give them something to lessen its power over them, but it won't eradicate it by any means." Holly was pleased to hear she'd devised the best way to treat them and that there was something that would calm them down, if and when men triggered their insanity once more.

Later, Holly asked Dita about her best guess as to Cezar's ultimate plans for Tierra. "He's effectively gotten Norwood removed from ruling Bettingham. I know he is working on similar arrangements with a number of the other kingdoms, and he's still modifying witches every other day; it seems that is his pattern. I have no idea why he is helping put the COG bishops in as the rulers of the kingdoms. That makes no sense to me, but then nothing he is doing is making any real sense."

Zosia interrupted, "Perhaps he is looking at this as being nothing more than an experimental lab, and we are his rats. He has definitely come up with a new technique for behavioral modifications, one that appears to be working. If so, he will probably publish his papers on it and become quite famous as a Psychman."

"I can see that," Dita replied. "But why these ignorant priests? Why have them running the kingdoms?"

"To control all the people on Tierra," Holly answered her. "Look, you put ignorant, superstitious, uneducated men in charge — men who put their faith in an unseen god, who has yet to actually do anything visible for them — men who because of their own egos and self-importance cannot ever even look at the truth of a matter — men who enforce their perverted wills upon the common man by force of arms, and you have the recipe for a Dark Age, where brutality and slavery, death and disease, and a lack of knowledge and a pride in being ignorant run rampant. Take their own supposed doctors. Their cure for all man's maladies is to blood let. Mark my words, a Dark Age is coming to Tierra."

"Yes, I can see that. You are anthropologically quite correct," Dita observed. Holly was impressively wise, she thought. "Now I can see why Cezar is pushing for this. If the planet retrogresses into a Dark Age, then he'll be able to far more easily control the whole planet and get more workers for the mines. Thus, he'll be able to produce more of the precious fuel and at a cheaper cost to the Imperium. Makes twisted sense, but at the destruction of all of us." Dita noticed now she included herself in the "us." *Well, I am one of them now.*

As January turned into February, Vivian and Sheena slowly improved. Meanwhile, life slowed down as the depth of the snow increased. Nearly two feet of snow covered the ground, and as usual, most folks stayed indoors much of the time. True, the children came out to make snowmen, and occasionally some adults did go for sleigh rides.

Dita and Norwood took the lead in going for sleigh rides, thoroughly enjoying this quiet time for themselves. For a month, all the cares of the world were lifted from the two.

Doctor Zosia, on the other hand, was having a hard time adjusting to the primitive conditions. She was used to her well-ordered life. Now, her world was turned upside down. Among these humans, she felt like the alien she was, unlike Dita who fit in perfectly and was obviously in love with Norwood. She'd just turned twenty-five and was finally filling out well. Rigels bodies reached their sexual maturity much later than humans, around twenty-six years old. However, Zosia had no illusions about her appearance; she was anything but pretty. Back on Rigel-3, she did not expect to find a mate, not with her looks. That was one reason she'd gone into the medical field, spending all her time studying and cramming from the time she was eighteen until her deployment six months ago.

Now life slowed down, way, way down. Worse, she didn't know how to relate to these humans, who seemed to her alien in every way. She felt miserable and began to wonder if being Behavior Modified might not have been such a bad idea after all.

Captain Able Smith was also very bored. Now twenty-six, he'd spent most of his career in the service of Norwood, one way or another. They had been good friends as children and being almost four years older, had looked after the king's son. Later, as they grew into their teens and began to see King Aaran for what he really was, a tyrant at the very best, Able had kept himself close to Norwood. In fact, when the cavalrymen of Rockton had invaded, he'd been the one to advise the prince to take charge of their northwestern defenses. Now that he'd saved his friend from the diabolical plan of the alien and bishop, they were in true exile, cooped up in a small gate house outside Wyth with nothing to do but wait. But wait for what? Norwood had not been specific, and Able had assumed he meant springtime, when they could travel easily once more.

One day, while the others were out on a sleigh tide, Able said, "So doctor, you probably find this life here is terribly dull and boring, compared to what you are used to handling. I heard you healed Norwood's sister and her friend last year, after her hands were cut off. I bet was a most challenging operation. I've seen what the butcher's around here who call themselves doctors actually do. It's pretty grim. We saw a whole lot of that in the war last summer. A guy gets a sword cut on his arm, and all the doc can do is chop it off. Heck, more than half of those poor victims later die, probably from what the doc did. Me personally, I think if it wasn't for the witches, no one would get cured of anything. I'll wager you've been able to work tons of what we bumpkins think are incredible miracles," Able made conversation with Zosia over tea. Nearby their fire crackled, adding a bit more warmth to the room.

"Well, I am feeling rather miserable and a little, well bored," she admitted. "Yes, I treated the two young women. I was really appalled at their physical condition and felt obligated to treat them. From what Dita has told me, you are right about your so-called doctors. They don't even realize the simple medical fact if you just sympathize with a person and tell them this pill will make them well, then one in five will get well, even though you've actually done nothing at all. That's their curing rate, according to what Dita has dug up."

"Amazing, one in five? Well, that is useful to know. I will remember that and try that one. One in five. Thanks for the tip," Able replied, sincerely pleased to know this trick.

Zosia sighed, "As for being so highly skilled, all I did was push the right buttons on my medical machine and in the right order. The machine did all the surgery and healing." She sighed again, before admitting, "In many ways, these witches here know more about real healing than I do. Yes, I have lots and lots of modern technology to use, some of the very latest in medical tools, but if I am really honest with you, I am a glorified button pusher. That's what the medical field has become. We've lost touch with real healing and have invented machines to do it for us. I am going to be utterly useless as soon as my batteries use up their charges. I've got no way to recharge them now."

She added, "And no, the only people I've had to heal since we landed here last summer have been those two women. Now that you mention it, I was incredibly bored on the base. I kept running down my checklist, you know, being prepared, but nothing ever happened. No one on the base needed any medical attention."

"But didn't you get into medicine because you wanted to help people — people who were sick or injured?" Able asked.

"Well, yes, I spent many long years studying to become a doctor, but so little of all that now has real relevance out here in the primitive world. I'm sorry. I don't mean to offend you," she suddenly realized her gaff.

"None taken, Zosia. We must seem pretty primitive to the likes of you and your people. Still, some of us are okay. Maybe you can get the witches to work with you and help you learn how to apply your skills here. Lord knows we need real healers, maybe even more so now that the COG has effectively gotten rid of the only true healers we had, the witches. I bet if you combined their practical, hands on skills with your advanced knowledge, why, you could be a phenomenal doctor here on Tierra."

"You really think so? I really do want to help cure people. I guess it doesn't matter if they are your people or mine, really. Actually, my people want to Behavior Modify me or probably now Mind Wipe me, and yet all I ever wanted to do was help people."

"Yes, I think you'd be fabulous as a doctor. That's what keeps me going too. I like to help. I've been looking after Norwood since we were kids. I knew his dad was the king, and probably someday he'd be king too and that he'd need looking after. He needs my help now more than ever before. That's what friends are for, to be there and help each other over the rough spots. Bet you are glad you have Dita or you'd be in bad trouble with your leaders. A Mind Wipe sounds awful, even if I honestly don't have a clue what it involves. It sounds terrible, Zosia."

"Dita saved me. I've never really had a friend, not like you and Norwood or any of these others here. They are all so close to each other. Back on Rigel-3, only married couples are close, but even they are nowhere near as intimate with each other as Dita and Norwood seem to be. She's happier with him than I have ever seen her since I first met her."

Able chuckled, "You can say that again. Norwood is head over heels in love with her too. I can see why too. You are both exotic beauties, as well as being incredibly able and smart."

Zosia chuckled, "Able, I am anything but pretty. I am actually quite homely."

"Homely? Well, maybe the standards are different on Rigel-3. I admit, you are a bit thin compared to us and tall. I'm pretty tall myself, but you are at least six inches taller than me. Still, that doesn't make you ugly or anything. I think you are quite the exotic beauty, Zosia. Surely, you have had many men dating you over the years. No husband yet?"

Zosia laughed. "No husband, no dates. I'm very homely. Okay, I admit it. That was another reason I became a doctor, rather to avoid all that. I knew that going to be asked out on a date, let alone to marry someone." She sighed. *I do feel incredibly relieved having finally actually said this to another person, even if he is a primitive.*

"Incredible, Zosia. I get it. Me either. No dates really. Now Palmer, he's dated half of the young women in Wycombe, but me, I was always watching Norwood's back and never had time for dates. Heck, if it wasn't for me doing just that on my own time, I'd never have overheard Cezar and the bishop planning to modify Norwood, and he'd be wiped out by now."

Zosia smiled, "Well, aren't we two fine losers."

"We aren't losers, Zosia. We have higher priorities in life, helping others."

She smiled at Able. On impulse, she asked, "Do you really see me as an exotic beauty?"

Able chuckled, "You bet I do, and so does nearly every man around here. Perhaps your people are blind, but we humans aren't."

The ice was broken at last between the two. These unlikely people struck up a strong friendship. Day by day, their admiration and respect for each other continued to grow. At his insistence, she asked Holly about learning their methods of healing, and to her surprise, Holly was quite enthusiastic about it. "Come spring, we will get started. First, you need to learn the various plants, which have medicinal properties. That's going to be very useful when your machine no longer works for you."

At Able's insistence, Zosia started going on the sleigh rides with Dita, Norwood, and himself. By the middle of February, Zosia finally relaxed and began enjoying herself and her new life. Dita too relaxed; she had been terribly worried about how Zosia would fit in with the locals. She was an anthropologist and trained to do this; Zosia was not. Still, the doctor was finally becoming far more cheerful than Dita could ever recall.

Chapter 14 Countermoves Begin

Alford didn't like the turn that the weather was taking. Dark clouds and the chill air suggested an early December snowstorm. In these open wagons, if a blizzard struck them, his party would not fare well at all. They were approaching the port town of Villa del Rey, Trujillo, located at the mouth of the second largest river in the Westerlings, the Alcantara River. Flowing from Valen close by the Plateau Grado southwesterly, it emptied into the Southern Ocean here at Villa del Rey, a port town of some ten thousand.

As they finally reached the edge of Villa del Rey at late afternoon, the dark clouds burst, sending giant descending flakes, which quickly turned the road from brown to white. While the children thought this was great fun, sticking their tongues out to catch the giant flakes on their tongues since three of them had no arms or hands to catch them, Alford knew soon that they would be wet and cold. He needed to find them shelter and soon. Worse, they could get stuck in deep snow, if it kept falling this heavily, to say nothing of perhaps losing sight of the road. He and Aiden felt particularly responsible for the large group. Did they dare chance trying to find an inn in Villa del Rey?

Via Holly, Aurora had been kept abreast of all the wild happenings across Tierra. Already the bishop in Almendia had struck, carting off two dozen witches from Arabella, that kingdom's capital city, giving them to Cezar for Behavior Modification. The twins knew the insane chaos was slowly spreading. Somehow, they had to get their group safely back to Wyth. Neither gave any thought about just why they would all be safe in Wyth when Cezar's madness was spreading to every kingdom on Tierra. In truth, though neither twin dared speak this thought aloud: there would be no place on the planet that would truly be safe any longer.

The light was failing rapidly, aided by the dense snowfall. Ahead, Alford could still see the road and the dark mass of the city and made for the first possible entrance road. This afternoon, they'd seen few travelers, probably most knew this storm was coming and were already hunkered down. Suddenly, a man on horseback moved out before him, un-shielding a small lantern. A jolt of adrenaline shot through Alford's body. Taken by surprise, he felt vulnerable and a bit guilty of having let the party down. He was leading the column of wagons and carriage. *Wait!* He thought, *the man doesn't have a sword drawn.*

"Hail strangers. Snow is coming pretty heavily now. Are you the Aurora Bettingham party?" the young man called out, a bit too hesitantly for a highway man.

"What if we are?" Alford replied not wanting officially to commit to this openly. He could be one of the bishop's men out looking for witches. They were still officially in Trujillo, if only for this last city.

"Mom sent me out to look for you. It is not safe for you to enter Villa del Rey. The bishop's men are rounding up witches even as we speak. They are somehow going to destroy them. I am supposed to lead you to a safe place. Mom and the others are already there," he replied.

Ally, who had been sitting beside him bundled up from the cold, spoke up, "Son, what is your mother's name?"

"I'm sorry. Francisca de la Cantara. I'm Eduardo de la Cantara." He pleaded, "Please, you are to follow me before the bastard COG finds you."

Recognizing the name, Ally said, "It's okay, Alford. Aurora said that Holly sent her word that Francisca was one of us and would be helping us. Lead on, Eduardo," she added. Alford nodded and slapped the reins over the team's back. The horses responded, and the wagon began moving once more. The young man quickly mounted and led them off the main road, heading northeast paralleling the Alcantara River.

Alford quickly saw this was a main river road, heavily traveled, though wisely no one but them was out in this snowstorm. They moved very slowly primarily because they could only see a few feet in front of their horses. The lad kept moving his lantern about, allowing Alford more readily to follow him. Before long, they turned left, and he sensed this was a barely used rut; he began to relax. The lad led them unerringly to a farmstead and subsequently into a large barn, where several loaded wagons were parked. Eduardo dismounted and called out, "We think we've made enough room for all your wagons. Pull in close and tight. I'll shut the door. Mom, they're here!" He called out enthusiastically.

The large barn just barely held the wagons and carriage; it was a tight squeeze. After shutting the door, a half dozen lanterns were un-shuttered, revealing a small group standing beside the barn's hearth, where they could see a steaming pot and the red glow of a warm charcoal fire. An older woman with a lantern held high, said, "Welcome. Welcome. I am Francisca de la Cantara. We are safe in here tonight. The farmer owes me a big favor for having saved his wife and child during her last childbirth. He's putting us up for the night. I've a hot pot of stew waiting for you. Come warm yourselves. You must be freezing by now."

The large group got down from the wagons and moved towards the warmth of the hearth. That's when she and the others finally noticed Drina and her three children really didn't have any arms. "Oh my goodness! Holly was right! Oh you poor dears," Francisca exclaimed.

"It's been pretty hard on us to be out like this away from our home where things were built by my husband just for us, but we are making it," Drina replied, sensing what the woman wanted to know. "Thanks for the hot food. Nasty outside. I'm Drina, by the way."

Aurora apologized about being so tardy with introductions, and she introduced her party, one by one. Francisca then did the same. She was forty and had two sons, Eduardo, nineteen, and Escobar, seventeen. Her companion was Gracia del Mar, thirty-five. She had two daughters, Juana, fifteen, and Lola, thirteen. Francisca explained they had married sailors who spent a lot of time at sea, which is why their children were two years apart and had almost the same birthdays. Both men had been lost at sea some twelve years ago, and the two witches had joined together after that, helping each other get by.

"Holly's been in touch with us, nearly every day now. This COG-alien plot is monstrous. If you don't mind, we are coming with you. Holly said we should come to her, that together we could survive the coming darkness," Francisca explained.

"We could use the help; it has been tough on me and our three children," Drina admitted. "We do fine as long as our environment is set up properly for us so we can use our feet, but out here in the wild and cold, I admit, it is a bit challenging for us. Thanks for your help, Francisca."

Already Juana and Lola were hovering over Elena and Felipa, helping them off with their wet cloaks, and getting hot stew in them. Escobar did the same for little Emilano. Only as they began to help themselves to the hot stew did they see Aurora and Ally's missing hands and gasped yet again. Everything Holly had told her was precisely correct, though Francisca had hoped that she was exaggerating a bit.

Once warmed and fed, Aurora felt more like chatting. "We are very pleased to have you join us, Francisca, Gracia. I expect we will pick up some others as we get closer to home. Yes, things are rapidly going down the drain, but we few witches are going to arrest the total destruction of our people on Tierra. It will take time, but we will succeed." Few here truly believed her, she noted, but that was to be expected.

Meanwhile, Eduardo and Alford held a discussion on the best roads to take. They had to bypass Almendia's capital of Arabella. The COG was running rampant there, abducting witches right and left. "Some of the women aren't even witches," Eduardo claimed. That troubled Alford, and he had Aurora relay that tidbit to Holly the next time she made contact with her.

Ally observed the two older women. Francisca was a portly woman, used to eating well. She later learned that Francisca was a superb chef. Both women had long black hair and eyes, typical of the Westerlings. In contrast, Gracia was a very attractive woman at thirty-five. Her facial features were angular and gave her one of those faces that one cannot ever get out of your mind, rather like an angel, Ally thought. She noted that both women's children were quite close and probably had been raised together since early childhood. She smiled, as she watched them hover over the Esteban children like mother hens.

"Now when we leave, I absolutely insist the children and you women ride in our carriages. Eduardo and Escobar will drive our two carriages," Francisca declared. Thus, after that, Drina and her three children rode with Francisca and Gracia, divided up equally between them. Their two carriages and Alford's were winterized, that is, the occupants tended to stay a bit warmer inside, buried beneath many blankets. The windows were shut, of course.

The next day after the storm abated, they had to travel some twenty miles upriver before they could get a ferry to take them across the wide Alcantara River. After Alford got the first carriage across, Aurora became excited. The snow had already mostly melted, and she called out, "Alford, we must stop here a while. Get me down, and come with me. We have to find it. I know it is around here someplace; this is the right spot!"

"What's here, Aurora?" asked Ally, helping her friend down from the carriage.

"A very large psi-crystal, which we really must have, Ally. I've seen it. We are to find it somewhere around here. The river has exposed it, that much I know," Aurora replied. "This place is just like I've seen it!"

"Okay, we have time. It's going to take at least a half day to get all nine across the river. Come on; let's look for your psi-crystal. How big is it?" Alford asked.

Aurora held her stumps about eight inches apart. "This big, a really large one. We must find it, it is vital."

The three began searching, joined shortly by Inez, Isabel, and Luisa. Before long, Marisol and Ria decided to get their boots muddy too and help out, leaving Benita behind to watch the carriage and their stuff.

An hour's search later accompanied by very muddy boots, Marisol cried out, "Over here!" She'd found a psi-crystal, which was nearly nine inches long and eight wide.

"Yes, that is it! Thank you Marisol!" exclaimed Aurora. She bent to pick it up, but glared at it frustrated.

"Allow me," Aiden teased her, picking it up for her.

"Thanks, so damnable annoying," Aurora muttered beneath her breath, hoping the others hadn't seen her failure or heard her vocal disgust.

Marisol whispered sympathetically, "It's okay, really it is."

When they got back to the carriage, others had crossed, and all gathered around to admire the largest psi-crystal any had ever seen. "What's it for?" asked Marisol.

"This and more like it will be what we use to save ourselves and our whole world," Aurora said without revealing anything critical. Now was not the time, she knew. Aiden stowed it safely in the carriage. Late afternoon, they continued on their way once more, having finally gotten across the natural barrier between the kingdoms of Trujillo and Almendia, the latter kingdom now executing its witch purge, compliments of their COG bishop. From now on, travel would be dangerous for all of them. Aurora cautioned everyone to never mention or even let on that they were witches, for obvious reasons.

As they neared the capital city of Arabella, Holly relayed the news that Norwood had abdicated his throne and fled to Wyth. Thus, the party learned of the latest plot of Cezar and Bishop Gil. Not long after that, they also learned Dita and Doctor Zosia had fled their own people, becoming exiles themselves. Aurora only smiled when she learned this news, since she had already foreseen this happening, but had said nothing of it.

While the Bettinghams cursed and swore revenge against the bishop, the COG, and the aliens for destroying their kingdom, Aurora only looked very pleased. "It is all coming to pass, just like I saw it would. Guys, Dita and Zosia are supposed to be with us." She would say no more, but that was enough to calm them down.

As they skirted the capital, twice Ally had to intervene and take control over two groups of bandits attempting to raid their party. Of course, her actions shocked all the others, who began to see the immense power that Ally and Aurora now carried within themselves. They did learn the chaos was spreading in Almendia. Their king had become under the control of the bishop there, and the population divided up and began taking sides. Skirmishes between COG members and the anti-COGs became commonplace within the city and slowly began to spread beyond — hence the rise in banditry.

Just outside of Arabella on the eastern edge, a family of six begged to join them. Marita and Alamo del Fuego, their four children, and their hastily packed possessions were packed into a large carriage. She was forty-three, and he was forty-five and a city engineer, but that was before they heeded Holly's warning and fled just as their local bishop began his reign of terror. Marita was twenty-one, their eldest. Ramira, Amador, and Beltran came next, each a year apart.

The two sons took over for Sammi and Abby, allowing them to ride in the comparative warmth of a carriage. Now, they had ten wagons and carriages in their ever-growing party. More were going to be added, though, as they continued heading for home, just as Aurora predicted.

When they finally reached the southern point where the Goza Mountains touched the Southern Ocean, they encountered more bandits that were attacking a carriage, which had broken down. Again, Ally went into action, while Alford and Aiden drew their swords and headed into the action. The dozen bandits fled from the combined threat. Another family of six, who were headed to Bettingham from eastern Almendia, joined them. It took the men a day to repair the broken axle of the carriage, however. They had not gone ten miles when two more wagons joined them, carrying another pair of advanced witches and their families fleeing the chaos erupting down in Bashir. Further north, upon entering the southern portion of Bettingham, some three hundred miles south of Wycombe, another two carriages joined them. These witches came from neighboring Pinewood to the east. Wisely, Alford steered them close to the border between Wycombe and Bashir, hoping somehow to bypass the capital of Wycombe and its chaos.

Finally, on the fifteenth of February, the large group finally pulled into the Bettingham estate just outside of Wyth, home at last. For a day, organized chaos ruled the Bettingham manor house. While it was large and mostly unoccupied for years, all the new arrivals had to be given rooms. Alford insisted Norwood's group move into the manor too. They were part of the large group now. Many introductions followed, along with numerous questions.

Alford took charge and had each person relate what details they knew. Poor Vivian and Sheena, upon seeing so many men in the large manor house, had their insanity triggered again. Both constantly hounded any available man, begging for some way to help them. However, this time, they were not quite so insane about it and were easily sidetracked into helping with the children.

By the end of the hectic day, at last everyone knew what everyone else did. There were no secrets withheld. The curiosity of the two Rigel-3 women ran its course among the new arrivals, who as yet had not actually seen one of the aliens before. Unfortunately, the unusual situation of Drina and her three children continued to attract the attention of many for some days, much to her embarrassment.

The next day after breakfast, Doctor Zosia took Aurora and Ally aside. "I brought a set of prosthetic hands for each of you." She opened the cases. "I know the skin color doesn't match yours, but they will fit your arms perfectly. They run off battery power. You insert your arms into them like so, and they will apply a little suction to secure themselves to your stumps. They work by picking up the electrical signals, which would normally have been passed on down to your real hands. Let me show you how they work."

She helped each into a pair of the hands. "Okay, now imagine you were opening and closing your fists. Yes, see, they work just like your real hands did."

"This is a miracle! Look, I can pick up a spoon," Aurora exclaimed, wide-eyed.

As Ally experimented with her new hands, she asked, "There must be a catch. This is too good to be true, Doctor Zosia."

"There are severe limitations. First, you can't pick up anything more than around a couple of pounds. If you try, you'll simply pull the hands off your stumps. Still, they will allow you to eat, to write, to dress yourselves, and many other tasks. Second, the batteries need to be recharged periodically. That's the catch, Ally. If we were not exiles or if we were living at our base, you would just plug them into the recharging dock when they ran low on power. Unfortunately, exiled as we are, I can see no way to recharge them. It is not my field, but I'll try, Ally. Third, you can't feel anything with them as you could with your own hands, so be careful. They are programmed not to grip overly tightly so you won't crack any pottery, for example, or hurt anyone when shaking hands with them."

"We can live with the weight limitations. Just to be able to easily feed ourselves and to write — that's fantastic," Aurora replied. "Thank you, thank you!"

"Yes, but how long before they run out of power? Isn't it really merely prolonging our agony, just putting off for a time our being so helpless?" Ally asked. The hands were fantastic, but if they ran out of power, they'd be useless once more.

"If you used them for say an hour total each day, I expect that they would run out of power in about three years. However, even if they did, we could always tie a fork or spoon to the fingers allowing you to eat rather easily. At least, they would be of some use to you both. I am so sorry I cannot do more for you," Doctor Zosia said sighing. *If only we had access to a simple electrical recharge station.*

"Ally, if we can at least do a few things for ourselves, these hands will be a blessing," Aurora countered.

"Yes, but I think we should continue working with Drina and continue learning her ways," Ally decided. "When they no longer operate, we're still going to have to be able to do things for ourselves, Aurora." They chatted and experimented with their new hands, but both agreed not to rely totally on them and to continue to learn from Drina.

After that, the others wanted to see their new hands and how they worked. Doctor Zosia received high praise for her timely and generous gifts to the two women from everyone, especially from Alford and Aiden. The doctor whispered to Drina, "I am terribly sorry there is nothing I can do for you or your children." Drina smiled and thanked her for thinking of them.

After lunch, Aurora asked all the adults to meet together once more. "As we explained yesterday, my gift is to be able to see into the future a little ways. I have seen the path we must follow if we are to survive as free men and women.

We can all see a Dark Age is descending upon all Tierra. The COG will soon be in control of all the kingdoms; it is just a matter of time before their bishops work out deals with this Cezar. Instead of enlightenment, these religious fanatics will bring on an era of darkness, violence, slavery, and ignorance passing as wisdom. Somehow, this is also what the Rigel folks desire as well. Against the COG, we might have a chance of defeating them by using normal means, but against the vastly superior technology and weapons of the Rigels, we have no chance at all if we fight them with swords."

"The only people standing between the slavery of the Dark Ages and freedom on Tierra are us who are gathered here today along with those who are making their way here from the other kingdoms. Yes, it will be we few against the very many, but there is a path we can follow that will allow us to be successful in the very long span of years. As you are suspecting, we have an unseen ally in the psi-crystals themselves. We three who recently received our gifts have been given a gift that is a quantum leap from all of you who have gone before us. Ally will be able to ensure no one can harm any of us while we are here in this estate. Sammi can spy on any area of Tierra and see what is going on, and I can see the future and what we must do."

"Many things will happen and must be handled properly by us. If we do these things, ultimately we will be victorious. The first of these has already occurred. We have acquired the first of four enormous psi-crystals. Three more are waiting for us to find, which we will, when the time is right. On the table, you can see it. As long as this psi-crystal is in this manor house, all our powers will be greatly magnified, particularly those of Ally, who is our ultimate protector."

"Let's not dwell on the distant future, rather let us focus on those steps which we need to take in the present. Here is what we must accomplish by August, when our first true test will come upon us all. The first action will be to establish here above South Fork Creek a sixteenth kingdom, the Kingdom of the Angels. Yes, we will be calling ourselves the Angels, a fitting slam against the COG that has brought Tierra into its Dark Ages. From Bettingham to the east over to the Goza

Mountains, then on up to us in Wyth and up and over to the Wyndl River will be the triangular Kingdom of the Angels. Eventually, our kingdom will stand alone against the fifteen COG run kingdoms and the other aliens from Rigel-3."

"To that end, we must drive all the COG supporters and worshipers from this triangular area. We will do it peacefully; no need to kill them or burn them out, for they have already chosen their own path to a slavery far worse. Ally will handle those who offer resistance. Beginning tomorrow, we'll post posters to this effect and then begin making lists of those we know who must move out before spring comes."

"By spring, we need to have our new kingdom rid of all those who support the COG. Next, many of our young are ready to receive their gifts from the psi-crystals. There will be an early snow melt around the end of March. At that time, all these young women will be taken out into the wilds, there to locate their own personal psi-crystals. Yes, many will be receiving powerful gifts, gifts that will enable us to achieve our goals, as long as we all stick together and work as a coordinated group and not as a bunch of individuals. Such a group is vastly more powerful than a similar number of individuals acting alone."

"The third action is we must begin work on the construction of three stone towers that rise a hundred feet in the air and are a hundred feet across at their base. One will be located here at the Bettingham estate. Another will be located at the Bettingham's other estate in the far eastern village of Bettingham. The third will be located at the headwaters of the Wyndl River, from where we gain our precious psi-crystals. While these towers are critical in the years to come, they will take many years to build, and thus we must get started on them now so they'll be ready when the time comes. Between them, they will act as a sort of force field protecting our kingdom. I am not exactly sure how this works. I have not seen enough of them in operation, only that they are crucial to our long term survival."

"Finally, as time progresses, many others will want to immigrate to our kingdom. While we must be alert to traitors sneaking in, we must allow those who genuinely desire to help us in our battle to come. Those who only seek their own personal protection are coming for the wrong reasons and will be asked to change their outlook or to leave."

Aurora continued, "How about our organization and leadership? I've thought a lot about it. I believe we need to have an Angel Committee composed of some of key individuals, representing many critical aspects. I don't want you to think of me as the top leader; heck, I cannot even write out an order yet, though Drina is working with me on learning how to write again. The Angel Committee should be well informed and make the decisions that impact us all. Still, I expect anyone in our kingdom ought to be able to give advice to the committee who will consider it. We all have to work together as a powerful group to make this work."

Alford held up a map of the old Kingdom of Bettingham. He drew in the boundaries of their new Kingdom of Angels. "It's kind of small," Ally noted. "It's an isosceles triangle on its side." The Wyndl River northern boundary was eight hundred miles long, running to the southeast, while the southern boundary was also eight hundred miles long, the South Fork River, which met the Wyndl River a hundred miles further east of Bettingham. The base of their triangle was the Goza Mountains to the west, some five hundred miles long. Brom was the last village in the north some twenty miles from the headwaters of the Wyndl River and close to the mountains. Also close to the mountains, their southern village of Bedwurth lay barely twenty miles from northern edge of Plateau Grado. These two villages and Bettingham closely marked the three vertices of their new kingdom, perhaps a fifth of what had been the Kingdom of Bettingham. All the villages and hamlets that had been destroyed by King Chester's cavalrymen and subsequently rebuilt last fall by Norwood lay within their kingdom, further ensuring their loyalty to Norwood, as soon as they learned he was part of the new kingdom.

Abby, Adam, Jordan, and Sammi volunteered the challenge of getting the town of Bettingham prepared. All four were eager to throw out all the COG followers there. Additionally, several of the new arrivals and their families joined them, and their wagons set out on the long, cold journey a week later.

Ally was impressive in her uncanny ability to "convince" the Wyth COG supporters to pack up and leave for Wycombe. True, Alford and Aiden posted the many signs in the town first. Naturally, the COG supporters and the new priests from Wycombe refused to move and began making trouble. One by one, Ally, accompanied by Alford and Aiden, merely visited these men and women. While they threatened them and argued, Ally said not a word, though the twins had to fight their natural impulses to counter the filth coming from these people's mouths. They followed Ally's order to say nothing and not react, allowing her to "do her thing" with them.

Uniformly, each man or woman promptly shut up and began to pack up and make arrangements to leave Wyth. "Ally, you are absolutely amazing! How are you doing this?" Alford asked, breathing out clouds on the cold morning as they walked to the next COG supporter's home.

"I give them mental images of what will happen if they don't move and then give them an overriding order to move immediately. Simple really. My psi-crystal is converting my thoughts and wishes into something they can't resist obeying. You know, I wished my father dead on many occasions, but my wish, my postulates didn't have enough force and power behind them. Now they do, thanks to my gift."

"Remind me never to mess with you, my dear," Alford teased her. She giggled.

A week after they posted their proclamations, old Leo Wyth came to visit them at the Bettingham's estate. Like nearly all the larger towns and villages, Wyth was founded by one or more noblemen, whose heirs now controlled the towns and villages. Leo Wyth was the current head of the extended Wyth dynasty, which controlled much of the town. As one might expect, Leo was fuming that something of this magnitude had not been first discussed with him. "Alford, how dare you secede from the kingdom! You should have consulted me at the very least!" He was quite angry and intended to put a stop to this nonsense. His voice was so loud Norwood heard him there in the main hallway and came to see if he could calm the nobleman down.

Alford didn't try to counter the man, but said, "Come on inside. You need to understand what is going on, *Jefe* Wyth. Please, this way." He used the formal greeting due all noblemen, appeasing the older man, but only slightly.

As Norwood entered the hallway, Leo spotted him. "Sire, King Norwood Wycombe! What brings you to Wyth? Why was I not informed of your Royal Visit?" His attitude softened. *The king is here? What is going on? I must find out.*

"*Jefe* Leo. So good to see you again. Come on in; please take tea with us. I will explain," Norwood took over for Alford, whose relief was most apparent. He was a man of action, not diplomacy. He smiled to Norwood and nodded his appreciation. As they entered the dining room, Dita rose to greet the newcomer. Leo looked even more surprised to see one of the aliens here as well. *Something **is** going on! I must find out what!* He thought.

"*Jefe* Leo Wyth, this is my fiancé Miss Dita Ewa. Dita, this is the nobleman and head of the Wyth family, who founded Wyth so many years ago, *Jefe* Leo Wyth," Norwood explained formally. She picked up on his intention and greeted the elderly man with due respect.

A minute later over tea, Norwood began a lengthy explanation, sparing few details. He realized they had to get the ruling noblemen on their side as priority number one. If the noble families backed their plan to secede and form their own kingdom, then there would be little other resistance to it, save from isolated folks who could be handled, one on one as needed. In this case, King Norwood was highly respected here in Wyth. Not only had he put a stop to the atrocities committed by his father, the late King Aaran, but he'd also saved Wyth from King Chester's cavalrymen, ended the war, rebuilt the nearby destroyed villages and hamlets. Leo had thought, *Now we really do have a king who is worthy of the throne.* That Norwood was here in Wyth and no longer in Wycombe was a powerful motivator for Leo Wyth, whose attitude changed by the time the lengthy discussion ended. He left fully backing Norwood, still calling him King Norwood.

Leo commented, "Well, I am behind you all the way,

King Norwood! Some of us think the COG already has too great an influence over our lives. If what you say comes to pass, that the COG bishops are taking over control of the other kingdoms, then you'll see noblemen there resisting as well. Mark my word, son; other kingdoms will break apart too! Kings rule because of the *support* of us nobleman. Few of us want fanatical religious leaders running our lives and businesses."

Jefe Leo Wyth was precisely correct in his prediction. Within a month, *Jefe* Harold Oakham, *Jefe* Ben Haverhills, and *Jefe* Able Rusden came to meet with King Norwood. All were seceding from the Kingdom of Bettingham. *Jefe* Ben Haverhills controlled some eight hundred miles of the foothills of the Goza Moutains just below the South Fork River. Ben would be their southern neighbor. *Jefe* Harold Oakham controlled the remaining eight hundred miles of the foothills down to the Southern Ocean. *Jefe* Able Rusden controlled the rolling grasslands along the southern border of the Kingdom of Bettingham and the Kingdom of Bashir. After all three seceded from the Kingdom of Bettingham, all that remained under the control of Bishop-king Gil Granville in Wycombe was that huge city and the central lands over to the border with the Kingdom of Pinewood. The bishop, lacking any army, was powerless to stop the seceding noblemen, who did have their own troops now. The noblemen had quickly rehired many of the returning soldiers from Norwood's disbanded the army, guaranteeing their autonomy. By the summer of 1001, what had been the large Kingdom of Bettingham was now fragmented into five smaller kingdoms.

This pattern played out during the summer of 1001 all over Tierra. While some kings were Behavior Modified to do the bidding of their local bishop, some abdicated and some cast out their bishops and COG. The many noblemen, embolden by what happened in Bettingham and dismayed at what the COG was doing in their lands, seceded from their kingdoms as well. By the winter of 1001, the number of smaller kingdoms now numbered close to one hundred! Only fifteen were ruled by the COG bishops. However, these did include all the fifteen largest cities in Tierra. This fact alone appeased the many bishops and Archbishop Mata Hatta, who saw they had control of the largest populations and now had clearly defined areas of non-believers to convert to the ways of the Lord God. Thus, the year of 1001 marked the beginning of the Dark Ages on Tierra.

Chapter 15 The Rise of the *Mentales*

"Where the devil are Dita and Zosia?" bellowed Governor Andrzej angrily. The two women had not reported in for two days. Security had found their id badges, a pile of RFI tags, and their shuttle ships' homing beacons on the flight deck.

General Janek growled, "No trace of them or their shuttles. They just vanished. Clever of them to remove their tags, though. I suspect they don't want to be found, governor. Perhaps they are on some kind of covert medical mission among the primitives." He made the only suggestion that made any sense to his military mind. *Why else would those two abandon this facility?*

"Well, I would not spend any more time worrying about them, gentlemen," Cezar broke in. Since both men were under his control, he knew what he said would be slavishly followed. He did slightly regret not having drugged those two, as he had done the others, but even now he saw them as being of no importance whatsoever. *After all, a Social-Anthropologist and a medical doctor are darn near useless in the first place. Well, maybe not the doctor. Still, my wife and I have enough medical training to be able to push the buttons on the large medical devices, should someone need emergency care. Besides, I am really busy with my huge Behavioral Modification program throughout Tierra.* He explained to the others, "Whatever they are doing, it's not going to impact our refueling program in the slightest. Let's forget about them for now. They'll return when they are ready. After all, who would want to live out there among these primitives, eh?"

"Preposterous, yes! No one would want to do that!" the governor exclaimed, shaking a little from just thinking about such nonsense. *Horrors of horrors.* "Okay, then. When they return, I'll file a formal reprimand on each of them. Let's get back to production, shall we?"

The refinery portion had been in operation for a full month. Essentially, the psi-crystals were pulverized into a fine dust and put through a chemical purification process. Once completed, the purified chemicals were compacted into fuel cells that would fit nearly every engine in the modern Imperial fleet. Eight hundred years ago, the Imperium had ordered all ships to be upgraded to use these standard engines, which varied only on thrust output and of course size. Thus, refueling was easily done, regardless of the ship.

The process created a rather large amount of psi-crystal dust, which floated above Plateau Grado. The prevailing winds took the enormous dust cloud off to the east by northeast, out over most all the original Kingdom of Bettingham, with the heaviest concentration falling on the new Kingdom of Angels. From there, it fanned out to most all the Midlands and then all the Easterlings. Only the southern portions of Bashir were missed by this initial expanding cloud's fallout. Months later, rains cleansed the upper atmosphere, dropping the last of the dust onto the Westerlings. There, the concentrations of the psi-crystal dust were the least of any area, save southern Bashir. Thus, beginning in the year 1001, the dust entered the food chain on Tierra.

"I'm hearing people's thoughts!" young Adele complained to Holly. The barmaid from Wyth had come to Holly for help and healing many times in the past. The snows were finally melting and she'd slogged her way on foot to visit Holly, having heard she was now staying at the Bettingham estate about two miles northwest of Wyth.

She picked up Holly's thoughts, *This can't be. Telepathy? Has she ingested a large quantity of our psi-powders?*

"No, I don't even know what psi-powder is, Holly," Adele added. Holly looked up very surprised. "At night when the pub is packed, I am nearly driven out of my mind from the noise of so many people in my head. They are there all at once. Sometimes, I can't tell whether someone just said something to me or whether they were thinking it. Can you help me, Holly? *Please*?"

"I can give you something to completely deaden the whole effect," Holly suggested. Adele picked up, *Of course, then you would not hear anyone's thoughts. It is so useful to know what another is thinking.*

"I know, sometimes, knowing what another is truly thinking is a blessing, especially in my line of work," Adele responded to Holly's unspoken thought. "I wish there was some way I could control this thing. Am I sick or something?"

"No, you are not ill, but I am going to have Doctor Zosia examine you just to make very sure. Is that all right with you?"

"Oh yes! She's one of the two Rigels who are living among us, right?" Adele asked, very eager actually to meet one of the aliens herself.

While Doctor Zosia gave Adele a thorough examination using her portable machine, Holly conferred with her peers. "This is the tenth case I've seen in the last week. Rogue telepaths are popping up all over Wyth," Holly explained.

"I think we are to start a training school for them," Aurora suggested. "I have seen images of ordinary townsfolk coming to our tower for training and education. I don't think it is limited to forms of telepathy only, Holly. I think you should start training these ten women on how to control their telepathic receptions. See if any can go the other way and send their thoughts as well. I'm sending Drina and Marisol into the town to check out as many people in Wyth as they can. Drina always knows what someone wants, and her abilities in this area have increased enormously since she arrived here. Marisol now has her gift and hers is so far unique. She can sense what another's powers or gift actually is. I think something fundamentally powerful is happening to us all, and we need to understand what it is. Dita and Zosia swear they know nothing about this, and that some alien bacteria is not behind it. Aiden, will you go with those two and protect them if they encounter any trouble?"

"Absolutely, I know it is strange, because I'm starting to pick up what you are feeling, my love," he said to Aurora. She flushed; she knew what he meant and forced her thoughts away from their bed.

When Holly rejoined Doctor Zosia and Adele, she was wrapping up her exam. "Hi Holly. Adele here has a clean bill of health. She's in perfect health. The only thing I found is that her pituitary gland is much larger than I would have expected. I am going to have to begin making similar observations on everyone and see what, if anything, this may have to do with it." She left to do just that, rather excited to have something medical-related to research.

Meanwhile, Holly advised, "Adele, I am going to teach you how to control your *mentales* gift. Some of we witches have the same abilities as you now have Adele. We too have to learn to control it or we find being in large crowds extremely disorienting. You are not alone. Nine other women in Wyth are experiencing similar *mentales* gifts. Can you come here in the mornings?"

"I'll do *anything* to get this under control! As I said, sometimes, this gift is very handy to have, but not so when I am working at the pub. I'll be here!" Adele responded favorably. The next morning, Holly began her lessons in how to control telepathic receipts with ten women from Wyth.

By the end of the week, Marisol made her formal report to the High Council. "Nearly half of those Drina and I examined in Wyth now have some kind of *mentales* gift. It is not limited to women, a goodly number of men also have it. Some are becoming quite ill as a result, while others are adapting. We found some are highly attuned to animals, such as falconers, dog breeders, shepherds, and horse trainers. These tend to be men. At least one man has somehow gotten a gift that allows him to make high quality weapons. Last year, he made normal swords, but since the start of this year, the results he is obtaining are just incredible. Some of the women and a few men as well are able to receive other's thoughts and/or emotions. It is like there has been an explosion in *mentales* gifts out there in Wyth."

Drina added, "Some of those who have gotten the *mentales* gift are suffering and have gotten very ill. I believe that some of those may die. What is wild is others in the same family have not become ill nor have they gotten the gift. What is going on? When I am in the vicinity of that large psi-crystal that Aurora found on our way here, I know my own gifts are greatly enhanced. Can all this be psi-crystal related?"

"There does seem to be a lot more dust in the air, coming from Plateau Grado," Alford pointed out.

Dita suggested, "They are now beginning to refine their

psi-crystals. I believe they first crush them into a powder. I would guess this dust is a fine psi-powder. Could that explain all that's happening?"

"Yes and no, Dita," Holly tried to explain the confusing situation. "We witches have long used psi-powders to temporarily increase our telepathic abilities for a few hours at most. Here, we are looking at a long term exposure to psi-powders. Doctor Zosia has examined a lot of us now and her results are quite interesting. Doctor," she turned the floor over to her.

Doctor Zosia rose and began rather timidly, quite unused to such attention. "Yes, those who as yet have no *mentales* gift have a normal pituitary gland. Everyone else has a greatly enlarged one. Aurora and Ally have the largest ones I have ever seen. All are way, way above the normal size, even among us Rigels. However, Dita and my own are also now somewhat larger than they were when we first came to this world. Somehow the unthinkable is occurring. These endocrine monitoring glands are increasing in size. At first, I thought this might be an infection of a sort, but I can find no such indications. Nowhere in the galaxy out there has any doctor seen these glands increasing in size like I am seeing here on Tierra."

She continued, "As your doctor, I would like to run a controlled experiment on some of us. The question is this: will these glands shrink back to their normal sizes if the constant exposure to the psi-powder in the air is removed or reduced? If so, then perhaps all these wild *mentales* gifts will go away if the dust clouds dissipate. On the other hand, I wonder what is going to happen to newborn babies? Will they too have enlarged glands or not? Is this effect permanent or not? What is happening to those who are becoming ill because of the psi-powder dust? Honestly, as your doctor, I really must have answers to these fundamental medical questions."

She faltered a bit and then admitted, "I too am being affected. It seems that I am getting better at somehow being able to monitor or sense how my patient's bodies are doing. Just yesterday, I sensed one had a tumor in her brain. When I used my medical monitor, there it was. I was able to remove it safely, but still, I am a bit spooked by my own apparent gift. I am going to have to find the answers."

"I agree," Aurora declared. "Doctor Zosia, the questions you raised are critical. I believe in time you will have the answers you and we need. Let's give our doctor all the assistance she is going to need to get these answers. Also, I sense it is time for us to retrieve the next of our large psi-crystals. The high mountain snows are finally melting. Alford, you and Ally need to ride to the Wyndl headwaters and find it. I'll draw you up a map of where I believe it will be found. I think the heavy snows have somehow dug it up and are bringing it down to us. The second one will be appearing in a few more weeks over by Betthingham. The spring rains will wash away a bank, revealing that large psi-crystal. I'll have Abby and Jordan find that one."

"What about the third one?" asked Drina.

"Not until summer. There will be a mine cave in. We'll send in some to help rescue the trapped miners, and they'll retrieve it," Aurora explained. Many heads nodded, particularly pleased to hear more of their future being revealed.

As the weather warmed bringing spring's rebirth to the lands, the two large psi-crystals were found and taken to two of the new towers under construction. Ernesto was in charge of the stone construction of the new tower here on the Bettingham estate northwest of Wyth. Ken Waters, Vivian's son, was heading up the construction of the tower at Brom. Alano del Fuego, Marita's husband, was handling the construction in Bettingham, not far from their second estate there. New arrivals Ben Nottingham and his witch wife Betsy were handling the construction of the fourth tower at Bedwurth. Estimates suggested they would be finished within three years.

Spring also brought Bishop Gil Granville into total control of Wycombe and the central lands of what had been the Kingdom of Bettingham. Eager to don the mantle of power and control, his religious followers jumped at the opportunities the bishop made available, from soldiers to guards, to city sheriffs, to local militia, to tax collectors, and even to advisors and spies. Daily, Bishop Gil solidified his iron-handed control over the city and lands, always guised in the form of Lord God's wishes for a Holy Realm. Those who resisted his new laws were severely beaten by the Bishop's GOT, the Gang of Thugs, as they were called by their many victims, or the Righteous Vigilantes by the bishop himself.

Into this ever-growing chaos, nobleman *Jefe* Vincent Wycombe, the sixty-three year old patriarch of the Wycombe family and the father of the late King Aaran Wycombe, had to take a stand. He was a businessman by nature. Throughout his long life, he'd amassed a large fortune and controlled many of the larger businesses in Wycombe. During the reign of his ruthless son, Vincent had turned a blind-eye to King Aaran's harshness. His profits only grew by leaps and bounds, pleasing him. With the assassination of his son, Vincent was annoyed, not saddened as one would expect a father to be. Why? Almost at once, he began to see his monthly profits declining rather rapidly, because his grandson, King Norwood, nearly bankrupted the country's treasury with his insistence on rebuilding all the devastated villages and hamlets that King Chester's cavalrymen had destroyed.

Worse still, the COG had taken over the throne. For weeks, Vincent tried to find out what had possessed King Norwood to vanish suddenly, yielding the throne to the despicable COG. Vincent was not a religious man. "Hogwash. The bishop preaches nothing but pigswill!" Vincent vocally proclaimed to other lesser noblemen every chance he got. Rapidly, he made enemies of the COG and of Bishop Gil, but as yet, *Jefe* Vincent was untouchable. He had the funds and the means to surround his estate and manor with dozens of well-trained, highly paid guards. More than a dozen GOT members were found dead in the streets of Wycombe during the spring months, infuriating Bishop-king Gil, as he preferred to be called as of May 1001.

At last, Bishop Gil took note of Vincent. "We have to get that nobleman under our control," the bishop growled to his advisors. Sitting regally in his scarlet robes upon the throne, he began to believe that he was going to have to contact Cezar and request another Behavior Modification, in spite of the fact Cezar's price was slowly increasing with each new request that he made.

"What the hell is the matter with me?" Vincent growled angrily. He was hearing voices inside his head this summer. He was having a hard time distinguishing if someone had actually spoken aloud or if he'd somehow magically heard their thoughts. He'd already embarrassed his long-standing butler this morning. William had said or thought — Vincent had no idea which — that he wanted to retire. *I am too old to keep on caring for this rich, stuffy man.* Vincent had replied rather antagonistically, "Well, then just retire, William!" William looked utterly shocked; his face crimsoned, and Vincent knew he'd just committed a major gaffe, but merely cleared his throat and said, "That will be all, William." His embarrassed butler left his room rapidly.

Just now, he'd done it again at the breakfast table. Twice. He'd upset his wife over something she'd not said, but likely only thought. Highly embarrassed, she excused herself and fled the room. Betsy, their maid, had said or thought that she was really annoyed with caring for them and their quirky behaviors. "Well, no one is forcing you to stay on with us, Betsy." His angry outburst spooked Betsy, who broke down into a fit of crying, as she fled the room, leaving Vincent quite red-faced and highly annoyed and agitated. *What the hell is wrong with me?*

Later in his study, he smoked his pipe. *I can't go to Babs and find out what's the matter with me. She's dead. Damn those COG folks anyway! Now, we don't have any reputable physicians, only their COG doctors. I'll be damned if I am going to let them bleed me! Who the hell can I go to for help?* His mind was a blank. He paced his study a while and then summoned his business coordinator, instructing him to quietly make inquiries to see if there was any witch still in Wycombe who would agree to see him on the quiet. "I'll pay five times her going rates," he added. As the man left, Vincent didn't hold out any real hope he'd find one.

"I am going stark raving mad!" Vincent exclaimed. As if backing that point up, his soft chair came sliding across the room, buckling up the carpet for some six feet. "What the hell?" he exclaimed loudly, growing more annoyed. He resisted pounding his fist onto the table. However, the table inexplicably shattered, as if he had pounded it with a sledgehammer! "What the devil?" he shouted, exploding in anger. Almost as if responding to the outward pressure of his breath, the six windows in his study exploded outwards, sending shards of glass flying onto the well-kept grounds of his estate! Vincent put his hands over his mouth, stifling any further words, and left the room and headed out for a walk on the street. *I have to calm myself down! This can't be happening to me, this can't. What is wrong with me? It must be some devilish plot of Bishop Gil! Yes, that's what it is! He is trying to drive me mad!*

His walk only exacerbated his problems. The streets in the morning were filled with men, women, and children. His mind echoed with a myriad of thoughts, often many received simultaneously. Again, he couldn't tell if they were speaking or if he were somehow picking up their unspoken thoughts. Worse, he couldn't tell who was saying or thinking what. It was just a confused jumble of random thoughts reverberating in his head. *Are they all using megaphones just to annoy me?*

For example, as he walked a few feet, he heard the following conversations in his head simultaneously:

I need to remember to bring home a slab of bacon or she'll fry me this time.

Damn Bill anyway! Why doesn't he get the lantern oil this time? It's his turn.

I want to lay that man. I bet he is good in bed. Wonder how I can make him?

Where the blazes did I leave my horse this time?

Oats, corn, carrots. Now what did I forget?

Why can't I sleep right anymore? These damn dreams are killing me.

Utter confusion swamped Vincent as he tried to stumble his way down the street past the many folks going about their business.

Hastily, he headed back to his estate and went into his

bedroom, locking the door. He ignored his wife's questioning if he was ill or something. He didn't know if it was really his wife talking or if he was imagining she would be saying that. "Go away!" He wrapped his head and ears up tightly into a pillow, and at last got some peace and quiet.

He tried to relax but was soon interrupted. Someone wanted to know who had attacked their mansion and destroyed the study windows and table. His own guards, fearing an attack had come, stationed themselves around his bedroom door and outside his windows. Once more, he heard their voices or thoughts but could not tell which was which, and buried his head in his pillows even harder, fearing to scream aloud once more. *They'll think that I've gone mad!* He dreaded what might happen to him if others thought that! Madmen were often hung just to put them out of their misery and from causing embarrassing problems to others.

Night came finally bringing with it stillness and silence into Vincent's mind. *Thank god! Quiet at last!* He roused, left his bedroom and raided his pantry. His hunger satiated, he sat back and thought. *Now this is more like it. I am back to normal at nighttime. It must be some new diabolical COG drug the bishop has been slipping into my food somehow. Well, I'll show him he can't get away with that. I will only eat food I pick up on the side.* He wrote out orders to his butler to fetch some freshly baked bread and cheese in the morning, and to bring them straight into his bedroom.

For the next couple of weeks, Vincent slept through the daylight hours and conducted his affairs only after everyone else went to bed. The wild, random noises in his head subsided to manageable levels, but he soon tired of eating only bread and cheese. He left new orders to his butler to purchase cooked meals, but never twice from the same location or inn. *That way, the bishop will never know just where my next meal will be cooked and cannot then poison me any further!*

Still, he heard the chaos of voices in his head, but minimized them by becoming a nocturnal creature, much to the utter annoyance of his whole household. He wrote out strict orders to all his many companies and businesses dictating they were not under any circumstances ever to sell anything to the COG or to the Bishop-king or his representatives. The penalty for doing so would be severe; they'd be fired.

Late September, Bishop-king Gil fumed, "This cannot go on. Vincent Wycombe has to be put in his place! I don't care if he's become a nocturnal bat! Bring him here to me today around two this afternoon or heads will roll!" He issued his orders to his COG guards and pressed the button to summon Cezar. He'd had all of this nobleman's interference he could stomach. The man's businesses had to start selling to his people today! There was no other alternative possible. *Well, I'll see he causes me no more trouble, not ever!*

An hour later, Cezar landed his shuttle near the palace and walked inside. He'd been here so often that none of the COG guards were the least bit surprised, and they motioned him to enter. "Well, Bishop-king Gil, why have you summoned me today? It can't be the witches."

"No, thanks to you, our problem of evil witches has been permanently handled. No, I have another problem." He outlined the myriad of troubles that *Jefe* Vincent Wycombe was causing. "Can you simply take him away from here permanently? I don't even want him back."

"Hum, you are saying this man is mine to do with as I please?" Cezar smiled. *Now this is more like it. A primitive upon whom I can experiment to my heart's delight!*

"Absolutely. I've sent guards to fetch him and bring him here. He is all yours. I hope never to see that man again. I don't care what you do to him, as long as he doesn't ever come back here. What will this cost me?" Gil asked, fearing the worst. *I've never asked him to get rid of someone for me. True, I could have him killed, but then the other Jefe nobles would be up in arms over it. I can't have Jefe Vincent becoming a martyr!*

"I take it he has been causing you a good deal of trouble?" Cezar replied coyly. *I dare not come right out and say it will cost you nothing.*

"Yes, so much so that he simply must vanish. However, I cannot be seen having him slain. He is a nobleman. If I have him killed, he'd become a martyr and rallying point for the other *Jefe* noblemen of Wycombe. I can't have that."

"I see. Well, Bishop-king Gil, since we are good friends, I'll take him off your hands for you this *once*. No charge. All in the name of good relations between your people and mine."

Gil looked relieved. "Now that is admirable of you, Cezar. I will owe you a big favor!"

"Indeed, you *will*."

Just then, three of his COG guards came racing into the throne room. Their uniforms were shredded, and they were bleeding from various wounds. "Your highness! We can't seem to take him! He is like a wild man! Five are dead already."

Vincent had been sleeping in his bed when a dozen COG guards attacked his own men on his estate. The noise of the battle roused him, and he watched from his window as his men were defeated, many lying dead, and their blood discoloring his green lawn. Soon, a half dozen men heavily armed burst into his bedroom. "Get out! Leave me alone!" Vincent screamed, thrashing around on his bed, tearing up his pillows, as if they were the men's heads. The men were tossed wildly around his bedroom by unseen hands. Necks were broken, uniforms shredded by unseen hands that gouged deep scratches on their arms, legs, and torsos. More men piled into the room and more men died. At last, the COG guards retreated, leaving Vincent fuming with rage. Dead bodies flew wildly out of his now smashed windows, scattering bodies and broken glass on the lawn, adding to the hectic scene.

"Okay, I'll take care of him for you, Bishop-king Gil. I can see that he must be a handful," Cezar offered, much to the great relief of the bishop.

Bishop-king Gil was stunned to hear how many of his men had been lost. *How could this nobleman have killed so many? He is but an old man?* Stupefied by the afternoon's events, he headed over to the Wycombe estate to survey personally the damage, but under a heavy armed guard. Meanwhile, Cezar returned to his ship, lifted off, and hovered briefly above the mansion. He zeroed in on Vincent and pressed his teleport button. One moment, Vincent was raving orders to his few remaining guards and the next moment, he simply vanished. Although quite shocked, his guards were relieved. The madman was gone and so were his outlandish orders.

"Where the hell am I?" Vincent screamed, pounding his fists onto the gold, metallic walls of the ship. Cezar pressed his buttons and an energy field flooded Vincent, causing his mind to register a tremendous pain. Cezar estimated this would keep the man quiet until he could get him to his laboratory. Five minutes later, Cezar sat his shuttle down at the spaceport and opened a viewer to the gold compartment. *Ah, he's unconscious. Good.*

Cezar knew better than to merely open the doors and drag the man into his lab. That would raise too many questions. Instead, he reset his teleport controls and beamed Vincent directly into his lab and into a holding cell, where he could perform many experiments on the primitive man. *Now this'll be quite exciting. I'll have to document carefully each result.*

Cheerfully, he walked briskly across the landing platform and into the main building, ignoring the dust-filled air all around the humming refinery. He stopped at the first intercom and told Jolanta to join him in his lab right away. She arrived shortly after he stepped into the spotless room, filled with his many pieces of equipment. "Ah, dear, we now have a primitive subject for our experiments. See," he pointed to Vincent, who was still in his pajamas, but was secure within a metal cage, six feet on a side.

Vincent came to. "God damn it! It's back again!" For a brief few minutes, he had felt peace and quiet in his mind. The intense pain blocked out all his perceptions and yielded a complete silence for the first time in months. Now that he was out of the gold room and the pain-causing device was no longer operating, all the outside noises returned. He heard the strange alien voices of hundreds of the Rigels; many were Drugi on patrol around the premises. He stared out of his cell, holding his hands over his ears. *Aliens! The aliens have me!* "Let me out of here! I am Nobleman *Jefe* Vincent Wycombe! How dare you take me away from my house! I demand you return me this very instant!" He yelled as loudly as he could, which was quite loud indeed.

Both Jolanta and Cezar adjusted the volume levels on their ULAT boxes, lowering Vincent's sounds to a tolerable level. Cezar said via the ULAT box, "Relax. You are now my prisoner. I'll be experimenting on you to alter your behavior patterns to whatever I wish. Bishop-king Gil was very explicit. You are never to return to Wycombe. Now relax while we work up the first Behavior Modification for you."

"The hell you are! Let me out of here immediately!" Vincent screamed. Anger seethed in him so greatly that his veins in his neck pulsed grotesquely. The metal bars on his cage began twisting of their own accord, giving Cezar the shock of his life.

"Jolanta, activate the pain level to ten immediately!" He raced to grab a syringe, intent upon injecting the wild man with asylic acid, as quickly as possible. Jolanta began punching in the desired levels of pain on the huge machine, which began a low electrical hum. The noise echoed like an entire orchestra of bass drums within Vincent's head. Unfortunately, this only increased his anger all the more. He bellowed and screamed all manner of curses towards the two aliens.

As Cezar approached him with syringe in hand, Vincent's anger crescendoed. The metal bars of his cage ripped off themselves, flying around the room, smashing into everything in sight. When they hit the pain generators, a huge electrical short-circuit occurred, flooding the room with electrical spark discharges. Vincent saw Jolanta and Cezar's bodies caught within the arcs, and they jumped around in place like some kind of puppets on strings. Then, their bodies exploded, spewing bodily remains all over the lab. The electrical short continued its wild arcing and before Vincent could do anything at all, a blinding white flash occurred.

Vincent came to. He was floating high above the Rigel spaceport complex. Below him he saw a huge mushroom cloud billowing upwards, pushing him on up even higher. He could see nothing on the ground. Plateau Grado was hidden behind the greyish mass, which grew larger and larger. He rose still higher. All thoughts were gone from his mind. Peace and quiet. No more noise, no more mental voices. Vincent was content. Now the cloud took on a reddish glow as it continued to grow and expand, pushing him far higher into the sky.

All summer, Aurora was plagued with her latest visions of the future. Until now, she could easily comprehend what the visions were about, but no more. At first, she kept them to herself, but the horrifying nature of them kept her very uneasy. At last, Aiden began to worry about her health, and she finally confided in him. "I've seen something in the near future, Aiden. It is so horrible, so awful, but I don't know what it means."

"It's not our child, is it?" he asked worriedly. Aurora was now two months pregnant with their first child, a boy, she'd said, though Aiden had no idea how she could be so positive about the unborn baby's sex.

"No, he's doing fine. It's the Rigel spaceport complex. It looks as if it is somehow blowing up or something. It is spewing red stuff. Our world will never be the same again. Oh Aiden, it is awful, terrible, but I don't know what it means."

"Well, if it involves the Rigels, let's get Dita in on it. She might be able to make some sense of your visions," he suggested.

A half hour later, Dita joined them, along with Norwood. She too was pregnant and sensed their child would be a girl. Dita, like many others now, had developed telepathic abilities and had been getting training from Holly on how to control it. For days, she sensed something was terribly wrong with Aurora, but had not said anything. *One must not pry into another's thoughts without their permission.* Holly had drilled that rule solidly into her head. Without that rule, chaos would prevail, that she knew. When Aiden sent her a telepathic message that Aurora wanted to see her, Dita just knew Aurora was going to let her know what had been troubling her these past weeks.

Hi all. What's up? She sent to Aiden and Aurora, as she and Norwood entered Aiden and Aurora's study.

"I've just got to tell someone about what I've seen of the near future, Dita. It involves the alien complex, but I just don't know what it means. It is just awful, terrible beyond words. I've been trying to figure out what it means myself, Dita, but I just can't." She didn't trust telepathy to tell Dita this. Indeed, she was shaking a little while saying these words aloud. What was to happen was just too horrible.

"You can trust me; let me see what you have seen," Dita replied softly and compassionately. "Maybe I can figure out what it means."

"I hope so. I must warn you, Dita, it is just awful. Put up a barrier so your baby won't be adversely affected by what you'll be seeing. I am protecting my little boy," Aurora replied. "You too, Aiden and Norwood. I'll show you three what I've seen of the future."

"Wait a second. If it is really this bad, we need a *regulador* to watch over us," Norwood interrupted. By now, everyone knew with all the *mentales* effects happening to so many people, the only safe way to explore potential disturbing situations was to have another person around whose job it was to monitor the physical bodies of those involved, safeguarding and protecting their bodies while they were otherwise distant from them. "I'll get Holly in here pronto. No, she's tied up with twenty students. Okay, how about Drina?"

Shortly, Drina came running into the study. "What's up? You need a *regulador*?" She had a worried look on her face, but she knew already they needed her skills as a *regulador*. Of all the others, Drina had the most talent and ability to monitor the physical bodies of others, save perhaps that of Holly. Norwood had only asked her to come to Aiden's study, but she knew from her expanded gift, her *mentales*, they needed her monitoring skills urgently. Hence, her worried look.

"Thanks for dropping everything and coming, Drina. Yes, we need you to monitor us all. Aurora is going to show us what is going to happen in the future. She says it is terrible, and we ought to take safety precautions," Norwood explained. Drina nodded, took a seat, and expanded her mind outward. Soon, she felt Norwood's body and knew he was excited and anxious, but also worried. She sent soothing impulses to his neural network, and he calmed down. She found Dita's body and did the same for her, then handled Aiden's body. Lastly, she joined with Aurora's body. Here, she had to do quite a bit of neural alterations; Aurora was really scared, frightened perhaps. *All set,* she sent to all four.

Aurora made contact with Dita, Norwood, and Aiden. Then, she began replaying the terrible images she'd seen weeks ago, scenes of their future. Drina was challenged. Suddenly, enormous fears flooded through all four of the bodies she was monitoring. It took all her skills to keep them nullified, and she nearly passed out from the huge expenditure of *mentales* energies she needed to use to keep their terrors nullified. She was about to give up and forcefully break the telepathic connections between them and Aurora, when Aurora finally ended. Drina nearly collapsed, as she then dropped her connection to the four bodies.

"My god, Drina! Are you okay?" Aiden asked, jumping up to keep the woman from falling off her chair.

"Food! Need food right away. I'm drained," she managed to whisper. Hastily, Aiden put his arms around her and carried her to the pantry. He began stuffing her with chocolate, bits of apple, and blackberry juice. She needed calories rapidly. *Well,* he thought, *we all do after that!* Once she was stable, he carried a tray of the high caloric foods to the others, who ravenously helped themselves.

Finally, Dita was able to speak coherently. "Thanks, Aurora. I believe I can make some sense of this all. The main purpose the Rigels have here on Tierra is to mine for psi-crystals." She no longer considered herself to be part of her own race. "They are converted into fuel for their spaceships. The fuel is highly combustible, and they take enormous precautions to guard against accidents. Yet, this is what I would expect to see if the fuel is somehow ignited. It would result in a massive explosion. That's what you are seeing, Aurora, the entire fuel depot is exploding. That can only happen if there is some kind of massive electrical spark to set it off." She paused and re-examined the very beginning of Aurora's images now in her mind too.

Using her scientific mind to analyze what she'd seen, Dita continued, "Damn that Cezar anyway. It looks like the origin point of the explosion is in his laboratory. The fuel is exploding, making that grey mushroom cloud you are seeing,

Aurora. However, if I am not mistaken, the red is lava. I don't know much about geology, but I'd swear somehow that huge explosion has ripped the very earth, tearing a gash in the crust of Tierra, releasing molten lava from the core of our planet here."

"That's really bad, isn't it?" asked Norwood. *I really don't know what that all means, though.* His thoughts were picked up by the others.

Dita answered his question. "Yes, really bad. I believe most of the space station on Plateau Grado is going to be destroyed. But, Norwood, that's not why it is so bad. Yes, that black-grey cloud is going to float over all Tierra for some time and may cause premature cooling, but there is something else that happens as a result. I don't think that cloud is going to cause the huge climate changes Aurora is seeing in the future. The moons are all wrong. I don't quite grasp it, though. Don't Echador and Palidez go around the middle of Tierra? Don't we see them rise in the east and set in the west?"

"Sure, they are our stable reference points," Aiden answered her.

"Well, look at the night sky near the end of Aurora's images of the future," Dita whispered.

"Funny, I'd swear they are rising and setting way down south," Aiden answered her, rather perplexed. "How can the moons be moved by an explosion on the plateau?"

"They can't, Aiden," Dita answered, fearing her own conclusion.

"But then how?" he asked nervously.

"I think the explosion has turned Tierra on its axis. It's moved the north pole southward."

"Huh?" Aiden scratched his head.

She took an apple in her hand. "Imagine this is Tierra. It spins around like this. The stem here is the north pole. For every action, there is an equal but opposite reaction — basic law of physics. At least I remember that much from my schooling. The explosion is giving Tierra a big push and it moves a little, like this. Now the north pole is here. See, the moons would now be seen rising down south."

Aiden scratched his head. "So what does all this mean?

So Tierra shifts a little."

"That means, Aiden, what used to be the Kingdom of Haruk is going to be closer to the north pole and a whole lot colder. Here in Wyth, we are going to be a whole lot colder. In fact, you can expect every kingdom is going to become a whole lot colder all the time. Without detailed analysis, I can't say how much. It is not my area of expertise. Possibly Jurek Kacper, their mining engineer could answer that question," Dita sighed, as she realized all those who came to Tierra with her were soon going to die a horrible death, all due to Cezar's constant psych meddling in the affairs of those on Tierra. She refused to call them primitives anymore.

"Will Tierra tilt back to normal in time?" asked Norwood.

"Not without another countering explosion of the same magnitude and properly placed. No, I think it will be a permanent polar shift, but I am no expert," Dita explained.

"What can we do about it?" Aurora asked. *This is what is really important. Somehow, we must be prepared for this. We are going to survive, that much I have seen, but how?*

"Unless we can stop Cezar, nothing, I'm afraid," Dita sighed. *If only I had found some way to stop Cezar and had not run away. Maybe I could have prevented all this.*

No, you did all that you could, Dita, Norwood sent. *Cezar has total control over the whole Rigel base, and you know it.*

"Well, we should notify everyone to lay in all the food supplies they can get a hold of, make tons of warm clothing, and many, many blankets," Aurora suggested.

"And lay in a drastically large winter wood supply," Aiden added. "We best get on it now. Too bad there is no way to truly alert all the other kingdoms of this impending disaster."

"You know as well as I, the bishops will not listen to anything we have to say and will likely blame us for it when it happens," Norwood countered. "We can at least let our two neighboring southern allies know, though." The ever-growing psi-dust became the wildcard, altering Tierra forever.

Chapter 16 The Aftermath

September 25 1001. The fall harvest was nearly done. Outside the Bettingham manor house northwest of Wyth, the men had stockpiled fifty cords of wood, preparing for the anticipated cold winter. Ordinarily, eight would have been enough for a long, cold winter. One whole room was entirely filled with blankets and extra cloaks, coats, and even heavy boots, imported from the far northern kingdoms. Their communal pantry was filled to overflowing. Aiden felt confident their kingdom could ride out the coming catastrophe. He'd sent riders to all their villages and hamlets making sure everyone was stockpiling food, blankets, and wood for the coming winter. Around three in the afternoon, the ground began shaking. Lanterns and crockery fell off shelves. Dishes scattered. Several yelled, "Earthquake!"

The shaking did not subside, and Aiden ushered Aurora outside. Many others soon joined them. All eyes turned to the south-southwest. A huge mushroom cloud steadily grew in the far distance, in the direction of Plateau Grado. "Well, it's happened," Aurora whispered. Even standing was challenging. Drina and her three children chose to sit down on the ground, unable to keep their balance. The rumbling of the ground beneath their feet subsided within five minutes, much to everyone's relief.

Before long, the black-grey cloud took on an orangish appearance and then reddened. By four, the cloud looked more like some giant finger of the gods protruding above Tierra. Watching in horror, Dita thought, *Well, it's finally happened. My people have wiped out an entire world!*

We are not dead yet, dearest. Don't write us off so quickly, Norwood countered. *You and I are still alive, and there is new life within you. We'll be all right. Trust me.*

After a hushed dinner, everyone again went outside to watch the moon rise, specifically Echador. Palidez would not rise until after midnight at this time in the month. "Where is it?" Aurora asked, staring off to the west where the moon always had appeared before. "It should be up by now; it's nearly full."

At last, Aiden spotted Echador rising in the far southeastern sky. "My god, look where it's at now!" he exclaimed. Dita's heart sank; the planet had indeed shifted its poles, just as Aurora had foreseen. From its location, she guessed the north pole had moved to within perhaps five hundred miles of Haruk. The two northern ports, Bafra and Kozan, would likely be frozen over most of the year now, forcing a population migration to the southern kingdoms. Inwardly, she wondered if everyone here would be forced to move south as well, staring over in some other kingdom.

Even spookier, dawn never came the next morning, though folks tended to rise at their usual times. Most quickly headed outside to see what was happening. The black-grey cloud now covered the entire sky over the Kingdom of the Angels, as well as all Bettingham and Brentwood to the east. Part of Pinewood also saw no daylight, only a dim illumination. Although they didn't know it, each day, more of the east-central kingdoms saw no daylight. For three days, the orange-red sun of Tierra was unable to pierce the heavy, high atmospheric dust cloud over Bettingham.

Finally, a greatly reddened orb appeared briefly on the fourth day. Quickly it disappeared and ferocious thunderstorms took its place. Never had anyone seen such an electrical display. Lightning was fierce, and the thunder shook the very foundations of the manor house, scaring the children. The falling rain was cold and dirty. Rivulets of ash turned the paved cobblestone entrance to the estate into a river of grey mud. "Nature is clearing out all the debris thrown into the air by the explosion," Aurora explained to the worried children. They took heart in her explanation.

A week after the explosion, the skies finally cleared somewhat. Although the sun was significantly redder than usual, the storms were passed. Dita and Doctor Zosia decided to take a flyby of their old base to see first-hand the damage done. With the help of the men, they got one of their shuttles out of the barn. Accompanied by their husbands, Norwood and Able, the two women boarded the shuttle and soon lifted off from the estate.

Dita took the controls and approached Plateau Grado with caution. "My god! It's gone," exclaimed Norwood. Most all the entire plateau had disappeared. A tall volcano rose in its place, its caldera was still red hot with vapors and heat waves rising above it. Dita flew over the tiny southern portion of the plateau that still remained and then looked over the western side of the mountain. She spotted the remains of the giant interstellar spaceship, which had brought them to Ashford-5 a year ago. Half of it was buried beneath the new mountain, half-protruding upwards like some kind of strange, silver monolith or gravestone. There was no sign of life anywhere around the peak. Hastily, they returned home, again parking the shuttle in the barn.

As they stepped out of the barn, Doctor Zosia said, "There but for the grace of you, Dita, go you and I. Thank you for saving our lives. If we had stayed on the base, we'd be dead as well. Thank you." Dita smiled.

Later that afternoon, Aurora asked Ally, "Do you think it is colder outside than normal for late September?" Her worry was the impending weather shift. If her visions were true, the weather would be changing for the worst.

Ally raised her hands to feel the air before she caught herself. With a sheepish grin, she felt with her face into the light wind. "I think so, a little. I keep forgetting," she admitted. Aurora grinned, *I do too,* she sent back.

By suppertime, more storm clouds replaced the clear skies. An icy, sleety rain fell, bringing with it the first hard freeze of the season, some three weeks earlier than last year. The next morning, all hands were called to the many fields and gardens around the Kingdom of the Angels. Everything that could be salvaged was harvested that day, hindered by a cold drizzle, sometimes accompanied by sleet. That night, giant snowflakes began falling at sunset, though it tapered off fairly soon. An inch of snow covered the grounds as October came. Speculation ran rampant over the significance of this.

In the warmth of the pubs of Wyth, many believed the growing season would now have three weeks cut off it in the fall and similarly begin three weeks later in the spring. Others declared it would be more like six weeks early, since they usually didn't get an inch of snow until the middle of November. At least the common folks had something to discuss for days.

The weather continued to be rather fickled. One day would be sunny, well relatively so, considering the high altitude dust was still obscuring some of the orange-red sun's warmth. The next day, a cold rain came with sleet towards the evenings. On the third day of the storms, the sleet gave way to snow — blinding snowstorms. Then, the sun reappeared, melting much of the snow.

On the tenth of October, precisely as Aurora predicted, all eyes gazed skyward. Another silver flying ship slowly descended from the sky, great jets of flames roaring from its bottom side. Dita guessed it was landing on that small piece of Plateau Grado, which still remained. Not long after it touched down, a dozen shuttles began flying off in many directions, obviously scouting the planet, possibly looking for survivors.

"One of us is going to have to go report in to whoever has come," Dita said with a sigh. Zosia grimaced. "Doctor, you are needed here more than I. I will take one shuttle and report in and see what I can do. We have to prevent another catastrophe from occurring. If they imprison me, I'll not reveal your presence, Zosia. You continue your healing works on Tierra."

Norwood cursed. "If they imprison you, I swear, Dita, I will find a way to rescue you and our unborn child!"

They may Mind Wipe me. I wouldn't even know who Norwood is after that, let alone who I am. "No, Norwood. You must promise me if I do not return, you'll forget about me. Zosia can explain why."

"I can't do that! I love you. You are carrying our baby. Surely they aren't that inhumane," he protested. "I should go along with you."

"No, you have to stay here and run the kingdom." *I'd dearly love him to come, but there is going to be hell to pay this time. I don't want him Mind Wiped as well!*

"You can't go alone!"

"I have to, my love. I have to."

"No, Dita. I will be with you," Drina spoke up,

surprising everyone. "Not with my pathetic body; I will use my powers, my gift, and be with you. I will maintain contact with you, and let you know what you need to say to appease them. You know I always know what another wants. We must make use of that now."

"Norwood, I will be there with Drina too," Ally spoke up. "I give you my word I will not let anything bad happen to her. Trust me. I can handle these aliens."

Sammi added, "Norwood, you can link to me, and I'll hover over them; we can watch what they do."

He smiled, greatly relieved. "Thanks everyone, but I swear I'll come after you if they hold you prisoner, dear. That's my final word."

Dita grinned and knew he would do just that. *There is more honor among these people than my own kind.*

Soon, she was airborne and felt the presence of Ally and Drina with her. Both women's bodies were sitting in a couch, covered with many blankets and monitored closely by Holly. Overhead, Sammi soared, as if she were an eagle. Holly was also monitoring her body as well. Norwood, linked with Sammi, felt nauseated from her eagle-like flight, and wished they'd hurry up and get there.

"Dita Ewa, ex-minister of Social-Anthropology reporting in," she spoke into the headset's mouthpiece. Already, her shuttle had been spotted and five others were swarming in towards hers. She repeated her message twice before she heard back.

"Go ahead and land Minister Dita. Are there other survivors with you?"

"No, just me. I know what happened, and I can explain it," she answered, not altogether truthfully. She was not about to divulge the fact Doctor Zosia was also alive, not just yet. She landed where she was instructed to land, though she saw the other shuttles were armed to the teeth, fully prepared to shoot her ship down if necessary. As she slowly hovered over the small fragment of the plateau that remained at the extreme southern edge, she saw hundreds of Drugi there; all were in full battle armor complete with large field guns.

After landing and stirring up a small cloud of ash, she

stepped out and was met with dozens of field guns pointed at her. Involuntarily, she found herself raising her hands into the air. "I'm not armed," she called out. She regretted not wearing her green uniform for a moment, but then she banished that thought. As pregnant as she was, it would not have fit her any longer.

She was marched into the bowels of the huge battle cruiser. She realized with the utter destruction of their key base here on Ashford-5, the Imperium had sent in a very heavily armed force to find out what had happened. For example, raiders could have taken over the base. Such was not unheard of, not this far out in the rim of the galaxy.

As she walked the metal halls, many faces stared at her strange clothing. *Well, they must think I have gone native. Well, I have,* she grinned to herself. At last, she marched into a well-lighted room. Two men stared at her. One was obviously the general; the other was not wearing a Drugi uniform.

"Please have a seat. Miss Dita Ewa, Minister of Social-Anthropology for Ashford-5. Correct?" the general stated dryly, while looking at the colony manifest in his hands.

"Yes. I was off the base at the time of the explosion and survived."

"I am General Cibor Borislaw. We have many questions for you. First, did enemy raiders attack the base here? Or was it sabotage by the primitives on Ashford-5?"

"You can relax. No sabotage, no enemy raiders," Dita tried to put him at ease at once.

He really wants to know what did happen, Dita, but he thinks he must follow protocols, whatever they are, Drina sent.

Dita spoke up, "I can give you a full account of what happened here on Ashford-5 if you like, General Cibor. During our year here, we have never seen any signs of any raiders, and the population of this world only has swords for weapons and cannot have possibly threatened the security of the base here." She defused his protocols.

He looked up and met her eyes. "Pray, tell us what catastrophe has struck this incredibly important facility," he barked.

"It is a long story, but the explosion was caused by our Psychman, Cezar Gerwazy. He blew up the base with his electronic machines."

"What? How is that possible?" General Cibor exclaimed.

"Long story. Shall I begin at the beginning?" He nodded.

"It began in all likelihood long before we left for Ashford-5. Cezar snuck a huge supply of asylic acid in liquid form as part of his supplies, enough to drug half of the primitives on this planet. He slipped the drug into Governor Andrzej's wine. He drugged everyone but Doctor Zosia and myself, and then implanted them to do whatever he told them to do."

"That's preposterous! Outlandish!" General Cibor burst out in anger.

He thinks you are lying. He wants proof, Drina sent her.

Dita said, "I have all the proof you could want of that. Have someone play tapes one, two, and three in my shuttle's console. Password: Cezar."

General Cibor snapped his fingers, and the other man headed out to relay the orders, returning shortly. "If you don't mind, we'll wait until that can be verified. Those are extremely heavy charges you are leveling against a reputable Psychman." *Oh that is nothing compared to the rest of it,* she thought. She sensed Drina giggling.

A half hour later, a soldier came running into the room. He looked slightly pale. "It's true, General. She has Cezar on tape doing just that! I have prepared copies for you, sir!" He saluted and left the room.

"My god! This is worse than we imagined. Okay, please continue, Minister Dita." General Cibor sat down at last.

"Once we got here, Governor Andrzej canceled Imperial Directive #5. I protested this action many times, but he overruled me. I believe Cezar wanted this directive canceled so he could perform his many experiments on the local inhabitants without fear of reprisals." She then began a lengthy description of what he had done. She explained about the local healers, the witches, and the Church of God who wanted to gain control over all the kingdoms. She described the Behavior Modifications that Cezar did to the captured witches, adding there were several of them who could be examined if the general desired.

She then outlined what Cezar had done for the COG bishops, namely driving the rightful kingdom rulers into exile or Behavior Modifying them to take orders only from their bishops. "You see, in less than a year, Cezar's actions have resulted in the complete disintegration of the ruling kingdoms. Before they had fifteen. Now, there are close to a hundred small fractions, all fighting each other for power. In short, he's thrown this whole planet into a Dark Age, where the COG doctors cure diseases by bloodletting! Beyond primitive! He's destroyed their entire civilization here on Ashford-5."

She then outlined the simple fact their refinery was not properly setup. It cast vast volumes of psi-dust over the entire lands, causing a great deal of terminal illnesses in the population of Ashford-5. She did not reveal so many were altered and gained powerful *mentales* abilities. Of this, she said nothing. If the Imperium discovered this aspect, they would swarm down on these people, abducting them and forcing them into service of the Imperium. Telepaths were a very rare commodity.

"About a month ago, Cezar was performing another one of his psych modifications on another victim when something went wrong, electrically. He was using powerful electronics to blast their minds, you see. That set off the initial explosion, which then struck the refinery. All the refined fuel subsequently detonated. So powerful was the explosion that the very earth cracked, and lava came to the surface here. Worse, I believe the explosion has shifted the north pole of Ashford-5. It has already wildly altered the weather here. Much of the northern population of this world may not survive the coming winter. I suspect there will be massive migrations to the southern lands where the weather, while far colder than before, will at least be tolerable by these people."

Dita summed up, "You see, failure to enforce Imperial Directive #5 has very nearly wiped out all the indigenous population of this world. Cezar has very nearly committed genocide of these people."

He wants to know how you and the doctor survived, Drina sent.

"When I discovered what Cezar was doing, I tried every way possible to stop him. Yet, there was no way I could with Imperial Directive #5 no longer in force. To avoid being Mind Wiped myself or getting a dose of his Behavior Modifications, I fled the base, taking Doctor Zosia with me. We hid out with the local people, waiting for a chance such as this to make our case against Cezar. Yes, we have married local men and are surviving well, at least until this devastating explosion struck. Lord knows what damage has been done to Ashford-5 and if it can be somehow remedied."

General Cibor glared, "Well, Minister Dita Ewa, you have to admit this is a lot to absorb. Please, visit our doctor and get a full checkup. She'll keep you in quarantine for a time, while we discuss your explanations, and see what we can determine ourselves. Part of the star ship survived. I'll summon you later on. That will be all." The aide led her out of the room and took her to the infirmary.

"Hello, I am Doctor Genovefa," a middle aged woman dressed in a sterile white apron over her mandatory green uniform said politely.

She is very curious about your dress, Drina sent. Dita replied, "I am Dita Ewa, our Minister of Social-Anthropology. What do you think of my native dress? It's a linen weave, quite comfortable."

"Not very practical, I suppose. Such tall boots!" the woman replied, beginning her analysis of Dita's health.

"Highly practical. The snow gets very deep out there. These are warm and have good traction in the snow. The natives here are very practical about their dress."

"Well, no signs of nasty parasites. I half expected to see your body riddled with them, considering you've been living among the primitives for some time," the doctor admitted.

"They cook their food well. Our doctor made a thorough study of their dietary methods and found them satisfactory. Actually, I've put on some muscle in my field work," Dita added.

The doctor chuckled a little. "And you've gotten yourself pregnant too. The baby is doing fine, I might add. I assume the father perished in the explosion?"

She really wants to know who the father is. I think she actually wants to know if the father is a primitive, Drina sent along with a giggle.

Dita smiled, "No, my husband is very much alive. I married one of the natives. He is one of the key leaders of the kingdom that I am studying." *Drina, I added that for her benefit. Otherwise, she is not going to be able to accept it, thinking I must be mad.*

"You see, the late governor abolished the Imperial Directive #5, and our Psychman totally interfered with the local population. Specifically, he wiped out their best healing physicians, replacing them with men whose only answer to illness is the ancient art of bloodletting, whose only answer to a sword wound is to cut the appendage off. Brutal beyond belief. My husband and I have been trying to preserve a small number of those older healers, who had been very effective physicians here on Ashford-5 for hundreds of years. I just couldn't let Cezar wipe out all effective medical treatment on this planet. Surely, you can understand that, Doctor Genovefa."

"Incredible! Why in the world would the Psychman do such a thing? It is beyond belief!"

"He wanted free reign to conduct Behavior Modification experiments on these people. Plus, he wanted to be in total control of this entire world. Well, he succeeded, but then he managed to wipe himself and our whole base out, to say nothing of causing irreparable damage to this entire world and its people."

The two chatted for a time, while the doctor continued her examination. Finally, the doctor said, "Well, that's that. I find you are in perfect health, Dita. Compared to your previous checkup on file in the Imperium data base, you are actually in substantially better health, if one can believe that."

"Field work always brings out the best in we anthropologists," Dita half-teased her, but the doctor missed that point.

"The only detail is somehow your id marker in your shoulder is missing. I'll have to get a new one fabricated and inserted. Meantime, let me show you to your temporary quarters and the mess hall. I'm sure General Cibor will summon you as soon as he's ready to continue your interrogation. I half-expected to find a large number of patients here, what with the explosion and all. Obviously, the explosion was more devastating than any of us expected. Imagine, five hundred sixty-one dead and only two survivors!"

"If it is any consolation, they died instantly, as far as I could tell. Massive explosion — the whole fuel depot went up at once," Dita explained.

A bit later, Drina sent, *You actually eat that stuff?* She was watching Dita down a tiny plate of supper. It looked more like pellets than food.

Yes, condensed proteins. It is a perfectly balanced meal, highly compact, nourishing, but I now greatly prefer your food to this. This stuff tastes awful. I can't wait to get out of here. Drina laughed.

Late the next morning, the general again summoned Dita. This time, she found a dozen men and women in the large meeting room, a far cry from yesterday. Several faces looked apologetically at her. *They are feeling sorry for you,* Drina sent.

"Good morning, Minister Dita Ewa," General Cibor began. He introduced the various personnel around the table. "First, we have been verifying your story. You have to admit it is pretty far-fetched. Yet, our Psychman's monitoring of our discussion yesterday indicated you're telling the truth. Our own observations are backing up your point of origin for the explosion. The geosynchronous satellite telemetry and visuals confirm an initial explosion from within the base personnel building that subsequently ignited the refinery. Plus, we've been able to gain access to the remains of the ship and have been able to bring up the interior plans for the base housing. We are fairly confident the initial explosion came from the Psychman's laboratory. We did some further investigation and have also verified Cezar did indeed bring along a massive load of his mind altering drug, in liquid form. The only conclusion we can reach is that Psychman Cezar Gerwazy did indeed cause this entire mess."

He turned the meeting over to Ania Anka, the Sector ID Minister, that is, the Intelligence Division. Ania was forty and tall. Her countenance was beyond stern. Dita got the impression this woman would tolerate no nonsense and was a stickler for rules and regulations. She rose slowly, as if her very presence demanded everyone's strict attention. Dita had never before been in the presence of such a high ranking Imperium figure, certainly not in the Intelligence Division, which had broad powers even over the battleship cruiser's General Cibor.

She cleared her throat and began speaking. Dita noticed everyone else in the room hung on her every word, paying rapt attention. "Gentlemen, ladies, what we have here is a textbook example of just why the Imperium has long ago adopted the Imperial Directive #5. Psychman Cezar, whatever his motives might have been, has disregarded this directive in total. The results on Ashford-5 are catastrophic, to say the very least. His actions have totally altered the culture and society on this world, plunging them into what can only be called a Dark Age. Kingdoms have been destroyed; thousands of lives taken; hundreds more have been permanently Behavior Modified. The local healing arts have been lost, replaced with utterly barbaric practices. Yet, it goes far beyond even this."

"I am afraid to say this, Dita, but we have been hard at work, analyzing what the results of the explosion have been to Ashford-5. Our geologists have verified the North Pole has been shifted some thirty point two degrees. Even worse, the planet will now be permanently wobbling wildly. It is not just that the polar axis has shifted. Rather, roughly each day, it'll be wobbling through a thirty degree variation. As you have indicated, the climate has been irrevocably altered, for the worst, I am afraid. Our meteorologists have been hard at work preparing their best predictions for the new weather patterns for the continent here. It's grim indeed. We can expect wild swings in the daily weather along with fierce, cold winters, except in the southern extremes of the continent. In this area alone, the growing season will be foreshortened by at least four weeks. In short, this perfectly pleasant planet has been turned into a planet of nightmare weather, especially here in the mountains where the Imperium wants its spaceport to be located."

"The spaceport must still be located here in these mountains. The extra cost of the fuel needed to rise from the lower elevations is prohibitory. Thus, our ideal spaceport is no longer going to be ideal, far from it. On the more positive side, no further planetary mining will be done on Ashford-5. Rather, our geologists have discovered vast deposits of psi-crystals on the larger moon above us. Already, a new mining colony is being established there. The refineries on the moon will supply the fuel that is so desperately needed by the Imperium. Shuttles will bring the fuel cells down to the spaceport. Thus, the Imperium's critical fuel needs will still be met and, I might add, far more readily and cheaply than would have been done with the original planet-side operation."

"That said, the problem the Imperium now faces is what to do with Ashford-5, given the horrific breach of the Imperial Directive #5 here. There can be no question of the magnitude of the destruction inflicted upon the population of this world by our vastly superior technological society."

Dita raised her hand, hoping she could ask a question. She had no idea if such was permitted, but felt obligated at least to try. "Yes, Dita? No need for such formalities here," Ania asked, without breaking her stern delivery in the slightest. All eyes turned to Dita, and she flushed from the unexpected attention.

"Anthropologically speaking, the results of the polar change and the resultant weather alterations are disastrous. Is there any way we can somehow move it back, restore it to what it was before the explosion? I know this is way out of my area of expertise, but that would go a long way to helping the indigenous population cope with the damage done." Dita thought she'd stated her case reasonably well. This was the burning question she needed answering, for so much depended upon it.

"Good point," Ania replied sternly. Dita could not help see the others relaxing a bit. Evidently, they all feared this

Sector ID woman, either feared her or held her in the highest respect. Perhaps, it was a combination of both, Dita thought.

"I've have our geologists working on that one. The simple answer is no. While they have been able to make some educated guesses, they cannot guarantee that any counter-action they could take would not make matters worse. If there was a way to undo what has been done and with a one hundred percent chance of success, I would consider taking that action. However, I will not consider any that could potentially make things worse here. I'm afraid the population on Ashford-5 will have to adapt to the drastic climate changes that are already in progress here. As you well know, humans are highly adaptable, and in time, I am sure the locals here will adapt, just as humans have elsewhere."

"So with that said, the next question becomes what else do we do here on Ashford-5? The answer to that one lies in the fundamental basis of why there is an Imperial Directive #5 in the first place. Minister Dita, this is your area of expertise. Care to enlighten us on the why of the directive?" All eyes again focused on her.

Dita explained, "When a highly technological and advanced society encounters a vastly more primitive society, culture shock inevitably arises. Lacking the education and knowledge, the more primitive society then must somehow weave the new society into the fabric of their understanding. Such can range from treatment of the new arrivals as gods and utter worship of them, to the other extreme of all-out warfare against them. People fear what they do not understand, and that fear can lead to wars at one end of their reactions to that of an utter apathy and a total succumbing. Our history books are filled with examples of both. On Cotterman-3, the primitives there simply just gave up and starved themselves to death, all the while praying to these new gods to provide food for them. They ceased doing anything for themselves. On Begil-4, out of ignorance and fear of the new arrivals, the primitives attacked and slaughtered the entire colony."

"In essence, when one faces a serious threat, there are only five actions that they can take. They can attack it; they can flee from it; they can ignore and neglect it; they can lay down and succumb to it; and they can try to avoid it somehow. Thus, when a technological society encounters a more primitive one, the natives will invariably take one of these five routes. As you can imagine, none of these are healthy to the long term evolution and survival of the primitives. Attacking us is fatal; obviously, our stunners and disintegration guns can wipe them out. Thus, the most optimum solution for all concerned is to wholly avoid placing that serious threat before the indigenous population in the first place. Hence, the hands-off policy of the Imperial Directive #5, which history also shows is clearly the best policy for both parties." She sat back, confident she'd explained the underlying rational in fairly clear terms that invoked no anthropological nomenclature.

Evidently, she was right, Ania actually smiled briefly for the first time. However, her stern look reasserted itself almost at once. Ania then said, "Minister Dita is precisely correct. Now then, Minister Dita, I have a very important question to ask of you. Does the population of Ashford-5 already know about us, that is, the former Rigel-3 colony here on this plateau?"

"Absolutely, every one of the fifteen original kingdoms is acutely aware of it; many of the rulers and even common folk know about the Behavior Modifications," she replied. There was no hiding that fact.

"I see. Then, does everyone also know Cezar was the cause of the massive explosion and subsequent pole alteration and attendant massive weather pattern shifts?" Ania asked.

Dita thought long and hard on this one before answering. "Our new Kingdom of the Angels certainly does. Our two southern neighbors, the Kingdoms of Haverhills and Oakham, the latter of which borders this plateau or what is now left of it, most certainly do know the explosion has caused massive damage. We do not know about the other large population city of Valen on the western side. I would presume folks there also know it. However, in all honesty, I suspect the more distant kingdoms are not yet fully aware of the cause and effect and may never be. Communications across the continent are in their infancy. With the breakup of the fifteen kingdoms into hundreds of smaller domains, communications are apt to be vastly poorer, especially now that the weather is going to become a huge factor."

"Interesting," Ania said, rubbing her chin lightly. "First, the spaceport must be built here at this location. That is not at issue; the Imperium needs this vital spaceport for further rim explorations. It has to be built here, period. Second, given that it will be built here and that we 'aliens' will have a visible presence here on Ashford-5, it is my decision that from this point onward, the Imperial Directive #5 will be strictly followed with regard to the local inhabitants. There will be no further violations tolerated in the development of the local culture."

"That preventative measure taken for the future, it remains to decide what, if anything, we can do to rectify the horrific damage done here. We simply cannot undo what's been done. Period. Instead, we must look to the future and repair our relations with the denizens of Ashford-5. This must be done on the quiet in so far as that is possible. No, we cannot just provide our technology to these people — that would violate the directive. We must work behind the scenes, so to speak, aiding where we can."

She continued, "I will be personally in charge of the planet-side operations of the new base. All encounters with the inhabitants shall henceforth with go through me, no exceptions. That said, I will need close liaisons with those in power. Minister Dita, I would like to request that you remain with your husband and continue your field work there. Likewise, it is to everyone's benefit if Doctor Zosia does so as well. She may well be able to improve the overall medical practices, at least in the area in which she dwells. I do insist you both get your ID markers inserted into your shoulders once more. Besides, we can track your shuttles from the satellite anyway. I will expect periodic reports from the both of you, however. On the whole, we will avoid any direct influences as per the directive, but on the QT, we will endeavor to assist as we can. However, Minister Dita, such assistance *must* be cleared with me first before it is given. Further, I am appointing both Minister Dita and Doctor Zosia to ID Field Agent Status."

That surprised everyone present. "But," General Cibor protested slightly.

"No but's. She and Doctor Zosia have earned our trust and respect. They alone stood up to the plot of Cezar, and they have taken responsibility for the people of this planet when no others did. Besides, they are now both well-established members of the local society. Who better can provide us with accurate and timely information?" The stern face of Ania silenced any further objections.

Everyone here is terrified of Ania, even General Cibor! She must wield huge powers, Drina sent Dita. *She wants something from you, but what it is I can't tell yet. Her ideas are too vague. She probably has not yet fully formulated her wishes.*

The meeting broke up. Ania spoke hastily to Dita. "Minister Dita, please go fetch Doctor Zosia here at once. I need her to get her physical. Then, let's get your ID tags reinserted into your bodies. We can't risk losing you two. Once that is done, we'll get your official ID badges made so you can have proper access here. Now get going, Minister Dita." She saw that Ania wanted no further words from her, and Dita hastily left.

A half hour later, she chatted with everyone else back at the Bettingham manor house, Doctor Zosia in particular. Everyone wanted to know what had happened.

Finally, Doctor Zosia said, "Okay then, I guess we'd best not keep her waiting. Isn't it strange a Sector ID Minister is going to be in charge of the spaceport? Such a person usually controls a whole sector of the galaxy and countless battle cruisers and many planets."

"I know. She must be a very powerful person. If I can get to a communications terminal, perhaps I can look up her biography and find out more about her," Dita suggested. "I'll see what I can dig up while you are getting your exam."

Another half hour passed before Dita landed her shuttle at the edge of the volcano on the small remnant of the Plateau Grado. Already, the weather had changed. Blinding snow and sleet replaced the relatively sunny morning. Shivering from the cold, a guide was waiting patiently for them and subsequently led Doctor Zosia to the medical lab aboard the huge ship. That done, he gave Dita a quick tour of the public portion of the ship. He left her in the dining quarters. Dita spotted a computer terminal and discretely wandered over to it and did a quick search for information on Ania Anka. Only the barest details appeared on her screen. Ania was in charge of all Intelligence Gathering for the entire outer rim sector in which Ashford-5 was a part, a very tiny part. Her rank in the Imperium exceeded that of the generals on board the many battleships stationed here in the rim! Dita was impressed.

An hour later, Doctor Zosia joined her along with the same guide. "If you will follow me, I will take you to the ID tag station and then on to get your ID badges." The two followed the young man. Soon, they received a tiny shot in their left shoulders, implanting the tag that all Imperium people carried within their bodies. Such tags allowed their bodies to be tracked wherever they went. Dita hated this aspect, but could do nothing about it. Besides, with the satellite now in operation, they could follow their shuttles anywhere and even zoom in on her manor house if they so desired to spy on her.

At the badge station, the guide punched in their codes, and the machine took a photograph of each and soon ejected their new badges. "Impressive, ID Field Agents. You both have incredible clearance, you realize," he said, very much impressed with the two strangely dressed Rigel-3 women. Dita smiled and followed him to Ania's private quarters.

Somehow, Ania knew they were arriving and opened her door as they walked up. She summarily dismissed the guide and beckoned the two women to enter. She put her finger to her lips, indicating silence. Ania pressed a few buttons on her desk. Then, she sat down. "Okay, it is safe to talk now. The room is cloaked in an anti-scrying field. What we say in here cannot be overheard by anyone outside this room. The walls are sound proof as well. I wanted our first talk to be very private, just between you two and me. Please sit down." She was just as stern as she had been. Dita wondered if she ever smiled.

"Now then, I assume you have your ID badges." Both waved theirs. "Good. I have put your past year's pay into your private accounts along with a little bonus. Plus, you each have a substantial ID Field Agent account you may use as needed. Just clear major expenses with me first, please. Now then, one of your duties will be to fully train our linguistics specialists so we can program our ULATs appropriately." She went on outlining their duties, but all were reasonable and nothing out of the ordinary. Briefing the local Social-Anthropologists on the cultures found on Ashford-5, briefing the medical staff on the diseases found on the planet — just routine actions.

She really wants to know about your mentales skills. She's seen the doctor's report on your greatly enlarged pituitary glands. She knows something is going on with you two, Drina broke in on the two women's mental thoughts.

Dita spoke up. "Well, by now you have seen our medical results. We are both in excellent health." *I'll be damned if I am going to tell her about the mentales effects on Ashford-5! She'll start wanting to take people as guinea pigs for experimentations!*

"Yes, funny, I was just thinking about them. You do realize there was one singular anomaly in both of you women that was most definitely not present when you shipped out from Rigel-3," Ania said sternly, but with a hint of coyness in her voice.

She knows! Zosia sent to Dita, rather panicky. *What do we say? I don't want her probing me and testing me or anyone else for that matter!*

"Yes, our pituitary glands have enlarged," Dita said in a matter of fact manner, as if it was of no importance.

Ania eyed both women closely, and then spoke, "Yes. We see this effect in the exceedingly rare Imperium Empaths and Telepaths."

She knows! Zosia fairly screamed into Dita's mind.

Dita thought fast. If Ania knew hundreds if not thousands of the locals were now exhibiting all manner of *mentales* powers, what would she do? Would she begin to snatch them up and press them into service with the Imperium? Would she try to test them, experiment on them? Some were her dear friends. Dita hedged a little. "For every action, there is an equal and opposite reaction. My professors drilled that into my head, Sector ID Minister. Here on Tierra, that's their name for their world, we set up a refinery without any regard for the environment and impact on the local inhabitants."

"Are you saying there was an impact of the refining process on the people here and yourselves?" Ania replied astutely picking up on her words.

She's no dummy! Careful does it. Dita answered, "There is always an environmental impact."

"Are you saying your enlarged glands are part of that impact?" Ania probed her eyes bright and drilling into Dita's causing her to flinch.

"Yes, we believe it has, though Doctor Zosia cannot either prove or disprove it," Dita countered.

"I see." Ania stared long at the two women before adding, "Well, let's be quite frank. I know what you are both trying to hide from me. I also know that you, Dita, looked up my public file while you were waiting for Doctor Zosia's exam to finish."

Dita flushed! *How can she know that?*

Ania answered her unspoken question, rather startling her. "I *am* head of this entire sector's Intelligence Division. How do you think I got this position? Not by my good looks. Ha. Not by my charming personality! I am a Class V telepath, but that is not well known. Do not repeat this outside this room. It is highly classified information, known only to my staff and my ID Field Agents, which you two now are. You cannot hide it from me. I suspected it from our first meeting. What I want to know first is who is also touching your minds? There is a third presence here with you." She added sharply, "Who is this Drina person? She is not listed in the Imperial Settlement Force Thirty-three personnel roster." Involuntarily, Dita's mind glanced at an image of Drina. "Ah, a local, I see. My god! She doesn't have any arms?"

"No she doesn't. A genetic birth defect," Doctor Zosia spoke up. "Unfortunately, her three children have inherited the same birth defect. I've verified that detail. Prosthetics will be of no use to her, I am very sad to say."

Dita volunteered, "She is one of only a handful of the

true healers left on Ashford-5. Cezar got rid of the vast majority of their healers, replacing them with the COG quacks."

"I see," Ania replied, "and how is it that she is with you and why?"

"Drina always knows what a person deep down wants to know. We didn't know what your intentions were when we saw the battleship setting down. We thought it prudent to protect ourselves and the locals as best we can," Dita justified. This was not a lie, and she felt comfortable in saying what she had.

Ania answered, "Indeed, most prudent of you." She flashed them both a brief smile before her stern look reappeared. "What concerns me now is just what are your *mentales* abilities? I need to know; it is obviously a matter of top security. I must know the skills of my Field Agents, if only to best protect them."

"We both can send and receive thoughts with ease. We can pick up others' thoughts," Dita answered, trying hard not to reveal any more than needed. "However, you must realize all this is new to us, and we are still learning what we can do and how to do it."

Ania nodded. "That makes sense, since you did not have this gift before you came to Ashford-5. Something here has obviously changed all that. But I sense that you are withholding far more about this from me."

Dita sighed. "Yes, we are, Ania. I don't want my friends and the people here to be stolen away in the night to become experimental subjects or to be forced into Imperium services without their consent. These are human beings. Besides, much of what is happening is in reaction to the devastation our people brought to their world. It may well be a reaction that will help them evolve out of the nightmare into which their civilization has been plunged without their consent."

"I see. Yes, I can grasp that concept. Lacking other information, it is a good operating theory for now. I sense there is a whole lot more that you both are not saying. Look, I have given you my sworn word, from this point on, Imperial Directive #5 will be rigorously enforced on Ashford-5. You can speak openly about it. I will not be stealing locals away or conducting experiments upon them, but I must know the full situation if I am to be an effective administrator here and help undo the immense damage that we've done to these human beings."

Doctor Zosia sighed. "Okay, then. I believe the psi-dust from the refinery floating out over the entire world has caused the massive changes we've witnesses in the last many months. The refinery dust spread over all the plants and was eaten by the people and animals and via the animals, by the people. Further, they inhaled the dust for months. It was after this we first began noticing the changes."

She continued. "My direct observations have been limited to the old Bettingham kingdom, closest downwind from the refinery. I have limited data that suggests the process is also occurring planet-wide now. Locally, one in four are wholly unaffected by it. One in five of the others goes totally insane and usually dies from it. Two in five have shown some changes, though the 'gift' appears to be relatively marginal in them. One in five has undergone massive changes and must be handled by our wise healers if they are to survive the transformation. One in five undergoes the massive changes on their own without outside assistance to deal with it. However, what has me worried the most is what will happen when some of these women give birth? What state will their offspring be in? Only time will tell, I am afraid. It could be really bad or perhaps good. I just don't know. We in the medical profession have encountered nothing like this before."

"Good god! A whole planet of telepaths!" Ania exclaimed, visibly shocked by the doctor's statements.

"Er, not telepaths, not entirely. All manner of *mentales* are occurring," the doctor explained. She then outlined some of the "gifts" she'd personally observed. She then added, "Like Dita, I believe this is Mother Nature reacting to the devastation that our people did to their world. I believe these gifts are Nature's way of trying to help the people adapt to their drastically modified world environment. Please, don't let the Imperium interfere with the people's development here on Ashford-5," Zosia begged.

"Thank you. You have my word that Imperial Directive

#5 will be strictly enforced here from now on. Obviously, the Imperium has a vested interest in helping Ashford-5 prosper and evolve so one day they can join the Imperium. Still, you have given us a valuable clue, psi-dust. I don't fully understand the manufacturing process, but I will report this potential development on up the line. It may be we can spare some of the highly valuable psi-crystals for some experiments of our own. I give you my word that such will absolutely not occur here with the local population of Ashford-5."

Ania then asked, "Do I have your permission to contact you telepathically when I need to do so? That will save us both a whole lot of time and inconvenience."

Dita smiled, "Yes, that is fine with us. Please, don't let others know of our *mentales* gifts just yet. Please."

"You wish to remain on Ashford-5 with your local husbands and soon to arrive children," Ania replied, reading the two women's thoughts. "Of course I will not tell others. None of what we've said here today will ever become part of your official records. It is merely between the three of us. Let's keep it that way. *Mentales* trained Field Agents are *extraordinarily* rare and thus *highly* valued. I'd rather lose this battleship here than either of you!" Dita sensed she was being sincere about her proclamation and relaxed a little.

Doctor Zosia asked, "May I requisition a prosthetic battery charger? Two of the most powerful women on Tierra had their hands brutally chopped off right after we initially landed here. I healed them and later provided them with prosthetic hands. They know they have at most three years of power in them before the hands become inert. I'd like the ability to recharge them for the two women, if I may."

Ania again flashed a brief smile. "Very well, as long as you alone possess the charger. Now then, there are a myriad of details I need to discuss with Minister Dita. One of the more pressing ones is the lease. The spaceport will be built here, but we must sign a several hundred year lease for the land. Which kingdom owns this plateau?"

"Three, I believe. Our Kingdom of the Angels, our southern neighbor, Kingdom of Haverhills, and on the western side, the Kingdom of Valen," Dita answered as best she could.

"I see. And what form of payment would be considered valuable here?" Ania asked.

"Ashford-5 is heavy-metal deficient planet. Even iron ore is scarce. Steel bars and gold would be very well accepted as payment," Dita replied.

"Excellent. I will see that this is handled soon. The construction here must begin soon. Okay, that will be all for today. I will contact you later on when we are ready to make the lease arrangements."

They shook hands and left. Outside, the winter storm raged and only with great care was Dita able to lift off successfully. Their shuttle swayed precariously but stabilized once she punched in the coordinates for home and activated the short flight. "That went better than I expected," Zosia admitted once the hectic buffeting subsided.

"I agree. I was really worried there when she admitted she was a telepath too. We will have to be careful around her. Still, if she keeps her word and allows Tierra to develop on its own, maybe we all have a chance," Dita replied.

Chapter 17 The Founding of the *Círculo de la Torres*

"We must have half of Wyth coming here!" Sissy exclaimed rather exasperated at the sheer number of men, women, and even children who were coming to their manor house and tower under construction. All had the *mentales* gift. Uniformly, they were in various stages of desperation to know not only what was the matter with them, but how to stop it or at least control it. Couple that with the wild winter storms beyond anything in living memory and you can see the level of frustration Sissy felt.

They all did. Outside, the snow depth was at least four feet with drifts approaching ten. The men worked nearly daily keeping a small path open across the two miles to Wyth proper so the needy townsfolk could manage to get here for their daily sessions. Yet, this was the least of their problems; this was one that could easily be solved with a little physical muscle. Not so with their ever-growing *mentales* gifts!

Sissy explained it all very well a few months back. "Look, we used to have control over telepathy. When we wanted it, we only had to squeeze our psi-crystals. When we were done, we simply let go of them. Now, I've got everyone in my head all the time, day and night, same as everyone else. It's nerve wracking to say the least!"

Holly calmed Sissy, "Hush child, you know we've managed to work out ways that can be taught to these *mentales*. In time and with our training, they are learning how to block their minds from others and to block out the background minds of others, when unwanted."

"Yes, but what about all the other powers? You know as well as I do, some of them we can't control. A hundred to one odds on the fire starter fellow. Fifty-nine to one on the fellow who can think a person dead," Sissy countered.

Holly sighed; she knew Sissy had a point. In the last few months, they'd seen people doing things they never imagined possible. Holly thought of the man who could start a fire just by thinking the wrong thoughts, or so he claimed. Well, a bit of juice from a *bacal* leaf had temporarily handled the man. She was then able to train him a little so he could control his thoughts that started fires. He'd left with a small vial of the juice, promising to use it daily, if he found he was unable to keep from starting small fires.

As if picking up on the women's thoughts, Aurora joined them, waddling slowly along. She was two months from her anticipated delivery date of Anna. Already her heightened senses knew that she and Aiden were having a little girl. They decided to continue the A-game, that is, naming their children's first names with that letter. "Hi, I think we need to divide up the folks who come to us for help with their *mentales* gifts. We'll keep those who seem to have some talent in the healing arts here in our tower, since Doctor Zosia is here with us."

"Well, that makes sense," Sissy declared. "We can send those who now have a gift for detecting the truth or making perfectly believable illusions over to Bedworth tower. Inez, Isabel, and Luisa are good at that."

Holly added, "Right, Aurora. Each of our towers has some special skills, gifts. Those who deal with perception gifts, send them over to the Bettingham tower. I hear that Sammi and Francisca are doing a good job helping those with such *mentales* gifts. The fire gifts and some of the healers, we can send to the Brom tower. Tammy and Val are doing pretty well handling folks along those lines."

"Yes, it makes sense to do this," Aurora replied. "We shall call our towers the *Círculo de la Torres*. I just heard that *Jefe* Harold Oakham and *Jefe* Ben Haverhills wants us to help them build similar training towers in their kingdoms. They used telepathy to talk to Norwood about it this morning. Last week *Jefe* Able Rusden also asked Norwood for something similar. I can see in the future there will be many of these towers across Tierra, helping to heal and train all of us who suddenly have *mentales* powers."

"Yes, that's all well and good," Sissy replied, "but will it do any good, really? I don't want to be a spoilsport, but I've already told you we only have two to one odds on this being successful. Isn't there any better answer?"

Aurora sighed, slumping into the nearest chair. So much weight fell upon her shoulders, for she was thus far the only known case in which the *mentales* gift allowed one to glimpse the future. That she was also heavily pregnant didn't help matters. "I honestly don't see anything else, Sissy. Nothing. I wish I could, but I can't."

"Well, things are going to only get worse," Holly declared. "Once the spring comes, if it ever does, food production will likely suffer dramatically. Plus, the animals! Did you see that herd of reindeer wandering through here yesterday? Until now, they are only found up in what used to be the Kingdom of Haruk."

"I thought they were rather cute," Sissy admitted. "Of course, I've never seen one before. I did hear tales the northerners often tame them for riding animals, much as we use horses here. Ten to one, the reindeer are moving south because their homelands have grown too cold for them." That was a sobering thought. The ten feet of record snowfall backed up her hunch.

"Expect massive changes," Holly spoke up. "The altered climate will be devastating, as will the proliferation of people with forms of *mentales* gifts. Couple both of those with the total disintegration of the kingdoms into all these smaller kingdoms and we have a recipe for chaos. Change has come to Tierra in a huge way. I don't think Tierra will ever be the same. At least, according to Dita and Zosia, the Rigels will no longer interfere in our affairs."

"Sometimes, Holly," Aurora sighed, "I kind of wish that they would. They might be able to spare our people a mountain of grief in the coming years."

"Well, I'd just as soon wish they wouldn't meddle ever again!" Sissy declared. "Just look at the disaster they've already caused us!" None could deny that point.

Aurora looked at her hands and sighed again. *They are not all bad. Ally and I have workable substitute hands and that alone is huge for us. I'm glad for some of their meddling.* She countered, "Sissy, let's not condemn them all. At least two have been the best. Rather, some of their advanced technology and metals are very good for us, but there are always rotten apples in the bottom of the barrel."

"True, but you'd think the newcomers would have the decency to fix up *some* of the damage their kind did here on Tierra," Sissy countered, unwilling to budge much from her opinion.

Dita waddled into the room. Like many of the younger women in this tower, she too was very pregnant. With her heightened sensitivity, she'd overheard their chatting. *It is so hard to get used to all this openness between all our minds. We all are so intimately close now. There just aren't words to describe how close we all are, shared beingnesses perhaps. Tierra is becoming a telepathic society now. I am so lucky to be here at the start. No anthropologist has ever had such a field to study. I supposed I ought to comment upon Sissy's thought.*

After pleasant greetings, she spoke up, "The Imperium has enforced a hands-off policy towards us for good reasons." She wanted to use the word primitives but chose her words more graciously, "The Imperium is a very advanced technological society. We here are certainly not. When two widely disparate cultures encounter each other, ignoring whether or not it is good or bad, the non-technologically advanced society is always very heavily impacted and influenced, while the technologically advanced society remains wholly unchanged. The hands-off policy gives the non-technologically advanced society the best chance at evolving gradually without losing its own culture and values. Sissy, here on Tierra, we've seen what happens when the Imperium does not follow that policy. We should be thankful that at last they are adopting it here. I don't think there is any feasible way for the Imperium to undo all the damage done to our world, not without making things even worse here for us all."

Sissy sighed, "You are right, the odds are nine hundred sixty-three to one that their continued intervention here would make things worse for us. Still, it is a mess."

"You won't get any argument from me on that point," Dita teased her. "However," she grinned mischievously, "I wouldn't want to give up our *mentales* gifts now. You are all so dear to me now, so close, like we were the dearest of sisters."

Sissy laughed, "Don't forget our men." Each woman present could not help thinking about their incredibly close bonds with their husbands. Touching minds while also touching bodies went so far beyond ecstasy — an ultimate satisfaction and bond of love that none present had even remotely any words to describe this merging of two souls. All were silent for a moment, all lost in their own precious memories, all sensing the similar memories in each other as well. They were closer than even identical twin sisters. At last, Sissy asked, "But will it last?"

"Will what last?" asked Doctor Zosia. She'd just entered having finished her physical exams of five new arrivals. She could not help but pick up the combined groups' thoughts, merging with her own feelings of ecstasy with her husband, Captain Able.

"Our heightened *mentales* gifts," Sissy added. "I mean they stopped polluting our air with the psi-dust. In time, will we all go back to normal, the way that we were before the dust came? God! I'd hate to lose this!"

Doctor Zosia grinned. She could not help but remember the utter ecstasy she and Able had shared this morning when they awoke. His fingers lightly touched her skin, electrifying her wholly. The feather touch of their lips had nearly caused her body to have an orgasm. Flushing, she hastily threw up her mental barriers, hoping to block out these very private thoughts from the others. Too late, from the faces of her companions, her "sisters," she saw similar memories had been stirred in them as well. She flushed. Regaining her composure, she answered Sissy.

"So far, I've seen no reduction in size of the glands in anyone, Sissy. It's been nearly a half of a year since the psi-dust last went up into the air. I think if the glands were going to shrink in size, then they would already be showing signs of it. I've seen nothing to indicate that is happening, Sissy. However, as your doctor, I am always on the lookout for such signs, and I will let you all know if I find anything that might suggest the alterations are reducing. Oh yes, I am done with the five new women. They are just fine and are ready for your first lessons now."

Aurora, who had slipped slightly out of the present time stream, returned to the present. Dreamily, she said softly, "Sissy, we will not be losing our *mentales* gifts. On the contrary, there will one day be even more of our *Círculo de la Torres*. I can see only a few years from now, there will be ten of them, all nestled up against the Goza Mountains. The *Círculo de la Torres* will become the stabilizing influence for all of us on Tierra. I just wish the weather would improve though."

Dita could not help thinking once more the thought that kept recurring to her, *Then, we all do have a chance!* This was what she desperately wanted, more than anything in the entire universe. Although born on Rigel-3 and her tall, greyish body considered alien to this world, Dita knew Tierra was her home, her life. She had found a happiness here that was entirely absent throughout the thousands of worlds within the Imperium.

She smiled, as she realized the Psychmen were completely and utterly wrong. People were spiritual beings with a mind and living within these bodies. Those supposedly learned men had no concept or notion that people were spiritual beings! The people who now possessed this precious *mentales* gift knew they were not their bodies and not their minds. They knew they were far more than the animated mud of the Psychmen's theories. *Could the salvation of the whole universe start here with us?* She wondered.
The End.

Other Books by Vic Broquard

Without Warning (fantasy)

The Trident Series: (fantasy)
>Volume 1 The Trident and the Book
>Volume 3 The Trident and the Scepter
>Volume3 The Trident and the Resurrection

The Adventures of Elizabeth Stanton Series: (science fiction)
>Volume 1 The Evolution of the Path
>Volume 2 The Great Messiah
>Volume 3 Of Kings and Queens and Troubadours
>Volume 4 Chaos in the Aftermath
>Volume 5 Power Plays
>Volume 6 Age of Exploration
>Volume 7 Abducted
>Volume 8 The Emperor and Empress
>Volume 9 A Job Worth Doing
>Volume 10 Degradation
>Volume 11 The Second Crusade
>Volume 12 When Worlds Collide
>Volume 13 Dark Ages

The Lindsey Barron Series: (fantasy)
>Volume 1 The Rod of the Apocalypse
>Volume 2 The Board of Governors
>Volume 3 The Crown of Moses
>Volume 4 Dominus for President
>Volume 5 The National Health Care Program
>Volume 6 States Justice
>Volume 7 Cross and Double-cross

Zoran Chronicles Series: (fantasy)
>Volume 1 A Dragon in Our Town
>Volume 2 Dragons, Power, Courts, and War

Planet of the Orange-red Sun Series: (science fiction)
    Volume 1 When Kingdoms Fall
    Volume 2 Dark Ages
    Volume 3 Age of the Towers
    Volume 4 Difficillis Exitus
    Volume 5 Age of the Lords
    Volume 6 The Renegade Tower
    Volume 7 Rebellions
    Volume 8 The Aliens Return
    Volume 9 Power Struggles
    Volume 10 Guilds, Genetics, and Gods
    Volume 11 Magi, Witches, Swords, and Superstitions
    Volume 12 The Voyage of the Eagle's Seed
    Volume 13 Justifications
    Volume 14 Responsibilities

The Return of the Wizards: Twelve Companions – The Making of Wizards (fantasy)

www.ingramcontent.com/pod-product-compliance
Lightning Source LLC
Chambersburg PA
CBHW072131250626

47159CB00007B/2648